Dark Wilderness
& Other Stories

By
Vin Morreale, Jr.

Cover Design by Susan Coleman Layman

ISBN 978-0-9991473-2-0

academyartspress.com

TABLE OF CONTENTS

Exquisite Anxiety — 1

Last Request — 15

There's Someone in the House — 28

Don't — 37

Second Income — 51

Ghosts — 64

Them — 69

Other People's Treasures — 98

Dark Wilderness — 108

Wake Me Up! — 154

Mark of a Champion — 162

Monster — 184

That Healing Touch — 189

The Promise — 212

Buried Alive — 221

*Imagination is
Nature's victory cry,*

*the only true
currency of the soul.*

Exquisite Anxiety

The fierce splash of colors danced and leapt across the canvas like a multi-hued assault on the senses.

Valerie Myra Lambert took five steps back from the painting she had just spent the last six days giving birth to, and tried to envision the huge artwork through the eyes of her critics. It was vibrant and colorful, no one could deny that. And so impressively disturbing, in that distinctive Valerie Myra Lambert style.

She could imagine the pompous gallery owners on the Lower East Side gushing and gurgling over its outpouring of 'positively primal emotions' forged in the crude sensuality of each fiercely delineated brush stroke. Students of fine art would craft elaborate doctoral theses on the underlying sociopolitical impact of this work, in relation to other examples of Early Twenty-First Century neo-modern impressionism. Carla, her agent, would quickly translate all that buzzing enthusiasm into an obscene amount of fame and dollars, both of which Valerie was pretty sure she had seen enough of already.

She poured an Amaretto from the wet bar and carefully dropped four ice cubes into a French crystal glass. As the cubes cracked and sputtered against the warm liqueur, the celebrated artist carefully searched the undried canvas for the soul of her creation.

She could not find one.

Others would surely concoct an underlying meaning to prove or bolster their own artistic imagination, but Valerie knew the truth.

It was shallow.

Explosions of scarlet, yellow and vermilion alone do not make great art.

She grabbed the painting with her free hand, and flung it wildly across the room. Art in motion. It careened, bounced, broke and eventually rested, the still-wet paint creating a new form of art on the sofa and far wall. Only this time the message was painfully clear…

This world-renowned painter had lost her touch.

The sad truth was that Valerie Myra Lambert's career as an artist had peaked seven years ago. Any work since then had been a futile attempt to recapture past glories, each recent painting a cheap and shameless parody of her own renowned style.

The stunning use of colors remained, but the depth of emotion, the searing heat that epitomized what *The New Yorker* once dubbed the Lambert mystique, had long since vanished. Without the passion, her subjects became strained and lifeless things. Mockeries in oil. Vibrant blotches of despair. The fact that they continued to command exorbitant prices made her feel even more wretched.

Amaretto was quickly followed by Sambuca, which eventually gave way to Kentucky Bourbon. A lot of it.

Van Gogh had it right, she decided. Die at your peak, so that your work may live forever. A well-timed and highly publicized suicide can make even something as mundane as sunflowers seem brooding and filled with meaning.

As the proper blending of alcohol and self-pity began to blunt her sensibilities, Valerie Myra Lambert spit on an empty canvas, just to see what kind of pattern it would create. She stared at the multi-sided splotch intently, then laughed out loud.

"I could probably convince some pretentious private collector that even my spit is a statement and a significant work of art!"

She laughed bitterly, sobbed for a while, then passed out on the newly paint-stained sofa.

****

Like most artists, Valerie Myra Lambert dreamed in a succession of vivid flashes and images. Joyous hues and vivid pigments swirled around her, like the caress of a living rainbow. Yet she could not escape criticism, even in her dreams. Jackson Pollock rose from the dead to stand before her artwork and scoff.

Henri Matisse mocked her signature unrestrained use of color as *'derivative, at best.'*

Georgia O'Keeffe simply turned away in disgust.

And then there was Van Gogh, sneering at her. disapproval pouring out of his frighteningly cold eyes. *"You know nothing,"* the legendary artist seemed to mutter. *"And express even less."*

As always, Valerie's dreams eventually narrowed to Peter, the heavenly scourge of her life. Peter Winthrop. Her paradox incarnate. The man who made her life complete, even as her artistic talents seeped away.

Of course, Van Gogh would sneer. He cared less for his art than his tragically flawed relationships. It was not glory and inspiration that drove the gentle painter to madness...it was something infinitely more mundane.

In today's cynical world, he would be just another sad, comic character on some low-rated soap opera. A simple, self-pitying fool who placed love above art.

What a sap.

"Just like me..." Valerie whispered to herself, even before she realized she was actually awake.

It was the annoyingly persistent ring of the telephone that brought her back from the delicious, liquor induced dream state, which was becoming her preferred habitat these days. She reached out an arm heavy with sleep. It failed to follow her brain's precise instructions and swung wildly about in the general direction of her phone. A twelfth ring. A thirteenth. She cursed loudly and repeatedly, until her frustrated profanities cleared enough of the drunken fog from her mind to enable her to find the antique, black rotary telephone mere inches from her hand. She growled into the receiver with a voice usually reserved for insurance salesmen and telephone solicitors.

"This had better be real friggin' important," she growled.

The voice on the line matched her anger with an irrepressible wave of affection.

A man's voice; warm, deep and caring.

A voice she knew well.

"Good morning to you, too, sweetheart." said Peter Winthrop, cheerfully. "I'd say by the tone of your voice, this was an Amaretto to Maker's Mark day."

"With a little Sambuca thrown in."

"No luck on the new painting?" There was no trace of condescension in that voice, no pity or contempt. The gentle support which reverberated through the fiber-optic cable brought tears to Valerie's eyes.

"Damn it, Peter! Why can't I paint anymore? Why can't I find the...heart, or the humanity which used to just pour out of me? What the hell happened to me?"

A painful pause. Then, Peter answered, with a tone both soft and sorrowful.

"I did," he said.

The truth of his answer shocked and shook the last bit of intoxication from her. Her work had lost its signature power, that desperately pleading edge, the distinctive Valerie Myra Lambert style, lost it all the very day she fell in love with Peter. Her personal joy had rung the death knell for her professional creativity.

"It...it shouldn't have to be that way," she muttered apologetically. She felt on tremulous ground here. She knew long ago that her happiness had been her artistic undoing, but she had jealously guarded that terrible secret, hoping Peter would never realize he was guilty of breaking her art.

"But it is, and we have to find a way around it. I can't watch you waste away, always torn between me and your love of painting. And I won't deny the world its most beautiful and passionate artist."

Suddenly, Valerie understood why Peter had undertaken this particular assignment for the Discovery Channel. Why he had suspended work on his own beloved Encyclopedia of Entomology to disappear into the Amazon rain forest for more than half a year. He was a laboratory scientist, not a field researcher. She knew that well. He hated being away from his computer files and electron microscope. He was the rare naturalist who hated the outdoors. But now, he was tramping through Peru, Paraguay or some other South American hell hole, just for her.

"Peter...I..." Dammed by tears and emotion, her voice welled up in her throat and would move no further.

"Don't sound so despondent, sweetheart. I think I've found the answer to your problems."

"I don't want to lose you, Peter. That's not an acceptable answer."

"I'm not talking about that..." A new excitement had crept into his voice, the same boyish enthusiasm that burst forth whenever he bragged about her talents to people they met on the street. "I'm sending you a present," he said, with a smile she could hear right through the phone.

"What is it?"

"I can't tell you yet. But the moment I saw it, I thought of you and the magical things you do on canvas." He was obviously having a difficult time containing his secret. The effort caused his voice to rise in pitch. "I'm hoping it can infuse you with some new inspiration."

Valerie curled closer to the phone, as if this could draw the secret from him.

"You've got me intrigued."

"That's what I was hoping."

"You bug-sniffing bastard! You can't leave me hanging like this! Without giving me an idea as to what it is. Not even you can be so cruel."

"Sure, I can," Peter laughed. "You should receive the package by tomorrow or the day after. But you have to promise me one thing..."

"I don't make promises to scientists."

"This one you have to. It is extremely important that you don't open the package until Christmas."

"Are you crazy? That's more than three months away! I can't wait that long!"

"You have no choice. Listen to me, Valerie. I couldn't be more serious here. I do not, under any circumstances, want you to open the package 'til Christmas. If you can't promise me that, I'll call up and cancel the delivery right now."

"Oh, all right," Valerie sulked. "But if you are going to torture me with suspense, you can at least give me a little hint as to what it is."

"Okay," Peter responded after a long breath. "It's the genie in the bottle. The inspiration that has eluded you these last few years." He could hold it in no longer. "It's the Valerie Myra Lambert style come to life!"

"Ugh! You mean it's alive?"

"Not exactly." His voice was suddenly serious again. "Just promise me you won't open the package until Christmas, Valerie."

"I promise. I hate you, but I promise."

"I hate you, too." Peter's voice was light and airy again. "I hate you for making me miss you so much while I'm thousands of miles away. I hate you for distracting my thoughts while I'm supposed to be focused on research. I hate you for…"

Angry voices rose in the background. Harsh, guttural sounds in a language she did not understand.

"What's going on, Peter? Sounds like a fight?"

"Nothing. It's nothing," he tried to hide the tension in his voice. "Just another friendly disagreement between our guide and the cameraman. I better go before they break out the machetes."

"Are you going to be okay, Peter?"

"Yeah. Nothing but sunshine and fun times down here in the Amazon. I'll see you in January. I love you, Valerie."

"I love you, too, Peter..." But the line had gone dead before she could finish her sentence.

Valerie stared at the old black telephone long after the call ended. She hated uncertainty. She hated not knowing where she stood: with Peter, her career, or life in general.

Tossing her blouse on the bed, she stomped over to her easel, mounted another frustratingly blank canvas upon it, and tried desperately to capture the spark that was once again missing in her life.

****

Nine days.

Nine agonizingly long days.

That's how long it took Peter's surprise to arrive from the Amazon.

It was a large box, three feet long, two feet high and eighteen inches deep, covered with a collage of stampings, those redundant bureaucratic ink marks which allow items to cross international borders. The words; FRAGILE: GLASS handwritten in both English and Spanish. Valerie recognized Peter's precise scrawl, an artistry of his own. The UPS delivery man, with thinning hair and a face overcome with freckles, insisted that it was not heavy, not like the last delivery he had to lug up three flights of stairs...only about twenty-six pounds. In response to her anxious questions, he pointed out there were no air holes in the box, so anything that might have been alive when it was packed, would not be now.

The contents of the carton were insured for the maximum amount. The bill of lading described it only as 'art.'

The delivery man placed the carton, as Valerie suggested, on the piano bench in the right corner of the room. On the way back to the door, he asked her if she was some kind of artist, he had noticed the paintings and canvases. She told him that she was no kind of artist anymore, signed for the package, and closed the door quickly behind him.

She stared at the box. In large, block letters, Peter, damn him, had repeated his stern instructions.

DO NOT OPEN UNTIL CHRISTMAS!

Valerie returned to her easel and tried to ignore the strange package.

****

A week later, Valerie accepted the fact that she could not possibly ignore the cardboard mystery which had been forced upon her.

Even from its position in the corner of the room, it dominated her attention, daring her to look away. She paced around it, swore at it, even painted bright cartoon flowers on its side.

Still, it would not let her go.

In deference, she moved it onto a coffee table in the center of the room. Although she almost tried not to shake it, a certain amount of lateral movement while she was transporting it from bench to table revealed...nothing. Something insubstantial may have slid, packing material perhaps, but the carton was either so well packed as to resist all movement, or completely empty. Its weight denied the emptiness, and meticulous packing would be consistent with Peter's fanaticism to detail, so she assumed he had buffered it solely to infuriate her.

Men could be so vicious.

From its new position of power in the center of the room, the package wound its invisible tendrils into the recesses of her mind. She tried to paint, but kept on turning to judge how the light was casting shadows on the carton; how the dull tan cardboard subtly altered its hue as her eye made the journey from the middle to the left edge of the box; how odd the Spanish language looks when written; and how well designed the official Brazilian customs symbol was.

She spent hours dusting it for no reason. She tried to cook, but nearly chopped her fingers, along with the scallions, because she was distracted by the box. There was nothing she could do without its annoying presence creeping up on her at least four times an hour.

Then it was every four minutes.

She knew she could not let it win.

Eleven days, three hours and fourteen minutes after it arrived, Valerie Myra Lambert broke her promise and opened the box.

With a loose razor blade, she sliced through the many layers of packing tape. The blade neatly bisected the instructions:

DO NOT OPEN UNTIL CHRISTMAS!

With her fingernails, one of which broke, and later a screwdriver, she removed each of the large copper packing staples.

She tore open the flaps.

Then gasped.

Inside the carton was another box, slightly smaller, and wrapped as a Christmas present. The paper decorating the box was a cheap reproduction of one of her colorful early paintings. Little white letters on the paper's edge trumpeted Hallmark's 'Great American Artist Series' of holiday wrapping papers. On the top was a tag, again covered with Peter's infuriatingly precise handwriting. Its message made her turn away with shame.

It read: *"If you truly love me,*

you will not open this until Christmas...

I know I can trust you.

Love always,

Peter."

Valerie stumbled into the bedroom, threw herself on the flowered mattress cover, and cried until she fell asleep.

Still, the box would not let her go.

In her dreams, it loomed menacingly from the ceiling, a crushing weight or the promise of salvation. No matter how much she ran towards it, it always remained just beyond her reach. She dreamed of all manner of creatures and creations inside, alternately wondrous and horrible...a Siberian tiger cub of purest white...the Venus de Milo...a dead tarantula with curled up legs...soft mounds of pink and purple snow...Van Gogh's Sunflowers...then his ear...the baby she never had...the Mona Lisa...a box filled with Mayan art treasures...and Peter's severed head. It could be anything and everything, both wondrous and deadly.

The inanimate carton began to develop its own silent personality, the brooding tormentor of her subconscious.

Valerie knew the only way to exorcise the demon of the box was to attack it in the best way she knew how...with paint. After three too many Scotches, she set upon a new canvas with a passion and fire she had not felt in years.

Over the next three and a half weeks, Valerie painted night and day, grabbing nourishment only when she felt too weak to stand, sleeping only when her arm could no longer bear the weight of the brush, showering only when she could no longer tolerate her own body. She unplugged the telephone, ignored the mail which piled up in her mailbox, and completely seceded from humanity. It had been years since she had felt so maniacally driven, so hopelessly desperate.

And she loved it.

****

Valerie sipped the sweet port wine with a slight intake of breath to enhance its tawny flavor. It was the first alcohol she had tasted in nearly two months. She felt energized and exhausted, as a tall, slender woman with white-blonde hair circled her paintings.

Carla Weintraub, 52, paced with her back towards Valerie, her well-coifed hair and abundance of expensive jewelry a silent testimony to her success as one of the art community's most powerful agents. Valerie admired her straightforward criticism in a way she would not tolerate from any other person. Carla was brutally frank. She would not hesitate to tell Valerie if these new paintings had any merit whatsoever, or were merely further examples of her artistic self-indulgence. She would still sell them, no matter how shallow they were, but she would always let the nervous artist know how she really felt.

The agent uttered not a word for nine full minutes. Valerie was dying with anticipation, but she knew better than to interrupt Carla when she was appraising a work.

Carla stood before the seven paintings, her brows pulled together, her lips pursed. Each canvas displayed the same image: an exquisitely colored box in various suggestions of suspense.

One box bore a tag that said; *DO NOT OPEN...EVER!*

Another painting tantalized the viewer with a single flap of the brightly hued box dangling open.

A third showed the box from a different angle, so that, even with flaps fully open, it was impossible to see what was inside.

The fourth and fifth similarly teased the eye.

The sixth box oozed blood.

The seventh exploded upwards with a vivid shower of colorful butterflies.

Carla Weintraub considered each, then spoke with her back still facing the artist.

"What do you call this series?" It was a professional voice, devoid of emotion.

"I call it *Exquisite Anxiety*," Valerie offered quickly. She was as nervous in front of Carla as she had been that first day, fifteen years ago, when this powerful New York agent had visited her Greenwich Village apartment to become the first person on Earth to see her paintings. The first to take her talents seriously.

"Exquisite Anxiety," Carla repeated to herself. Then she turned to face her fearful client.

"Valerie Myra Lambert," she said with a broad smile. "You're back!"

✳✳✳

11:43 PM.

Traffic noises drifted into the lavish apartment from the street below. Valerie sat alone in the pale darkness. Alone with the brightly colored box on her coffee table. Carla had left with the seven paintings, amid promises of a new unveiling of the resurgent Lambert style. The two had celebrated with champagne and bruschetta, buzzing with enthusiasm, until the alcohol blended with the physical trauma of the last few weeks, and finally caught up with the emotionally drained artist.

In her hand was a wrinkled letter bearing a South American postmark.

The world is more wondrous than even I could imagine.
Miss you terribly.
REMEMBER, DO NOT OPEN THE BOX UNTIL CHRISTMAS!
Love always, Peter.

His notes had gotten briefer the longer he was away. The weekly seven page epiphanies had dwindled to this. Four sentences. One, a command. And worst of all, she was painting again. Painting better without him. She walked to the bar and poured herself another Maker's Mark.

She was sure he knew what he was doing. The box was probably empty, it was the hunger, the curiosity, the frenzy he had given back to her. That was his Christmas present, she was sure of it. She stared at the tag on the top of the box again.

She did love him. And she had made him let her go, so she could paint again. She had even celebrated her triumph with Carla. But when it came to sharing her joy with the one person who really mattered most in her life, she was left stranded, once again, in a cold, empty bed.

True artists are forged in hunger, shaped on the anvil of despair. Need and self-denial polishes them to a bright, potentially blinding shimmer. Yet too many choose to become warped and pitted by the corrosive power of contentment.

Damn Peter for understanding that better than she did.

He transplanted half her life to South America, and left her sitting alone with a damn Christmas present.

A present she couldn't even open for another two and a half weeks!

"Damn him," she yelled, her voice echoing through the darkened room. She stood slowly on wavering feet, as she glared at the box that tormented her from its defiant pedestal in the center of the room. She raised her empty Bourbon glass, and in a fit of frustration, suddenly flung it at the object of her drunken anguish.

The glass shattered.

As did something within the box.

Even in the shadowy stillness that filled the room, Valerie could see the gaping hole torn in the wrapping paper where the projectile had struck. Shards of glass like dragon's teeth dangling above the opening.

She was horrified. What would Peter think when he came home in January? Did her alcohol-fueled anger shatter some prehistoric artifact that could never be replaced? Could she have just destroyed Peter's career by reducing a truly important scientific find to mere rubble?

How on earth could she have been so...

She never completed that thought. Her first glimpse of the small black things swarming out of the hole in the side of the box froze the breath in her lungs. She could not move at all. There were hundreds upon hundreds of them, all crawling and slithering out of the ruptured box, across the coffee table, and hitting the floor with a slight, squishing sound. She could not even scream. In the eerie darkness of the apartment, the miniature army of misshapen creatures unfolded like a nightmare.

The...things, whatever they were, glistened black and slimy against the pale ivory carpet. They crept up on the last pieces of bruschetta that lay by her plate on the floor, the remaining vestiges of her celebration with Carla. The creatures quickened their pace, as they swarmed over the greasy morsels. Valerie's ears caught the almost imperceptible sound of little gnashing jaws, and found it horrifying. The remaining bruschetta was devoured in seconds, as still more of the disgusting things slithered from the box.

How could Peter send her something so horrible? So ugly and disgusting?

Then she noticed the creatures were moving – no, swarming – straight towards her.

Something in Valerie's body compelled her to stand and run. She staggered to her feet, never taking her eyes off the dark, grotesque wave, which continued to undulate irresistibly towards her. She reached out for the lamp, but as she did, her foot caught on something under the sofa. The broken canvas would have been no problem for a sober person, but clumsied by an excess of champagne and bourbon, Valerie could not recover her balance. She seemed to fall in slow motion, seeing the coffee table rush towards her head, hearing the dull thud of impact, and feeling the warm trickle of blood pooling on the carpet around her.

Time stopped.

Valerie briefly wondered why she was lying down in the darkness. Then she caught sight of the swarm of black creatures moving ever closer. She saw their pinpoint eyes of demonic light, the undulating arch of their backs as they slithered towards her. She felt a hundred stabbing pains on her leg, then closed her eyes and saw no more.

****

Dr. Peter Winthrop, sunburned and caked with glory, lugged his heavy suitcase up the stairs. Beside him, Dr. Emmett Anderson, Peter's mentor and a world-renowned scientist in his own right, chattered endlessly about Peter's find.

"This is the most exciting entomological discovery in the last one hundred and fifty years," the elderly scientist gushed. "Imagine, a species that is both aggressive and carnivorous in larval stage, as well as a docile post-chrysalis herbivore! Your career is made, boy. All you need now is sufficient shelf space to mount all your awards and honoraria!"

Peter smiled. Anderson had been droning on about his discovery ever since the return flight from Brazil.

He never knew how wearying thirteen straight hours of praise could be.

"The part that means the most to me," Peter interrupted. "...is that they so perfectly capture Valerie's spirit. It's as if her artwork had actually come to life. That's why I named the species after her."

"Lambertus Lepidoptera. She should be thrilled. Until she sees them in their larval stage, that is."

"She won't for a while. The specimens I sent her were dormant in that, odd non-breathing way of theirs. They were set to mature around December 20th. I made her promise that, if she loves me, she wouldn't open the package until Christmas."

"Then let's hope she loves you, Peter. Otherwise, she's going to come face to face with some of the ugliest and most ferocious caterpillars the world has ever seen."

Peter shook his head. "I trust Valerie. Besides, even if she did open it, they're safely encased in a glass tank. And she'd have to really rattle the box to rouse them from their dormant state." He imagined her stunned expression. "She would be pretty upset, though," he grinned, mischievously.

The two weary scientists finally reached the apartment door. Peter was mildly annoyed when Valerie failed to answer the doorbell, despite repeated ringing.

"She's probably painting," he sighed. "I bet the Lambertus Lepidoptera really inspired her."

Peter fumbled with his keys, a jolting reminder of how greatly the civilized world differed from the tribal societies of the Amazon rain forest. He held the door open, while Dr. Anderson lugged his suitcase inside. As Peter entered the apartment and closed the door behind them, he was startled when a butterfly with an eight-inch wing span rested gently on his shoulders. It's vibrant scarlet, yellow and vermilion coloring made it unique among tropical butterflies.

"No matter how many times I see them, they are still absolutely breathtaking to me," sighed Dr. Emmett Anderson.

"Valerie must have let one loose to capture its soul on canvas."

The two scientists moved deeper into the apartment. Peter smiled at the scene of canvases and paint splatters that proved Valerie had indeed been inspired to paint.

Then he screamed, a gut-tearing howl of pain.

His eyes landed on Valerie's snow white skeleton.

Around the pale bones fluttered hundreds of the world's most beautifully colored butterflies. As if the distinctive Valerie Myra Lambert style had suddenly come to life.

Last Request

"Oh, God. If you exist, don't let them do this to me..."

Despite the icy sweat that dampened his forehead, Carl Edward Braddock couldn't help but let an ironic smile assault the steep contours of his hardened face. Who exactly was this God he called out to now? The God of his mother, who left her to rot out alone on the dry plains of Oklahoma, an Apache arrow in her throat? The God of his father, who watched from some ethereal vantage point, as the worthless old drunk worked himself up to a whiskey lather and beat the tar out of his seven scrawny children, simply because they dared let their innocent eyes confess to a painful, unrelenting hunger? Or the God desperately invoked by any of the two dozen men and eight women he had gunned down on his way to becoming the most wanted man in the Arizona territories?

No, he had little room for religion in his life before. To Carl Edward Braddock, the only higher power was the silent end of a Colt 45 revolver. No God had ever interfered with his plans up until now, and he reckoned that no self-respecting deity was going to interrupt the justice they had planned for him tomorrow.

Braddock stood six foot one, with deceptively warm eyes and an angry scar that meandered from his right cheek to his chin. The beard he had grown these last three weeks of captivity helped soften his appearance, flecks of steely gray danced among his rough brown whiskers like a winter's frost on the prairie, a frost many said was born in his outlaw heart.

As the lonely shadows on the cell wall creeped quietly towards the ceiling, Braddock picked at the cold slice of stringy beef laid out on his battered metal tray.

Army food.

He should have known better than to kill that soldier. Then again, the young fool should have known better than to accuse him of cheating at poker. What the young soldier had said was true, of course. He had been cheating. But to call a man out on it was just begging for a bullet in the belly.

What the soldier didn't realize, and what most people - the ones who liked to call themselves civilized - could never understand, was that killing gets to be instinctive after your first five or six victims. Before you know it, taking a life becomes nothing more than a reflex action for a fiery temper. Like closing your eyes when you sneeze.

Braddock jabbed at his supper with the three-tined fork, and let loose a cruel laugh. He left that young soldier as much a cold slab of flesh as the beef they had laid on his tray.

Life was funny like that, sometimes.

At some point during the night, sleep ambushed him, dragged him down to its warm, inviting cave, and entertained its hapless prisoner with frenetic images of terror and life. The two had always been inextricably joined in the mind of Carl Edward Braddock. In life, you either imposed terror, or surrendered to it. Terror invaded your body with each tainted breath, crept through your lungs, and stole its way around to poison your entire system. The only way to escape this cruel immolation, to keep yourself from being devoured, was to store it tightly in your backbone, then blow it out the barrel of a gun straight into the chest of some other cowering sonuvabitch.

Ruth St. Martin, the pretty blonde hooker he used to run with, never quite understood his philosophy of terror...until he was forced to teach it to her one bloody night in a Dallas flophouse. He dreamed of her now. The tears. The terror. The contagious thrill of her abject fear. He drunk in her horrified supplications like an elixir of pure, sweet evil. All too quickly came the last dying gasp of possible redemption, which she haltingly drew into her broken body, then stole away with that awful night so many years ago. His solitary ramblings hadn't been as satisfying since.

She came to him now, a pale lover for his own newly-made corpse. He ran from her rotting sheaths of gray-white flesh, unsure where hers began and his ended. This time, he could not outrun her. She had suffered the rules of death longer than he had.

In horror, he threw himself to the cold, unyielding earth and begged for mercy with the same trembling voice she had used that night in Dallas. She hovered over him, silhouetted against the black sky like some vengeful demon. She hesitated now, as he had then. But her brief hesitation was cured in a dizzying swoop of savage swiftness. The hawk and the prairie dog. Only this time, he was the victim. She tore open his chest with yellow boned claws, while he howled the rabid cry of the newly-ravaged dead. He could only watch as she devoured him, his blackened blood dripping from the cadaverous mask that was once her gentle, loving face. He was dead, but dying still. Then his stationary eyes widened. Hideous streams of shadowy worms poured forth from the gaping cavern in his mutilated torso. The terror come to life. Life surrendering to death.

Carl Edward Braddock screamed himself awake.

A light bereft of all comfort crept across his quivering face. It took three long gulps of stale air to dispel the chilling images of Ruth and the grave. But Braddock knew he had only exchanged one nightmare for another.

It was morning.

The morning of September 13, 1892.

In a few short hours, he would die.

****

After a bitter breakfast of boiled eggs and hardtack biscuits, Carl Edward Braddock rested his head on the stiff straw cot, and listened to the harried preparations, which creaked and groaned from the courtyard outside his cell window. He was almost tempted to peer through the rusting iron bars, though he knew too well what he would see. A squad of uniformed, but surprisingly colorless men practicing the motions of his execution. Marionettes in cavalry blue, endlessly spinning their comical dance of death on clockwork gears. They would be nervous, he imagined. A little frightened maybe. More frightened than he would be. Raw recruits, who had yet to acquire the sublime taste of killing. He would die with pieces of lead tearing through his body. They would live with the gnawing memory.

He smiled, knowing who would suffer the greater pain.

He could picture their pale and trembling faces as they raised their virgin rifles. They had probably shot at targets, or maybe bottles before. But targets merely ripped. Bottles shattered. They had probably never watched precious life leak into unforgiving sand from the bullets they had fired.

A few soldiers might have shot at renegade Indians, but they were usually on horseback galloping away, or charging your patrol, forcing you to shoot back in self-defense. He'd wager that none of those uniformed idealists ever looked a defenseless man square in the eye and gunned him down.

They just didn't have the belly for it. Or the lust.

"Ready..."

He heard the Sergeant-at-arms call out the command...

"Aim..."

...saw, through his closed eyes, the small platoon raise their rifles in unison...

"Fire!"

He heard the confident clicks of seven empty Springfield rifles, no questions, no hesitation. Braddock flinched, then sneered. That was the easy part. Those soldier boys had yet to look him dead in the face.

He would make sure that the next time they pulled those triggers, their Springfields would be loaded with anguish.

✶✶✶

A long, agonizing hour later, they came for him.

The echoing clang of the cell door roused his thoughts and propelled him to his feet so quickly, that the fat Lieutenant drew his heavy revolver in panic. Braddock slowly eased back onto the straw cot.

The time had come, and he was ready.

The Lieutenant shuffled apprehensively into his cell, accompanied by a rigid, gruff-faced Sergeant and a bespectacled man clinging to a well-thumbed Bible. Braddock knew the man with the thin wire glasses was not the regular parson. The parson had been at the poker table with him that night the young soldier was shot. As the parson, holding a pair of fours, rose to object to the split-second slaughter, Braddock put a bullet in the clergyman's left eye. This afforded the holy man a premature glimpse of the pearly gates he so lovingly sermonized about every Sunday.

With no other priest, minister or rabbi in the territory, the army enlisted the aid of the county clerk to serve as presiding spiritual authority, a role the diminutive man clearly found uncomfortable, as he stood with his bony back pressed tightly against the cold iron bars.

Braddock had to smile at the tableau; a silent prisoner resting comfortably on an army cot; a grossly overweight Lieutenant with his quivering revolver still aimed at the prisoner; a stationary Sergeant with his eyes and rifle held at attention; and a little man pinned against the unyielding bars of the cell, clutching a Bible for dear life.

Even in the last few minutes before his execution, Braddock enjoyed being the one with the power.

Seeing that the Lieutenant was still unable to speak, the Sergeant stepped forward with a firm, but respectful, "It's time, sir,"

Braddock nodded. He lifted himself off the cot, which forced the fat Lieutenant to back away. Then he extended his arms in a long, luxurious stretch. The clerk began muttering some rapid, indistinct prayer, but even he wasn't sure whether it was for the prisoner's benefit, or his own.

Braddock walked over to the steely Sergeant, stared him straight in the eye.

"You ever kill a man just for fun, Sergeant?" he asked.

The Sergeant didn't flinch. He looked to the Lieutenant for permission to reply, but the quaking officer simply waved his revolver as if it was a crucifix warding off Satan. Clearly, Braddock's murderous reputation had crawled deep within the other man's soul. Years from now, he would tell his grandchildren how he single-handedly escorted the infamous Carl Edward Braddock to his death.

Braddock's voice grew louder. "I said, you ever kill a man for fun, Sergeant?"

The soldier looked between Braddock and his superior officer. He locked eyes with the notorious killer and wrestled with his own feelings of revulsion. Then, a small smile broke across his stern expression.

"Not until now, you cold-hearted bastard," he growled.

Braddock nodded with new-found respect. At least he wasn't the only wolf set loose in a world of crippled fawns.

"Then carry on, Sergeant," he said, as he began the long walk from his cell to the place and the moment that would end his life.

****

They walked the darkened hall in silence; the prisoner in the lead, followed by the corpulent Lieutenant with his meaty paw still gripping the handle of his holstered revolver, the stiff legged Sergeant, and the temporary parson, who was still searching frantically for an appropriate passage out of the Bible.

As the odd parade broke free of the building and spilled out into the blinding flash of sudden sunlight, Braddock felt his legs grow weak. He should run. Grab the fat man's gun and blast his way to freedom. Even if he were to die, he would...

No. He would not give them the satisfaction. A bullet in the back of a fleeing outlaw would be a great story, easily forgotten.

He would not allow his captors to escape that easily.

Braddock approached the old stone wall which ringed the fort. His gaze was immediately drawn to the bullet holes and bloodstains that marred its ashen face. He walked on, unable to pull his eyes from this enticing evidence of human destruction.

His legs weakened a second time.

"No! You cannot do this!" cried the raven-haired beauty, as she raced across the sand-filled courtyard. "You cannot execute this man!"

Braddock turned at the distraction, regaining his legs even as he admired hers. She was beautiful, indeed. Her flowing black hair fluttered as she ran, then wafted softly down, until it clung protectively to her delicate waist. She was that rare feminine flower that seldom bloomed in frontier outposts. Catherine Whitehall. The Major's daughter.

She stood face-to-face with the Lieutenant, flung her arguments at the corpulent officer so vigorously, he unwittingly sought out the handle of his holstered revolver. He caught himself doing so, and appeared twice as embarrassed. Still, she berated him mercilessly in front of the men.

His men.

"The Bible tells us we shall not kill!" she cried passionately. "Were we to execute this man, we would be just as guilty of murder as we judge him to be! Jail him if you must, but do not compound this unholy parade of death!"

She went on and on. The Lieutenant could only interject an occasional "...just doing my job..." and "yes, Ma'am, but..," while his men snickered at his widely reddening face.

"What you are doing is wrong!" she wailed, as she pummeled the officer's heaving chest. "Terribly, horribly wrong!"

Braddock paid little heed to her words. He was excited by the passion of her posture. She was his type of woman; delicate, yet savage. As she argued for his life, a grin welled up deep inside him. He wanted to see her naked on the sand. Imagined how enthralling she would look with fresh red welts swelling up along her fragile white skin, his rough hands grasping mounds of her coal black hair, twisting and pulling, until her lips curled back in that grimace of pain and horror that never failed to enflame his desire. If she succeeded in having him pardoned, he would thank her in ways he was sure she had never been thanked before.

"He could be redeemed!" Catherine Whitehall continued fervently. "If the Lord could forgive sinners, then so should we!" She looked at the bearded outlaw, the man scheduled to die in mere minutes.

He looked back at her with gentle eyes that had learned long ago never to betray his inner thoughts. His doe-like expression doubled her ardor.

"Are we animals, that we can take life without remorse? Are we..."

She did not get a chance to finish. The Major, no longer able to ignore his daughter's tirade, was forced to relinquish the isolated security of his office. He stormed onto the courtyard, and slapped his daughter full across the face. She stood startled, embarrassed.

A painful silence followed, broken only by the spontaneous, exuberant laughter of Carl Edward Braddock.

With the outlaw's cruel laughter as much a rebuke as her father's slap, the chastened young woman dashed off across the hot sand towards the familiar embrace of her living quarters.

The Major, equally shamed by the only hand he had ever laid upon his daughter, turned to the stunned Lieutenant.

"Get on with it!" he yelled, before the commanding officer also tramped off to the safety of his well-appointed cocoon.

****

The Sergeant placed Carl Edward Braddock before the thick wooden post standing ominously erect in front of the blood-spattered wall. He tied the outlaw's arms tightly behind his back, so that the post stiffened his posture, an external spine for those who lost their own. Braddock felt a wave of sudden panic surge through him, yet he fought it back down. The six-foot pole dug splinters deep into his back, while he tried to concentrate on the blue sky above. To calm himself, he remembered the faces of the first two men he had killed...back in the days he killed for money, not sport. He remembered the explosive horror that wracked their bodies as they suddenly realized their lives were ending. How their bodily functions rebelled and the stench of embarrassment soiled their pants.

As always, the gruesome images brought him comfort. He knew then, as he always had known, that he was a breed apart. A predator. Were he to be magically transported over these nightmarish walls, he would continue to be a predator. What else could he do? They had made it too easy for a man like him. It was the fault of the prey. And, like Catherine Whitehall, the guilty prey was always willing and eager to take responsibility for his bloody actions.

The Sergeant began to place the black blindfold over his eyes, but Braddock shook it off.

"I want to see their faces as they shoot me down," he growled.

After a moment's hesitation, the Sergeant relented. He walked proudly to a position to the right of the Lieutenant, whose face was still suffused in vibrant magenta.

"Company, Ho!" the Sergeant shouted, and the seven-member firing squad marched double-time to the center of the courtyard.

"Company, Halt!" came the musical grunt. The line of blue uniforms pivoted and froze, shoulder-to-shoulder, facing their victim.

Braddock's back fought the post, his wrists struggled with the thick rope that bound them together. Bound him to this dreadful spot. This stepping off point to eternity.

The last outpost to Hell.

"Rifles, Ho!" The Sergeant shouted, and like a well-oiled machine, seven rifles executed a precision pirouette, before they snapped neatly onto seven shoulders.

"Wait!" screamed Braddock, his voice cracking with desperation. "Where's my last request?!"

The Sergeant hesitated. The squad looked confused. The Lieutenant scratched his head. The custom of a condemned man's last requests had been forgotten long ago, lost somewhere on the wild plains of westward expansion. Yet why exactly had it been abandoned? Surely a man should be allowed one last comfort before he faces eternal retribution?

"Give me my last request!" Braddock yelled to them.

The firing squad murmured amongst themselves, their rifles began to droop.

The Sergeant and Lieutenant shared an increasingly angry whisper.

The Major peeked out the window of his office, and did his best not to be a part of these proceedings.

"I deserve a last request!" Braddock screamed again. Then added a plaintive, "Please..?"

Somewhere within the safe confines of the fort, his words reached a young girl with reddened cheek, who sobbed more deeply for the injustices of the world.

In the courtyard, the Sergeant and Lieutenant ceased their discussions.

"What is it you want?" the Lieutenant asked with a hollow echo of authority.

"Better make it reasonable." grumbled the Sergeant.

The man who had killed more than thirty men, women and children, took a heavy sigh. "It is reasonable. I simply want my final wish to be granted."

"Spit it out, Braddock!"

Carl Edward Braddock smiled. Life had been sweet and exciting, he thought. He would enjoy it to the end.

"I only want to be introduced to those brave men who are about to rob me of my life," he said simply, with no hint of animosity.

The Sergeant was furious. The Lieutenant merely shrugged.

"As you wish," said the senior officer. He gestured to the men of the firing squad. No one spoke. The Lieutenant, whose authority had been undermined all day, shouted at the first man in line.

"Tell him your name, soldier!"

The soldier hesitated, his face a battlefield of emotions.

"Quinn," he whispered at last. He put his rifle down, lifted his dark blue cap, and ran thin fingers through his close-cropped sandy brown hair.

"What was that, son?" shouted Braddock from his post, thirty feet away.

"Quinn, sir." the young soldier responded. "Private Jacob Quinn."

Braddock smiled generously. "Thank you, Jacob. You've made this day easier for me."

"You're welcome, sir." smiled Jacob Quinn in return. Then he tugged the arm of the man beside him. "Tell him your name."

"Uh, Markham. Private First Class," said the tall soldier with the thick black sideburns.

"And your Christian name, Private Marcus?" Braddock asked with apparent interest.

"James. James Markham."

"An honorable name, James. My father's name."

"Is that so, sir?" Markham relaxed. "Mine, too. I'm James, Junior actually."

"Get on with it!" growled the Sergeant.

"Private Wilson Halloran," waved the third man. Wilson Halloran was ten years older than the others, and by far the most relaxed.

"That's a New England accent, if I'm not mistaken, Wilson." Braddock said, nodding in friendly recognition.

"You're absolutely right, sir!" Halloran beamed. "I'm Boston, born and bred."

"A beautiful city, Boston." sighed Braddock. "I always dreamed of seeing it, before I..."

There was a long uncomfortable pause. The condemned man's head lowered with the weight of unfulfilled dreams.

The men of the firing squad had all removed the Springfields from their shoulders. They stood now with discomfort. The stifling silence was broken by the bark of the gruff Sergeant.

"Next man!" he shouted.

The next man stepped forward.

"Private Avery Martin, sir." The boy, barely eighteen grinned so broadly that his freckled face nearly split in half. "And may I say you are the first famous man I ever met, Mister Braddock."

Braddock returned the grin. "The pleasure is mine, Avery. For you are the most freckled young man that I have ever met!"

The squad all shared a good-natured laugh at this, and even Avery Martin joined in the humor at his expense.

Theodore Eckel was next in line.

"Private Theodore Eckel, sir," he was a tall man, with wiry brown hair, an unkempt mustache, and a flamboyant manner of gesturing with his hands. "Might I ask, Mr. Braddock, how you came to kill so many men?"

The others leaned in. They had been eager, but too well-mannered to ask the same question.

Braddock considered his response carefully.

"I chose to defend my family, my country and my honor, boys," he said softly. "Anything more you may have heard are just rumors made up for readers of those penny dreadfuls they sell back East."

"Did you shoot those five men in Loredo?" shouted the next soldier in line.

"Your name, son?"

"Forgive me. Private Christopher Osborne, sir," added the stocky young man with the brightly polished boots. "But my friends call me Chris."

"Then Chris it is." chuckled the man tied to the post.

"Is it true about the five men in Loredo, Mister Braddock?"

"Well, Chris...As I said, I was always willing to defend my family, my country and my honor. But sometimes, like in Loredo, I was pretty busy defending myself."

Their laughter was freer now. The famous outlaw, Carl Edward Braddock was one of them. They were sharing a conversation with one of the most notorious gunslingers of the West. Each of them suddenly felt as if he was part of the legend. The last man in line waved his hand high above his head.

"I'm Nicholas Reid, Mister Braddock. I've been hearing stories about you ever since I was a kid!"

"I hope you enjoyed them, Nick."

"That I did, sir!"

"Because, it is up to you...all of you...to write the final chapter in my story." Braddock's head bobbed again. When it raised, the tears could not be hidden. "I'm guilty only of being Carl Edward Braddock, boys. I've made mistakes...but I've lived my life as I believed was right...In your hearts, you must each remember that..."

The joviality vanished, punctured by the stark reality of the situation. In a few moments, they would kill this man tied to the post. They would be responsible for bringing to a close the enduring legend of Carl Edward Braddock. Chris Osborne began to sniffle. Theodore Eckel's expressive hands refused to fly. The seven riflemen stared at their life-taking weapons and seemed to breathe as one.

The Sergeant stepped forward, clearly irritated by the abrupt change that blanketed his men. He called out to Braddock in a harsh voice.

"You've have had your last request, Braddock. Now you must receive the sentence the courts have seen fit to give you!" He turned back to the firing squad.

"Ready!" he bellowed.

At his order, every man in the solemn group swung his carbine to his shoulder, a projectile of harsh lead loaded into each firing chamber.

"Aim!"

Each soldier stared down his barrel at the silent man tied to the post. His image filled their eyes. Jacob Quinn with the soft voice. James Markham, Jr., who shared his father's name. Wilson Halloran of Boston. Avery Martin with the abundance of freckles. Theodore Eckel and his expressive hands. Christopher Osborne, whom he had called Chris. And Nicholas Reid, who had grown up inspired by stories of this outlaw's colorful career. Each man fixed Carl Edward Braddock in the unforgiving sights of his Springfield .22 caliber.

"Fire!"

The briefest of pauses, then seven recoiling rifles shouted their angry message of death. Carl Edward Braddock's head snapped backwards, smashed against the pole behind him, and fell forward again. Blood flowed from his right ear. The bark of the rifles echoed, then died away across the open desert.

Each man in the firing squad slowly retracted his rifle, looking away from the motionless target.

The Lieutenant wiped a soiled white handkerchief across his damp forehead. He was about to murmur to the Sergeant to dismiss the men, when a chilling sound began to fill the courtyard.

Laughter, cold and brutal.

The soldiers looked at each other, then at the limp figure tied to the post. The sound grew louder. More derisive. All at once, Carl Edward Braddock opened his eyes and raised a wicked cackle to the pale blue sky.

The blood which trickled from his ear was caused by the collision of his head with the wooden post. The soldiers looked among themselves with shame and confusion. The Lieutenant was profoundly distraught. How had seven sharpshooters missed their target completely?

Carl Edward Braddock continued to laugh derisively. His experience as a murderer had served him well. He knew it was harder to kill a man once you saw him as a person, instead of a faceless object. And that's how Jacob Quinn, James Markham, Jr., Wilson Halloran, Avery Martin, Theodore Eckel, Christopher Osborne and Nicholas Reid perceived him now. Each had misadjusted his aim slightly, assuming the man beside him would fire the lethal shot.

Braddock's savage laughter reverberated throughout the courtyard.

"It's hard to kill a man you know, isn't it, boys?" he taunted. "Especially for men like you. I'm in your minds now. If you kill me, you'll be killing a friend. And that thought will torment you for the rest of your lives!"

His words tore through the hearts of the young soldiers like a rusted razor. His laughter rang in their ears, like the brutal clang and hum of a sword striking steel.

"You're fools, all of you!" Braddock shouted. "Pitiable, weak-hearted fools! I'll live in your memories long after I've taken your names with me to the grave, Jacob Quinn. James Markham. Wilson Halloran. Avery Martin..."

Suddenly, a shot rang out across the courtyard and burned its way straight into the throat of the condemned killer. Startled, Braddock began to spit long streaks of crimson onto the hot sand in front of him. Twenty feet away, the Sergeant aimed his Colt revolver a second time.

"My name is Sergeant Woodrow Allan Sweeney..." the angry soldier shouted, as he fired a second bullet into the chest of the notorious outlaw. "And I'm sending you straight to hell, you cold-hearted bastard!"

As he emptied the lethal contents of his pistol into the dead man's body, Sergeant Woodrow Sweeney understood that some evil was beyond redemption.

And that even Hell was too good a place for the likes of Carl Edward Braddock.

There's Someone in the House

Charley Hendricks slowly pushed his way up through the viscous fog of sleep to emerge, once more, cocooned within the familiar warmth of his king-sized bed. A single thought pierced his semi-conscious mind like a cold steel blade slicing through gelatin.

There's someone in the house...

There's someone in the house!

His eyes battled their way open to reveal the statue-like expression of Bernadette, as she sat upright in the bed beside him. The overstuffed feather pillow she now clutched in a death grip had coaxed her thick blonde hair to shoot out in impossible angles. Although her eyes never left the bedroom door, she whispered to him again.

"You hear me, Charley?" Her hoarse whisper taut and brittle as an overwound guitar string. "There's someone in the house!"

For an instant, Charley Hendricks struggled with the vague feeling that he might still be trapped within a dream. Yet the feeling passed as the unwavering consistency of his wife's expression sent an icy shiver up his spine. Fear and ferocity alternated in her eyes, the look all parents exude when their offspring are threatened.

Seeing her face, Charley immediately absorbed and emitted the same emotions. His heart pushed adrenaline into his limbs, and his teeth clenched tightly. He was halfway to the bedroom closet before Bernadette even realized he had left the bed.

Charley emerged from the shadows an instant later. The unfamiliar weight of a twelve-gauge shotgun heavy in his hands.

At the sight of the weapon, which they had bought precisely for this eventuality, but never really believed they would ever have to use, Bernadette slid deeper into panic.

"Grab your phone," he said softly, with what he hoped was a reassuring lilt to his strained voice. "If you hear me yell, you call 911. Then grab Sarah and lock yourselves in the closet." He started to move, then stopped. Turned to her again. "And you stay there. No matter what."

"Charley...," she whispered, neither question nor statement. He knew she just needed to say his name as a way of pushing her fear back down.

"You hear me, babe? Stay there until I come back."

The frightened woman locked eyes with her barefoot husband, and the two exchanged a brief glance that instantly and wordlessly communicated the gasping whirlpool of emotions between them. Was this to be the last time their eyes would ever meet?

"Whatever happens...you don't come after me," he said.

She let out a half-gasp/half-moan, that was the most painful thing he had ever heard come out of her mouth.

"Promise me. You have to be strong for Sarah. Promise me, Bernadette."

"I... I promise," she whispered and lowered her eyes.

Charley nodded. Paused to steady his ragged breath, for her sake as much as his. Then with clammy hands, he cocked the shotgun.

The distinctively brutal *ka-chang* of the shell being forced into the chamber made them both cringe.

It took him another twenty long seconds before he could find the safety. 'Safety' seemed a cruel irony now. His house was being invaded. His family threatened. The man in the flannel pajama bottoms cradled the butt of the shotgun against his thigh, then scoured inside himself for the detached courage he would need to actually use it.

He knew, without hesitation, that he would be willing to die to protect his family. But could he also muster that strange mix of ice and passion which would enable him to kill in their defense? The solemn black barrel of the shotgun seemed to mock his indecision.

Use me, it pleaded.

This is precisely what I was forged to do.

Slowly, carefully, Charley Hendricks opened his bedroom door. Sensing nothing but darkness and shadows, he slipped slowly into the hall and stepped into whatever future lay beyond.

The crushing blackness of the hallway seemed to amplify his hearing, so that every tiny noise crashed and echoed around him. His breath became a noisy bellows of fear. His own blood whooshed and pulsed in his ears. The groan of the wooden floor beneath each deliberate footstep reverberated louder than a car alarm to his heightened senses. Too late, he realized that he had cheated his family; he possessed neither the skill nor confidence of a hero. Would the next clatter of his clumsy, uncatlike movements push whoever was in his house to murderous rage? He silently begged a God he had prayed to only haphazardly for years, that his family would not be forced to suffer for his ineptitude.

He hesitated.

Took another step forward.

And another.

Sarah's bedroom still lay twenty agonizing feet beyond. It was a distance he would cross in a heartbeat whenever her five-year old voice cried out for Daddy to come rescue her from some lurking nightmare creature. On those precious nights, he would scoop her tiny, trembling body into his arms, brush the soft hair from her tear-stained face, murmur a father's litany of love and comfort. All the while trying to burn the smell and feel and image of this tiny frightened child into his memory, as a soothing balm for the time when she would be too old to need him. He had always been a heavy sleeper, but with the birth of his daughter, he would rouse and dash at the slightest murmur escaping from her room. Perhaps it was the constant illness this frail and trusting child had suffered through the first years of her life. Maybe it was his absolute dread at the thought of losing her, the only thing he could say with absolute certainty that he had done right in his life. Perhaps it was his own suffocating fear of being alone. Whatever the reason, he argued that it was both normal and wondrous that this thin child with the pale blue eyes needed her Daddy so much.

His mind snapped back to the hallway. The shotgun felt suddenly heavier in his hands. The door to his daughter's bedroom still seemed an eternity away.

It was half-open.

He never left it open.

Someone was in the house.

In his little girl's room!

At that very moment, the silence of the hallway exploded in a loud, echoing clang. He gasped loudly, then felt wretched for doing so. The grandfather clock downstairs continued to ring out the hour, and Charley cursed it under his breath. His element of surprise was gone. He raised the shotgun and bounded the remaining distance to his daughter's bedroom.

He crashed through the door, ready to fight Hell itself to save his baby. Yet he wasn't prepared for what he saw in that room.

Sarah writhed in the throes of a nightmare, her doll-like arms tossed randomly across the bed.

The shadowy figure of a man stood over her.

But Charley could not fire his gun.

He could only stare at the tall man, as the freezing claw of terror gripped his chest and spread its clammy fingers up to his throat.

The man turned to him with a smile.

Charley Hendricks never remembered hitting the floor.

****

From miles deep within the labyrinth of his mind, Charley could feel the brutal slap of cold hands against his face yank him back to consciousness. He did not want to wake up, but the hands were painfully insistent. As he came to, he could feel warm blood trickling lightly into his right eye. That's when he finally panicked. His arms swung blindly from side to side. The next slap was one of pure sound.

"Stop it, Charley!"

It was Bernadette's voice. And it jerked him upwards from the abyss.

Bernadette's face danced with worry. A handprint on her cheek blazed scarlet where he had slapped her in his momentary delirium. Beside her was the small face of Sarah, crocodile tears reddening her own pouty cheeks. Bernadette saw the consciousness return to her husband's eyes and she finally allowed herself a full breath.

"Thank God, Charley," she muttered. "Thank God."

The wail of the sirens drowned out the remaining words she mumbled. Charley tried to sit up, as the pounding on the front door flowed up the stairs to intrude on this bizarre family scene. But everything tilted and spun, he was too dizzy. He slunk back down to the floor.

"It's the police," Bernadette sighed again. "Thank God, Charley! Thank God."

****

Forty-five minutes later, Charley was still sitting in the downstairs kitchen, an icebag insulting his throbbing forehead. Sergeant Eberle, the shortest policewoman Charley had ever seen, was frowning at the notes she had jotted down on her paper. Her partner, Officer Michaels, was examining the outside doors and windows. They glanced at each other with practiced subtlety whenever they thought Charley was not looking. Bernadette had already retreated upstairs to rock Sarah back to sleep.

"So, to sum up, Mr. Hendricks..." this was actually the fourth time Sergeant Eberle had summed up his answers. "Your wife woke you, saying she had heard a noise. That someone was in the house."

"Yes. That's right."

"You proceed to arm yourself with a twelve-gauge shotgun, then walk to your daughter's room down the hall."

"I wouldn't say I walked exactly. More like, snuck and ran."

"Snuck and ran."

"Uh-huh."

"Okay. So, after you gain access to your daughter's room. You find your daughter asleep in her bed. After assessing the situation, you suddenly lose consciousness, receiving a large contusion on your forehead as you hit the floor. And you claim you don't remember anything else until your wife roused you. Is that about it?"

"I guess so."

"And you have no idea why you lost consciousness?"

"Look. The guy fainted..." Officer Michaels called from the far end of the kitchen. "Give him a break, will ya? I mean, we can't all be heroes." He looked down at Charley's wounded expression. "Um, no disrespect intended, sir."

"Thank you for your valuable input, Officer Michaels," Sergeant Eberle said without a shred of actual gratitude. "But *I* happen to be taking Mister Hendricks' statement here."

Officer Michaels nodded. "Sorry, Sarge." He tossed in an apologetic grin, then ducked out the back door. Eberle turned her attention back to the wounded man in the baggy pajama bottoms.

"So, Mister Hendricks...You say you saw nothing unusual prior to losing consciousness?"

"No."

"No sign of anyone else in the house?"

Charley shifted under her penetrating gaze. "Not that I remember." He squirmed again throughout the long, squirming pause that followed. An oppressive silence that was broken a minute later by Officer Michaels' blessed lack of timing.

"No sign of forced entry on the doors or windows, Sarge. Everything's still locked from the inside."

"And you double-checked the house?"

"Clean as an anorexic's lunch box. The lady musta just got a little spooked. Uh...no disrespect intended, sir."

"None taken, Officer Michaels," Charley offered up an overly dramatic yawn. "Can I go back to bed now, Sergeant Eberle? It's been quite a night, and I have work in the morning."

"Would you like us to leave a squad car out front for a while?"

"Thanks, but that won't be necessary," Charley rose to his feet. "I'm sure we all just got a little spooked. But I do appreciate you stopping by."

Sergeant Eberle skewered him with another long, appraising look that forced Charley to find some action with which he could comfortably turn away and occupy his attention. Finding nothing, he fiddled with an imaginary piece of lint on his pajamas. After what seemed like an eternity, the policewoman clicked her tongue and flipped over her notepad.

"Thank you for your time, Mister Hendricks. Feel free to call if you need any further assistance."

"I will. And thank you."

Charley escorted the two police officers to the back door without another word, then quickly bolted it behind them. He wiped his brow with trembling hands, before slowly making his way back up the staircase.

Outside, Officer Michaels was leaning against the squad car, as he watched the lights go out, one by one, in the Hendricks' house. He turned to Sergeant Eberle, maneuvering her way into the passenger's seat.

"So, whatta ya think, Sarge? Flake or felon?"

Sergeant Eberle snapped the shoulder harness of her seat belt, as she too, looked up at the darkened windows.

"He's lying," she frowned. "There was somebody in that house."

∗∗

Charley made sure that both Bernadette and Sarah were sound asleep before sneaking back to the kitchen with the shotgun once again in his sweaty hands. The strangling fear, surprisingly absent when the police were in the house, returned to continue its prickly pounding on his chest.

There was someone in the house. He knew it all too well. He had seen the face of the old man, and it had terrified him more than anything else had ever done in his life.

The shotgun, still cocked and ready, lay across his knees in the silent kitchen. There was no need to turn on the lights. He knew the man would return, and he was sure the man knew Charley would be waiting for him.

He checked the safety again. This time, he promised himself he would not faint, no matter what happened.

It was impossible to say how much time had passed, or even if Charley had dozed off or not. But suddenly, his spine stiffened and his fingers gripped the trigger of the shotgun.

The old man was there, only a few feet away.

Staring at him.

Neither the watcher, nor the watched said a word, they simply appraised each other without moving so much as an eye muscle.

It seemed forever since Charley last exhaled.

Finally, he could stand it no longer.

"Dad?" he whispered.

The old man nodded, and Charley abruptly collapsed into tears.

****

Most men share a similar, evolving relationship with their fathers; one that grows from childhood idolization, through the sudden realization of a father's humanity, and the crushing disappointment that brings. This is usually followed by an extended period of adolescent contempt, as paternal frailties become bitterly exaggerated when seen through teenage eyes struggling for their own world view. By the time the boy is thrust into his own position of fatherhood, he finally understands that the man who raised him was as much a confused little boy as he is himself, a carefree post-adolescent who suddenly found himself saddled with a crushing responsibility to a child that inexplicably idolizes him. If the relationship is allowed to mature, father and son may rediscover common ground as two men who desperately want to be free again, but would rather lose an arm than a single precious memory of fatherhood.

The relationship between Charley Hendricks and his father was never allowed to mature. It died in the adolescent contempt stage.

And Charley had always hated his father for it.

Now that same old man stared back at him from the night-infested shadows of his own kitchen. That same face had loomed over his daughter's bed as she slept. Charley raised the shotgun and carefully aimed the imposing black barrel at his father's head.

"You would only wake your wife and disturb my grandchild," the old man smiled softly. This was even more shocking, since Charley had few memories of his father smiling. Without knowing why, he lowered the gun.

"What are you doing here?" Charley asked in a hesitant whisper, though no actual words passed between them. The old man was suddenly at Charley's side and there they stood: father and son, face-to-face.

"I keep an eye on Sarah. Just as your grandfather once watched over you, and your great-great-grandfather once watched over me. Don't ask me how. Just accept it as truth."

"I hated you."

"I know, son."

"Don't call me son! How could you leave me like that?!"

"It was beyond my control. So many things in this world are," he sighed.

"That's an easy out."

"There are no easy outs, Charley. Only truth and self-deception. And I have too little to lose to lie to you now."

"Doesn't change anything," Charley sniffed, with insincere finality.

"I know," the old man's face was sorrow itself. "But believe me, I would change it all if I could.'

Beset by wave after wave of frantic questions, Charley had nothing to say. He simply stared at the stark linoleum and let the old man continue.

"Listen, Charley...Each of us stumbles blindly through an ocean of insignificance, only to find, much too late, that we focused on all the wrong things. Always the wrong things. We squander our precious time building walls of broken promises and missed opportunities. Then one day, we discover there's no time left to make things right. In those last desperate moments of realization, our hopes flounder. And we sink beneath an avalanche of bad choices, desperately pleading for a second chance..."

Charley was mesmerized by the way the old man conveyed a multitude of emotions without ever changing a single expression on his face.

"I had no chance to make it right with you, Charley," he continued. "For that I am eternally sorry."

"You never even gave me a chance to say good-bye."

"Few ever do. Even when we are there at that final moment, we always feel there's more we could have said. Don't punish yourself for that, Charley. But learn from my mistakes. Tell your daughter what's in your heart, while she's still young enough to listen and believe."

Charley had given up all hope of stopping his tears. He looked into his father's face and, suddenly, felt all those years of bitterness melt away.

"She's beautiful, isn't she?" he said at last.

"She's beautiful, my grandchild," the old man smiled.

"Will you always watch over her?"

"All her life. Just as you will watch over her children after you die. Believe what I say, son. Not even death can distance a father's love."

The silver shimmer of the early morning light intruded on the silent conversation. The old man slowly began to waver and fade. Charley stood quickly, trying somehow to prolong the moment.

"Dad, there's so much..."

"Say it to your daughter, Charley."

And these became his father's newest last words.

Weeks later, Charley Hendricks was again roused from a deep slumber to find his wife frozen upright in the bed beside him.

"Wake up, Charley!" she whispered harshly. "Someone's in the house!"

Charley tried to focus his eyes on the dark shadows which wavered through the open door to the hallway. He said nothing.

"Did you hear me?" Bernadette gripped his arm tightly. "I said there's someone in the house!"

"I know," mumbled Charley, as he slowly rolled back over on his side. "Isn't it wonderful?"

Don't

As the steel-booted guards escaped down the iron corridor, the denizens of Cellblock H bristled with anticipation.

Mangled knuckles, bulging forearms, and massive, tattooed biceps hung through the vertical bars like so many tentacles of a monstrous, ill-defined creature grasping at its prey. Eloquent in their dark blues, reds and blacks, the ornate tats screamed of anger, hatred, death, and occasionally even a strange form of love. The welts and scars echoed similar themes, though in more clandestine tones.

Cellblock H of Kaufman State Penitentiary was reserved for only the most dangerous inmates. The crème de la criminals. The self-appointed cancer of humanity. Despite the obligatory protests of innocence or discrimination, the men of Cellblock H sheltered no illusions as to why they were here. Most accepted their role, and more than a few reveled in it. They were simply part of the two percent of our species who, throughout history, had always possessed the unique ability to slit a throat for the simple delight of guessing how far the blood would spurt, and what expression the victim's face would reveal at that sudden, initial realization of impending lifelessness. Civilizations across the globe chose various methods of dealing with this unique breed. They were alternatively eliminated, isolated, tortured, or, in our enlightened age, condescended to, and thus, allowed to prey on the remaining ninety-eight percent who had no hope of ever understanding their vile and chaotic thought processes.

These were hardened men. Social mutations. And only the most self-righteous members of the parole board, along with a few first-year legal aides, ever spoke of actual rehabilitation without choking down a laugh.

The reason for today's excitement was etched on every calendar, and carved in nearly every drab cell wall. This was the first Thursday of the month. 'Sheep Day,' as the Rogue Boys of Cellblock H liked to call it. The day when the new inmates arrived, to catch their first gut-numbing glimpse of the concrete and steel tomb that would be their home for the next twenty years to life.

Sheep Day was one of the few bright spots in the numbing monotony of incarceration.

The men hooted and hollered as the hesitant parade of new inmates spilled into the corridor. The frightened novitiates were welcomed with catcalls, whistles, jokes and threats. Fists clenched and reclenched. Eyes darted nervously.

A few of these new inmates tried to tough it out; these would be the ones who best understood the unwritten code of the iron arena. They would have to hurt somebody right away, in order to prove themselves dangerous and worthy of respect, or at least, avoidance.

Others well-versed in prison life, instinctively scanned the already caged brotherhood for protectors; gangs or lovers who would often treat them just as brutally, but would, in return, shelter them from the far more terrifying possibility of random attack. Even though they were to be tightly confined with murderers, rapists and career prisoners, each man's worst fear was being completely alone.

And so, they filed in, twenty-nine in all.

Out of the twenty-nine shuffling, staring or strutting sheep, only one of the current group of initiates to Cellblock H had not been in prison before. And all eyes were irresistibly drawn to him. Not merely because he was unfamiliar, but rather that he looked as incongruous to this setting as a human being could possibly be.

Despite the muttered disclaimers of social scientists, most career criminals carry a certain look about them. A visual edge that warns others to stay away. The cold eyes. A predatory walk. An inadvertent sneer or too-easy smile. This new convict had none of those qualifications. He was a young man with the face of an angel, distant blue eyes, slim build, and a profile sculptors had long associated with saints and idealized lovers. All decided liabilities in a place like Cellblock H.

There was a strange purity about this one. His long, blonde hair curled long on his neck and shimmered silently under the harsh fluorescents. Although he lacked any mannerisms which could be considered effeminate, his gentle face reminded the desperate men of Cellblock H of women they had known long ago and abused.

His expression was gently shaped by sadness, not fear or regret, more akin to the ethereal sorrow of a doomed poet.

He walked amidst the jeering spectators lost in thought. An ideal victim, oblivious to his surroundings.

Not surprisingly, it was this new inmate who generated the largest share of catcalls and abusive comments. Yet he seemed completely at peace, or better put, self-contained, despite the cascade of vile threats and promises hurled in his direction. He walked through the clanging cacophony as if he were pacing alone in a wooded park. Many of the veterans were already drafting plans for this young novitiate.

The steel booted guards looked at him with pity and contempt, yet gave him an unusually wide berth.

Even they had to admit, there was a presence about this one that could not be denied.

****

By lights out, the rumor mill, fueled by the prison currency of crack, cigarettes and favors to come, had already sketched a composite of the angelic boy.

Name: Allan Lawrence Trent.

Status: Homeless.

This was the first time he had ever done time, a rare situation for anyone sentenced to Cellblock H.

Easy Eddie, who worked in the infirmary where all new prisoners are processed before being released to the general prison population, claimed the boy bore not a single visible scar on his frail body, and that the prison doctor had certified he was free of communicable diseases. A definite plus in the eyes of the prison counselor who exhorted the virtues of safe, if not always consensual, sex.

Age: 19, young for a place like Cellblock H.

Marital Status: None.

Sexual Preference: Unknown.

Crime: Nine Counts of First Degree Murder.

Sentence: Life, without possibility of parole.

Although the details of his crime were few, the guards had heard talk of that 'horrible massacre upstate.' At the trial, he offered no words in his own defense, except to vigorously dispute the insanity plea of his defense attorney. That alone had been important to him. He also pleaded with the judge that he never be eligible for parole, or he would inevitably kill again.

The guards whispered that the young man's court-appointed lawyer had thrown his file across the courtroom in frustration.

That was all anybody knew about Allan Lawrence Trent.

The new inmate, like all other first timers in Kaufman State Penitentiary, was given his own small cell in the back corner of Cellblock H. After thirty days, he would share a regulation cell with another inmate. At that point, he would either adapt to prison life, or die mysteriously in the night. Another concurrent life sentence for murder meant as little to these men as a clean bill of health to a hypochondriac.

Three hours after lights out, the cellblock breathed the uneasy sleep of caged men. The high-pitched hum of those few functioning fluorescent bulbs provided an odd counterpoint to the bass line of snores, gasps and whispers. In the softly heaving metallic hallways, Jake Graffis, a double lifer up for parole in three years, silently slipped a packet of rocky white powder to Willie Moynihan, the prison guard with the addict wife.

Willie's forehead glistened in the dim light, and his ears strained to catch any hint of steel-toed boots. Not that he should have cared. The warden and the other guards knew all about Willie's midnight commerce with the prisoners. They simply chose to look the other way. It was looked on as a minor infraction in an environment of structured abuse. They explained it this way; even the most brightly polished metal begins to exhibit pits and scars after prolonged exposure to corrosive elements. Though there were only occasional attacks on guards, no more than five a year requiring hospitalization or permanent loss of limbs, few were willing to work the graveyard shift in Cellblock H.

Willie's pipeline would therefore be tolerated.

The inmate hierarchy knew better than to jeopardize their relationship with Willie for something as unprofitable as blackmail. The dim-witted guard with the junkie wife provided a valuable service for all concerned. He was a surreptitious liaison for official warnings and inmate concerns. An unwitting pressure valve for this constant, concrete hell.

The terms of the deal were set only in nods and gestures. And it was left to Willie to offer up his part of the transaction.

"Don't exactly know how to explain it," Willie whispered in a high-pitched voice, which oddly suited his massive bulk. "There's something weird about this kid…Almost scary."

"Scary?!" Jake's laughter rang through the cellblock and splintered in a hundred pair of straining ears. "Hell, I've skinned bunny rabbits scarier than that fairy boy."

"He's not a fairy. He's not…nothin'. He carried a picture of some girl in his wallet. A real looker. But when they were going to hand it back to him, he tore it up into a thousand pieces. With his teeth."

"Yeah? So, he's nuts, huh?"

"Maybe. Maybe not. The whole time he only said one word."

"Yeah? And what did golden boy have to say?"

Willie hesitated, wiped a soiled white handkerchief across his damp brow. When no answer came, Jake reached a gnarled claw through the bars and grasped the bigger man's throat, just to help the answer along. "I said, what did the kid have to say, Willie?"

"Well, I was pushin' 'em all down the corridor, and I didn't care for the way he was just saunterin' along all casual like. So's I give him an extra shove with my nightstick and knock him flat on his ass."

"Then what?"

"I…I can't explain it. He didn't cringe. He didn't complain. He didn't even try to swing at me. He just stood up…looked me straight in the eye. He's got these real spooky eyes, that kid. At that point, I figure it's time to teach him a little respect for authority, so's I raise my nightstick to educate his skull a bit, and then…"

"Then what?" spit Jake, growing tired of this story.

"I…I couldn't."

"You couldn't?"

"I couldn't. It was the way he looked at me. And what he said. Or how he said it. I dunno."

At this point Willie was shaking visibly, even in the dim light. Jake thought maybe Willie's wife isn't the only one using these days.

"I ain't got all night, Willie. What'd the kid say?"

"He…he looked at me and said…Don't."

"Don't?" the convict coughed out a laugh.

"Don't," shuddered the guard.

Jake looked at Willie and let a breath of contempt escape through his yellowed teeth. He didn't think it was possible to have more disgust for this burly buffoon. Until now.

"Willie, man. I think the old lady musta cut something off while you was snorin' last night. If you let these guys know you let some wimp kid stare you down, you're dead meat in this place."

"No first-day sheep stares me down, Jake! You know that!" Willie pulled the black .45 caliber automatic out of his side holster. "I'll put two in the back of his skull! You know I will!"

His eyes reddened, as he waved the gun around for the benefit of other, unseen eyes and ever-present ears.

"No. Willie. Let me handle it, man. On the house."

Willie's relief came a little too quickly, and he reholstered his gun. "Yeah. Maybe you better. Warden's got his eye on me lately. I can't be seen breakin' any rules."

"Yeah. You're a real saint, Willie. Say 'high' to your wife for me."

"Go to hell," mumbled Willie, as he stomped quickly down the corridor into the retreating darkness.

Jake looked after him and smiled. "I'm already here, Willie. I'm already here…"

****

In a small holding cell in the furthest corner of Cellblock H, Allan Lawrence Trent sat motionless on his bunk with legs folded beneath him, yoga-style. It appeared to the night guards making their rounds that this strange kid had not moved a muscle in over three hours. They laughed to themselves at this weird golden-haired boy, who sat like some Southern California Buddha. Yet there was an uneasiness in each of their voices. He did not behave like any other inmate they had ever seen.

And that bothered them more than they cared to admit.

****

Thirty days later, and thanks to a few payoffs in the right hands, the new prisoner was assigned to share a cell with Jake Graffis.

No one was surprised.

As second in command of the Rogue Boys, Jake was the third most powerful man in the prison, right behind Crazy Eddie Farrow and the Warden...in that order.

Inmates in a maximum security prison like Kaufman State Penitentiary break off into a multitude of gangs, divided by color, religion, ethnic background, or even sentences. Cellblock H boasted, among others; the Black Gangstas, a Muslim brotherhood; the Chulas, a Latino group; the Ihtzaks, a Jewish gang; the Skinheads, a white supremacy group; and the Slashers, a fraternity of mass murderers. Other gangs were often built around a single personality striving for dominance. Out of these, the Rogue Boys were the most feared and respected. With sixty-six members, the gang pledged strict fealty to that six-foot-six, two-hundred and ninety-pound walking psychosis known as Crazy Eddie Farrow.

Although virtually everyone in Cellblock H had the capacity to kill, Crazy Eddie was a master of mutilation. Men who crossed him could wake up to a searing pain and a gusher of blood, only to find their eyelids or ears torn off. Crazy Eddie had earned his reputation one mutilation at a time, until even the guards knew better than to approach him when he was in one of his darker moods.

'Eddie's PMS' they called it.

Pre-Mutilation Syndrome.

And everyone knew better than to get in his way. The warden knew he had no weapons at his disposal to deal with Crazy Eddie, so he used the Rogue Boys to keep order in Cellblock H. In return, he would look the other way when an enemy of the Rogue Boys turned up dead or mutilated.

Since Crazy Eddie was in solitary confinement for biting yet another nose off a fellow inmate, his third in two years, that left Jake Graffis in temporary charge of the Rogue Boys.

Jake had long been second in command to Crazy Eddie, and had the honor of being the only inmate Crazy Eddie ever talked to about his past. They had become fast friends after Jake alone helped Crazy Eddie fight off an ambush by the Black Gangstas. Outnumbered, seven to one, they managed to put nine Gangstas in the infirmary, and bury two others.

During the fight, Eddie had used the bone protruding from his own broken arm to gouge out the eye of an attacker. Jake had torn open another's throat with his teeth. That had sealed the bond of brotherhood between these two psychopaths.

Now, as the cell door was flung open to scream its metallic complaint, Jake smiled. Allan Lawrence Trent was led into his cell without a word. Anton, the day guard, also said nothing, feeling a little like an executioner by leaving the new boy in the care of this human shredding machine. Anton softly pushed the expressionless inmate forward and quickly slammed the door behind him.

He forced himself to not look back as he fled down the hallway.

Allan Lawrence Trent let his eyes wander around the cell with dull curiosity. His gaze eventually fell upon Jake, who was baring his most vicious smile.

"I'll make this easy for you, kid," Jake began. "I'm the man, and you're a piece of dog shit. You got that?"

The new inmate said nothing, as he simply sat down on the lower bunk.

Jake continued. He had used this speech many times before.

"You may think this cellblock is hell, but you ain't seen hell until you piss me off. The last guy in that bunk shoved his own arm in the license plate stamping machine, just so's he could get away from me." Jake smiled as he remembered the screams. So few things bring you joy in prison, so you have to rely on those happier memories. But he roused himself, remembering he had a new cellmate to terrorize. "He ain't never gonna pick his own nose again, but he felt like it was a good deal. You may not be so lucky."

Still, the new cellmate said nothing. He stretched out on the bed. Looked curiously up at his oversized cellmate.

"That's right, boy. You don't talk unless I tell you to. You don't move until I say so. You don't breathe, unless you ask my permission first. You don't take a crap without my approval. You don't even live without me allowing it. You're mine, and nothing on earth can help you now."

And then the young inmate did something that left Jake almost speechless. Just at the point in the speech when every other new cellmate had begun begging for mercy, crying uncontrollably, or cowering in the corner, Allan Lawrence Trent fell asleep.

Jake was so stunned by this reaction, it took almost eight seconds before he exploded with rage. Pretty or not, he intended to kill this golden-haired kid, who didn't even have the decency to listen to the rest of his speech.

Jake let out a howl of pure rage and everyone in Cellblock H knew instantly that Allan Lawrence Trent was a dead man sleeping.

Jake saw only blood in his eyes as he grabbed a pillow from his cot and slammed it toward the face of his sleeping cellmate. As he was about to choke the life out of the boy, an arm shot up to block the pillow. The boy's blue eyes flew open, and caught Jake's blood engorged stare in a vise-like grip. There was a fury in those steel blue eyes, more horrifying than anything Jake had ever seen. They seemed to bore right through him and explode inside his skull. The big convict staggered backwards, unable to break the gaze. Those beautiful, terrifying eyes seemed to suck the breath right out of his lungs.

The boy didn't even bother to sit up. In a soft voice, horrifying in its absolute control, he spoke a single word...

"Don't."

Then, he closed his eyes and went back to sleep.

Jake Graffis fell backwards until he felt the concrete wall pressing into his spine, then sunk to his knees on the opposite side of the cell. He tried to make himself as small as humanly possible; the murderous pillow still clutched in his hands, though now in a strictly defensive position. His breath burned in his lungs, coming only in sharp, ragged gasps.

The image of that stare burned inside his brain. It was a full minute before Jake could even muster up the courage to blink.

On the bunk, Allan Lawrence Trent began to snore softly, his face even more angelic in slumber. Then, from down the corridor, a plaintive voice carried forward.

"Damn it, Jake. Why'd you have to go and kill the kid? He was the prettiest thing we ever seen in this place."

Jake didn't answer.

He sat cowering in the corner, staring across the stark cell at the sleeping boy with the golden hair.

And for the first time in his life, Jake Graffis knew real fear.

Over the next two weeks, the other convicts began to notice a gradual change in Jake. No more was he the arrogant second-in-command of the cellblock's most feared gang. He still had the same hair-trigger temper, but it began to look more like the paranoia of a cornered animal than the unpredictability of a fearless predator. He developed a noticeable twitch in the right corner of his mouth. Dark, sagging circles under his eyes bitterly confessed to his increasing lack of sleep. His skin became noticeably paler, and his movements more agitated whenever his new cellmate approached.

Jake wasn't the only one who shrank away from the odd boy with the beatific face. Whenever he passed, the other convicts gave him a wide berth. There was something about Allan Lawrence Trent, something intangible, that made even these desperately sadistic men a little queasy. It wasn't that they were afraid of him. There was nothing specific in his movements or demeanor that could be seen as overtly threatening. On the contrary, he seemed the most unassuming of men. A pitiful sunfish who had unwittingly wandered into a pool dominated by hungry sharks.

Yet the bloodthirsty pack continually circled, never struck.

It was only a matter of time before he would be taken out, and a small pool was drawn up to see who would be the one to cut this punk kid down to size. Somebody had to break him into the prison routine. After all, it had been over two weeks, and he hadn't even been raped or beaten once. That was far too long for a new sheep to be left unsheared. A few inmates even grumbled that Cellblock H was losing its edge, but those who complained also kept a safe distance from the silent convict with the strange eyes.

For his part, Allan Lawrence Trent spoke only one other time during those first two weeks. When it became clear that Jake had, for some unknown reason, failed to cower him into accepting the protection of the Rogue Boys, a rival gang decided to make their move. Although their target was clearly not Latino, the Chulas decided it would be fun, as well as major status points for their gang, to have this golden-haired sheep as a pet.

The moment was set for the Tuesday lunch shift in the cafeteria. As always, Allan Lawrence Trent sat alone. In the crowded cafeteria, his was the only table enjoyed by a single occupant. He kept to himself, and appeared not to notice the noise, the crowded hall, or the inmates that scowled at him from a distance, each with lowered gazes and clenched jaws. Yes, he would certainly be major status points for the Chulas.

The leader of the Latino gang was a thin, almost emaciated Puerto Rican with a reputation for being especially adept with a knife. Outside the concrete cocoon of Kaufman State Penitentiary, Julio Guzman had sliced open twenty-seven prostitutes. The police had found only enough evidence to charge him with two counts of murder, which he plea bargained down to one case of aggravated assault. He was up for parole in three months. While inside, he was rumored to have cut-up fourteen inmates, even though the warden could not find a single living witness to point the finger at Guzman. Even the usual snitches were far too fond of their tongues and genitals to consider implicating Julio.

On a signal from their leader, nine Chulas rose as one from their table against the wall. Raoul and Manuel walked directly over to the heavily armed guards by the doors. This was the sign language of Kaufman State. The guards, took the silent cue and turned their backs on what was to follow. The prisoners' personal matters were not their concern. If the whole business was handled swiftly, silently, and with a minimum of commotion, they would not get involved.

The other seven Chulas walked behind their unassuming victim. Julio cast a quick glance at the guards, and confirmed that they were intensely occupied with some unseen debris or markings on the far walls. All the other inmates had also taken their cues and began concentrating intently on the lunch trays in front of them. None dared raise his head. You could not be forced to testify to what you never saw.

Allan Lawrence Trent ate his gray lunchmeat slowly, unaware of the hovering presence behind him.

In the wink of an eye, a homemade knife with a four-inch serrated blade appeared from beneath a prison workshirt and was quickly handed down a line of seven men to Julio. The other Chulas assumed a casual formation with their backs to the scene, effectively blocking the view of anyone who would be foolish enough to look at what was about to transpire. The choreographed action was executed with clockwork precision. A paramilitary strike on an intensely personal scale. With rabid swiftness, Julio flashed the razor-sharp blade in a sweeping, downward arc, until it rested tenderly on the throat of his victim. At the same instant, he grabbed a fistful of blonde curls and yanked Allan Lawrence Trent's head sharply back. This exposed the boy's throat even further to the icy ministrations of the blade. The whole movement took a fraction of a second. The Chula leader's face pressed against the ear of his victim.

Julio rocked the blade with the precision of a surgeon, enough to inflict pain and terror, but without sufficient pressure to break the skin.

Not yet.

He whispered into the young man's ear with a cold voice forged by years of unrelenting hate.

"Yo, Goldilocks. You belong to the Chulas now! You belong to me. Comprende?!" To emphasize his point, he allowed the blade to slip lightly beneath the outer layers of skin. The thin sliver of blood communed in a single red drop, which fell ever so slowly down the exposed throat of Allan Lawrence Trent, and onto his plate of gray lunchmeat.

Julio smiled, as he looked into the eyes of his victim.

And that was his big mistake.

Because the Chulas were positioned to block the scene from prying eyes, nobody could later report to the warden exactly what happened. The initial blood-curdling scream was unusual for this type of confrontation. Julio was a master of the quiet kill. But as the scream turned into an agonizing howl, the guards, themselves, whirled around in surprise. The unspoken rule of swift and silent had been violated and they would now be forced to break up the party. This made them angry. Questions would be asked and explanations would have to be concocted. The Chulas were usually much more professional than this. The guards leapt forward with their blue steel revolvers and lead-filled nightsticks.

They reached the table just as the body hit the floor and began convulsing wildly. Blood splattered everywhere in a surreal mockery of the type of modern art that might have commanded hundreds of thousands in a New York gallery. The two burly guards received no resistance at all as they pushed aside the six stunned, but equally massive Chula bodyguards.

What they saw froze the hearts of even these jaded professionals.

At the table sat Allan Lawrence Trent, quietly eating his unstained carrots and mashed potatoes. On the floor beside him, Julio Guzman writhed and screamed, as he clawed savagely at his own face and head. A flap of ragged skin and muscle that had once covered an area from his right temple to his lower jaw flapped open, exposing the bones of his skull to the silvery harshness of the fluorescent lights. Julio was wildly tearing a similar gash in the left side of his face, when his heart, in a rare act of mercy, stopped beating.

Everyone looked with horror at the silent, mutilated face of Julio Guzman. Everyone except Allan Lawrence Trent, who swallowed the last morsels of his lunch, then gently dabbed the thin line of blood on his throat with a paper napkin, before rising to return his tray to the proper area for washing.

Suddenly, the vacuum of sound left by Julio's final scream was filled with a roar of confusion and anger.

The guards aimed their pistols at Allan Lawrence Trent and prepared to fire.

Three Chulas rushed towards him with their own homemade shivs.

A fourth threw the table aside, and leaped at the silent inmate with clawed hands and hatred.

In a flash, Allan Lawrence Trent pivoted on his right heel and faced the wave of fury head on. His eyes immediately burned into the brain of every attacker. A look of sheer malevolence and searing rage shook even these experienced killers to their very souls. As they stood around him, frozen in mid-gasp, Allan Lawrence Trent uttered a single word.

"Don't..." he said softly.

And no one did.

****

When Crazy Eddie Farrow returned from solitary confinement ten days later, he was surprised at the massive change in Cellblock H. There was a new, hushed tension that was visible in not only the traditional victims, but also the victimizers. Shouted, good-natured abuses, and bloody jocularity were replaced by paranoid whispers. Cruel men appeared to shrink behind their bars for protection.

There were no fights. No threats. No coarse laughter.

It was the hell that outsiders imagined prison life must surely be. As if some terrible disease was devouring the carefree spirits of these violent men. And Crazy Eddie was determined to do something about it.

He found the Rogue Boys in the recreation yard, huddled against the east wall, turned in on themselves like a herd of zebra when the scent of lion is in the air.

Other gangs paced nervously along similarly small plots of jealously guarded footspace.

Only one face appeared oblivious to the surrounding gloom.

An angelic face.

The face of a victim, not a convict.

"Who's the pretty boy?" Crazy Eddie asked Jake. He could not help but notice the constant twitch on his second-in-command's face, and the anguished expression that had become his constant companion.

"Name's Trent. Allan Lawrence Trent," Jake whispered, with the slightest of tremors in his voice. "Been here 'bout a month."

"What's he in for?"

"Murder."

"Gee, I'm scared," Crazy Eddie smirked. His voice rose louder in defiance of the hushed tones of his friends. He knew this Trent kid could hear him, but the golden-haired kid with the poet's face didn't even look up. For Crazy Eddie, who wasn't used to being ignored, this was an unconscionable lack of respect.

"Who owns him?" he bellowed.

"Nobody."

"Nobody?!" Eddie choked in disbelief. "A sheep like that, and nobody's sheared him yet? What the hell's wrong with you guys?!"

"He's...he's different," whispered Jake. "Real different."

Crazy Eddie spit on the ground, then kicked disgust at his solemn gang. "You guys don't deserve to be Rogue Boys! You ain't never gonna get respect if you let one little sheep scare you off. I'm gonna show that punk bastard who runs this cellblock!"

As the big man's angry boots stormed across the yard towards the silent figure of Allan Lawrence Trent, thirty inmates and four guards turned to him with a single, frightened voice.

"Don't," they said.

Unfortunately for Crazy Eddie Farrow, he didn't listen...

Second Income

How could she?!

The words tumbled through Alex Bailey's consciousness, a cerebral roller coaster careening out of control.

How could she?

Married less than three months and already...

He loved her, there was no doubt. Yet it was more than love, something far more desperate and intense. A sublime addiction he nurtured and craved with every furtive and indulgent glimpse of her, every casual touch of her shoulder, every subtle sniff of her fragrant hair. He was addicted to her irrepressible smile, the constant glint of amusement in her sapphire eyes, the refreshing optimism which radiated a gleeful warmth straight into his heart. She exuded life as some people exuded arrogance and insecurity...himself, for example.

It was four years ago at a Halloween party when he first met Michelle. He was the quintessential friend of a friend of a friend, who could not bear even one more claustrophobic evening entombed in a dark and meager apartment, surrounded by his possibly brilliant sketches of architectural opulence. While inane party chatter swirled about him like a manic emotional symphony, Alex Bailey leaned against a kitchen wall, caressed a warming Budweiser, and cursed himself for being one of only two people not in costume. The other, he noted, was a strikingly morose woman with hip-length black hair, and an equally Goth attitude.

"Michelle," his friend of a friend informed him. "She's a strange one." Alex realized at that moment that he didn't like this friend of a friend, who looked at his own warm beer as if it were the culmination of life's ambition, and then smirked. "I'd call her a spider woman, but even spiders mate occasionally."

With well-rehearsed casualness, Alex Bailey sauntered over to the girl in black, but ran feelings-first into an unexpected blast of frosty hostility.

"Couldn't think of a costume? Or just too pretentious to wear one?" she said, looking him up and down like a laser scanner.

He thought he detected a tone of amusement in her voice, but her hard stare convinced him he was dead wrong.

"Neither. I'm dressed as a successful architect." He cloaked himself in his finest, lost puppy charm. "It's what I want to be when I grow up."

"Ahh. When you grow up..." she nodded sagely, then returned a devastating smile. "And when exactly will that be?" She leaned in, her wit sharpened to deadly precision by a fierce lack of mirth. "Don't tell me I'll be lucky enough to witness some instant emotional puberty, some career coming of age by the end of the night." Her smile, the sweetest he had ever seen, could not hide an internal sneer. "How fortunate for me. I do hope I'm dressed for it."

She expected him to turn away with a shuffled apology, as they all did after her initial barrage, as his own feet encouraged him to do. But something inside him stiffened, and he refused to give her the satisfaction.

"Ever think of hiring that mouth out as an assault weapon?" he replied with forced casualness. "Or do you just enjoy racking up the male body count?"

She steeled.

Then smiled.

Warmer now. Almost captivating, as she said, "A backbone in a man. I almost forgot what one looked like." She held out a slender hand. It was warm, so incredibly warm. He wondered what it would be like to kiss her. "I'm Michelle. And, yes. I believe most self-satisfied, pseudo-creative males deserve to be cut down without mercy."

"Alex. Nice to meet you. And I'm guessing you consider yourself a one-woman logging company for the male ego?"

"I prefer emotional strip mining. Leaves more scars." She hesitated, but only long enough for dramatic effect. "Uh, I came in with that hand. I would like to leave with it."

He blushed, and immediately hated himself for doing so. Her hand felt so strangely comfortable, so natural wrapped around his own fingers, he had forgotten to let go. He dropped it quickly and said nothing, while she studied him with those tragic, enticing blue eyes. Only after a long, disconcerting pause, did she speak again.

"If you're not too poor to buy me a burrito..," she said softly. "...you can pick me up tomorrow night." She turned and left him standing there, but couldn't resist a final shot over her retreating shoulder. "Don't expect to get lucky, Alex the architect."

Alex got her number from another friend of a friend of a friend, along with a dire warning of impending emotional castration, should he decide to use it. He stared at the beer-stained paper for a long time.

Michelle...nobody seemed to know her last name.

642-7756.

With a sad, staccato breath, he felt his courage lapse. Eventually, he placed the paper in his top desk drawer, and let the weeks slip away.

Two months later, his phone rang. The friend of a friend. Same slurred voice. "What d'ya do to her, man?"

"Who?"

"Michelle. Michelle Thornwall. She tried to commit suicide last night."

He listened to the litany of details, but could concentrate only on putting failing oxygen back into his throbbing lungs.

It wasn't his fault. Why should it be his fault if she was a screwed-up lunatic? The girl had problems, that was for sure. More problems than he had time to deal with. After all, he just met her once at a party, and let her carve him up. He wasn't responsible in any way.

So why did he feel like a part of him was dying too?

All that night, he tried to convince himself there was no reason to be affected in the least by the tragic act of this strange woman.

At four in the morning, he telephoned the hospital to check on her condition.

Critical.

An hour before his alarm rang, Alex Bailey finally fell asleep remembering the warmth of her hand.

So very warm.

The next morning, he postponed a job interview he had tried to set up for months. He had to see her. If only to let her know it wasn't his fault.

She had to know that.

He lied to the gruff-faced nurse by saying he was Michelle's brother. He held a meager bouquet of carnations, which cost him the equivalent of three indigestible frozen dinners. When he saw her ashen face, her disturbing stillness, he wished he had brought more. Despite a spider web of IVs and sensors, her skin remained frighteningly close to the color of the hospital sheets.

He had never seen anyone so close to death before.

"Coma," the burly nurse clicked her tongue and harumphed. She seemed to blame him for being the only visitor to bother with this pathetic waif who felt the need to end her own life. After the nurse left, Alex sat alone for two hours with the comatose girl. Watching her.

Aching.

Before he left, he scribbled a note to go with his pitiful bouquet, the only flowers in the room.

The note read: *'I never should have let go of your hand.'*

Because that is what his throbbing chest was telling him now.

There were tears in his eyes, when he finally allowed himself to escape into the judgmental light of day.

****

"Hi, Alex. Remember me?"

It had been three years since that bitter night in the hospital room, but the voice on the answering machine was unmistakable. Or maybe it wasn't. The tone was Michelle's, but the voice seemed strangely...perky.

As he listened to the rest of the message, Alex's mind flooded with images of the caustic woman in black, who now sounded as chipper as a Disneyland cashier.

He met her for lunch, he had to, at an upscale cafe on the Lower East Side. Afterwards, he could not recall a single word of their three-hour conversation. He could only wonder at how incredibly beautiful she was in that pale pink sundress. How happy and full of life she seemed now.

On their fourth date in as many days, she confessed it was his handwritten note that had pulled her through, that had made her want to go on living.

By the end of the week, they were engaged.

Party etiquette to the contrary, neither of them had many friends, nor any family to speak of, so they decided on a simple ceremony with a surly Justice of the Peace. His happily weeping wife served as witness to the union. The sparseness of the ceremony didn't matter in the least to Alex

Bailey. Michelle was the most beautiful bride he had ever seen, and the unabashed joy she radiated cloaked him in an energizing veneer of pure, storybook love.

****

Despite the fact that he was barely making ends meet as a struggling freelance architect, Michelle and Alex were ridiculously happy in their cramped studio apartment. Then he lost the Curtis-Hoffman account, one of his few steady clients, and suddenly the future looked bleak indeed. But again, it was Michelle who rescued him from his own morose nature. One month into the marriage, she confessed she had a part-time job, plus a little money saved up.

"How much?" he asked with nervous enthusiasm.

"Ninety-six thousand," she replied, and his jaw dropped.

"Ninety-six thou...Why haven't you mentioned this before?"

She curled up in his arms; laughed at his stunned expression. "I was so happy just being with you, I guess I forgot about it."

"How did you save that much money?"

"I picked up a job right after I got out of the hospital. It's pretty steady work."

"But what do you do?"

"Personal services."

"Personal services?" He had never seen her this evasive before. "That could be anything from foot massage to amateur proctology."

Suddenly, Michelle's face darkened and Alex was reminded of the dour girl he had met years ago.

"Look, Alex." she said with tightly drawn lips. "This is something I'd rather not discuss right now. We can use my savings for whatever you want, but don't pressure me about my job. It's a long-term contract, but I got a month off for our honeymoon. It helped me turn my life around."

Alex was all fluttering kisses and tactile apologies. "I don't mean to pressure you, sweetheart. I was just trying to understand..."

"Don't try." she smiled, the new Michelle once again. The woman he married. The woman he loved. "Besides, a little mystery helps keep the fire burning in a relationship. And a second income means you can devote all your time to being the world's most brilliant architect-to-be." She clung to his lips in a long, passionate kiss. "Well, almost all your time..."

"Uh, if you put it that way..." he grinned, as he eased her down on the sofa for the second time that morning.

✶✶

The next day, Michelle installed an odd-looking fax machine in the far corner of the dining room.

"For business," she explained, then asked him as politely as she could never to touch it.

"Who even uses faxes anymore?" he asked, but a single look from her dark eyes convinced him not to pursue the matter.

Ten minutes after she plugged the aging device in, it began to spit out a single page of information, something she would not let him see. She removed the page, folded it twice, then kissed her husband as she walked to the door.

"I'll be back in an hour," she smiled. "Business."

And that's how it went for the next two months, with three or four business meetings a week. Each lasted no more than an hour. And each time, an envelope would arrive in the mail the following day, containing one thousand dollars in brand new twenty dollar bills. No receipt, no pay stub, just cash. The return address on the envelope was always the same.

Terminal Bliss, Incorporated.

The money was a godsend for the young couple. With financial worries diminished, plus the loving support and encouragement of his new wife, Alex was free to pursue his dream, the creation of a fifteen-story mixed-use residential complex that would usher in a new age of architectural design. Exterior frame concrete lattice work and three cantilevered walkways enhanced a nine-story atrium, with interior circulating pond and garden area. If he could work out the physics of the dual glass elevators, which would rise upward at 82° interior angles, he was sure he could win the prestigious Frank Lloyd Wright award for architectural excellence.

Yet even though he was happier and more creative than he had ever been, Alex Bailey slowly succumbed to a nagging curiosity that consumed an ever-larger section of his attention. Michelle's regular disappearances, coupled with her reluctance to talk about them, flung him into the surliest of moods. He imagined all sorts of bizarre employment: part-time stripper, government agent, Mafia hitman. The more time he spent at his drafting table, the more he concocted elaborate fantasies of his wife and her mysterious employment.

He hovered around the fax machine, ached to see the secrets it shared with her, but the strange device was conspiratorially silent whenever she was not standing by it.

Almost as if someone knew where she was at all times. As if they were watching us, he thought almost out loud, then waved away and washed away the paranoia with a hefty swig of Fireball. And then another.

He reminded himself that Michelle was the ideal wife, closest friend, and most enthusiastic lover he had ever known. Her gentle laughter flowed easily and often, her loving caress, as warm and comfortable as a soft blanket fresh from the dryer. He came to know and enjoy her completely...except for that single facet of her life she refused to share.

And he gradually began to resent her for it.

By the end of their third month, he was poised on the fragile edge of ecstasy and anxiety. If only she would let him in on her secret, their life together could be the stuff of legends and romance novels. Once again, she refused, gently but firmly, and Alex retreated to his drafting table and silently fuming conspiracy theories.

The next time the fax machine sputtered to life, he pushed her aside and tore off the sheet before Michelle could reach it. He acted like it was an affectionate game, the naughty child stealing the cookie, but she would have no part of it. She stunned him with a solid left hook that sent him sprawling in pain and amazement.

"Don't you ever do that again!" She raged, staring down at him with eyes on fire. She grabbed the paper and stormed out the door without another word.

Alex's aching jaw curled into a smile. Although he had only a brief glimpse of the paper, he finally knew the secret.

A single name. Marvin Waxman.

A photo of a well-groomed, fifty-six-year-old man.

And an address. The Westview Motel on the edge of town.

Taking side streets and driving his aging Ford Fiesta at speeds it was never designed to achieve, Alex managed to reach the Westview Motel before Michelle arrived. As he waited in a hidden corner of the parking lot, he wondered what he should do now. Should he burst in on the two of them, the raging husband, catching the woman he loved in the midst of some $1,000 tryst? Or should he drive away before witnessing the awful truth with his own eyes.

Hadn't Michelle given him more happiness than he ever expected to find in his life? Must he demand fidelity, too?

Alex felt wretched as he slunk further down behind the red vinyl wheel of his Ford, and waited for his wife to meet the well-groomed Marvin Waxman in some dank room of this seedy motel. His eyes misted as he saw her black Mercedes pull up beside the battered neon sign.

There was his wife, beautiful as ever, wearing dark sunglasses to hide her cheating eyes. Michelle looked around carefully. Content that nobody was watching, she locked the car door, checked the paper one more time, then walked purposely towards room number eight.

Then she did something Alex never expected.

She walked right through a wall and disappeared inside the motel.

Less than forty seconds later, she reappeared through the undamaged wall, scanned the parking lot for intrusive eyes, then climbed inside her Mercedes and drove away.

It took Alex Bailey another seven full minutes before he could finally stop shaking.

****

When Alex arrived home, supported by a bottle of Jack Daniels he had picked up at a package store on the way, his wife was waiting for him. Michelle kissed his bruised jaw and apologized for hitting him so hard.

He had caught her off guard, she explained. She would never, ever do anything to hurt him. She begged his forgiveness with a gentle massage of his sagging shoulders.

Alex, confused beyond belief, cringed under her touch, then surrendered to the tender ministrations of the woman he knew he loved more than life itself. He yearned to ask her who, or what she was, but dared not jeopardize the only true happiness he had ever found.

Later, when they made love, he clung to her with reckless emotion. She felt his pain, softly reassured him with feathery touches and whispers of forever. While she slept, her angelic face painted pale by moonlight intruding through the bedroom window, he refilled his veins with Jack Daniels and wept for the lost innocence of the unknowing.

He was not surprised by the small article in the morning paper about a fifty-six-year-old salesman found dead in the Westview Motel.

Natural causes, it said. Alex stifled his sobs to avoid waking his lovely wife.

Later, as Michelle was luxuriating in a hot shower, Alex unplugged the fax machine, hoping somehow, that simple solution would return everything to normal. He went to the mailbox and removed the package from Terminal Bliss, Inc., which contained another $1,000 in cash.

Blood money.

Their second income.

As she stepped into the room, looking irresistible with tousled wet hair, the fax machine immediately sprang to life. Alex moved towards it far enough to confirm that it was still unplugged. Michelle saw it to, and quickly plugged the cord back into the outlet, muttering some lame exclamation about the wonders of new technology.

It took three more weeks before Alex built up enough courage to confront her. Three weeks of cringing every time the fax machine would ring. Three weeks of seeing his wife's sinister hand in every obituary. Three weeks of avoiding the mailbox for fear that a package of cash would signal the termination of another person's life.

They were lying in bed, Michelle's body folded into his like a pair of old spoons in a kitchen drawer. He kissed her hair, the back of her neck, then sighed.

"I was at the Westview Motel." he whispered. "The day you met Marvin Waxman."

Immediately, her body went rigid. He felt the blood drain from her skin, her back turn cold, the slowly building sobs which began to quake within her. She turned to face him, her wide eyes illuminating the darkness.

"Oh, Alex," she sobbed. "Why?!"

"I couldn't...not know." He wiped the tears from her eyes, ignoring his own. "I...I'm sorry."

"What did you see?"

"Everything...nothing...I don't know." He turned away from her. "You walked through a wall, for Chrissake! You walked through a wall, and that guy died! He died!"

There was a long silence. He was afraid. Not of what he suspected she could do to him, but that she would rise out of their bed and leave him forever. Slowly, she spoke words laced with pain and resignation.

"I don't want you to think I killed him. That's not what I do." She took a heavy breath. "I helped him. Helped him make the transition."

"The transition?"

"This is so hard to talk about. To explain," she shuddered, then steeled herself. It was time he knew the truth. She was a fool to think she could avoid it so long.

"When I was in the hospital, I was close to death...closer than you can imagine. I was about to cross over, when suddenly, some part of me saw you come into the room. I could feel your sorrow. Feel it stronger than my own heartbeat." She could not hold back her tears. "I tried to commit suicide, because I felt my life didn't matter. Didn't matter to anyone. I was irrelevant. A sad, stupid footnote in a world of pain and ignorance..."

"Michelle..."

"But you changed all that, Alex! You cared. I could feel it. I don't know how, but I could feel it." She turned away from him, pressed her back into his hungry chest and arms. "And from that point on, I wanted desperately to live. To live for you. To live *with* you..."

Her tears racked her body so hard, Alex was afraid she would shatter into a million pieces. Then she stiffened, and the sudden rigidity in her limbs was even more frightening.

"It was then, he offered me a choice..."

"Who did?"

"Death."

Alex laughed, then hated her for turning this moment of confession into some sick joke. Then he felt a cold hand on his spine when he realized she actually believed what she was saying. His crazy wife actually believed that she...

"You talked to...Death?" he whispered, slowly and carefully.

"Well, not Death himself. A representative of his actually. With almost eight billion people, you can imagine how busy he is these days."

"Uh-huh."

"Anyway, I was told I could come back if I worked this region. Subcontracted for him in this territory."

"Uh-huh."

She grabbed his face in her cold hands. Stared deeply in his eyes.

"I know it sounds crazy, Alex. But it's true. You have to believe me."

Looking into her eyes, seeing the longing and confusion raging in them, Alex Bailey desperately wanted to believe her. In spite of the insanity of her explanation. In spite of the betrayal he knew she was covering.

"So…you help people die?" he muttered, and hated himself for participating in the obvious lie.

"No. No, Alex, I would never do that. I've come to realize how precious life is. It was you that helped me see that." She kissed him. He did not pull away, though part of his consciousness begged to run and hide.

He could tell she really believed what she was telling him. That she had to believe it, or he knew her carefully constructed psychosis could fall apart, leaving her even more damaged than that night in the hospital.

He nodded for her to continue, because he didn't know what else to do.

"It's like this, Alex… People die when they are destined to. I just show up at the right moment and touch them. I help ease the transition from life to afterlife. It's always been that way."

"Michelle," he sighed. "You do understand how…hard this would be for me to wrap my head around. To believe."

"It wasn't easy for me, either. They told me they had set up a corporation, Terminal Bliss, made up of people like me who were near death, but who learned to appreciate life at the very last moment." She again grabbed his face in her hands. "There are millions of us, Alex. All over the world. We provide a service. We make the moment of death easier, more comforting. It's no longer a lonely process. One gentle touch and they're on their way to a better place."

Another long pause, only the ragged rasp of her frightened breath disturbing the silence.

"Please try to understand, Alex. I came back for you."

"I… I have to sleep on the couch."

He got out of bed, suddenly shamed by his nakedness in the moonlight.

"I love you, Alex."

He should have taken that moment to say, *'I love you, too, Michelle.'*
But he didn't.

As he sprawled out on the living room sofa and pulled the knitted blanket over his quivering shoulders, he could hear Michelle's sobs calling to him from the bedroom which had been their special haven what seemed like a century ago.

****

A distance had come between them that Alex knew was entirely of his own creation. No matter how hard they tried to make things appear normal, the ring of the mysterious fax machine would remind him he was married to a psychotic killer, who believed she was Death's service representative. When his friend's mother passed away, Alex could not speak to Michelle for a week, wondering if she had anything to do with it.

As he pulled back emotionally from her, Michelle grew more fragile, more despondent. He had been the reason she wanted to live, and now here he was, blaming her for the mortality of the entire world. Most nights of their formerly perfect marriage ended with him on the couch and her crying herself to sleep on their cold queen-sized bed.

Alex took to drinking, and in a fit of frustration, burned all the sketches that represented his life's work. The unique fifteen story mixed-use complex with its innovative angled glass elevators, cantilevered walkways and nine-story atrium, disappeared in smoke and ash before anyone could ever recognize its brilliance. It was a foreshadowing of the inevitable, and both of them knew it as such.

The next day, a drunk and despondent free-lance architect sat by his drafting table. A pile of obituaries torn from newspapers of the last three month spilling over onto the floor.

All those names...

All those faces....

All those lives...

Alex stared at each one, trying to imagine a past and a personality that was suddenly wiped out, arbitrarily erased from the world. Then he turned to the bridal portrait of Michelle he kept always on his desk. He kissed his finger, then touched it to that smiling face safely encased in unfeeling glass.

When Michelle emerged from the shower, with those ever-enticing tangle of wet curls, she wore an expression of pure sorrow that made her seem even more beautiful.

She did not seem surprised to see the .38 caliber revolver he had pressed under his chin. She just seemed sad. So wretchedly sad.

"I'm sorry..." she whispered.

"Yeah, me, too."

She tried to move towards him, but he cocked the gun and pressed it tighter against his head. She froze, her only movement, the bitter tears streaming down her face. "I love you so much, Alex."

"I love you, too, Michelle. But I just can't take it anymore."

"I know." she collapsed to her knees. "I'd die for you if I could."

"I know that."

Suddenly, a middle-aged woman with gray-streaked hair walked into the room, though no door was open. Michelle looked at her with fear, hatred, sorrow, and finally resignation.

"This is Natalie, Alex," Michelle whispered. "She works with me." Alex nodded. "Natalie, this is Alex. My husband..."

Natalie looked at Alex with the kindest eyes he'd ever seen, other than Michelle's.

"Don't be afraid, Alex," she whispered in a gentle, soothing voice. "I'm here to help you."

Alex nodded again. He turned to Michelle with eyes that betrayed all the fierce love and anguish in his tortured soul. She smiled back at him through bitter tears, and silently whispered the last words he would ever hear;

"Soon, my precious love."

Alex Bailey closed his eyes. As he squeezed the trigger on his .38 Special, he felt the strange comfort of Natalie's warm and gentle touch on his cheek.

And it felt wonderful.

Ghosts

I hate ghosts.

Not with your typical shivering fear, but with a tangible, all-consuming disgust that gnaws at my soul with a bitterness even I can't control.

Ghosts ruined my life, and I can never forgive them for that.

I hate the way they suddenly appear at the top of the stairs, sending icy fingers of dread through your heart and straight up the back of your neck. I hate the way they fill the shadows in a room; watching...waiting... crouching on the very edge of human perception.

Always behind us.

Always hovering.

Always hungry.

I hate the way they turn the soft comfort of darkness into something cold and menacing.

And I hate what they did to me.

Ghosts, spirits, specters, apparitions, poltergeists, manifestations of the dead...call them what you will, they are the hidden evil which infests our deepest nightmares. Supernatural maggots, they exist only to plague us, torment us, and feast on our fears like so much decaying meat.

The biggest lie in the world is that ghosts can't hurt the living. That they are merely harmless wisps of psychic vapor, powerless in daylight, unable to choke the life out of someone foolish enough to enter their terrible domain. It's a cruel lie.

Believe me, I know.

I had a pretty decent life before I came to this old mansion. I had a family who loved me, a good education and a head full of plans for the future. I also had a chip on my shoulder as big as old New York.

I remember that awful night, so long ago. Caleb, Warren and me. Three of us crouching in the weeds before the dark, deserted mansion. Trying with the rash bravado of young men to prove who was the least scared. To prove which one of us was man enough to spend an entire night cowering in the old, abandoned house under the sinister prodding of a full moon.

Warren was the smallest of the three of us, and therefore, felt he had to talk the loudest.

"What's the matter, Jonathan? You scared?" he sneered at me. "Did all those ghost stories your momma told you about this place turn your spine to pudding?"

Caleb, the silent one, looked at me with giggling fear, glad that he wasn't asked the same question.

"I simply don't see the sense in it," I replied, trying my best to sound reasonable, despite the awful shiver that crept into my voice. The huge mansion loomed over us as if it were eager to hear our decision. "This place hasn't been lived in for years. We could fall through a rotted floor board, and they wouldn't find our bodies for months."

"Then *we* would be the ghosts that parents warn their children about," Warren smiled wickedly. "Wouldn't that be delicious?"

Caleb had heard enough. "I want to go home," he mumbled nervously.

"I agree with Caleb," I said, then turned quickly, before Warren could see the telltale trembling of my lips.

"Do that then! Both of you! Dash off to the safety of your momma's arms!" Warren's eyes were wild and flaring, as one possessed. "I, for one, will spend the night doing battle with the unliving!"

Caleb and I felt this was a reasonable time to saunter away. That is, until Warren added...

"And tomorrow, I will tell Elizabeth Williams which of us had the courage to brave this old house!"

Elizabeth Williams, the beautiful, pig-tailed girl who filled our dreams almost as much as this mansion infected our nightmares.

Caleb and I stopped, then turned back to Warren.

"I don't care at all what Elizabeth Williams thinks," I lied. "I have no interest in catching cold by spending the night in such a drafty old shack."

Warren only smiled, realizing that sometimes silence can be the cruelest rebuke of all. Then he dashed up the broad stairs of the old mansion, broke the lock with his father's hammer, and was swallowed up by the massive wooden doors.

Caleb and I shifted uncomfortably in the cold night air, wordlessly balancing our courage against our childhood pride, only to find our courage came up woefully short. Warren's challenge didn't bother us, we were used to his foolish boasts. But the thought of Elizabeth Williams' sparkling laughter reddened both our faces, even in the lifeless pallor of that eerily cold moonlight.

"Are you going in?" Caleb whispered, though there was no one else around to hear.

"Not me," I replied. "I have better things to do."

"Me, too," Caleb nodded, though either of us would be hard pressed to list a single item on our agenda that night.

Yet something held us rooted to that spot among the weeds, shifting back and forth under the malevolent stare of the old house. I was about to make another of my casually clever remarks when the screaming began.

I had known Warren since we were babies. I had known his wicked sense of humor and his flair for the dramatic. And I could tell a shout of pain from a rehearsed yell meant to frighten his friends.

This was neither. These were screams of pure, unadulterated terror.

I raced across the weed-choked yard up the steps of the old mansion. I could hear Caleb's footfalls behind me, providing a sinister beat to the ghastly screams which spilled out the broken windows of the old, abandoned house. We were about to throw open the huge wooden doors, when the screaming suddenly stopped, freezing us in our tracks.

I turned to Caleb, whose face was now deathly pale. I felt a suffocating pain in my chest, and only then realized neither of us was breathing.

Slowly, I opened the creaking door and crept inside.

It was dark, of course, only that thin, cruel moonlight leaking through the jagged, broken windows. And it was cold as death. I stumbled forward, pushing aside cobwebs and bumping into objects I would rather not identify. My footsteps sounded like the echo of a tomb, filling the stifling blackness with its only hint of life.

At one point in his maturation, every boy must approach his own particular threshold of fear. He will either cross it with bold steps of manhood, or shrink back in trepidation. For some, the threshold is embracing a dream, or standing up to a dominating parent. My threshold, however, was far more literal. Against every part of my being that shrieked for escape, I had to will my legs forward through that gloomy, silent house.

My teeth were vibrating. My stomach drawn in so tightly, I again forgot to breathe. Still I moved forward through the engorged darkness.

Through the dangling cobwebs.

Through my own paralyzing terror.

I was halfway across the room when I saw Warren. Or what was left of him. His twisted form lay crumpled at the bottom of the large staircase, a look of unbridled horror permanently etched onto his now ashen face. Blood leaked out of his open mouth, frozen in mid-scream. So much blood, though I knew at once his heart no longer pumped it through that lifeless body.

He was no longer my friend, rude and baiting. This was a corpse, broken and repositioned in some ghastly mockery of life.

My mind tried frantically to make sense of that horrible image. I wanted to run, but a fear-fueled paralysis crept over every inch of my body. Try as I might, my legs simply refused to move, as if they blamed me for carrying them here, pushing them this far.

I stood rooted in the shadows, able only to stare in shock at that terribly contorted face. A face that was once Warren.

What had happened to my friend?

What could have done this to him?

At first I dismissed it as a trick of the shadows, only moonlight dancing off the cobwebs. But as my eyes grew accustomed to the darkness, a sharp tingling of horror permeated my flesh.

Above Warren's corpse, three dreadful spirits hovered, their own pale faces streaked with the fresh blood of their victim.

Their victim.

I tried to scream but couldn't. I could only stare at the grisly scene in wide-eyed panic.

Until they came for me.

That was more than a century ago.

Caleb never entered the house, and so was the only one of us who lived through that terrible night.

Now, under the sterile caress of a full moon, Warren and I wander the abandoned halls of the old, deserted mansion, hungrily waiting for the next brave and trembling mortals to cross their own personal threshold into our world.

They will come, and we will be here.

We will always be here.

The old mansion decays with each passing decade, ignored by the living, populated by the dead. A legion of evil apparitions crowd this place like an infestation.

I hate ghosts.

But I do love the living...

Them

From the moment he first saw the attractive couple walk into the all-night diner, all giggly and sleepy-eyed, he knew it would be them.

He had no idea how he knew, he had never met them before, had never even seen their faces before tonight. Yet he knew it had to be them. The realization slammed his body back against the red vinyl bench like a sudden jolt of electrical current.

They looked so young, so happy, so full of life. He shuddered to think what awaited them. Why couldn't it be someone older? Someone tired of his pitiful existence? Someone who no longer care whether he lived or died. Someone like him, maybe. Or someone evil, who was better off removed from this world? But as he scanned the smiling faces of the newlyweds through his own tired and frightened eyes, he knew there was no denying it.

It had to be them.

And he knew, beyond a shiver of doubt, that someday soon, he would have to kill them.

In a desperate attempt to keep his eyes off the young couple, Clark Mendoza riveted his gaze on the cold fried eggs congealing on the white ceramic plate in front of him. It was just past 4 AM, and he had been jacking cup after cup of strong black coffee to jar himself awake, at least until he reached Omaha. Four hundred and fifty miles of unrelenting highway behind him, with one hundred, thirty-seven more to go. He was numbed and weary and scared as he sat in the red vinyl booth of the plastically cheerful Denny's Restaurant on Interstate 80.

All his life, people had accused him of being aloof and ambivalent, as if the world around him was no more than some hazy distraction. Nothing ever got to him, because nothing ever really mattered that much. Even the worst problems would lose their edge a few miles down the road, and a good trucker knew there was always enough road to put between you and any hassle. To Clark Mendoza, the outside world was like the annoying hum of an old refrigerator, the kind you can tolerate once you tune out that incessant, low-level buzzing. That's why driving a big rig was the perfect career choice. His truck's steel frame cocoon, animated by the rough vibrations of the road, distanced him from everyone and everything else. He preferred to live on a low simmer setting, while others boiled and seared with burnt-out relationships and the scalding heat of introspection and self-doubt. Clark Mendoza? He just drove, and was content to watch the world blur by him through his ultrawide windshield.

But now, as he sat in that Denny's on Highway 80, it took every ounce of sinewy strength to keep him from screaming. His right hand was shaking, as it always did in times like this, so he tried to steady it by grasping the coffee mug even more tightly in his meaty fist. So tightly, he was afraid the smooth porcelain would shatter like his nerves into a dozen jagged and scattered fragments.

God, he thought to no one in particular, why did this have to happen now? Why did this have to happen at all?

Maybe it was the road. Maybe it was one of those killer headaches that plagued him on a long run like this. Maybe it was the rough suspension on the eighteen-wheeler, that had jangled his nerves all the way from Albuquerque. Yet even though he tried to avoid all the side effects of his internal alarm, the truth kept staring him down like a deer in his headlights.

He knew he would kill this couple.

And he hated himself for it.

With an abrupt slap of the counter, Mendoza flagged down Cybil, the laconic waitress he always asked for on this late-night Omaha run. As she sauntered over to his booth, he tried his best to appear calm.

"What's up, Clark?" she said, without looking at his face. "Eggs not to your liking?"

"Eggs are fine, Cybil," he hated the quiver in his voice. "I just...I need you to do something for me."

"Sorry, darlin'. My tush ain't on the menu tonight." She flashed him a toothy smile. "But thanks for askin' anyways."

"This is serious, Cybil. I..." He tried to keep from gasping out the words. It was important he appear somewhat in control of his flailing emotions.

"What is it, doll? You don't look so good." She scanned his face with genuine concern. She liked this one. He was a regular. Quiet, but always a good tipper. A few times she had turned around and caught his eyes following her as she bent over the counter, and she liked that, too. But now her eyes were drawn to his clenched and shaking fist, then up his bulging arm to the terror leaking out his eyes. She chose her words carefully. "What is it I can I do for you, honey?"

Although her voice was soft and comforting, it was a long agonizing moment before he gathered the strength to answer.

"That couple sitting at the counter…"

"The lovebirds? What about 'em?"

"I want you to put their order on my tab."

This surprised her. In the eight years this middle-aged trucker had been driving this route, she had never seen him so much as buy a cup of coffee for anyone else. In fact, he made a point never to talk to anyone but her. Now, for some reason, this silent loner wanted to play nice with others, and that was usually dangerous. She plopped herself down in the booth beside him. Reached out to steady his trembling hand.

"Friends of yours, hon?"

"Sort of."

"Relatives?"

"No, Cybil." She winced at the pain in his expression. "Truth is…I never saw them before today."

She nodded, then laid out her words slowly and carefully. "But you wanna buy them breakfast?"

"I need to." He was surprised by her concern. Impressed, really, but it was the last thing he needed at the moment. His only hope was to climb down deep inside himself until this icy feeling passed.

"I, uh…don't feel much like talking about it, okay?"

She'd been a truck-stop waitress long enough to know you don't push an irritable trucker past the point he'll let you ride. She stood up, smoothed the hem of her wrinkled white uniform down to a less suggestive position, and tugged an errant wisp of hair from her eyes.

"Whatever you say, sugar. It's your money." She looked across the dining room to the young strangers. "But if you ask me, those kids look like they can buy a big jerk like you wholesale."

He tried to muster a smile.

"Wouldn't take much, Cybil. Wouldn't take much…"

Clark Mendoza clasped his hands tightly together and blew on them. Then he realized this probably looked too much like praying, so he pulled them apart and drummed his thick fingers on the table top. He dragged his right hand through his matted black and gray hair, and tried desperately to appear casual, as he watched Cybil talking to the young couple at the counter. They seemed confused and argued with her for a moment. Then, they followed her gesture to Mendoza's table. He nodded weakly in reply, and they looked even more confused. He buried his head in his hands, while embarrassment burnt hot, jagged tracks across his cheeks.

Why was he doing this? Why couldn't he just let what was going to happen just happen? Why was it so important that he do something for them? Something, anything, before he had to...

His thoughts were interrupted by a sudden outstretched hand bearing a thick gold ring.

"Andrew Ross," the man said in a voice, less friendly than suspicious. "This is my wife, Natalie. It appears we have something to thank you for, mister."

"No big deal," Mendoza mumbled. He uncomfortably shook the outstretched hand and dropped it quickly. Too quickly. He didn't like the way Andrew stood over him. Peered down at him. The guy was too tall, too elegant. His carefully groomed blond hair and finely chiseled features that made the burly trucker's arm hair stand on end.

Mendoza could read this guy like a book. It was the dispatcher's son all over again. Arrogant and smart. Even the handshake and stance were typical 'power moves.'

"Forget it," Mendoza added, wishing he could escape their questioning faces, "It's nothing."

As quickly as he disliked the man, he was just as swiftly taken with the young woman. Natalie Ross scanned his face with gentle curiosity, accompanied by a soft smile that spread over him like a warm summer breeze. She was a slight woman, no more than five-four. And thin, with a face slightly rounded, but not distractingly so. But he couldn't help but be drawn to her oversized brown eyes, brimming with warmth and secret humor.

While Andrew had come to interrogate this stranger for such an unexpected act of generosity, Natalie had come over to the table to express appreciation, and to get to know her mysterious benefactor. She was real.

Genuine. The trucker liked her immediately, and that bothered him more than he expected.

He couldn't afford to like her.

An uncomfortable silence followed, as Mendoza shrunk under Andrew's withering gaze. The young newlywed said nothing, realizing that silence can often be the most powerful negotiating position. Finally, for no other reason than to break the silence, Mendoza gestured for them to sit down. Natalie sat first and Andrew slowly fell in beside her.

"I hope you don't think us ungrateful, but do we know you?" she asked, her voice disarmingly childlike in tone.

"No reason you should," he grunted. "The name's Mendoza. Clark Mendoza." He could tell by Andrew's narrow eyes that he was trying to place the name or face. "I drive a rig along this route."

"So why did you insist on buying us breakfast, Mr. Mendoza?" Andrew pursued. "Not that we're not appreciative, I mean."

"It was very sweet of you."

"Yeah. Well, it seemed like the thing to do."

"Why, exactly?" Andrew's eyes narrowed.

"Huh?"

"Why us?"

Clark hesitated. How he hated that question every time he heard it. But how much should he tell them? Was his guilt over his future crime already evident in his face?

He had to think fast...

"Well, you two looked so happy and all. And I figured with the new baby coming, you might..."

"How did you know about that?" Andrew snapped, cutting off the big man's words.

"Really," Natalie added with surprise. "We only found out for sure yesterday."

Stay calm.

Don't let them trip you up.

Whatever you do, don't let them know what you already know.

"I dunno. I guess when you have six of your own, it's easy to spot things like that." Clark squirmed under Andrew's unflinching appraisal. Hated him for it. Wanted to smash his perfect features with the coffee mug.

"You work in a doctor's office?"

"Like I said, I'm just an old Texas trucker."

"Who was just in the mood to buy breakfast for a pair of strangers?"

"Look, I'm sorry I bothered you. It's just that..." What should he tell them? The truth? How would they take it? How would anyone? "It's just that your wife there kind of reminds me of my daughter."

This delighted Natalie. "How sweet. How old is she?"

He sighed heavily. Why the hell was he doing this anyway?

"About your age," he said softly. "About your age when she died."

It was Andrew who bolted first. Tried to stand up and leave the booth, but Natalie put a restraining arm on her husband and coaxed him back down with just a look. Then she turned her sympathetic gaze to the nervous trucker.

"I'm so sorry, Mr. Mendoza. How did she pass away?"

With panic as his inspiration, Clark spun a story, embellishing it as he went along. His daughter was her age, looked a lot like her, too. And pregnant, about eight months. Then a car crash less than a mile from her home. The other driver walked away, but she and her husband died before an ambulance could reach them.

Natalie's eyes reddened with tears. Andrew squirmed with discomfort. Clearly, this was not the explanation he expected. And way more than he wanted to know about some raggedy trucker in a low-rent diner.

Mendoza continued. "I got to the car before anyone else did. Grabbed her hand and tried to convince her to hold on. That help was coming. But we both knew it wouldn't get there in time. So I just held her hand as she was bleeding out. And she looked up at me with this sad, confused expression and said..."

He had tears in his own eyes now. Natalie put a soft hand on his rough, trembling one.

"Said what?"

"She said, 'Why us?'" Mendoza gulped his coffee as if it were a shot of whisky. "But I didn't have no answer for her..."

The young couple watched the big truck driver lose the battle to hold back his tears. Andrew squirmed, but Natalie was all patience and kindness.

"And that's how she died?"

"Yeah. Her husband and unborn baby, too."

"What about the other driver?"

"Like I said, he just walked away. Left the truck right there. Nobody ever found out who he was."

"He walked away and let them die? You didn't try to stop him?"

"No."

"Why the hell not?!"

"Andrew! The man was holding his daughter's hand. He probably didn't even get a good look at the other driver."

Mendoza flinched.

"Nobody did. I guess they all thought he was dead, too. Or hoped he was. He walked away before I even noticed he was gone."

"Christ. Guys like that should burn in hell."

"Probably will." Mendoza had run out of story, and didn't want to stick around while Andrew realized the flaws in his tale. He stood up, and at six-foot-five, it was his turn to tower above the seated couple. "Look, you don't need to hear my troubles. Besides, I got a long drive ahead of me." He dropped two crumpled twenties on the table beside his untouched eggs. "That should cover all our breakfasts. But you go leave a big tip for Cybil. She's an all right gal."

He was free of the table at last. He moved quickly toward the doorway, when he suddenly felt Natalie's hand on his thick biceps. He whirled around as if stunned, and looked down at her. Surprised by the tears in her eyes.

"I'm so sorry for your loss, Mr. Mendoza. You must have loved her very much."

"Yeah... Never told her though."

"I'm sure she knows."

Mendoza could say nothing. He wanted to crush her in his bearish embrace. Tell her he loved her. Apologize for what he was going to do to her. Tell her to run as far away from him as she could.

Then she uttered the words that would ultimately seal her fate.

"Mr. Mendoza. You seem like a kind man. If you're ever in Indianapolis, look us up."

Andrew was shocked, but not as shocked as Clark Mendoza.

"Natalie and Andrew Ross. We're in the book."

Mendoza managed to grunt out an uncomfortable goodbye, before fleeing the restaurant for the safety of his eighteen-wheeler.

From behind the counter, Cybil watched the burly trucker with the pale expression dash across the parking lot like he was running from the devil himself. She turned to the pretty young couple arguing in the booth.

And she knew in her heart something was wrong.

Very wrong.

****

He watches them come towards him, can see the expressions on their faces; anxious, but unsuspecting.

His own body appears to be floating. He is closing in on them, but no longer feels in control of his body. He briefly wonders why he isn't behind the wheel of his truck. Where he feels protected. Safer than any other place on Earth. The dashboard and cab interior are the boundaries of his cocoon, the steering wheel his umbilical cord. If he was in his truck, maybe he wouldn't have to be doing this to them. Outside of the cab, he is just another potential victim.

Like Andrew and Natalie Ross.

Andrew and Natalie Ross of Indianapolis.

He can see Natalie's small features offset by those wide, generous eyes. She is frightened, but not by him. She has yet to notice him coming towards her.

But he is coming towards her.

Fast and deadly.

Just before he strikes, he catches the flicker of recognition in her face. Hears her sharp intake of breath. Her abortive scream.

It all happens so quickly. He sees the blood spurt from Andrew's forehead, painting his face in a vibrant red grimace of surprise.

The merging of metal, bone and flesh compresses into a singularly macabre medley of destruction.

Then the silence. That horrible silence.

And the whimpering.

He knows Andrew is already dead, head twisted at an impossible angle. Rivers of blood staining his clothes a dark burgundy. The sickeningly sweet smell of liquid humanity assaults Clark's senses, as he tears away the last barrier between him and Natalie.

He must get at her. With the fury of a savage animal, he will not be denied. He must get at her.

His hands are coated with blood as he grabs her at last. She is fragile as a broken butterfly wing. The soft hiss of air from her chest reveals the gaping hole in her lungs.

As his fingers move up to her neck, her face is almost serene.

He grasps her shredded hand, feels the terrible coldness seeping into it.

Then, with only the slightest movement of her head, Natalie Ross looks deep into the face of her killer. She stares into Clark Mendoza's eyes, and whispers two words he knows will haunt him forever...

"...why...us?" she whispers amid painful gasps.

He has no answer for her.

He feels her slip away, taking part of his own life with her.

And then the dreadful realization of what he's done. Still clutching her lifeless form, he lets loose a ghastly shriek, a scream born of horror, betrayal and rage. He screams until he feels his lungs will explode.

Then he wakes up.

At that same moment, he always wakes up.

This time he woke up in a Knights Inn on the outskirts of Akron, Ohio. Screaming, as always, cold sweat gluing his t-shirt to his chest. He woke up terrifyingly aware of every facet of the dream. The only dream he has ever remembered in his life. Every cruel detail burned into his conscious mind.

He turned to the red numbers on the digital clock.

3:47 AM, of course.

This time he was lucky enough to wake up in a motel. Most nights he woke, shaken and shivering, in the sleeping compartment of his truck. It never made a difference. The dream never changes. The dream that has haunted his sleep for the past three months.

But tonight was different. Tonight, he knew the names of the people he would kill.

And now he knew where they lived.

Natalie and Andrew Ross of Indianapolis.

****

The life of a long-haul trucker is a strange combination of boredom and freedom. There's a seductive power to sitting so far above the other commuters in their little metal boxes, hurtling down the highway with eighty or more tons of steel at your command, a self-contained seventy mile-an-hour empire, which you alone control with your hands on a steering wheel and shift. The roar of the engine is a primal scream in your ears, the bellowing challenge of an animal under your command. The shriek of your air horn and the sight of your massive grill in a rearview mirror is enough to unnerve the most confident driver.

It is easy to say truckers are kings of the road, but they are more than that. They are predators, chewing up time and distance, and town after town, according to their individual appetites.

At the same time, their moving palace of armor is also a prison. The radio offers merely an illusion of human contact. Disembodied voices drift into their leather and steel upholstered world, and then fade out of range. Like the relationships in Clark Mendoza's life; eager voices promising intimacy, but fading away before he ever found something substantial to cling to. He had never married. Never had a best friend that he could remember. Never spoke to anyone but truck stop waitresses and gas station attendants in countless cities spread across North America. The arm's length at which he held the world had grown to an insurmountable distance. Not at all what he had planned, but exactly what he had created.

He longed to share his fiery thoughts with a woman; his decades of emptiness, his cold despair. Yet he could never utter more than a breakfast order, or ask for a well-done cheeseburger with extra onions. He was even too afraid to ask for a refill, unless he knew the waitress.

A couple of times a year, he visited a Nicaraguan hooker in Arizona, he had been seeing her since 1983. Her name was Imelda, and he thought maybe she liked him some after all this time. She was dark-eyed and gentle, and soft to the touch. He loved to tenderly stroke her long black hair, which had been kissed with streaks of gray over the years.

Yeah, he could tell by the way she would let him hold her after they were finished, just hold her and let their chests rise and fall in unison with peaceful afterglow, surely that meant she liked him a little? But he wasn't sure, because she never spoke any English, except "Twenny Dollahs. And use rubbah, be sure." The rest of what she said was in soft, lyrical Spanish, a language he enjoyed, but never took the time to understand.

He was thinking of Imelda when he saw the green highway sign herald the next big city on his route. Indianapolis, it proclaimed.

Indianapolis.

Where Natalie Ross lived.

Before he realized what he was doing, he had hit his turn signal, and was already careening his rolling prison toward the off-ramp of 65 North.

It had been months since he had gotten their address. Although he was never good with numbers or addresses, this one lodged in his mind like a bullet in his gut; dangerous, but not yet lethal. Not yet. He had looked at it once, out of curiosity, then never forgot it. Now he wished he could purge it from his mind.

Andrew and Natalie Ross.

423 Meridian Parkway.

Indianapolis, Indiana.

And he was heading their way.

It had been four months since the encounter at the Denny's on Interstate 80. He knew Natalie would be swollen with child by now. He would not have to make up flimsy excuses about how he knew she was pregnant. By now, everyone would know. But only he knew that she would never live to see her baby.

And he wished he could drive that evil thought out of his constantly pulsating skull.

Meridian Parkway was an upscale suburban neighborhood, with rows of mature oaks lining the sidewalks like silent sentinels of status. Clark Mendoza knew his eighteen-wheeler would stick out like a sore thumb on this quiet street, but he had to see where they lived.

He couldn't help himself.

The house was just as he pictured it. A two-story French colonial, with a gray brick and stone front. It was every bit as brash and ostentatious as Andrew Ross. However, it also held touches of Natalie's sweetness. A small rose garden, neatly trimmed and colorful. A cement goose dressed with a pale blue hat and country smock. A too-cute welcome mat with embroidered bunnies, that must have annoyed Andrew to death every time he stepped over it. A swing set in the yard, purchased months before the baby was to be born. Clark knew instinctively that these were Natalie's touches, and they brought a familiar tear to his eye.

He had seen the house, now he knew he should leave. Get back on the road while there was still time. But, of course, he couldn't. He had to locate the exact spot where he would kill them, so he drove up and down the side streets until he found it. A quiet little street facing a vacant lot. Too many trees, in an area of the subdivision that had yet to be developed. A spot where he would be able to walk away after they had died, knowing no one would remember his face.

He pulled the eighteen-wheeler to the curb, stepped down from the cab. He walked over to the spot, rehearsing his lethal role in that fateful scene he knew by heart. He could almost hear their screams in his ears. He could almost picture the blood pooling at his feet. And then he could hear Natalie's voice, calling to him.

Calling to him.

"Mr. Mendoza?"

He looked up, shaken from his horrific vision, to see her standing on the opposite sidewalk. She had her hair pulled back in a ponytail. A pair of gray flannel sweat pants covered the lower half of her swollen belly. On top, she wore a vibrant blue sweatshirt emblazoned with the words, "Baby Under Construction." She was waving to him and calling his name. He wanted to run, but his legs were frozen to the spot.

The spot where he would kill her. His heart raced, and his breath escaped in accusatory gasps, as she looked both ways, then crossed the street to meet him.

"I thought that was you, Mr. Mendoza!" She was beside him now. So real. So alive. She reached out a soft and slender hand. "I'm Natalie Ross. Remember?"

He could only nod. If only she knew how foolish a question that was.

"What are you doing here in Indianapolis?"

He looked down to the pavement, hoping she wouldn't hear the agonizing screams it would soon contain.

But she couldn't hear them yet. Only he could.

He looked deep into her eyes.

"Looking for you," he mumbled, his face turning red with shame.

****

"Would you mind telling me what the hell he's doing here?!"

Clark Mendoza jumped at the sound of Andrew's angry voice. He had been having such a wonderful time getting to know Natalie Ross, her hopes, her fears, her childhood joys, even the painful idiosyncrasies of her young marriage, that he had somehow lost track of time and place. He had forgotten that he was in the very home of the couple he was here to kill.

Andrew's poorly hidden rage brought it all back to him. He would not even think twice about killing Andrew. Natalie was too good for this pompous, authoritarian jerk. She answered her husband with controlled impatience, embarrassed by his appalling lack of manners.

"Mr. Mendoza was in the neighborhood, Andrew. I invited him in for a cup of coffee. That's all."

"In the neighborhood?"

Clark nodded.

"And exactly what cargo were you delivering in our neighborhood?"

The two men glared at each other in undiluted fury. Yes, it would be no problem at all killing this guy, Clark thought. Andrew's expression revealed similar thoughts.

"I came by to see your wife," Clark grumbled, a bit too forcefully. "I was on an unfinished furniture run to Fort Wayne. Natalie told me to come by whenever I was in town. Remember?"

"You'll have to forgive my wife," Andrew pursed his lips with disgust. "Natalie has a nasty habit of picking up strays."

"Andrew!" She was on her feet in an instant, eyes blazing. "Mr. Mendoza is our guest. How can you be so rude?!"

"It's okay, Natalie," the trucker said, as he rose to his full height. "I'm not here to cause no trouble." He stood uncomfortably close to Andrew, his huge frame allowing him to look down on the younger man. He would be looking down on what was left of him soon enough. "Time for me to hit the road, anyway."

Clark Mendoza turned and stomped toward the door. Natalie was beside him in a moment, her gentle hand once again on his arm. How he would miss that touch.

"I'm sorry, Mr. Mendoza. We haven't been married all that long, and Andrew is still a little jealous. I hope you understand."

"No problem," he muttered, then escaped out the door before they could see the cold sweat beginning to erupt on his forehead.

As the door closed behind him, he could hear Natalie's murmur to her husband, "You really can be a son of a bitch sometimes."

****

For the next few weeks, Clark Mendoza forced himself to stay away from the young couple, though his thoughts were frequently hijacked by the image of the enchanting Natalie Ross. The enticing crinkle around her soft brown eyes, the endearing smile, the alluring expression of innocence that masked a truly playful spirit. He told himself she had opened up to him in ways she probably never would to her husband. After two brief meetings and one cup of coffee, he felt he knew her soul. Felt he had always known her. And he knew he loved her.

Which made the idea that he would have to kill her even more painful.

For six weeks, he turned down any job that would take him anywhere near Indianapolis. He knew he could not resist the freeway onramp, which beckoned him with the siren's song of a life he deserved. A love he would never know. He turned down so many jobs, that he was in danger of missing his truck payments. Caught between poverty and temptation, there seemed little choice but to take on another Fort Wayne run.

Back on the road, the freeway signs pulled at him like an electromagnet. The truck almost drove itself through the streets of downtown Indy. Clark knew it would be too dangerous to be seen again in their neighborhood, so he pulled the big rig into a U-Drive-It Car Rental Agency, and tried to rent a car with a fake license he had picked up years ago under the fictitious name Felix Esperante.

Sammy Schechter, the silver-haired bastard who ran the car rental lot spotted the fake license instantly. To Clark's surprise, he passed it through anyway, but demanded an extra five hundred 'cash security' on the rental, which would probably never officially be tallied into the day's receipts. Unfortunately, all Clark had on him was three hundred and twenty-eight dollars in crumpled bills. Sammy sighed heavily, then shoved the cash in the back pocket of his brown, pinstriped pants.

Sammy Schechter led Clark to a dark green Dodge Neon which had obviously been the loser in a recent traffic accident. The door was bashed in and the left front fender looked like a Picasso painting, but it would do. Without knowing why, Clark pulled his ever-present companion, a Smith & Wesson .45 caliber, from his truck and quietly slipped it under the front seat of the small car.

If the furniture manufacturer back in Texas knew a truck full of his unfinished merchandise was sitting unattended at a car rental lot, Clark Mendoza would lose his job for sure. Such irresponsibility would ruin his reputation in the trucking business. Yet the temptation to see Natalie Ross again was impossible to resist.

He parked the Neon across the street from the Ross' house, downed a cup of cold McDonald's coffee, and wondered aloud what the hell he was doing in this situation.

Why couldn't he just leave her alone? Maybe if he stayed half a country away, he wouldn't have to kill this young couple. Maybe he could let their child be born. But that was just wishful thinking.

It had to be them. He knew it from the moment he saw their happy, innocent faces that night at Denny's.

He wasn't a murderer, had never killed anything bigger than a dog before, but he knew he was destined to kill Natalie and Andrew Ross.

No matter how miserable he felt about it.

Clark Mendoza was so caught up in his dark spiral of thoughts, that he almost missed Natalie's car as it pulled out of her driveway. Her blue minivan fled down the street with the staccato urgency of too many suburban errands. There was no time to lose. He smashed the Neon's gear shift forward, feeling oversized and clumsy in anything but his spacious truck cab, and followed Natalie's retreating tail lights down the tree-lined street.

Without knowing why, he shadowed her through all her morning errands: to the pharmacy where she picked up a two-month supply of pre-natal vitamins; to the bank's ATM machine to get a little extra cash; to a small strip mall, where she wistfully window-shopped outside a store specializing in designer baby furniture. When she was in line at the grocery store, she glanced up from her checkbook, and he was sure she had spotted him watching her through the large windows. She looked right at him and her expression was troubled, as if she had a sudden premonition of the evil he could not prevent. When she handed the cashier her last remaining check, her expression softened and he was sure she hadn't seen him.

He didn't want her to think he was stalking her, or anything like that. He wasn't the typical psycho stalker. He honestly did not want to kill her.

He just wanted to be free of the nightmares.

Shortly after noontime, Natalie drove to a small restaurant and sat down at the only table facing the window. She sat alone, lost in thought, as if she could sense what he was trying to do. Though he was parked at least fifty yards away from the restaurant, he swore he could see a teardrop tracing a single line of distilled sorrow across her pale cheek. That teardrop screamed to him with the eagerness of a head-on collision. Even though he knew it was a mistake, he squeezed out of the tiny car and threaded his way through the parking lot. He hesitated before entering the restaurant, then took a deep breath, pushed open the double doors and walked quickly to her table.

He was right. She was crying, alone at that table, and his heart pounded to see her in such distress. He just stood over the table, watching her cry. Without looking up, she said,

"Why are you following me?"

"W...what?" the big man stammered.

"Why have you been following me all morning? What are you trying to do to me?"

"Nothing," he lied, knowing the truth would only bring her more pain. "I was in town and..."

"Let's cut the crap. There's nothing you want in this town except me, Mr. Mendoza." This time she fixed him with a cold, hard stare. "You're a truck driver. You don't expect me to believe you drove to Indianapolis in a Dodge Neon, do you?"

"No."

"Where did you get the car?"

"I...rented it."

"Because you didn't want to be seen following me?"

He nodded, then whispered, "Because I didn't want to be seen following you."

"Why, Mr. Mendoza? Why me?"

How he hated that question. It reminded him of the dream, the way she was at the end, all bloodied and oozing life, the way she was when she asked him those exact words. He didn't have an answer for her then, and didn't have one for her now. The tall Texan crumpled weakly in the chair facing her, knowing it was probably the last thing she would allow him to do, the last thing he should do. But knowing also that if he didn't sit down now, his trembling legs would spill him to the floor.

She studied his face; her own expression, strong, but softening. Compassion overtaking her fear.

"I don't really remind you of your daughter, do I?

He shook his head, although everything in his soul screamed at him for abandoning the pretense.

"No. you don't." He knew she could see through to his very soul.

"You don't have a daughter, do you, Mr. Mendoza?"

He looked up at her, more tears in his eyes than hers now. He shook his head again. She understood, and that scared him to death.

She pulled a small notebook from her purse, glanced at the notes she had taken. "In fact, you don't have any family at all. You are a forty-nine-year-old truck driver from Abilene. Texas, who has never been married. You served one year in a juvenile center for aggravated assault when you were sixteen, but haven't had any trouble since then."

"It wasn't aggravated assault."

"It wasn't?" She looked curiously at the information a friend in Texas had dug up for her.

"It was…attempted rape."

The color drained from Natalie's face. She tried to keep her chin from trembling as she continued to look at him, defiantly.

"Is that what this is all about, Mr. Mendoza? After more than thirty years, you've chosen me as your next rape victim?"

He reached across the table and grabbed her hand so quickly, she didn't have time to pull away. She was surprised by the speed of his movements, the sudden contact, and the gentleness of his touch.

He was surprised that she didn't pull away.

"This isn't like that, Natalie! I'd do anything to keep from hurting you, I swear it!"

"Then why are you following me?"

"I don't know... To warn you, I guess."

"Warn me? Warn me about what, Mr. Mendoza?"

He took a deep, staggered breath. He might as well tell her. He knew by this point she had probably told the grocery store clerk to call the police.

That they would bust through the restaurant door any minute now. He let her see him as he was. He wanted to convince her how desperately sorry he was. Sorry for everything.

"Warn you about me..."

There was fear in her eyes now, yet she tried to control it, and he loved her even more for her courage.

"Because you are planning to hurt me?"

"No...yes..." He realized he was still holding her hand, and he slowly let it go. "I'm going to kill you. You and your husband. I'm so sorry."

He expected her to run. To kick over her chair and dash, screaming, for the door. Although her eyes quickly flitted about for possible escape routes, she held her ground and fixed him with a stare. He knew she was frantically wondering when the police would arrive.

"Are you mentally ill, Mr. Mendoza?"

"No. At least I don't think so...I mean, if somebody's crazy, really crazy, do they ever know they are?"

She didn't answer.

"Look. I'm a normal guy, or thought I was...Up until like six months ago, when I started having these dreams...This couple drenched in blood and I did it to them...I did it to them, but I don't know why or how...Every night, I see their faces as clear as I see yours looking at me now...Only I didn't know who those people were until a few months ago, when I was sitting in a Denny's outside Des Moines at four in the morning."

"When we walked in."

"You and your husband. And suddenly I knew who those faces belonged to."

He looked deeper into her eyes, tried to somehow share with her the images that had been destroying his life. And as he looked at her, she seemed to understand, at least that's what he thought, until her eyes flickered up past his shoulders, and a look of relief washed over her face.

"Freeze!" shouted a voice behind him. "Put your hands up! Do it now!!"

They sat for a moment, the confessed killer and his intended victim, while all hell raged around them. Their eyes continued their silent dialogue, as the tearful truck driver slowly shoved his large hands into the air.

Two policemen barked orders he only half heard, then yanked his arms roughly behind his back. The handcuffs sliced into his wrists, but his eyes never left Natalie, even as the angry cops forced him up out of the chair. They turned him, dragged him out of the restaurant, and shoved him into the back seat of a squad car. He squinted from the pain in his wrists, but said nothing as the overweight policemen read him his rights.

Suddenly, Natalie's face was at the window of the police car, entrancing him, once again, with her tear-filled eyes.

"It's just a dream, Mr. Mendoza." She said in a voice burdened with sadness. "Nothing says you have to make it real."

If he had a reply, the police siren would have drowned it out. Instead, he watched her disappear from view as the squad car pulled away from the curb, its blue lights flashing.

****

The next few days were a blur to Clark Mendoza.

He spent a sleepless night in jail, then arraigned the following morning. The list of charges included terroristic threatening, possession of a fake driver's license, and fraud for entering into a rental contract with falsified identification. Judge Russell Fitzgerald, who happened to be Andrew's uncle, also slapped an injunction on the truck driver not to attempt any further contact, or go within twenty miles of Natalie or Andrew Ross. The surly judge told Clark he would hold the other charges in abeyance, if the truck driver left the city and vowed never to return. If he was ever spotted in Indianapolis again, Judge Fitzgerald would personally make sure Mendoza did serious time in an Indiana state prison.

When the police escorted him back to the U-Drive-It lot, Sammy Schechter insisted he receive an additional four hundred "lot storage charge" for keeping the big rig parked overnight. The ensuing argument became so violent, it took both police escorts to keep the truck driver from making the silver-haired manager's head resemble the crumpled fender of the Neon. In accordance with Judge Fitzgerald's orders, the two policemen tailed Clark Mendoza's truck all the way to the Indianapolis city limits.

Yet the thing which bothered Mendoza most were Natalie's words. Maybe she was right. Maybe a dream could stay just a dream. Maybe if he never set foot in that part of the country again, he would never have a chance to kill the young couple. Then his torment would only be restricted to his nightly ritual. He would suffer, but she wouldn't.

He pondered this all the way to Fort Wayne and beyond.

The first thing Clark Mendoza did when he returned to Abilene was sell his tractor trailer and give up trucking entirely. He reasoned this would keep him more than a thousand miles away from Natalie Ross and her husband. If he was nowhere near them, how could he possibly kill them?

Unfortunately, driving a truck was the only life Clark Mendoza had ever known. At forty-nine years old, he was left without a job, without an income, and without the spiritual release that cruising across country in his huge rig provided. He spent each day curled up on his worn brown sofa, watching daytime television and sneering at the scum of humanity he was asked to sympathize with on every talk show. Condescending hosts with their cheap veneer of sincerity expected him to understand the plight of some foul-mouthed teen degenerate, who refused to listen to her overly indulgent parents, or some angry trailer park transvestite who beat his wife regularly because she looked better in silk lingerie than he did. Years ago, these 'lifestyle choices' would have caused whispers of private embarrassment and societal scorn. Today, they meant instant fame and national pity. To Clark, these proud examples of social sewage were artificially honored for the sake of high ratings, and so the viewing audience could feel alternately compassionate and condescending. Each jobless day, he hated them, and all of whining humanity a little bit more. He had sacrificed his soul for Natalie and Andrew Ross, traded his life for theirs, and although he had done it voluntarily, he could not prevent the feelings of smugness and bitterness which accompanied his noble decision.

Eventually, he took to drinking again, but found it only stoked the constant fire in his gut. He drank in suicidal quantities. Drank to suckle his self-pity. Drank to be comatose. Drank to silence the demons within him. His passport to serenity, a bottle of cheap tequila a day.

Although he could feel his insides rotting away, his continual binge at least postponed the terrible nightmares.

He was usually too drunk to dream about killing anybody.

****

He heard her voice on the line and his breath caught in his throat.

"Hello?"

"Natalie...It's me. Clark Mendoza."

He heard a soft gasp, then a click, followed by the cruel mockery of the dial tone. He dialed the number again. This time she did not say anything as she picked up the phone.

"Natalie, I've got to talk to you…"

"They ordered you not to contact me anymore, Mr. Mendoza. Please. Just leave me alone…"

Another click, another dial tone. He pressed the redial button. Let the telephone ring twenty-two times. Her voice betrayed her anxiety when she finally picked up the receiver.

"Why are you doing this to me, Clark?!"

"Natalie, don't hang up! I just wanted to tell you that you have absolutely nothing to worry about anymore."

She didn't speak, yet he could hear her frightened breath on the line.

"I wanted you to know that you're safe now. I sold my truck. Gave up the road altogether. I won't ever get out of Texas again."

No reply.

"I did it for you, Natalie. So you'd be safe."

There was a long pause. When her voice returned, it was filled with fear and pity.

"They said you killed a man, Clark…"

"What?!"

"It's all over the papers this morning. They didn't mention you by name, but they said the chief suspect was an out-of-state truck driver who police witnessed fighting with the victim."

"What are you talkin' about?! That's crazy! I didn't kill anybody! I haven't even been out of my house!"

"They say it was your gun that killed him."

"Who?"

"Some guy named Samuel Schechter. He runs a car rental agency."

Now it was Clark Mendoza's turn to retreat into stunned silence.

"Why did you do it, Clark?"

His breath escaped in quick gasps and he could feel the tequila rise in his throat. He let the telephone receiver fall back to its cradle, then stumbled slowly to the bathroom, where he threw up violently.

His gun. His Smith & Wesson .45 automatic. He had left it under the seat of that piece of shit Neon he had rented, had forgotten completely about it when they picked him up and ran him out of town. And now someone had negotiated a better deal with that silver-haired bastard Sammy Schechter. The absurdity of it made Clark laugh out loud, his laughter echoing madly off the walls of his dingy apartment. He laughed and vomited until he passed out on the bathroom floor.

When he awoke, two Texas rangers were standing over him, pistols pointed at his head. The smaller of the two held an arrest warrant in his hands.

Clark threw up on their black polished boots.

****

The next day, Clark Mendoza was extradited to Indiana, handcuffed and accompanied on the Southwest Air flight by the smaller of the two Texas rangers. It was the only time in his life he had ever flown in an airplane, but the handcuffs and leg shackles distracted him from any enjoyment he might have experienced. He felt the eyes of the other passengers on the airplane lathering him with pity, compassion and loathing. Somehow, he had become just another piece of social sewage. Maybe, he would even be featured on a daytime talk show.

That afternoon, Clark Mendoza, unemployed truck driver, was arraigned on first-degree murder charges. They had found his rental contract, identified his gun as the murder weapon, and discovered nearly a pound of cocaine stashed under the driver's seat of the beat-up Dodge Neon. Add to that, the charges of terroristic threatening, plus the likely testimony of the two policemen who had witnessed his volatile argument with Sammy Schechter, and Clark Mendoza was facing almost certain conviction. Yet he refused a court-appointed lawyer when it was offered. He would defend himself, and his defense would be pure defiance.

Fate brought him back to Indiana, uncomfortably close to Natalie and Andrew Ross, but he would cheat its machinations by putting concrete walls and steel bars between him and his potential victims. It didn't take a legal expert to know he was looking at twenty years or more in prison, and this comforted him. In his dreams, Natalie Ross was always young and pregnant. If he served twenty years of hard time, the dream could not possibly come true. The key was not to be released prematurely. Clark Mendoza would see to it that he would never be paroled for good behavior.

The next day, he demanded to be brought in front of Judge Fitzgerald, where he pleaded guilty to the murder of Sammy Schechter. For good measure, he spat at the judge and the bailiff. Judge Fitzgerald, red-faced with rage, sentenced him to forty-five years in Indiana State Prison. Clark Mendoza, about to embark on the longest haul of his life, winced at the sentence, but was inwardly satisfied.

The irony of the situation was not lost on the new inmate. His life had fallen apart because he tried to stop himself from murdering two innocent people. Now, he would lose the remainder of his years because of a murder he did not commit. As they marched him down the concrete tomb of his new home, a fleeting memory of Greek mythology bubbled up from some long forgotten tenth-grade social studies class. The Greeks believed the gods amused themselves by devising intricate traps for the unsuspecting humans they chose to watch over.

Clark Mendoza figured the Greeks might not have been that far off.

He used his one allotted telephone call to contact Natalie. He wanted to tell her not to worry, that he was never going to hurt her, that she would be safe with him in prison. Unfortunately, Andrew answered the phone and swore at him repeatedly before hanging up. Clark could hear Natalie crying hysterically in the background.

Prison walls aren't truly solid, they are sponges engorged with the sinister thoughts of diseased minds. The evil musings leak out into the brains of each recipient of their claustrophobic embrace. Jung spoke of a collective human memory. Prison walls are its darkest repository.

Forced into sobriety, Clark Mendoza's nightmares return with a vengeance, even intruding into his conscious thoughts.

He again watches them come towards him; their faces, anxious but unsuspecting. He can see Natalie's pretty face, her wide, generous eyes...frightened, but not by him. She hasn't seen him yet.

Then the flicker of recognition, the abortive scream.

He sees the blood explode from Andrew's forehead. Hears the screams, the silence, the whimpering.

He sees Andrew's body awash in red, his head twisted savagely on a freshly broken neck. Clark sees himself clawing to get at Natalie, feels her dying body in his arms. He grabs at her shredded right hand and feels the coldness seep into it.

"...why...us?" she asks him as she dies.

And, as before, he has no answer for her.

****

The sharp clanging of the steel cage roused him from painful thoughts. Raymond, a massive prison guard, loomed over his bunk, baton in hand.

"Inmate 7200893, gather your things!"

Mendoza stretched and yawned, the disinterested pretense of a man with little to lose. "What for?"

The guard shrugged. "You're being released. Now move it. We need this cell for some other piece of excrement."

The details filtered through the trance-like state in which Clark found himself, as he was pushed through the numerous steps involved in processing a convicted criminal for release. He learned some strung out junkie had popped Sammy. Spreading cocaine around was his particular way of making the neighbors happy and becoming the big man in the 'hood.' The kid had rented the Dodge Neon to make a drug buy. When he stashed the coke under the seat, he must have found the .45 automatic Clark had left behind. Sensing a shady deal and some easy money, Sammy Schechter tried to squeeze the kid for an "extra security fee," a dangerous thing to do to a cokehead under any circumstances. With chemically induced bravado, the junkie emptied a full clip into the back of Sammy's silver hair, before he realized that this might not be the smartest career move. He panicked, dropped the gun, left the coke in the Neon and ran. The police finally caught him three weeks later, as he tried to break into the same rental car parked at a police impound yard, desperately searching for the cocaine. He confessed to the murder ten minutes after he hit the interrogation room.

Judge Fitzgerald reluctantly issued an order for Mendoza's release, with a warning that he leave Indianapolis on the next flight out. The judge personally sprang for a first-class ticket back to Texas.

A dazed Clark Mendoza sat sprawled out in the back of a police car on his way to the Indianapolis airport. Frank, the cop in the driver's seat was laughing about what an idiot the kid was, trying to break into a police impound yard. But Clark wasn't laughing. He promised himself he would not laugh again until he was back in Abilene, safely anesthetized inside a bottle of tequila.

He was not angry or bitter by this latest twist of fate. The truth was, nothing surprised him anymore. He'd come to realize that everything was beyond his control. He was an ant that had stumbled across a tornado; all he could do was watch helplessly as the shards of time and reality swirled in maddening chaos before his numbed eyes, until the maelstrom eventually crushed him in its ambivalent path of destruction. So he did not think it unusual when the freeway traffic outside his window slowed to a crawl, then came to a complete stop. Frank cursed loudly and turned the cruiser toward the nearest off-ramp.

"Isn't the airport up ahead?"

"Yeah," Frank sneered at the traffic. "But the radio says some fool truck driver jackknifed a big rig across all four lanes. If you wanna make your flight, we gotta take a shortcut."

This news bothered Clark more than he imagined, and he had no idea why it should.

"Is he dead?"

"Is who dead?"

"The truck driver. The one you said jackknifed on the road."

Frank turned on his police siren and lights to speed past the slow-moving cars. "Who the hell knows?" he shrugged.

Clark sat back, closed his eyes and sadly realized he didn't care either.

He fell asleep for a few moments, only to awaken in an even more dreamlike state. The world around him seemed to be spinning in slow motion, as if he, the car and everything, were suddenly moving through an ocean of thick, translucent liquid. The trembling began in his shoulders and reached down into his spine. He sat upright. Every sense enhanced -- his sight, his hearing and...something else.

He knew, without asking, where they were headed. Frank turned to see the panicked look on his face, and misinterpreted his growing anxiety.

"Don't worry, buddy," the gruff voice lagging, as if captured by some malfunctioning tape recorder. "This will get us to the airport in time."

"No, it won't," were the very last words Clark Mendoza would ever speak to Frank the policeman.

As the squad car hurtled toward its destructive rendezvous, Clark Mendoza could somehow feel what was happening to Natalie Ross at that exact moment. She was in pain. Terrible pain. The months of terror and anxiety since he first told her he would kill her had taken its toll. Now, as she read the morning newspaper trumpeting his release from prison, she sobbed hysterically. Her panic was heightened by the sudden stabbing pain in her abdomen, and she knew immediately her unborn child was in jeopardy. A scream of pristine agony ripped through her body as the hemorrhaging began. She collapsed, and would have hit the floor, if Andrew had not run into the kitchen and caught her as she fell. Her blood flowing more freely now.

Although neither would say the words, each understood it was the beginning of a late-term miscarriage. Andrew grabbed a thick roll of paper towels, pressed it between Natalie's legs in a vain attempt to hold back the bleeding. He picked up her quaking body and carried her at a full run to the car in the driveway. He was too distraught to close the front door behind him.

Frightened by the prospect of losing her baby, Natalie sobbed uncontrollably. Andrew backed the car out of the driveway, slammed it into gear and screeched down the oak-lined street in a desperate run to reach the hospital in time.

Neither saw the police cruiser racing towards them.

Clark Mendoza saw it all, not with his eyes but with...he didn't know what. He experienced all the pain and fear that she felt, even before the car was visible. He wanted to scream to the cops to turn back, to be anywhere but on that doomed street, but deep down inside, he knew it would do no good.

The dream had already taken over.

From the back seat of the police car, he watched them race towards him. He could see their faces through the windshield of their car, anxious but unsuspecting. Every nerve and fiber in their bodies were stretched and straining, as if they could save the struggling fetus by willpower alone. Andrew kept glancing over at his wife, and at the growing pool of blood spreading across her lap.

Clark Mendoza felt as if he were floating, like he was some disembodied observer unable to prevent the horror to follow. He knew he was moving towards them, but no longer felt in control of his body. He wished he was behind the wheel of his truck, the one place he felt safer than any other on Earth. As the two speeding vehicles barreled toward each other, he could see Natalie Ross's small features offset by those wide, generous eyes.

She had yet to notice him hurtling towards her.

Suddenly, she looked up and saw the police car in the opposite lane. But more than that, she saw Clark Mendoza's face, just as he had seen hers. Despite impossible distance and prohibitive speeds, their eyes locked. She knew then he was right. That he would be the instrument of her death. Yet the realization made her strangely calm, as she embraced the inevitable.

She turned to Andrew in a voice as cold as death and simply said,

"It's over."

Her eerie calm sent a surge of uncomprehending terror through her husband. What was over? The baby? Could she feel it die? Was she dying, too? Would he be left alone in the world after finally finding the one person in all humanity who could make him feel accepted and alive? All these thoughts flooded through his mind, as he turned his head to his wife and the strangely serene veil that had overtaken her expression.

And that's when he let his speeding car drift into the oncoming lane.

Clark Mendoza locked consciousness with Natalie Ross in the fraction of a second before the two cars collided, and that eerie communion held firm as the steel projectiles that held them apart crashed head-on at a combined velocity of one hundred and seventeen miles per hour.

Andrew screamed, and tried to jerk the steering wheel to the right, but it was too late. The deafening explosion of metal on metal echoed in the ears of both dying drivers. The vehicles consumed each other like two ravenous beasts, crunching steel and glass in a self-destructive orgy of death. The occupants of each car were tossed about like dolls. The engines merged into one screaming, smoking mass of broken and twisted metal, then were thrown violently apart.

After an interminable blackness, Clark Mendoza's head raised slowly amid the smell of blood and destruction. Frank's lifeless body was mangled by the crumpled engine now sitting where his lap should have been. The windshield was a mosaic of spider webs colored crimson by the impact of his partner's compressed skull. The agonizing silence, interrupted only by the cruel hissing of escaping radiator steam, made the macabre image even more terrifying.

Perhaps because he was alone in the back seat, the only one in either car wearing a seatbelt; possibly because his body was so strangely relaxed at impact; or maybe because he was simply not meant to die in this terrible accident...for whatever reason, Clark Mendoza was able to kick open his twisted door and crawl out of the smoldering police car. The Ross' car lay on its side, thirty feet away. As Clark limped towards it, he could see Andrew's fragmented body compressed against the pavement, a spurt of blood painting his face in a vibrantly red grimace of surprise. Andrew was dead, his head twisted at an impossible angle. All that blood staining his clothes a dark burgundy.

Clark heard the soft whimpering he knew would come, and it ignited a violent rage within him. He threw himself at the passenger side door; the last barrier between him and Natalie Ross. He wrenched and pried at it like a savage animal, screaming his curses at the crumpled metal. Blood was dripping from his own hands as he finally struggled it free. The sickening smell of fresh blood filled the car, and there she lay, torn and broken and strangely beautiful. A dying angel in a world gone horribly wrong.

A soft hiss of air oozed from the puncture wounds in her lung. She slowly looked up at him, not with hatred or fear, but with a tragic resignation. There was no urgency to save her, they both knew her fate had been sealed long ago. Despite the terror and carnage around her, the young mother's face appeared almost serene.

The quivering truck driver cradled the dying woman's head gently in his arms. He sobbed like a child as he held her, fragile as a broken butterfly wing. He reached out to find her shredded right hand, and felt the terrible coldness seep into it.

Then, with only the slightest movement of her head, Natalie Ross looked into Clark Mendoza's eyes. She whispered two words that would haunt him for the rest of his life.

"...why...us?" she asked, between painful gasps of breath.

The words drove straight into his heart, and he let out a soft groan of despair. He gently stroked her blood-soaked hair, then slowly felt her slip away, taking part of his own life with him.

He held her this way for a brief eternity. Then he screamed, a terrible feral shriek born of rage and injustice. He screamed until he felt his lungs would explode.

A small crowd had already begun to form, as the neighbors of Andrew and Natalie Ross spilled out of their homes, drawn by the irresistible attraction of someone else's misery.

Through tear-clouded eyes, Clark looked up at the suffocating circle of faces etched with pity and cruel curiosity.

He wanted to kill them all.

Instead, Clark Mendoza softly kissed the lifeless head of Natalie Ross. He stood up slowly, and limped alone down the tree-lined street, away from a mocking catastrophe he would never be able to escape.

Other People's Treasures

The cramped, three-room apartment was stuffed and cluttered with more than sixty years of well-worn remembrances. Although memories are priceless, their tangible manifestations are often far more affordable.

The two-dollar and fifty cent chipped bud vase, that Louisa's granddaughter had bought *with her own money* only seventeen years ago. The seventy-eight-cent softball her son, the next Babe Ruth, had autographed in 1966, two years before he was killed in the Vietnam war. At only sixteen years old, he had hit that ball so hard, it sailed right over the rusted chain link fence of the neighborhood sandlot to land smack in the middle of Old Mr. Wingate's garden, God rest his soul.

On the sofa lay the frayed, red and gray afghan her sister had crocheted twelve years ago, to keep her mind off the cancer ravaging her lungs.

There were other items, each painful and sweet. The extensive collection of specialty salt and pepper shakers, which friends and family members had sent from all over the country. The four-dollar puzzle she had finished and then framed for the wall. The small black and white television set her daughter's family had sent from Canada for her seventy-fifth birthday. The four-inch plastic Jesus with simulated wood cross, which she had ordered from that televangelist, who was still in jail, the last she heard. Turning the other cheek in ways he never imagined, no doubt. The toaster oven. The battered old rocking chair proudly bearing teeth marks of two generations of infants Louisa had helped raise. The plastic fern in the sunroom window, a blue light special from K-Mart. Her first hymnbook, embossed with the name of a vibrant church that had long ago given way to a parking garage. The peeling wallpaper her dear, sweet husband had hung all by himself the very year his heart gave out. Her pink house shoes, as old, worn and frayed as she felt today.

Eighty-year-old Louisa Mae Tyler poured boiling water from the small ceramic pan into a rose-covered teacup she had bought thirty-seven years ago. She reached into the top kitchen drawer and pulled out a dull, stainless steel spoon that was once part of her original wedding set. The tea bag, a day-old slice of lemon, and a drip of clover honey all mingled with the steaming water in the flowered cup. She carried the it to the rickety kitchen table, and sat in an equally rickety chair to bask in the sunlight streaming in through her tattered screen door.

The street outside was no longer filled with the laughter of children at play, the smiles of dear departed friends, the chattering of fat squirrels, or that unique serenity which can only be found in your own neighborhood. These days, motorcycles roared and police sirens screamed and whined their way through the screen. Strange faces with suspicious eyes peered in whenever the door remained open too long. At night, an occasional gunshot announced the latest casualty in the undeclared war of urban lawlessness.

Louisa sighed. She was now a stranger in a formerly familiar land. Somewhere along the line, the world beneath her feet had changed. Hostility festered on cracked sidewalks, where whole families once took their nightly stroll. The neighborhood she had refused to leave after sixty years was no longer her own.

Louisa used her thumb to press the tea bag against the dull silver spoon. Like her, it was brown, wrinkled and drained of purpose. It had brought flavor to its surroundings, done the job God intended it to do, but now was simply waiting to be discarded.

As she sat at her worn kitchen table in the little three-room apartment that both encased and reflected her life, Louisa Mae Tyler rested her weary head in wrinkled hands. With words no one could hear, she prayed again for someone to talk to.

****

Saturday morning. The one time each week Louisa Mae Tyler allowed herself to escape the oppressive confines of her tiny apartment, and venture out into no longer familiar streets to inventory the changes in her old neighborhood.

The Williard's house was gone, gutted by a fire last month. Of course, the Williards did not care. They had moved away back in 1962. The old homemade candy store on the corner now peddled liquor and filthy magazines. Margaret Maisley's house, where the old gang used to dance and play cribbage until all hours of the morning, was now campaign headquarters for a press-hungry reverend trying, yet again, to be elected to the city council on the grounds that all of the world's problems were inherently racial. The venerable Burgess Groceries, dating back to the 1940's, had burned to the ground under dubious circumstances nearly twenty years ago, taking kindly old Mr. Burgess with it. All that was left of that friendly corner store was a jagged jaw of blackened bricks and a vacant lot that became a midnight mall for drug dealers and prostitutes, the street in front littered with the skeletons of stripped and decaying automobiles, as well as the occasional overdose victim.

Louisa Mae Tyler harbored no illusions about her neighborhood. She also had no intention of becoming a victim herself. Her arthritic hands clutched the large black purse slung tightly over her good right shoulder. Her short steps were steady and purposeful, impressive for a woman of eighty. A can of pepper gas remained hidden in the pocket of her white, button-up sweater, and she had no qualms about using it, if she had to.

At Fourth and Plymouth, she started to fall short of breath. At Sixth and Plymouth, she discovered one of the few guilty pleasures she still permitted herself.

The front yard at 622 Plymouth Avenue was a rarity in the neighborhood, in that it was always meticulously trimmed, and bordered with a carefully spaced line of scrawny rose bushes in every color imaginable. This lawn was always an expression of tidiness and pride, though not today. This Sunday morning it was strewn with dark wood furniture, antique bottles, cheap ceramic figurines, kitchen utensils, old books, and the other semi-precious paraphernalia of a life well-lived. Dozens of people stepped over the rose bushes to pick and paw at the items for sale. Many browsed, some haggled, very few bought.

Although the last thing she needed was a sampling of other people's discards, Louisa indulged herself by perusing the flimsy card tables and TV trays overflowing with knickknacks and well-used items. She pursed her lips as she examined a set of eight coasters imprinted with the words, "Atlantic City." She clicked her tongue at a chrome-plated Timex with a cracked crystal face. She scrunched her eyebrows over a set of red quilted place mats with matching napkin holders. And she sneered at a chipped brown lamp that was priced at an unimaginable $8.00.

In short, Louisa Mae Tyler was having the time of her life.

Louisa was suspiciously eyeing a set of salt and pepper shakers in the shape of cows, when a voice rose from behind to startle her.

"I see you know your knickknacks," the smiling woman chirped, with uncontainable warmth. "Not everyone does, you know."

"How much for these?" Louisa harumphed. There was no room for friendliness in the traditional rite of yard sale haggling.

"I don't know...Three dollars?"

"Three dollars?!" Louisa repeated incredulously.

"Is that too much?" The woman looked genuinely concerned. She tugged at an errant strand of snow white hair which had somehow escaped from its bobby pin restraint. "Well, fifty cents then."

"Fifty cents?" Louisa pursed her lips again. This woman knew nothing about how to haggle. "Fifty cents each, or fifty cents for both?"

"Whatever you think is fair," The old woman smiled again. "To tell the truth, I'm just enjoying being out of the house and meeting new people again. It's so magnificently sunny, don't you think, Louisa?"

Louisa frowned at the woman. "How did you know my name was Louisa?"

"Why, it's embroidered on your sweater, dearie. And nicely done at that."

Of course, it was. This was the sweater she wore every Sunday when the weather was not too warm. "My daughter made it for me. A long time ago."

"She certainly did a wonderful job."

"She's dead now," Louisa said, as she carefully pulled two quarters from her purse, and slowly counted them into the older woman's hand. The woman never glanced at the coins in her hand, nor lost her friendly grin.

"Well, that happens when you get to be our age, dearie. But they never die in our hearts, do they now?"

Louisa stared hard at this strange woman with the inexhaustible cheer. She appeared to be in her nineties, her ankles swollen by poor circulation. The black and silver glasses seemed oddly appropriate to her broad, smiling face. Louisa couldn't help but relax in her presence.

"No," she agreed softly. "They never do die in our hearts."

"My name is Miranda Hathaway. I'm ninety-one years-old, and tomorrow my grandson is putting me in a nursing home."

"I'm sorry to hear that, Mrs. Hathaway."

"Call me Miranda, please. You have a very attractive face for an elderly black woman. Has anyone ever told you that?"

"No one I know would be that rude!"

Again, the woman appeared genuinely concerned. She shook her head sadly, even though the hint of mirth never left her twinkling eyes.

"Was that rude? I didn't mean it to be." She hit her head with the palm of her hand and giggled. "This old brain doesn't work like it used to, I guess. I can't remember when exactly I turned into such a silly, old woman." Again, the mischievous eyes. "I guess that's why my grandson is putting me in a nursing home tomorrow." Suddenly, the swollen ankles appeared to give way, and the white-haired woman had to grab Louisa's arm to steady herself. "I'm sorry, dearie. I have to sit down now. Would you like to sit beside me for a few moments? It really is a comfortable chair. Only $35.00."

"$35.00!" Louisa repeated as the two women shuffled over to the matching upholstered chairs set by the front porch.

"Well, $15.00, then..." She executed a slow bend at the waist, and eventually sat down with a stifled groan. "Do you live by yourself, Louisa?"

"Yes. Since 1976, when my youngest granddaughter went off to college." Louisa lowered her own tired body in the chair next to Miranda's, though she refused to show how much she appreciated the rest.

"Do you miss them terribly?"

Louisa hesitated. Miranda knew nothing of yard sale etiquette. Yet Louisa couldn't stop herself from opening up to the strange old woman.

"Yes." she said finally. And that was all she would admit.

Miranda leaned back and smiled. As she closed her eyes, her voice became lyrical, almost trance-like. Louisa had to lean in close to hear her words.

"When I was younger," she began. "You know, when I had a house full of children, I used to insist on dinner at 5:30 every evening. I'd have everything prepared when my husband sat down at the kitchen table at 5:30 sharp. Bernard was very fussy about time. What's that word?"

"Punctual."

"That's right. Punctual. Bernard was very punctual. And after Bernard died, I guess I got punctual, too. I insisted that all of the children had their hands washed and were sitting at the table at exactly 5:30 every night."

Miranda's eyes fluttered open, and she pointed to the large mahogany kitchen table set out by the driveway, and the six matching chairs carefully placed around it.

"After my husband died, my eldest...Bernard, Jr. sat there. At the head of the table. The proper place for the new man of the house. Wanda sat beside him, and would usually fidget all through dinner. Agnes, the one with my long blonde hair, sat beside Wanda. Agnes had the biggest appetite you ever saw for a skinny girl. I sat on the far end, once all the food was ready. On the other side of the table sat Allen and Anthony. They were my youngest...twin boys. Handfuls, the both of them."

Miranda closed her eyes again, as she seemed to sink deeper into her chair. "We always felt that a child's chair was theirs forever. Once someone moved out, or...left us, nobody ever took that chair. We didn't even move it from the table. We just...retired it."

"Where are your children now, Miranda?"

The question was like an unexpected slap in the face, and the ninety-one-year-old woman recoiled from the shock of it. For the first time, Louisa could clearly read the pain in the other woman's eyes, but like a dark and brooding ocean tide, that, too receded. When Miranda finally answered, no trace of that fleeting pain could be found in the serene resignation of her voice.

"My children? They're all here now," she touched her chest lightly. "Here in my heart. Bless them."

"They're all..?" Louisa groped for the right words. Words that would not reignite Miranda's heartache. But there was no reason to worry. The cheerful old woman was already back in control of her emotions.

"Dead? Yes, every one of my babies. Bless them all." She pointed to the chairs around the table, as if she could still see them sitting there. "The twins were the first to leave me. Polio. Anthony came down with the disease in October, and Allen just watched him twist up and get weaker. You know how twins are. Anthony had never done anything without Allen, and I guess they felt this should be the same. Polio crippled some children. Mine weren't so lucky. Allen didn't catch the disease until two weeks before Anthony died, but he passed away just three days after his twin brother. They were seven years old. God bless them."

"I'm sorry," was all Louisa could think to say.

"That's kind of you. But that's the way life is, isn't it?" Miranda's eyes became distant again, as she looked at the table, now being smudged by a greasy teenager with the last eighth of a Big Mac on his fingers. "That table's for sale!" Miranda called happily to the young man, who seemed shocked to be noticed at all. He dropped the remnants of his burger, and fled the yard as if everything in it was contagious. His actions didn't trouble Miranda a bit, as she continued her remembrances.

"Bernard, Jr. fought in World War II and was a big war hero. We were all so proud of him. They said he saved his whole squad in France, by jumping right on top of a German tank and throwing a hand grenade inside. At the time, I felt sorry for the mothers of those poor German boys in that tank, but they got some of my tears, too. Bernard, Jr. was put in charge of a division in the Ardennes Forest when the Germans attacked." She sighed heavily. "The Battle of The Bulge, they called it. A waste of precious boys, I say it is."

Miranda pulled off her glasses and wiped pure, distilled emotion from her weary eyes. Louisa laid a comforting hand on the older woman's arm, as she continued her painful history.

"Wanda, who sat right there, died in 1967. A car accident. She was always so full of life. That's her son, my grandson Robert, trying to sell my best china to that young couple over there. I love to see young couples, don't you?"

"They make me sad, Miranda. I feel I should run over and warn them. Tell them to hold onto each other real hard. Tell them how short the time they have together really is." Louisa, too, pulled out a ragged handkerchief to wipe her own tired eyes. "What happened to your other girl? Agnes, I think you said."

"What a clever memory you have, Louisa!" Miranda seemed genuinely thrilled. "How kind of you to remember Agnes' name." The old woman's smile glowed so brightly, a few people browsing through items stopped to stare at her. Miranda didn't seem to notice or care. "Agnes, was such a sweet child. My joy and comfort these last few years. She'd come to see me three times a week, and insisted on calling me every night before she went to bed. She was a good woman. A kind woman. You would have liked her very much."

Louisa nodded, but said nothing.

"Agnes didn't remain a skinny girl. She was sixty-two when she died, and almost as big as I am. I guess she needed room for that magnificent heart of hers. She was so good to everyone, that girl. It was only last February that I buried her. The last of my children."

"It's hard to bury your children, I know."

"I don't think Nature meant for parents to outlive their children. It seems wrong, in a way. But what do I know about Nature? I'm just a silly old woman who's headed for a nursing home tomorrow."

Louisa placed her hand on the older woman's arm, and the two elderly women sat this way, side by side in silence.

Suddenly, a tall man with a buzz haircut walked over to them.

"How much you want for the toaster?"

It took a moment to draw Miranda back from her silent reveries. "The toaster? Oh, I don't know. Four dollars, I guess."

"Four dollars?" The man repeated incredulously.

"Is that too much?" Asked the old woman, genuinely concerned. "Then how about..."

"Four dollars!" interrupted Louisa. "Not a penny less. It's a good toaster."

The man with the buzz haircut looked at the toaster and sneered.

"I'll give you two," he said, finally.

"That seems fair," smiled Miranda cheerfully.

"No, it doesn't." snapped Louisa, as she pulled herself up from the chair to look up at the man, hands on her hips. "Four dollars. That's it. If you don't like it, go to Walmart and buy a shiny new one for $19.95!"

The man looked at Louisa, then at the toaster. Then at Louisa again. He pulled four wrinkled bills from the front pocket of his tattered jeans. He handed them to her.

"You're one tough lady," he grinned.

"Damn right. And don't you forget it!"

Miranda's eyes widened, as Louisa handed her the four wrinkled bills.

"You've done this before, haven't you, dear?" she smiled.

It was then that Louisa taught her new ninety-one-year-old friend how to execute a fist bump for the first time in her life.

****

That night, Louisa sat by the large mahogany table, which took up most of the walking space in her kitchen. She had left the apartment willing to buy a salt and pepper shaker, and ended up with an antique kitchen set.

Not that she wanted it.

Miranda's grandson had priced the table at $250.00, a bargain for antique mahogany, but when it hadn't sold, Miranda insisted to the point of tears that Louisa take care of it for her.

"At least until I break out of that nursing home," she winked.

Louisa, who had never taken charity in her life, was adamant about paying for the table. The two elderly women haggled joyously, until they settled on a final selling price. Fourteen dollars, including delivery and set up.

To say Miranda's grandson was angry would have been an understatement of historic proportions.

Now, Louisa Mae Tyler sat at the far end of the large table, wishing she had met her new friend years ago. The nursing home was eleven miles south, which was as far away as Alaska to an eighty-year-old woman without a car. Louisa sadly put her rose-petal teacup down, and rested her weary head in her hands.

"What's wrong, Ma?" The child's voice was strangely familiar, although she was certain she had never heard it before.

Louisa looked up from her teacup, and they were all there, sitting around the large mahogany table.

Bernard, Jr. at the head of the table, looking proud and important. A handsome boy of twenty, with a beard too light to shave.

Beside him sat Wanda, fidgeting still. Her eyes catching the slightly mischievous glint that Louisa had seen in Miranda.

Then there were the twins, Allen and Anthony, fighting over the wishbone of a roasted chicken Louisa had never cooked.

And Agnes. Kind and gentle Agnes. The girl with the long blonde hair, that looked so much like a young Miranda, Louisa had to tear up.

"Leave her alone," said Bernard, Jr. judiciously. "She's probably thinking about Dad again. Sometimes, Ma just needs to cry it out."

Louisa looked at the small clock built into her compact gas oven. It was 5:30 sharp. Miranda's family was gathered around her table. They looked so real. So alive.

"I'm not your mother," Louisa whispered tearfully. "Why are you here?"

"Ma's being silly," said Allen.

"Yeah, silly," agreed Anthony.

Agnes put a comforting hand on Louisa's wrinkled brown arm. The touch was warm and soft.

"Don't worry about it, Ma," Agnes said, a voice as soothing as warm milk. "Whatever happens, at least we have each other."

Louisa looked into the young girl's compassion-filled eyes and immediately believed her tender words. The elderly black woman whispered a silent prayer of gratitude for Miranda's precious gift.

She knew she would never have to eat another dinner alone again.

Dark Wilderness

Ira Kaplan strolled dramatically into the command center to address his troops. The command center for his Nature Defense Brigade was actually little more than the cramped basement of his cheap duplex apartment. Bare concrete walls lined with angry posters decried environmental atrocities, both real and imagined. Rising sea levels, with whole nations underwater. Fields of wheat withered and fried by intense solar radiation. The depletion of fish in the ocean. A young child looking quizzically at the last tree left on earth. Lists of extinct animals celebrating man taking his last agonizing breath. Such was the gospel according to Ira Kaplan. The self-proclaimed last true believer standing between modern life and what he saw as the coming environmental apocalypse.

His latest batch of conscripts lay scattered in various poses of discomfort on the cold basement floor. Young, eager and motivated; fresh from the fertile recruiting grounds of Portland State University. Each dedicated to doing whatever it takes to further the cause, no questions asked. As Kaplan scanned their freshly determined faces, he felt renewed by their commitment; confirmed once again, in the righteousness of his own beliefs.

True leaders seldom act in darkness. More often, they become addicted to that peculiar social illumination which can only be supplied by the adoration of like-minded followers. That alone charges them with the energy and unwavering purpose necessary to accomplish their goals.

Kaplan ran long whitened fingers through the wild tufts of gray and brown hair fleeing his face in all directions. He wanted to extend this moment as long as possible, understanding the impact of a dramatic entrance on minds eager to be persuaded. Positioning himself directly under the dangling light fixture, he removed his wire rimmed glasses and polished them with the tail of his flannel shirt. The crowd of thirteen hushed in anticipation. After a long pause, he placed the glasses back on his thin nose, before flashing his trademark grin.

"Are you ready to save the planet?!" he suddenly shouted to his gathering of devotees, and this latest incarnation of the Nature Defense Brigade roared back its approval.

****

The joke among most cynical financial analysts is that you could feed a village for a year on what S. Rod Harris spent on his hair alone each month. What many of these critics failed to realize was that Harris himself started the rumor; because he understood that to be criticized for lavishly obscene spending, you first had to be recognized as being ridiculously successful. And that perception of unstoppable success had helped him bully his way to the top of the corporate world.

S. Rod Harris was fit, forty, and the fastest-rising executive in the history of Portman-Decatur Industries, a reputation he was quick to publicize at every opportunity. Some called him ruthless in his inexorable rise to the top. Harris preferred to redefine his actions as basic business acumen, minus the standard sugar coating. He knew the value of meticulously assessing your enemy's advantages, while simultaneously ensuring your enemy underestimates your own skills. Firing the man who first hired him at Portman Decatur might not have been beneficial from an efficiency point of view, but it was a brilliant tactical move in his career climb. It warned present and future coworkers to never take him for granted.

Now swaddled in the comfortable confines of his executive office suite on the fifty-third floor of the Portman-Decatur building, Harris swiveled his $30,000.00 calf-leather chair to face the handful of grim employees seated in front of his massive mahogany desk. Although he failed to serve in the military, S. Rod Harris loved the concise poetry of army slang, and he often surrounded himself with those who spoke his chosen language.

Phillips from Operations. McNulty from Acquisitions. Wellman from I.T. Support. Stoltz and Santiago from Marketing. All ex-military, settled comfortably into corporate life.

Until tonight.

It was Harris's unique talent to keep them supplied with enemies, real or imagined.

"Gentlemen...and lady..." he nodded to Ellen Stoltz, the lone female in the ensemble. She visibly bristled to being referred to his condescending tone, as he knew she would, and he had to hide his mischievous smile. "Our mission is simple. After a long, hard-fought battle in the legislature, we have finally captured the exclusive logging rights to the Old Tehanmar National Forest."

They applauded politely, then stopped on cue.

"However, as you know, Portman-Decatur Industries is far more than a paper and wood conglomerate. We have the technology, the talent and the customer base to quickly exploit any mineral resources we may encounter in the area. The solution to our country's energy needs may lie here. Buried under a patch of trees hundreds of miles from the nearest anything. A smudge of forest most Americans have never heard of."

Wellman was the first to respond. "The wildlife preserve?"

"What's to preserve? Wildlife and shit. Nothing you can't find in a hundred other places. The region has been under the strictest federal regulation since the Indians – excuse me, the Native Americans - were driven out a couple of hundred years ago. So, it's up to us to conduct some low-profile reconnaissance. Is there oil under that land? Lithium? We simply don't know. That is why we need a small, well-equipped tactical incursion to gain intelligence on the forest and its resources. If we strike quickly, we should be able to acquire full mining rights for the Old Tehanmar before the environmental lobby even has a chance to respond."

"We're talking boots on the ground, people." That was Borrell, Harris's Vice President in charge of 'Special Projects.' Harris was sure Borrell had a first name, though he had no idea what it was. Still, if you needed something done that was quasi-legal or borderline ethical, you called Borrell. "Each of you was chosen because you have some degree of military training in your background."

Looks of silent panic spread through the room. Phillips was the first to cough up a reply.

"That was a long time ago, Mr. Harris." He patted his newly acquired dad-bod. "I'm not exactly Rambo these days."

"We don't need Rambo. More like Indiana Jones."

"What is the anticipated duration of the mission, Mr. Harris?"

"What's the matter, McNulty? Gotta date?" This comment sparked a little good-natured chuckling. Chaz McNulty was newly married, severely so, and less likely to stray than a deceased nun.

"Estimated duration is eight days. Two days in, two days out and four in field. We hike in to avoid recognition. Carry all necessary equipment and supplies in our backpacks. Right, Borrell?"

"Exactly, sir," Borrell nodded with a humorless grin. "We already have fully outfitted kits for each of you. And we have taken the liberty of cancelling all your appointments for the next week."

Silent expressions of annoyance rippled across their faces, but only Phillips raised an objection.

"I have to visit my…"

"It's been cancelled." Borrell cut him off with a look that quashed any further discussion. "She will understand."

"Listen, people. This is for the good of our shareholders, and our country." Harris leaned in, eyes blazing. "We don't need to strike a gusher here, or find the Hope Diamond. Just a few soil samples and some ground sonar readings should do it. The engineering and analysis boys can take it from there."

"Isn't Old Tehanmar federally protected as a plant and nature preserve?" That was Wellman, the geek in the crowd.

"A portion of it is. And that's where we anticipate the greatest return on investment. That is also the reason for the maximum degree of secrecy on this mission."

"Anyone else know we're coming, boss?" Harris hated when Stoltz called him that.

"Not even the trees, Stoltz… Not even the trees."

****

The woods were quiet today, Tommy Ray Connors mused. That was always a bad sign. As much as he loved these woods, he never felt completely comfortable here, like he had in the Smokies back in his native Tennessee. The Old Tehanmar Preserve was every bit as beautiful in a primeval sense, but it was far less inviting. The ancient trees closed in on you here. The woods seemed dark and brooding, while the Smokies always felt like they smiled just for him.

Tommy Ray chuckled to himself, kicked at a large clump of weeds, and once again counted the months to his retirement. Thirty-one. Just under three years left on this forest ranger job. Then, once his federal pension kicked in, he could leave this gloomy place behind and build his dream cabin back in the Smokies.

But today he had more pressing concerns. It had been three days since that distraught call from Wanda Hammuck, and there was still no sign of her fool husband. Connors knew Ellery Hammuck well enough to know what kind of an idiot he was. Ellery was a middle-aged weekend warrior, who thought a fifth or two of bourbon would magically transform him into the Great White Hunter, the modern-day scourge of the forest. In that condition, Hammuck was twice as likely to shoot off his own toes than a buck with a twelve-point rack. He was probably sleeping it off in a deer blind somewhere, well-hidden because he knew hunting wasn't allowed in this section of the Old Tehanmar National Forest. Five hundred and sixty-two thousand acres of the country's most pristine woodlands, and only twenty-four hundred of that off-limits. Yet whenever any fool disappeared, it was usually in this old growth part of the forest.

He could hear the excuses now...

'Just got myself turned around, Mr. Ranger, sir...'

'Could've sworn my campfire was over here somewhere...'

'Guess I shoulda stayed a city boy, huh, Tommy Ray?'

Searching this deep into the old growth preserve was never easy. Tommy Ray spit on the ground in frustration, as he scanned the dense treeline for any hint of red flannel. He got so used to looking up, that he nearly tripped over Ellery Hammuck when he found him; or what was left of the drunken poacher, which was pretty much picked white bones and shredded fabric.

When the Forest Ranger brushed away the swarm of ants and flies, there was enough left of the face to prove it was Hammuck all right. Insects were great recyclers, and they were already returning the pools of spilt blood and decaying flesh back to the environment. Judging by the bits of shattered bone protruding through the body's jaw and pant leg, Tommy Ray guessed it was a grizzly that had done in Ellery Hammuck. A big one, probably attracted by the strange smell of whisky that permeated the clothing of the dead hunter. Hammuck was probably asleep on the ground, when the bear came nosing around. If he woke in a drunken stupor, the bear might have misinterpreted his panicked swaying as a challenge...not the best way to communicate with nine hundred pounds of aggressive grizzly. It would be quick and bloody. After the victorious grizzly ambled off, there would be plenty of other forest animals and insects to pick the bones clean.

On the other hand, the Forest Ranger knew that bears rarely roamed this section of the preserve. As he pulled the plastic body bag from his backpack, Connors scanned the area for any signs of that other lethal predator in the woods...homeless people. Actually, he had received official orders from the Parks Department not to call them that. Whenever the homeless committed a crime, they were to be referred to as drifters. That way, the public would never assign any negative associations with the homeless. Drifters hid out on public lands all the time, a few bad ones pilfered campsites, committed the occasional armed robbery, and according to federal statistics, accidentally started more than half of the forest fires that ravaged the Northern Pacific Coast each summer. By contrast, homeless people were unfortunate martyrs who roamed city streets in a daze, trailing after shopping carts filled with junk. The only real difference was in the accepted media label. That's why Tommy Ray loved the woods so much. Out here, there were no pretenses, no posturing. Things were what they were in nature. Only man redefined reality to make himself more comfortable with unfashionable thoughts.

As he shoved the broken remains of Ellery Hammuck into the black plastic body bag, Tommy Ray was relieved to see no footsteps around the body. That would eliminate all the paperwork of a murder report. However, there were no bear tracks either, and that was strange. Glancing up, he solved the mystery; a cracked branch with a piece of torn denim blowing in the soft breeze. The overweight hunter must have climbed a tree, and through drunkenness, stupidity, or sheer belly mass, broke the branch that was supporting him, crashing to the ground and broking his jaw and leg upon impact. He must have had just enough strength to turn himself onto his back as he died. Tommy Ray hoped the hunter was gone before the animals had started eating away at him.

Nature showed little mercy to the helpless.

****

/

"We've just received detailed information," Ira Kaplan informed his followers, "...that the assault on Old Tehanmar has begun! Not satisfied with stealing the logging rights for this venerable old growth forest, Portman-Decatur Industries is, at this very moment, setting in gear a wholesale strip mining operation for the most ancient part of the preserve!"

The outcry was loud and immediate. The expected shouts rang out. *How can they do that? Has Corporate America gone insane? That's our children's legacy!*

*What about the rare Steller's Eider and blue-tufted North American finch?! They'll
never get away with it!*

Ira Kaplan let the tumult boil just long enough to scorch the consciences
of any remaining pacifists in the room, then quieted them with a single
commanding gesture.

He would know what to do. He alone could save the forest from
industrial rape.

"My confidential sources tell me they are planning to introduce a small
squad of arboreal assassins into the heart of Old Tehanmar. Their mission
is to assess its profit potential and exploit any new resources they can find.
If successful, they will turn our country's last remaining old growth forest
into a Kuwaiti oil field. But that's only the first step! After that, they will
begin plowing up two thousand-year-old trees to dig for lithium and who
knows what else? The strip-mined West Virginia hills at their worst will be
nothing compared to what they have planned for Old Tehanmar!"

More indignation. Two graduate students rose to their feet, fists raised
in defiance. Ira played the moment to maximum effect.

"I know. I know. I feel just as betrayed as you do. What they are planning
is illegal, and they damn well know it! The question is...are we going to let
them get away with it?"

"No!" the small gathering screamed in unison.

"Are we gonna let them commit their greedy corporate atrocities on
Mother Earth?!"

"NO!"

"Then who's going with me into the woods to make sure they never
come out again!"

The echoing shouts and applause let Ira Kaplan know he had won them
over, heart and soul. In the on-going war over the environment, he had just
baptized another band of die-hard militants.

****

August ninth was dubbed 'Incursion Day' for S. Rod Harris and his
reconnaissance patrol. He had set in motion all equipment, excuses and
plausible deniability for his team of six. Stoltz was there, as was Santiago,
Wellman, Borrell and McNulty, with himself as the leader, of course.

Although they were careful to bear no markings or identification which could tie them to Portman-Decatur Industries, they were well-equipped by the company. The two jet black Ford Explorers that crossed into the Old Tehanmar National Forest's main entrance were loaded down with lab equipment, ground sonar devices, soil probes and automatic weapons, all carefully hidden within their folded tents and camping supplies. They would unload at one of the approved campsites, empty the vehicles, then hike in to the center of the restricted area for four days of undisturbed monitoring.

Spirits were high, even without the ongoing patriotic exhortations of S. Rodham Harris. He lived for moments like these. If he could find a profitable new source of income which could further propel him up the corporate ladder, all the better.

"We'll set up a diversionary camp here," he told his crew as they piled out of the four-wheel drive vehicles at Primitive Campsite #329. "We erect three tents, and make it look like we're going the typical tree-hugger route. I want campfires and sleeping bags, all the usual crap. Wellman will stay behind with the diversionary camp. If any forest rangers snoop around, or if we attract too much suspicion among the touchy-feely nature crowd, he can divert their attention, and radio us to come back in. Got it?"

They nodded in turn, never pausing in their rapid set up of the mock campsite. They worked without speaking, all focused on their assigned tasks. These were professional problem solvers. Harris admired their efficiency, as he knew they looked up to his decision-making skills.

In less than twenty minutes, Bobby Santiago and Andy Phillips had set up three tents, two blazing campfires, plus a few lawn chairs, fishing poles, kerosene lanterns and cooking equipment casually scattered about the site. In two of the tents, they stuffed mannequins in sleeping bags, and positioned them so only the closest inspection would reveal they were anything but exhausted hikers.

Chaz McNulty and Ellen Stoltz carefully laid out the ground sonar and other scientific equipment they would need to accomplish their mission. Marty Wellman, the team's electronics expert, adjusted the state-of-the-art, high powered radio communicators to a specially selected scrambled frequency. This would let him stay in contact with the team members, without fear of detection by anyone randomly picking up a stray signal. In addition to the two-way radios, Borrell outfitted each person's backpack with a compass, snake bite kit, bug spray, bandages, insulated jacket and socks, sleeping bag roll, dried food products, and two water canteens.

Harris himself was responsible for the weapons. Each team member would be issued a high-powered fully automatic rifle with three hundred rounds... more than enough to see them through a small-scale battle. Unknown to anyone else, he also carried a nine millimeter Beretta strapped to his leg.

The last thing S. Rod Harris wanted was be caught out in the wilderness, unprepared.

When everything was set, he ordered his team to line up for inspection. Harris nodded with satisfaction. It had taken a surprisingly short time for these former soldiers and sailors to lapse back into military efficiency. Yet, aside from the automatic weapons, as well as the diamond-tough look in their eyes, the five hikers could almost pass for any other Sierra Club groupies. They synchronized watches at 6:42 AM, when he gave them one final pep talk.

"If any of you has doubts regarding the importance of our mission, you can stand down now. I love nature as much as anyone. But unlike those environmental whackos, I also respect it. Hurricanes, earthquakes and tornadoes prove that the earth is not some fragile egg-shell we have to tip-toe over. It's a tough competitor with more than enough resources to kick our collective asses at the slightest whim. Hell, they say one super volcano pollutes the atmosphere as much as five years output of all the factories in North America! You gotta respect that. And hundreds of thousands of years ago, there were volcanoes all over the damn place, spewing sulfuric acid and all kinds of other crap into the air on a twenty-four-hour basis. This went on for centuries, yet the earth survived. It survived and flourished. That proves Mother Nature is no wimp. She's a kick-ass, ball-busting beauty that can take whatever we throw at her, and give back every bit as good as she gets. The kind of lady that deserves respect, not pampering. Tell that to the global warming crowd.

"Even if we cut down every tree in Old Tehanmar -- which we won't -- but if we did, new trees would sprout in their place. Within thirty or forty years, this would be a full-fledged forest again. Nature takes care of itself.

"Now our mission at Portman-Decatur Industries is to make life better for people. For *people*...because this planet was made for us. If birds or fish could think, if squirrels and bunnies could build hospitals and research labs, then I'd probably be willing to share it. But in the meantime, I protect my species...human beings. Everything else is just God's window dressing."

Phillips and McNulty chuckled politely. They had heard this speech many times before, and were eager to hit the trails. But S. Rod Harris wasn't finished yet.

"If Portman-Decatur is to prosper, if we are to serve our millions of shareholders and safeguard our own jobs, we damn well better find something profitable underneath this forest, before the environmentalists shut down our factories to save some ugly-as-sin beetle, whose sole purpose in life is to eat, shit and make a million more ugly-as-sin beetles. Anyone who thinks insects and plants are superior to people is just plain crazy. And we all know how dangerous crazy people can be. They've been known to kill a human to protect a bug or a plant, so I want you to watch yourselves. I don't intend to lose any men on this mission."

He could tell by their faces they were ready to go. The morning sun was rising in the sky and they were eager for the covering shade of the inner forest. With a simple, "Let's do this," S. Rodham Harris led his team of hand-picked employees into the heart of the Old Tehanmar National Forest, for what he thought would be a simple four-day incursion.

That was his first fatal mistake.

****

In another part of the preserve, members of Ira Kaplan's Nature Defense Brigade plotted their ambush. They had detailed information on each member of the Portman-Decatur group, knew the weapons they carried, the purpose of their mission. Although they did not know the exact point where they would enter the old growth section of the forest, Kaplan knew where Harris and his band were heading and approximately when they planned to arrive. This gave him a significant advantage over his sworn enemy, who still believed they would be alone in that restricted portion of the forest.

Four months ago, Kaplan had determined that S. Rod Harris was the most likely instigator of anti-environmental action within the massive Portman-Decatur conglomerate. Harris' love of publicity and his hard-to-disguise ambition made this assumption fairly clear-cut. Harris' speeches on the economic benefits of exploiting the Old Tehanmar National Forest were widely quoted throughout the mainstream news media. His 'people over bugs' arguments on Fox News had been dissected and dismissed as heresy throughout the environmental press. In the guise of negotiating a truce, Kaplan had bluffed his way into a rare fifteen-minute meeting in Harris' office. The only productive aspect of that meeting was the small electronic listening device he had planted under his seat. It was that tiny bug which helped him stay one step ahead of Harris' plans, including this secret incursion into the heart of Old Tehanmar. Ironically, it was this hidden electronic transmitter that had done more to dismantle Rod Harris' 'people over bugs' strategy than anything Kaplan could have done on his own. And the irony of Harris being brought down by an electronic 'bug' was too delicious to overlook.

Ira Kaplan had never told anyone in his organization about the listening device. He preferred to have them think one or more employees of Portman-Decatur Industries had a guilty conscience over the company's environmental atrocities, and were serving as double-agents. This played better with his group's avowed anti-technology philosophy.

Kaplan was smart enough to realize nothing was ever gained by undermining your core beliefs with trivial facts.

S. Rod Harris had five well-armed, well-trained employees. Ira Kaplan had thirteen highly motivated college students, who had only recently accepted the reality that sometimes, people had to suffer in service to a truly righteous cause. In a head-on confrontation, Kaplan's Nature Defense Brigade would be slaughtered, but by employing stealth, fear, and the hit-and-run tactics of the Native American Apaches he so admired, Harris' group didn't stand a chance.

Kaplan would wait until they reached the deepest part of the Old Tehanmar preserve before crushing them completely.

And his place in environmental history would be assured.

****

Back in his cramped ranger station, Tommy Ray Connors tried in vain to rub the day's tension from his throbbing temples. The shock in Mrs. Hammuck's voice, and her unflinching assertions that her husband must have been murdered, still echoed in his weary brain. He hated having to make these calls. There was just no easy way to tell a woman her husband was dead, no matter what a jerk he was in life. Yet her certainty that her husband was murdered struck a nerve in the forest ranger. Too many experienced hunters had died mysteriously in that old growth section of Old Tehanmar. There was something wild and disconcerting about the place. In that dark heart of the forest, the trees were too densely packed to allow anything but a motorcycle to maneuver inside. The rate of vegetation was unusual, perhaps because of the section's advanced age. Paths were quickly overgrown and far too costly to maintain. With no paths to follow, mapping had proven virtually impossible because of the size of the interior and lack of discernible landmarks. And due to some magnetic abnormality, compass readings were strangely inconsistent.

No one knew the forest as well as Connors himself. Yet it had taken him a day and a half to pull Hammuck's remains out, because he had gotten lost four times and spent half the journey hiking around in circles. To save money, the Parks Department cut the number of rangers to a handful spread over hundreds of thousands of acres, and declared the center of Old Tehanmar off-limits to the general public. Even so, there were at least a half-dozen poachers and hikers who hopped the barbed wire fence surrounding the preserve each month, eager to prove they were Robin Hood or the Great White Hunter. Most ended up freezing to death or becoming hopelessly lost in the unfriendly woods. The fortunate ones would emerge, frightened, half-starved and spilling over with tales of shadowy figures and looming death.

To complicate his job, Tommy Ray had recently learned some big, international company had bribed the legislature to conduct limited logging operations in Tehanmar. Although they were not permitted to fell trees in the old growth section, he knew it was virtually impossible to tell a logger alone in the woods exactly where he could and could not go. Especially if he was armed with a chain saw. Tommy Ray would be forced to flash the badge on a regular basis just to keep the loggers in line, but this was an awfully big forest to patrol for just one man. There'd be abuses for sure, which he'd be forced to either fight or overlook. If the environmentalists came to protest, the likelihood of violence could be very real indeed.

Tommy Ray rubbed his temples again, as he wondered how someone could love his job so much...and like it so little.

****

Rod's Rangers, as Harris decided to call them, moved through the dense woods at an impressive pace, considering each member of the team now spent most of their days stuck behind a desk. Yet S. Rod Harris had chosen his squad carefully. McNulty served in Iraq and Afghanistan. Phillips was an Army sniper, and had once been a member of the U.S. Olympic rifle team. Stoltz was Army Reserve, and held a black belt in Chinese Kenpo. Santiago was a former Navy Seal, with a handful of medals and commendations. And though juvenile records are supposed to be expunged at age eighteen, Harris learned Borrell had done time in a juvenile detention center for involuntary manslaughter. He also found out that, in truth, there was nothing involuntary about it. For all his electronic wizardry, only Wellman lacked the talent or personality to kill when required, and that's why he was left to safeguard the base camp. If a bear, a wolf, or with any luck, a militant environmentalist crossed their path, Harris wanted to know he could count on his people to do the right thing, without question or hesitation.

The silent squad hiked on a northeasterly course for ten miles without uttering a word. It was Santiago who spoke first, and his news was not good.

"We're being shadowed," he whispered to his boss. "Don't turn around."

Harris nodded, he had expected this. "How long?" he whispered in reply.

"At least two miles back. As soon as we entered the old growth section." They kept hiking, pretended their discussion was casual.

"How many?"

"Can't tell. One, maybe more. Someone who knows what they're doing. Knows how not to be seen."

Harris felt the hairs on the back of his neck stand straight up. He sensed the danger, loved the thrill of it. At the same time, he was afraid he would start shaking like a baby in front of his more experienced men.

"Think they're armed?" He tried to erase the fear from his voice.

"Hard to say. No glints of sunlight, so they're not scoping us. Nothing hostile yet. They might just be tracking us."

"Or waiting," Rod Harris said ominously.

"Or waiting." Santiago agreed.

Harris held his breath. He tried to glance casually over his shoulder, but quickly realized that if an experienced Navy Seal like Santiago couldn't pinpoint the followers, he didn't stand a chance of seeing them.

"Pass the word down the line," he whispered. "Nobody's to let on we know we're being watched. But I want everybody to be prepared in case all hell breaks loose."

"You got it, boss."

With impressive casualness, Santiago dropped back and whispered the news to McNulty, who was next in line. Harris decided to give Santiago a raise as soon as they got back to the office. The man was that good. In the meantime, he would simply enjoy the adventure.

'I know you're out there,' he smiled, with thoughts directed at the unseen watcher. *'And I'm gonna eat you for lunch, you stupid piece of excrement.'*

And the wary hikers moved ever deeper into the heart of the Old Tehanmar National Forest under a pair of watchful, malevolent eyes.

****

No place on earth brought Ira Kaplan more serenity and comfort than a virgin forest. The unspoiled beauty harkened back to a time of peace, millennia before man's corrupt practices and vile ambition made a mockery of nature's complex perfection. Nature creates, man destroys. The equation was simple as that. Bolstered by the sinister forces of advanced technology, the battle became even more slanted. What nature needed was someone willing to fight on her behalf, and that's what Ira Kaplan believed his role in history would be. He was the White Knight of Old Tehanmar, a curly haired savior willing to stare down the barbarians at the wooden gate, to slay the huge corporate dragon intent on devouring this precious natural resource.

However, even Ira had to admit the deepest core of this ancient forest made him a little uneasy. It was too dark, too cold in the shadowy teeth of these ancient pines; too easy to lose one's way in its maze-like thickets. This was a fiercely primeval spot, he could imagine it looking the same when man was still some barely-evolved simian monstrosity. The Old Tehanmar preserve was virgin woodland, one of the last in the United States. These trees had never known the destructive screech of a chainsaw. This arboreal floor had never been scarred by man's cruel footpaths. These plants and animals flourished without human interference. It was Eden reborn, although he professed not to believe in that biblical fairy tale. Still, this pristine sanctuary needed to be protected, no matter what the cost.

As these thoughts cascaded through him, Ira Kaplan sat with his back pressed against a towering redwood older than the United States, and felt as one with the tree's glorious longevity. He hoped future generations would one day be able to experience this moment for themselves. He envisioned himself years from now, leading a ring of white robed children laughing and prancing through the sun-speckled shade of these very trees.

His imaginings were disrupted by Bert Jennings, who crashed through the clearing in the trees like a bellowing moose.

"Ira! Ira! We've got 'em!"

The activist sprang to his feet.

"You found them? Where?"

"Angie spotted them about a mile and a half east of here. They're almost to Trap 49."

Ira smiled. Preparation was everything when conducting guerrilla warfare. The booby-traps they had set for the Portman-Decatur crew were sprinkled liberally throughout the old growth preserve, strategically placed along the most likely routes of travel. Those that were not tripped would remain an effective deterrent for poachers in this protected part of the forest for years to come.

"Angie is sure it's them?"

The tall grad student nodded. He still hadn't regained his breath after that last frantic dash through the forest. "Just like you said, Ira. Six hikers with automatic weapons. Rod Harris in the lead!"

"What about the communications specialist at the campsite?"

"We sent Fielding, Naharij, Scopes and Jefferson. They'll take him out."

"Are all our people armed?"

Jennings hesitated a moment. He had yet to fully accept the need for violence. "Yes," he said softly. "Two shotguns, a machete and a revolver."

Ira noticed the pained look in his young companion's eyes. "Well, we all hope they won't be forced to use them," he said, as cheerfully as he could. "What are the odds the others will trip 49?"

"I'd estimate a ninety-two percent probability," Bert was a math major, so his probabilities carried far more validity than the average environmentalist's guesswork. "They should be hitting it in the next few minutes."

Ira smiled. Things were unfolding exactly as planned. He threw an encouraging arm over his young follower, and slapped him gregariously on the back.

"Then it looks like the battle for Old Tehanmar has finally been joined, my friend!"

****

It all happened so quickly, Rod Harris never had time to react.

His team had been slogging through the forest for nearly two hours after the watcher first appeared. It bothered him to feel like he was a specimen under someone's microscope, but he was determined to let the watcher make the first move. If it proved to be an attack, he'd be more than happy to blow the hell out of everything in the forest. He used his frustration to tramp harder through the thickening underbrush, even though his legs were growing rubbery from exhaustion.

Unfortunately, as he often instructed employees under his command, exhaustion increases the probability of error. Perhaps that was why he never saw what hit them, until it was too late.

His heavy legs trudged forward, when something yanked him to the ground. Branches scratched his faces as he stumbled, yet it was that same fall which saved his life.

As he crashed into the moist, musty soil, a heavy log streaked overhead, striking Chaz McNulty full in the chest. McNulty didn't even have time to yell. The sickening thwack echoed the shattering of ribs throughout the forest. McNulty was picked into the air and thrown backwards into Borrell, the hikers behind him tumbling to the ground like a row of dominoes. Only Santiago escaped the collision, his Navy Seal training kicking in automatically. The former Special Forces warrior ducked and rolled to the side, his weapon at the ready. In an instant, Santiago pinpointed a target and fired a quick burst of crackling death into the treeline to the right of the stricken party. The chaotic sound of gunfire was amplified by the surrounding trees. The painful echo punctuated by a woman's scream.

Dazed and bleeding, Harris turned his head to Stoltz, but she was already up and tending to McNulty, whose gasping breaths and hideous moans filled the forest long after the echo of automatic fire faded away.

Harris struggled to his feet, wiped the trickles of blood from his face, and conducted a rapid inventory of his condition. Aside from a sore knee and a minor cut above his right eye, he appeared to be in good condition. Santiago was crouched in a military position, his hawk-like eye sweeping the perimeter through the telescopic sight on his M16 rifle. On a nod from Harris, the young commando dashed nimbly into the woods to overtake their assailants. Feeling scared and vulnerable, Harris wished he had brought along a dozen more like Santiago.

The surviving members of the squad hunched over McNulty to assess the damage. It was worse than they expected. The quarter-ton tree limb, which still swung languidly over their heads on carefully secured ropes, had accomplished its evil task. The broken man lay twisted on the ground, his glazed eyes staring up at the dark canopy of tall branches which covered them. Chaz McNulty's chest had caved in, two ribs jabbed outward through a tear in his shirt. Blood covered his shattered torso and leaked slowly from the corners of his mouth. His tortured breathing was painful for the others to hear, a grotesque wheeze gurgling with fluids and the hiss of puncture wounds.

Only then did Rod Harris realize how foolish he was not to have included someone with medical experience on the trip.

In the end, it wouldn't have mattered. McNulty was dying and they all knew it. Strangely enough, no one said a word, except Ellen Stoltz who whispered a desperate stream of useless encouragement to her critically injured friend, encouragement not even McNulty was buying. He coughed violently, which must have been torture with his jagged ribcage, then wheezed out two final words.

"...my...wife..." he sputtered softly, but that was all he said.

S. Rodham Harris had never heard a death rattle before, that slow and mournful last release of life which can chill the spines of those who hear it. Chaz McNulty slowly exhaled his humanity, and was no more. His abrupt silence and bloody corpse sucked the bravado out of the remaining team. They were no longer boardroom pirates confident of their abilities; bludgeoning their enemies with balance sheets and stock transactions.

They were three scared people alone in the woods.

Three people and one corpse.

The whole situation seemed so unreal. Things like this didn't really happen. This wasn't the movies. People didn't just die like this.

Yet the shattered remains of Chaz McNulty; newlywed, Gulf War veteran, acquisitions analyst for Portman-Decatur Industries, bore guilty testament to the deadly reality of the moment.

Stoltz cried softly. Borrell swore repetitively, while Harris absorbed the staggering responsibility of a true military commander, the gut-wrenching knowledge that someone under your command was dead. Dead because of your casual decisions. Dead because of your mistakes. He wished he was back in his office; wished he was anywhere in the world other than these accursed woods. He staggered a few feet away from the others, bent his head, and threw up behind a thorn bush.

"You okay, Mr. Harris?"

Stoltz was at his side. There was an edge to her voice he would never have allowed in the office, her eyes red with accusation and tears. He hated to have one of his people see him like this, on his knees, stricken and whimpering. However, in light of this sudden tragedy, none of it seemed to matter.

"Yeah," he said, as he wiped foul traces of vomit from his mouth. "I'm all right. Is he...?"

She nodded, tightened her jaw and willed the tears not to flow.

"What are we going to do with his, um...with McNulty?"

"I don't know. Take him back, I guess."

Borrell came up to them now. "Sonuvabitch!" he cursed as he displayed the tripwire Harris had stumbled over. The tripwire that sent the heavy log swinging straight into McNulty's chest. "Look at this!"

The sight of the tripwire helped Harris realize the awful magnitude of the situation. McNulty didn't die because of his mistakes. McNulty was murdered! Murdered by whoever, or whatever was following them. And that meant they were all still targets. They were all still vulnerable.

"Just give me one clear shot at them, Mr. Harris. That's all I want!" Borrell sneered, gripping his assault rifle with deadly intent.

The stunned executive found himself pinned between Stoltz's questioning expression and Borrell's hateful one. If ever they needed a leader, it was now. But what should he do? They were beyond metaphors and slogans now. It was real war this time, where the outcome couldn't be predicted with pie charts and statistical projections. War with bodies and blood, where the losers didn't pick themselves up to try a different defense.

In these woods, the losers never got up again.

With rising panic, Rod Harris grasped that he was way out of his league here. He would have to scrub the mission, face whatever humiliation and retribution waited for him back at the company. Word would get out. Inquiries would be made. Possibly with criminal action to follow. His meteoric career was finished, and he knew it. He reached for the two-way radio strapped to his belt and tried to raise Wellman. Tried again and again.

But there was no reply.

There was no Wellman.

Oh God, he thought. *They got Wellman, too.*

"Sonuvabitch," spat Borrell weakly.

And that's when they heard another vicious barrage of gunfire erupt in the woods behind them.

****

Ira Kaplan eyed his prisoner with cruel disinterest. He toyed with the pistol in his hand, so the frightened man could visualize how quickly and casually his life could be terminated. The middle-aged executive was gagged and lashed to the trunk of a sturdy Canadian birch with ropes that had been tied tightly enough to inflict a reasonable amount of pain.

"We know what you're up to, Mr. Wellman." He saw the other man's eyes widen in surprise and fear. "Yes, I know your name. Yours and Harris'. And Stoltz's. And Santiago's. And Borrell's. And McNulty's...I know everything from the serial numbers of the weapons you are carrying to the color of your underwear."

He paused. Best to let that sink in.

"I know Rod Harris' true intentions towards Old Tehanmar. I also know it's never going to happen. We are going to stop you. We are going to bring Portman-Decatur to its knees, whatever it takes. These woods are older than you, or me, or every person you've ever met in your entire life. They're older than your precious constitution, capitalism and your hypocritical Protestant work ethic combined! They deserve to be respected, not raped."

He pressed his pistol against Wellman's temple and clicked back the hammer. He could feel the man's uncontrollable trembling vibrate right through the handle of the gun. He could see the wet indicator of fear gradually stain his prisoner's lap.

"Is that what a tough guy like you gets off on? Huh? Raping a defenseless woodland?"

Suddenly, Jennings leaped out of the bushes and grabbed his arm. If Kaplan hadn't had the safety on, he would have blown a hole in Wellman's skull out of reflex. He turned on his young protégé with immediate anger.

"Don't ever jump up on me like that when I'm holding a goddam gun, you idiot!"

Jennings cringed, but pulled Kaplan aside with surprising strength. He whispered a flurry of panic into his idol's ear.

"What are you saying? Who's dead?"

More whispered nonsense. It had to be nonsense.

"That's impossible. The branch I told you to use in that trap wasn't big enough to kill anyone!"

Jennings outlined how badly things had gone in the last half-hour. Someone screwed up big time. Instead of a two-foot branch, the trap was set with a seven-foot log that caved in a man's chest. It was a mistake, a big one, and now a man was dead because of it. But not just one man. The one named Santiago, the ex-Navy Seal, shot Lisa Goodings down. Murdered her in cold blood. Kaufman and Jefferson shot back and Santiago killed them, too. It was a massacre. They came to protect the trees, and now bodies were scattered all over the forest.

Ira Kaplan stumbled back on his heels, trying to absorb the insanity he was hearing. Lisa dead? Kaufman and Jefferson, too? And now some crazed ex-military psycho was gunning them down one by one?

This was not the kind of battle he expected. He didn't want to die like a hunted animal in the forest. But what choice did he have now? If any of Harris' people escaped, Kaplan would be sent away for murder. Doing time for public disobedience was one thing, facing the death penalty for murder was something else entirely. The malignant absurdity of the situation, coupled with the suffocating closeness of the trees made his head spin.

"What are we gonna do?!" moaned Jennings, tears of panic streaming down his face. And that question was all Kaplan needed. When faced with the pitiful indecision of others, he would do what he was born to do.

He would lead.

"Round up all the others and have them meet back here as soon as possible! Gather all the weapons we have! If these corporate bastards want to start gunning down our people, they'll find we're not going to die easily!"

Ira Kaplan's confident air of command calmed the young activist.

"What do we do about him?" Jennings gestured to the prisoner roped to the tree trunk.

The two turned to Marty Wellman, saw the terrible side effects abject terror can impose on a human being.

"He's our hostage. Maybe we can work out some kind of trade." Kaplan hid his trembling by running shaky fingers through his wild hair.

"But the odds are...we may have to kill him."

****

Rod Harris, Ellen Stoltz and Arthur Borrell crouched nervously behind a clump of trees, guns at the ready. The last angry shot of the firefight had faded minutes ago, but they dared not move without knowing the true strength or location of their enemy. They felt like deer in a hunter's sights, afraid to bolt, or even breathe.

They heard a rustle in the bushes behind them, and there stood Santiago. The sight of their bloody compatriot was both a source of relief and terror. Relief, because their most experienced warrior had returned. Terror, because he had circled and appeared at their backs so easily. Had it been one of those environmentalist murderers, they would probably all be dead by now.

"They're gone," Santiago said simply.

"Gone...or dead?" Stoltz voiced the question they were all afraid to ask.

Santiago looked away, as if searching for the answer in the mocking gloom of the trees.

"Both," he finally muttered.

He led them to the body of Lisa Goodings, only thirty feet from where they were crouching. Lisa was a nineteen-year-old blonde with a graceful figure and pale skin. Her face had been shot off.

"Christ," groaned Borrell. "She's a friggin' kid! Did you have to kill her?"

Quick as a flash, Santiago's rifle butt slammed into Borrell's stomach, doubling the bigger man over. As he collapsed to the ground, Santiago tossed two automatic pistols by his feet.

"You wanna play nice with these kids?! Then you take the guns away from them!" he growled. "I, for one, don't intend to end up like McNulty over there!"

It might have gone worse for Borrell, if Stoltz hadn't pulled Santiago aside to calm him down. Harris helped Borrell to his feet, and they listened to Santiago yell at Stoltz.

"I don't care! This is war, goddam it! I don't need nobody to tell me how to do this kinda job! It's what I do best."

After Borrell caught his breath, Harris waved the others back to assemble his small battalion.

"Look. It's time to circle the wagons here. We've got a fight on our hands. We're bloodied but still alive. We've lost one of our own and they've lost three. We also have to assume they got Wellman, so maybe we're down two. That also means they know where our base camp is. As I see it, even if we try to double back, they're going to be gunning for us. Personally, I'd rather go down fighting than take a bullet in the back."

"So we proceed with the mission?" asked Stoltz nervously.

"Screw the mission. I've lost one, maybe two men." He raised his gun menacingly. "I say, it's time we do a little hunting."

****

Out of the thirteen dedicated student activists he started with, Ira Kaplan was down to eight frightened children. Goodings, Kaufman and Jefferson were massacred by that psycho Santiago. They discovered Pickert's body at the bottom of a small hill, his body broken by the fall. Marquez was nowhere to be seen.

The survivors were trembling like rabbits. Four wanted to surrender to the Portman-Decatur assassins, but Ira managed to convince them that those conscienceless bastards would shoot them down on the spot. This deep in the woods, with no other witnesses around, they would revert to the killing swine they must be deep down inside.

"These are people that kill for pleasure," he told them, "as well as self-preservation. Portman-Decatur Industries can't afford to let any of you live long enough to testify against the company in a court of law."

Pickert's body had been the proof he needed to sway the undecided. Cybulski had argued that Rod Harris' people might have killed in self-defense, considering the screw up with Trap 49. But Pickert was unarmed, and far from the scene of the gun battle. His body had been so badly mangled, it could only be the desperate, sadistic act of a psychotic mind.

"There are only four of them left, and there are nine of us." He tried to sound both confident and calm at the same time. "Our best defense is to make it to the campground in groups of two. We will be harder to spot that way."

He could see them eyeing each other carefully, appraising which frightened partner would be most likely to help them survive this nightmare.

"What...what if they catch us?" That was Miranda. He couldn't remember her last name.

"If they catch us, they'll kill us. So my advice is not to get caught."

A little nervous laughter. Miranda looked like she was about to burst into tears.

"Listen. We're not completely helpless here. We are creatures of the woods. They are stiff corporate suits. They have guns, but so do we. On top of that, we know where all the booby-traps are. That gives us a certain advantage."

"I don't want to die..." That was Miranda again. Ira put a comforting arm around her trembling shoulders.

"None of us do, Miranda. And none of us have to, as long as we stick together. Okay?"

She looked up at him with desperate, tear-filled eyes, and nodded. It was frightening to Ira how much they trusted him.

"One other thing... Once we make it out of the forest, we all have to promise never to tell another living soul what happened in these woods."

Their objections gushed out with a flood of angry emotion. He hushed them quickly, no sense giving their position away to the enemy.

"I know! I know! They should all burn in hell for what they've done! But remember who you're dealing with here. Portman-Decatur has the government in its back pocket. That's how they stole the logging rights to a protected forest in the first place. They can hire the best lawyers in the country to go up against you! By the time they're finished putting their corporate spin on this thing, they'll make it look like you were the killers. Like this was all your fault! Each one of you will end up doing twenty years to life in a maximum security prison. Is that what you really want?"

"But they've got to pay! For Lisa and the others!"

"They will be held accountable, I swear to you. But out there, they win. They always have. Our only hope is to bide our time, and vow to never say another word about this to anyone. Agreed?"

Their silence was deafening. He moved into the center of the circle. Held their wavering gaze, one by one.

"Agreed?" he asked again.

He held out his hand, palm down. Jennings slowly placed his hand on Ira's, and one by one the others followed this physical representation of their oath of silence. The last hand on the stack was Miranda's.

"We can survive this," Ira Kaplan assured his terrified followers. "But only if we promise to stick together."

They wanted to believe him, but their desperate faces revealed the doubts they held. Still, they had little choice in the matter. They were alone in the woods with four well-armed killers.

Ira knew they would do as they were told.

****

The next attack came from an unexpected source.

S. Rod Harris and his employees crept through the increasingly dense foliage, Santiago in the lead, his special forces training helping them avoid nearly a dozen booby-traps spread throughout the claustrophobic forest.

The further they moved into the center of Old Tehanmar, the more hostile the environment turned. Insects clung to them like bad perfume. Branches reached out from nowhere to savage their arms, legs and faces. Hidden holes in the forest floor wreaked havoc on their weary feet and ankles. Yet the small group pushed forward. They had a murder to avenge and more than enough firepower to do it.

Harris himself was having the most difficult time keeping up. Although a terror on the racquetball courts, this less structured form of exertion left him gasping for breath at every turn. He had to order them to stop every few miles, so he could get his wind back.

That was his second fatal error.

It had been over four hours since Santiago led them to the bodies of his victims, and since that time, they had encountered no other attackers. None could deny, however, the fact that they were being watched. Sometimes they caught a brief glimpse of menacing eyes, heard a twig snap nearby, or the mysterious rustling of leaves behind them.

Once, they thought they spotted an old man moving swiftly through the trees, but figured the weakening sun and their tortured nerves must be playing tricks on them. Most of the time, they just felt the stare like an icy hand on the back of their necks. Santiago tried twice to outflank their pursuers, but was himself out-maneuvered, not an easy thing to do.

The exhausted band finally stumbled into a small clearing, the first in at least nine miles. As the forest grew thicker around them, the thickening trees virtually abutted each other, choking out the less sturdy life in between their roots. For hours, Harris and the others had to rest standing up, because they could find no place large enough to sit, or stretch their aching limbs. This clearing, no more than a nine-foot circle, suddenly appeared like divine intervention to the weary hikers. Harris didn't have to ask the others to stop, they all collapsed the moment they penetrated the clearing.

Conversation had been sparse since McNulty died. With an enemy to pursue, or pursuing them, they were forced to leave his body behind in hope they could locate it when they returned with a much larger team. Nerves were stretched to the breaking point, and there was little they could say to dispel the mind-crushing tension of their drastic plight. The rasp of their breathing filled the clearing with a thick wall of individual anxiety.

Santiago was the first to speak. "I want you all to know I didn't mean to shoot that girl in the face. I'm not sorry about it, I intend to kill anybody who shoots at me. But I didn't mean to shoot hurt in the face. Guess my aim is a little rusty."

"Rusty. That's a good one," Borrell snorted. "I'm sure she'd take that as an apology."

"Like I said, I don't apologize to anyone stupid enough to shoot at me." Santiago's eyes narrowed to two evil slits. "If you've got the balls to take a shot, I wouldn't give a damn about killing you either."

The two men glared at each other with visual venom, and Harris was afraid the slightest involuntary twitch would result in a hail of bullets, with one, or all of them, lying dead in the clearing.

Fortunately, Stoltz stepped in quickly to break the tension.

"Bobby, you said your aim was rusty. Could it be someone tampered with our guns?"

"That's impossible," Harris objected.

"Is it, sir? I mean, this group, whoever they are, seem to know everything about us. They knew we were coming and when. They laid out booby-traps in exactly the paths we were walking. They obviously knew about Wellman back at the base camp. They must have someone inside the company feeding them information. Why is it so hard to believe they could have tampered with the sights on our guns?"

A long pause descended on the group as they contemplated this possibility. Again, Santiago was the first to speak.

"Ellen might have something there. Those other two I killed...I was aiming for their legs. They were just shooting into the trees like crazy people. Didn't even know how to aim the guns they were firing. But when I shot low, or what I thought was shooting low, they ended up taking it dead-center in the chest. Both of them. It was weird."

"What do you mean, 'weird'?" Borrell was curious now.

"I don't know, weird...like they almost dove right into my line of fire. Like they wanted to die, y'know?"

Harris waved it away. "Hell, maybe it's some new environmentalist strategy. Martyrs for the forest. Maybe it sends them all to environmentalist heaven." He hoped this lame attempt at humor would loosen them up.

It didn't.

The thick canopy of intertwined trees blocked out most of the sky, so it was difficult to determine how much light they had left. Harris looked at his Rolex watch. 5:13 PM. They each laid back and closed their eyes, the stress and exhaustion weighing down on them like a thick blanket of haze. The seductive whisper of the wind through the leaves and the lilting melody of the birds and crickets proved too relaxing. Almost hypnotic.

S. Rod Harris woke with a start to feel a pair of powerful hands grab his shoulders and shake him roughly.

"You've got to wake up, boss. We need to get moving!"

His bleary eyes gradually focused on the stern face of Bobby Santiago, pressed uncomfortably close to his own. It was dark. Why was it so dark? Then his entire body jerked forward as he remembered the awful truth about forests and bodies and death.

"What time is it?"

"After ten. We all fell asleep. We've got to get moving!"

Ten at night? Impossible. Harris staggered to his feet. He realized why Santiago was so upset.

"They could've killed us in our sleep!"

"Yes, sir. They could have waltzed right in here, slit our throats and none of us would ever be waking up again!"

His head was starting to clear now.

"Wake the others," he barked. "I want to get the hell out of here, now!"

Santiago crept over to Stoltz, asleep with her back to a tree, and roused her more gently than he had Harris. She mewed her displeasure at being disturbed from her slumbers. Then she snapped to attention, as she too, grasped the gravity of the situation.

"From now on we take turns on watch every time we stop!" Harris' orders were unnecessary. They all realized how dangerous their spontaneous nap had been. Santiago kicked Borrell's boot, who was still sprawled out on his back at the far edge of the clearing.

"C'mon, Sleeping Beauty. Get a move on!"

Borrell, who had a reputation as a heavy sleeper, as well as a heavy drinker, didn't stir. Santiago kicked his boot even harder.

"Move your ass, Borrell!"

But even the heavy kick didn't rouse him.

"Borrell, you moron!" Santiago kicked him so hard, his boot lifted off the ground. There was no movement. No sound. No reply.

Stoltz scrambled through the contents of her backpack for a flashlight, then pointed it at the sleeping man. Then gasped.

In the cold illumination of the flashlight, Borrell's expression was a picture of pure horror. His ashen face contorted. Mouth frozen in mid-scream. Wide-open eyes turned to the heavens.

The kick from Santiago's boots knocked a small black spider from inside Borrell's pant leg. Then another.

Then seven more.

In the ghastly chill of the flashlight, the others watched in terror as dozens of coal black spiders suddenly poured forth from every opening in the dead man's clothing. They streamed out his sleeves, his waistband, and up from his shirt collar to cover his face.

Hundreds of them.

Then thousands.

The horrible wave of arachnids crawled out of Borrell and covered the ground around him like some living blanket of pure evil.

Stoltz dropped the flashlight and screamed. Harris turned to run and smashed, face-first into a tree behind him. He fell backwards to the ground, his face numb with the promise of searing pain to follow.

Once again, it was Bobby Santiago who saved them. He grabbed Harris by the shoulders and jerked him to his feet, just as the ocean of spiders scrambled toward the dazed body of their next potential victim.

Santiago grabbed the flashlight and dragged both of his terror-stricken companions away from the clearing into the smothering embrace of the darkened woods.

****

"Justin? Justin, where are you?!"

The quivering in Miranda Williams' voice hung in the thick air like a bird too fearful to fly. She was crawling on hands and knees over the damp, musty smelling leaves, literally feeling her way out of the forest. Only a moment ago, the sound of moving branches ahead of them pushed them to the ground in ice cold terror. The sound passed. Justin, her appointed partner out of this nightmare, had vanished as well, leaving her feeling alone and claustrophobic in the threatening environment she had once sworn to protect.

"Justin!" she whispered as loud as she could without giving their position away to the corporate mercenaries she imagined were stalking her right now. A cry died in her throat, as something with a fierce grip grabbed her ankle, pulling her backwards. She was about to scream, when another hand clamped tightly over her mouth, knocking her flat to the ground.

"Be quiet!" whispered Justin Davis hoarsely into her ear. "Do you want to let them know where we are?!"

Miranda trembled. How did it all go so terribly wrong? She was doing well at school, had fallen in love with a shy, but brilliant computer programmer. She even had a job in an off-campus coffee house where revolutionary arguments flowed through the night, like the aromatic cappuccino which fueled them. There she had met Ira Kaplan, the legendary environmentalist, and was fortunate enough to be swept away by the sheer power and sincerity of his defense of Mother Earth. Through his eyes, she witnessed the history of man's violation of this sacred planet. Through his words, she had been motivated to take action to support the cause. And now, through his actions, she was fleeing for her life like a hunted animal, an animal whose life she would gladly sacrifice to be safely back in her small, over-priced campus apartment.

Lisa Goodings, the friend who had introduced her to Ira, was dead. Butchered. They said she had been shot in the face, a horrible way to die.

Miranda wondered if that was how she would die, too.

Even in the shadowy dimness, she could see Justin slowly rise to a crouch to scan the brush ahead of them, his pistol drawn and ready. Miranda would not allow herself to breathe until he gave the 'all clear' sign. When he did, she muttered a silent prayer of gratitude to a God she had not spoken to in years.

Ira had sent them off, two at a time, to escape the woods for the safety of civilization. She and Justin had spent hours circling around, losing their way, and desperately hoping they were headed in the right direction. In darkness thickened with fear, nothing seemed where it was supposed to be. The morning's landmarks had vanished in the night's eerie arboreal shadows. Justin dropped the unreliable compass after colliding with a tree limb, so they now moved by intuition alone. They couldn't use stars to navigate, because the oppressively tall trees spread jealous branches to blot out the sky. As much as she worshipped nature, she would have burnt down this whole ancient woodland to find a safe path home again.

Justin waved her forward, and she mimicked his crouching stride that made her shoulders scream in agony. It couldn't be more than a mile or two to the main campsites. They would be there in no time.

Poor Lisa wouldn't. But Miranda couldn't let herself think about that right now.

"Damn!"

"What's wrong?"

"I don't understand it? We have to be heading south…"

"What? Tell me." The trembling had seeped back into her voice.

Justin didn't answer. He simply turned a face as grim as death, toward a gnarled shape ahead of them. It was an old tree, an ancient one, possibly the oldest in the entire forest. Then she realized it was three gnarled and withered tree trunks twisted together, as if locked together in a death grip.

Three black trunks intertwined to form a shape vaguely resembling a monstrous, gigantic claw.

The sight sent shivers up Miranda's spine, not only because it looked so hideous in the uneven silvery stabs of moonlight, but because she knew they had passed this same growth three times before.

"We're going around in circles again, Justin!"

"I don't understand it."

"There can't be four trees that look like that!"

"It doesn't make sense. I did everything right...We had to be traveling in a straight line."

"We'll never get out of here!"

He turned to her with bitterness. "Shut up, Miranda! We'll get out of here if I have to carry your whining butt over my shoulders! Just let me think, okay?!"

The young woman moved a few paces away from her companion. She was frightened and frustrated, and wanted more than anything else to be out of these strange woods. She wanted to be curled up in an easy chair, with some book waxing philosophical about man's inhumanity to man. She wanted to be wrapped in a warm comforter, her hips resting gently in her lover's lap. She wanted to be...

The huge gray blur shot across her field of vision like a flash of lightning. The second followed behind it, so closely, she could smell its cruel scent. The third bounded forward, its green eyes flashing with hunger and savagery.

The wolves knocked Justin to the ground before he could even raise the gun in his hand. Sharp, angry teeth tore at his exposed throat, cutting off his scream in a gurgle of gushing blood. The spray of red gore whipped the other two wolves into a frenzy, and they all gnashed and ripped at the young man's flesh. The largest wolf remained at his neck. The other two rent open the boy's abdomen and fed hungrily.

Miranda could not move. The attack was too swift, the vision too horrible. She wanted to run, but her legs remained frozen to the spot. She could only watch in uncomprehending terror as the three gray wolves devoured her friend.

A low growl behind her set free her muscles. She turned slowly to see a huge gray specter, much larger than the other wolves, eyeing her with primitive malevolence. She watched the vicious saliva drip from its enormous fangs. Saw the massive leg muscles coil for the assault.

Fortunately for Miranda Williams, idealistic college student, her neck snapped at first contact with the pouncing beast.

She was dead before she hit the ground.

✳✳✳

Harris, Stoltz and Santiago ran through the blackened woods, oblivious to the thorns and branches that tore at their legs, arms and faces. With lungs exploding from panic and exertion, they finally stumbled under an opening in the thatched tree ceiling of the forest, skewered by the pale light of a new moon. They tore off their clothes and shook them wildly, until the three stood naked and panting. They checked themselves carefully, then inspected each other's bodies in the moonlight for spiders. There was nothing erotic or embarrassing about their actions, their minds simply could not escape the ghastly image of Borrell's corpse infested by that repulsive wave of crawling invaders.

Satisfied that they were free of the spiders, they crumbled to the ground, feeling its clammy chill seep through every inch of their bodies. They dressed quickly, shaking out each item of clothing a dozen more times. Although Santiago felt it was too dangerous, Harris insisted they make a campfire. He refused to let anything else sneak up on them in the night.

When the first sparks sundered the darkness, they again took stock of their situation. McNulty was dead, and now Borrell, probably Wellman, too. The only pack they saved from the clearing was the one Santiago had on before the spiders appeared. His M16 was the only rifle they had left. That, a hunting knife Stoltz carried in a sheath on her hip, and the small pistol Harris kept concealed on his right calf, comprised their only defense against armed assailants and an increasingly savage environment.

None of the sleeping bags were saved. Stoltz hesitantly suggested they go back to the clearing for their other gear, but the image of Borrell's body being consumed by legions of voracious insects quickly overruled that idea.

As the forest sank deeper into blackness, the three representatives of Portman-Decatur huddled around a small fire, surrounded by the woods they had so arrogantly planned to tame. Random cries, screeches and growls from the hidden inhabitants of Old Tehanmar made sleep impossible. The black periphery betrayed sinister pairs of green and golden eyes, which blinked open, then disappeared.

"There's something out there," Stoltz trembled.

"No. There's a whole army of somethings out there," Santiago added grimly. "And they all want us dead."

If only they knew then how true that was.

****

Tommy Ray Connors pulled his green Land Rover around to scan the primitive campsites along the western edge of Old Tehanmar National Forest. Calls had been pouring into his ranger station all night about sounds of sporadic gunfire emanating from the center of the forest. Although this area was restricted because of its environmentally protected status and impossibility to adequately patrol, it was not unusual for hunters to slip past the barbed wire fence for a shot at the ample game inside the preserve. However, the complaints spoke of automatic weapons, some complained it sounded like a war zone. One frightened camper said he was woken in the middle of the night by the sound of human screams.

An old Indian legend, which many still believed, claimed the old growth section of the forest was where the souls of dead warriors went to hunt. Of course, the Indians also believed the Great Spirit would drive the white man from the continent, and Tommy knew how well that idea had panned out. Every so often, he had to arrest a drunken teenager dressed up like a Sioux warrior prancing around to scare his friends.

Yet it was his job to check out every complaint, and that's what put him on the road tonight. He swept the beam of his door mounted headlight across a random display of designer tents and polyester teepees, the typical city crowd scheduling a little nature time. Everything seemed to be normal, at least until he reached Primitive Campsite #329.

An untrained eye might have missed the subtle oddities which triggered alarm bells in Tommy Ray's head: a pair of brand new, top-of-the-line Ford Explorers; same model, same jet black finish, same darkly tinted windows. Yet one bore a rusted Florida license plate, the other a used plate from Maryland. Judging by the newness of the paint job and tire tread, there was no way these vehicles had driven thousands of miles to this Pacific Coast forest. And there were other signs. Two brand new Walmart fishing poles positioned casually on the ground, though it was the middle of the night. Unburned logs in the campfire, despite the chilly weather. The flap of the main tent left open, permissible during the day if someone was tending the site, but unlikely in the middle of the night while everyone was asleep.

Tommy Ray slowly parked his Land Rover behind the twin Explorers. He called in the Maryland license plate number to Harvey Innis down at the local police station, and was not surprised to hear it had been reported stolen. The plate, not the vehicle. The same with the Florida plate.

Drug dealers were the most likely culprits. What better place to cultivate marijuana than a protected national forest too extensive to be patrolled on a regular basis? He pulled his government-issued revolver from the glove compartment. Being a forest ranger could be a lot more hazardous than most people imagined.

With weapon in hand, Tommy Ray slid out of his vehicle. Being careful not to close the door and make a sound, he crept toward the open tent. As expected, it was empty. What he didn't expect to find were two mannequins in the second tent, disguised to look like sleeping campers. He had to admit the dummies would have easily fooled anyone taking only a cursory look into the tent.

He walked out into the darkened campsite and scratched his head. No signs of a struggle. No weapons. No contraband. The whole campsite was a decoy.

And that meant whoever set it up was in the...

The distant shrieks of terror lasted only a moment, but they were jolting enough to launch him into action. The forest ranger sliced through the barbed wire fence with a pair of cutters, which always hung from his belt, then dashed headlong into the suffocating blackness that surrounded the heart of Old Tehanmar.

****

Ira Kaplan glanced nervously at his prisoner. Wellman was still gagged and lashed to a tree. Over the ten hours of his captivity, he had been released only long enough to crap in the bushes. Judging by the position of the moon, it was nearly 3 AM, and a decision would have to be made soon on whether to kill this man, or set him free.

Kaplan's nervousness revealed he had already made that decision.

Jennings, scared to the point of whining, crouched a short distance away, an early warning system in case the Portman-Decatur killers penetrated this deep into the preserve.

Alone, except for his silent captive, Ira Kaplan ran his hand over the rough bark of a gnarled tree older than any animal on earth, and envied its silent ambivalence to the course of human events. This majestic life did not suffer indecision, anxiety or fear. It did not suffer the crushing weight of responsibility for more than a dozen young lives, lost or endangered by his own reckless passion. It remained steadfast and unconcerned, and he envied it so.

Beset by the swarm of soft shrieks and whispers radiating from the darkness around him, Ira endlessly reviewed the series of decisions which had gone so wrong.

"They're all dead, you know."

In one swift movement, the activist spun around and raised his pistol at the voice behind him, its deadly black barrel pointing to an ancient, but amused face. The old man who stood there was wrinkled as tree bark, and his dark eyes shone with amusement.

"Am I that much of a threat?" the old man smiled.

Ira did not lower his gun. "Who are you?" he asked.

"Joshua...I'm not sure if I remember my last name after all these years."

"What are you doing here?"

"I might ask you the same thing."

"Answer me, or I'll shoot you down where you stand."

The old man narrowed his brows, quizzically. Once he determined this high-strung environmentalist was not bluffing, he slowly raised his hands.

"Forgive me," he said with a weak voice. "I have lived in these woods for so long, I've forgotten my manners. I did not mean to frighten you."

Kaplan would not relent. "Who sent you, old man?"

"Nobody sent me. This is my home. I live here."

Ira lowered his gun slightly. He carefully examined the old hermit in the undulating orange glow of the campfire. He had seen this man before on a hundred city street corners, in a thousand trash-strewn alleys. Homeless people always had the same creased and weary expression, carved permanently in their features by an overabundance of alcohol, cigarettes and rotten luck. The man's tattered gray coat was as filthy as the forest floor, his rumpled pants even worse. He wore no shirt to fend off the chill of the evening. Ira could see the man's bony chest dancing to the rapid breaths of the chronically ill.

Portman-Decatur Industries would not have even let this man rest on their sidewalk.

"Homeless, huh?" Ira removed his finger from the trigger, and relaxed against the tree behind him.

The old man spread his hands in a self-deprecating manner. "I like to think of myself as a simple spirit of the forest."

Ira snorted. "Like the souls of those dead Indian hunters?"

The man frowned in disappointment. "Please don't tell me you believe all those stories about ghosts hunting in these woods. I marked you for a more intelligent creature than that."

Ira shook his head. "There are things hunting in these woods, old man, but they sure aren't dead Indians."

"Ah, you mean the people from the logging company."

"You've seen them?" Ira's body straightened with interest. "You've seen those goddam murderers?!"

"Murder is such a subjective term...but yes, I have seen them. I have been watching all of you since you decided to play out your dirty little war games in these woods."

"This isn't a game! Don't you realize people are dying?!"

"Everything dies," the old man shrugged. "It's part of nature."

"There was nothing *natural* about the death of Lisa Goodings! Or Kaufman and Jefferson!"

The old man nodded. "Or McNulty. Or even your captive over there."

"What?" Kaplan whirled his head around. The sight of Wellman's head sagging to his chest pushed the words back into Ira throat. He ran over to where his captive was tied, and felt the man's neck for a pulse.

The veins were strangely silent.

"I don't understand...?" Ira stammered. Only then did he notice the strange copper and green snake writhing around the dead man's ankle.

"But...but there are no poisonous snakes in this forest?"

"Your friend there might disagree with you. Of course, you could always pick up the snake to find out for yourself."

His already frayed nerves unraveled at Wellman's unexpected death, and the stranger's casual sarcasm. Ira leapt forward and kicked the old man to the ground. He stood over him with his pistol pointed at the old man's chest. What had he to lose at this point? With all the death around him, what would the life of one filthy hermit matter?

Ira's fingers twitched seductively on the trigger.

At the last moment, he turned and fired twice into the snake that had started to slither his way. The serpent's head exploded less than a foot from his own shoe. Ira turned back to the stranger, struggling on his back like a wounded beetle.

"Tell me why I shouldn't kill you right now, old man?" He surprised himself with the cruelty in his voice.

The hermit was silent for a few tense moments. The whisper that followed chilled Ira Kaplan to the bone.

"Because then you would never know what happened to the others."

****

Exhausted, his mind screaming, S. Rod Harris scrambled frantically through the blackness towards the safety of the trees. He needed to find one with a branch low enough to grab, but high enough to protect him from the snarling gray beast which pursued him.

He saw it. A thick black arm in the darkness directly in front of him, maybe two feet above his head. With his last remaining ounce of strength, he leapt for the saving limb, and tried to hoist himself up. The gray wolf sprang at the same moment, and though it missed the vulnerable parts of his victim, the creature's powerful jaws sank deep into the leather boot being yanked into the air.

Harris howled in pain, as the wolf's brutal fangs tore open his heel and crushed the fragile bones in his foot. He hung from the branch as the ferocious animal hung from his foot. The result was inevitable. Though the muscles in his arms strained with anguish, his hands could not support his weight, plus that of the massive wolf. One by one, his bloody fingers peeled back from the branch, until both hunter and prey plummeted to the brush below.

Each was stunned by the fall, but the wolf recovered more quickly. It lunged for the frightened man's neck. The beast's maddened eyes and savage jaws filled his entire vision, then suddenly disappeared.

He heard the gunshot an instant later, then another and another, mingled with the dying howls of the four members of the brutal wolf pack.

S. Rod Harris let his head slump back to the cold earth, and wept uncontrollably.

****

"Tell me what happened to the others."

Ira Kaplan sat on the ground, his head buried in trembling hands. The elderly hermit leaned over the fire, warming his own bony fingers. He spoke slowly, but with little emotion.

"You know about the first three, who died in that first gun battle with the logging people. The one you called Pickert climbed a tree to spy on your enemies, then broke his neck when the branch he assumed was sturdy gave way below his feet. Marquez and four of the others, including that young girl Miranda, were torn apart by wolves."

"Wolves?"

"A pack of gray wolves. Quite vicious."

"Oh, God..."

"Fielding and Naharij tried to outshoot the Portman-Decatur people. They didn't. I believe that man Santiago didn't intend to kill them, but..." the old man spread his hands and shrugged. Ira Kaplan swore to himself he would kill this cold-hearted bastard if he dared make that gesture one more time.

"Did any of them make it?" Ira asked weakly.

"Angela Scopes almost made it to the campsites, but she fell into a huge nest of hornets. Seems she was deathly allergic to their stings. And Jennings..."

"Jennings?! He's right over there!"

"Yes, he is."

It was like being trapped in a nightmare. Ira jumped up and scoured the bushes where Jennings had been hiding. He found him face down in the dirt. When Ira rolled him over, he saw the grad student's face swollen and blotched. A grotesque white foam leaking from both sides of his mouth.

"Mushrooms. He got hungry," Joshua muttered from behind Ira. "He shouldn't have."

In a daze, Ira let Jennings' body flop back into the dirt. Dead. All dead. All those promising lives. All those young idealists who looked up to him. Who depended on him.

All of them dead.

He could see their eager faces in his mind, knew their images would haunt him until the moment of his own death.

He staggered back to the campfire, the old man moving slowly behind him. At the clearing, Ira Kaplan, environmental rebel, collapsed to the ground and wept.

"They didn't deserve to die..."

"Does anyone?" Joshua asked with indifference.

"Some do! The bastards who rape these forests! They deserve to die!"

The old man nodded. "And that is why you drive steel spikes into trees? So that when a logger's chainsaw hits them, it will explode in the sharp shards of your own personal justice?"

"Man doesn't deserve a spot on this planet!" Ira wrapped his words in bitterness and rage. "Our whole species is unworthy of the blessings of nature. We are a race of killers." He spat on the ground beside him. "If anything, this senseless waste of life proves that."

Joshua looked at him with a strange mix of curiosity and pity.

"You are so obsessed with death, Mr. Kaplan. Yet you fail to see it all around you. You say man is evil for killing, but the deaths of your companions should prove that nature is a far more efficient killer."

Ira waved the arguments away. After all that had happened in these last twenty-four hours, he was not about to debate philosophy with a crazy old hermit.

"It's not the same."

But the frail man was strangely motivated now. "You're right. It isn't the same. Nature kills, but with no feeling or emotion behind it. What is the difference between felling a tree for shelter, picking a mushroom for dinner, or being bitten by a poisonous spider for its own protection? Do you feel guilt for swatting a mosquito, or biting a carrot? Modern men are so elevated in their opinion of themselves, they don't realize they are merely another component of nature's feeding frenzy. Their destructive impulses are like the locusts, part of the cycle, and their inevitable passing will be likewise. Why should you agonize over your killing ways? Does a virus or bacteria agonize over killing you?"

"It's not the same. We humans are the only creatures that kill for sport."

"Really?" Joshua smiled. "Have you never seen a well-fed house cat kill a squirrel or a mouse? How he bats it around, relishes the feel of running it down. Same with a dog and a rabbit. Or a pack of wolves and anything that crosses into their territory. How many grizzly bears that attack people actually eat them after the kill? They slash and crush their victims with massive paws, because it feels natural for them to do it." The old hermit shook his head, as if he were lecturing a small child. "I challenge you to find one human emotion not reflected in nature...with the sole exception of guilt."

Ira didn't want to be sucked into this debate, but the intellectual challenge was a distraction from this horrible night, and a balm to his wounded vision of reality.

"Okay. Greed."

"Look above you. What do you see?"

"Trees. Hundreds of damn trees."

"Look more closely. See how the big ones spread their branches, so their leaves grab as much of the sunlight as possible? They hog the light, as you would say, horde it so they can prosper and grow at the expense of smaller, less established trees. If you assume sunlight is their currency, wouldn't you consider that greed?"

"Trees do not make conscious choices."

"Perhaps. But try taking a bone from a dog, even if he is not hungry. Try to steal honey from a beehive, even if is overflowing with the stuff. That's greed."

"Maybe greed was the wrong word. I meant envy."

Joshua's eyes sparkled in the firelight. "See that fir tree on the edge of the clearing? See how its trunk is being wound about and smothered by those thick vines? The vines know they can never stand as tall or as thick as the tree. They envy the girth of its trunk, something they can never develop. So they entwine the trunk. Wrap around its width. Steal their way up toward the light. With limited needs, the vine has enough sunlight to survive without breaking through the tree's canopy. Yet it continues to climb, choking the very life out of the tree, even though it means both will eventually collapse and die."

"Your argument doesn't hold. You're assuming that plants can feel."

"Would they be so majestic if they didn't? I thought that was the reasoning you used to recruit your followers?"

"This is pointless."

"Perhaps...but do you have something better to do before the morning comes, and your enemies find you at last?"

Ira shook his head. If he was going to die, this was a better way to spend his last moments, than shivering with fear. He took a long swig from the canteen by his side, then said, "I'll grant your point on killing. But what about genocide? Or war?"

"That is too easy. Think of a battle between red and black ants. Two species more alike than different. Yet they will turn most of their population into armies with the sole intention of destroying their rivals. Not over food or need, but solely because the other group exists within sensing distance of their antennae.

"And don't mention personal property, or possessiveness. Watch any animal mark its territory and defend it vigorously. The dog who barks at anyone approaching his yard. The lion, or moose, or ram who attacks any who dares approach his females. Hundreds of animals will drive off challengers to their power, even if it means death. Look in their eyes and you will see hatred. Pure hatred. A male chimpanzee will kill its young for no reason other than simple annoyance.

"It's all here. Every human emotion you condemn has its basis in nature. All except one."

"And that is?" Ira's eyelids were getting heavy. His thoughts spinning, as if he had been drugged.

As if he had been...

His brain shrieked with alarm. He looked down at the canteen, then up at the face of the old man dissolving into a blur in front of him.

"The difference," Joshua continued his speech, "...is that nowhere in nature do plants or animals feel the slightest remorse for what they do. They compete, they dominate, and sometimes they kill, because they are meant to do so. There are no psychologists in the forest."

Ira's head slowly sunk to his chest. The old hermit grabbed the other man's cheeks with powerful, claw-like fingers. He forced Ira to look into his hate-filled eyes.

"You must listen to me, Ira Kaplan. All your life, you have professed this great devotion to the environment, but you have missed the point entirely! Man does not behave like a savage beast because that is his nature... He behaves that way *because he is nature*."

A dense, viscous fog clouded Ira's thoughts. He listened to the odd pounding of blood in his ears, heard a terrible sucking rasp he did not recognize as his own struggling breath. His eyes fluttered open, as his head wobbled weakly in the old hermit's grip.

"You...you changed...the log?"

"In your little trap? Yes. The branch you chose was far too small to be lethal. We simply made it more...efficient." Joshua's expression turned cold and hard as the forest floor after an ice storm. "Just as we made Mr. Santiago's shots far more deadly."

Ira fought to get the words out, though his tongue was unwieldy and his head spin violently.

"Are you...are you going to...to...kill me now...?"

"Yes, Mr. Kaplan."

Ira tried one final stab at clarity. Tried to see the ancient creature's face as it really was. But the fog was too intense. The light too wavering.

"...why...?" was the only thing he could manage to say.

"Because it's my nature," said Joshua without emotion.

Then he pulled at Ira Kaplan's head with such a sharp, powerful twist, the cracking of neck bones echoed off the silent, apathetic trees.

****

The purple-black of night softly surrendered to its light gray companion, as Ellen Stoltz looked up with relief to the slowly brightening sky. As terrifying as their situation was, it seemed far less hopeless with the hesitant encroach of dawn.

They had survived their long night in the strange woods, but just barely. Half her right hand was gone, torn away by the monstrous gray wolves. If it hadn't been for Santiago returning in time...

She shuddered. The thought of the wolf's hot, foul breath set her body trembling once again. Mr. Harris lay beside her, asleep, his leg badly mangled. He would probably never walk right again. Bobby Santiago was unhurt, except for a few scratches. His training had saved their lives a dozen times that night. Things that came out of the darkness. Creatures he had killed for them.

She watched him now as he stood high in that tree, climbing up the twisted branches to scout the horizon, hoping to find a way back home.

The mission was over. It had been a catastrophe. McNulty was dead. Borrell. Wellman, probably. She and Harris should be dead right now, if it wasn't for Bobby.

She looked at him again, standing in that oddly shaped tree and had to laugh. He looked like such a child up there. A little boy having the adventure of his life.

"Ellen," he called to her from his lofty perch. "I can see the campsites from here! We're as good as home!"

This time she laughed out loud at his child-like enthusiasm, at the funny way he began to climb back down that strange tree...that very strange tree. She noticed now that it was not one tree, but actually three trunks twisted together, as if they were locked in some life or death struggle. The way they were turned, and the way the branches jutted up to the sky, almost made the strange growth look like some huge, claw-like hand.

A claw-like hand that Bobby Santiago was climbing down into...

She started to tremble then. Tremble at the cruel insanity of it all. She shook harder as Bobby's screams reached her, along with the creaking of the branches. Her own screams intertwined with his, as she saw it all unfold before her disbelieving eyes.

The huge wooden fingers closing on him, crushing the life out of Bobby Santiago. The branches and trunks moved inward, wrapping around him like a log cocoon, sealing him inside its grotesque grip. His shrieks were horrible, as he was slowly consumed by the wooden monstrosity. She ran to him, grabbed the rifle that had fallen from his shoulder. As he disappeared, bit-by-bit, inside the enormous claw, she fired, point-blank into its twisted trunks.

It bled.

The tree bled.

Not sap, or water, or amber, but blood.

Human blood.

The freakish insanity of it all tore the screams from her body. She shrieked so hard, she didn't feel the first tendrils as they wrapped around her legs. Didn't notice the fast-moving vines until they had climbed up her body, strangling her shoulders and arms, squeezing her like a hungry python. She howled and cried as the vines wrapped around her again and again and again.

She screamed until her ribs cracked and the lungs that contained her final gasps of breath collapsed and died away.

S. Rod Harris woke to see it all; Santiago, then Stoltz. The living forest wreaking terrible vengeance on those who thought to conquer it. He was on his damaged feet and running, hobbling as fast as he could, though the pain shot up his leg like fiery steel.

He ran until the very ground disappeared under his legs. The forest floor suddenly opened up beneath him, revealing a brain-like maze of roots and tendrils that pulled him down to it, then closed back up over him, shutting out any proof of his existence.

And just like that, the forest was quiet again.

****

By four in the afternoon on August 17th, Tommy Ray Connors had given up on his search. Despite three days of checking every clearing and trail in the forest, he could find no sign of drug dealers, poachers, errant hikers, or lost campers. No sign of human life at all.

No footprints. No shreds of torn fabric. No bullet casings. No blood stains. No litter. Nothing.

He let Harvey Innis impound the two Ford Explorers, because the registration papers were phony and no owner ever showed up to claim them. They would make a mighty nice addition to the local police force.

A big logging and mining conglomerate called a few times to see if any of their employees had registered at the campsite, but none had, despite their protestations. Tommy Ray wondered if they were somehow linked to the two vehicles, but couldn't see what possible connection there could be.

He figured he'd take one last sweep of the restricted section, just to make sure. He closed his eyes to focus on the complex, living fragrance of the forest. He breathed in deeply, absorbing its soothing cacophony. Finally, the ranger turned to leave, only to stand face-to-face with a strange old man in a filthy gray coat.

"Ranger Connors," the ancient face crinkled into a disturbing smile.

"Joshua," Tommy Ray nodded in return. "You know you're not allowed in this section of the forest."

This was the one blemish on his otherwise spotless record as a forest ranger. He didn't have the heart to run this aging drifter out of his park. Actually, he had never really been able to find out where the elderly hermit lived, even though he had run across him two or three times while patrolling the preserve.

"I'm at home here," Joshua shrugged, spreading his hands in a self-deprecating gesture.

"I know what you mean. I can't help but feel connected to this place myself. But I have a job to do. I told you last time if I caught you in here again, I'd have to run you in."

The old hermit smiled broadly, making his leathery face even more hideous. "I don't think you will."

A strange bird, no doubt about that. Still, he didn't see the guy doing any real harm.

"Did you know, Ranger Connors, that the largest living entity in the world is a mushroom?"

"Get lost."

"It's the truth. There is a single fungus over two miles long resting under the floor of a forest in Wyoming. It has been growing for centuries just below the surface, as oblivious to mankind, as mankind has been to it."

"We can all be pretty oblivious sometimes."

The old hermit offered that crinkled smile again.

"You don't have to be," he said, with an odd lilt in his voice.

Tommy Ray looked at him curiously. What was it about this guy? How could he be so...?

And then Tommy Ray Connors saw exactly what Joshua meant.

One second he was standing there, staring into the eyes of this strange hermit, and the next he was...everywhere.

His mind and body exploded with a billion simultaneous sensations, as he suddenly experienced the vast and frightening interconnectivity of Old Tehanmar. He was no longer a man standing in a forest, but a tree, a microbe, a bug, a fungus of incomprehensible dimensions. He was all of it, and they all were pieces of him. All the trees, and plants, and roots, and worms, and insects, and even the animals linked together like individual brain cells, firing independently, but contributing their own tiny spark to an overall consciousness of which they were only vaguely aware.

But this was no beneficent joining of life forces. It was a smothering, plotting thing. A heartless organic mass that protected itself by consuming everything it touched. He felt it where his stomach should have been, felt it flow through each screeching pore of his body. He felt each tree offering part of its strength. Each rotting carcass feeding and transforming into the greater life of the old growth forest.

Old growth that would never die.

Never.

Eventually, Tommy Ray regained consciousness in the center of a tight crouching of ancient evergreens. His limbs and face were scraped raw by uncounted hours of writhing on the hard ground.

Joshua was nowhere to be seen, and he was glad of it. Grabbing at the severe facial tic that would plague him the rest of his life, Tommy Ray Connors ran as hard and as fast as he could from the old growth section of Old Tehanmar National Forest.

****

Eventually, they would return. These man-creatures would stream through the woods like countless legions of ants, consuming everything in their path. The ancient trees would be cut down. The dense foliage cleared. The forest floor itself paved over with man's artificial rock.

But beneath it all, the old growth forest would survive, survive in a trillion interconnected root systems and dormant spores. A network of life lurking just below the surface.

And it would wait, extending a tendril here, a sapling there.

It would wait.

Soon, the massive roots would crack and buckle their expressways. The molds and insects would penetrate and decay their buildings.

And it would wait.

Eventually, the old growth would rise up again, as man faded off into extinction, giving way to the next dominant life form.

And it would wait.

After hundreds of thousands of years on earth, it could afford to wait a few more millennia.

Joshua eagerly drank in the thousands of individual sounds and smells that made up the old growth forest. Then, he turned toward the ancient claw-shaped tree and was himself absorbed, once again, into the heart of Old Tehanmar.

Wake Me Up!

The morning sun splintered into a thousand glittery reflections, as the big Buick slid through the crowded Chestnut Hill streets. The road was sleepily familiar, the same path he drove each weekday to and from college. He knew every curve and street corner by heart. Yet this time, the long trek down Commonwealth Ave seemed different, though he wasn't exactly sure why, until he realized that he could not remember getting up, brushing his teeth, or even leaving the house this morning, which was strange, to say the least. But like the road he travelled on, the wide black vinyl and wood dashboard of his 1971 Buick Riviera felt so comfortably familiar as he drove on.

He wondered why the radio wasn't on, when suddenly it was, and the first power chords of Bruce Springsteen's epic "Born To Run" reverberated through the interior cabin. The Riviera's 454 engine and four-barreled carburetor, the ultimate in 1970's Detroit excess, purred forcefully down the road along with the unrestrained freedom of the song.

Some songs have the power to pull you straight into their world, and his right foot instinctively pressed heavier on the gas pedal, as it always did with the audio lighter fluid of timeless rock ballads.

Life was good, until suddenly, it wasn't. On its own, the song surged in volume, to echo painfully in his head. The dashboard details grew grotesquely sharp, as everything crystalized into a hyper-focused version of reality.

His fingers stiffened, his hands melting right into the steering wheel.

Unable to pull himself free, it finally hit him that he wasn't awake. But unlike most dreams, which flittered and zagged across a frantic collage of disconnected images, this particular dream shocked him with its intense continuity. The crystalline visual clarity of the dashboard only brightened, refusing to waiver. The road he saw slipping past his windshield revealed the correct path, the appropriate speed, the current season, with every mailbox and trimmed lawn in its proper place. And all the while, Bruce

Springsteen hoarsed out his searing lyrics; verse after consecutive verse, in ways dreams never do.

The realization that he was pinned within a dream did not seem frightening, simply odd. *Dreams aren't like this,* he thought again, or maybe even dreamed he thought: it was hard to tell. So he surrendered to the dream and chose to see where it would take him.

The answer revealed itself around the next corner. The Buick thumped and leaped over an angry pothole, this was Massachusetts after all, as his head drifted to the passenger's side window to catch the first unfamiliar addition to the dream.

A stranger.

Standing by the side of the road, with a thumb out and a sheepish smile on his broad, friendly face.

He knew he had never seen this man before, but was impressed by the clarity of detail that shimmered around the hitchhiker, again so unusual for a dream. The stranger had a round, open face, splashed generously with freckles. The straight reddish brown hair extending halfway down his ears simultaneously retreated from his high forehead. He wore dirty sneakers, old jeans, and a faded brown leather jacket over a heavy knit sweater of dull orange, with a wide brown stripe running horizontally across the chest. A flat tweed cap, like Irish villagers used to wear, gave the man a somewhat European appearance, making him seem both out of place and perfectly positioned on this corner, and the driver in the dream could not look away.

As the stranger saw the car approach, he broadened his grin and wagged his thumb more vigorously.

Even though he realized he was still mired in this strangely episodic trance state, the driver remembered his father's droning advice to never, ever pick up hitchhikers.

"You never know who they are, or how insane," his father would grunt, in paranoid disdain for anyone who wasn't related by blood. That was his Dad all over. You were either family, or you could not be trusted. A code of bigotry hammered into his offspring at regular intervals from the moment they could walk.

But now, in this dream, his dream, the driver felt strangely free. Free from childhood fears. Unencumbered by parental enforced habits. He had never picked up hitchhikers before, but why not? He was not his Dad. He did not have to live in that angrily isolated world of us and them. Family and predators. Those definitions did not apply here. This was his dream after all.

His uniquely strange dream.

Where details never wavered, and the radio played on and on.

He watched the speedometer drop ten miles at a time - *How is this possible?* – as his hands, operating of their own free will, steered the massive Buick over to the curb.

The stranger half hopped and dashed with appreciation as the car pulled closer. The power locks clicked open of their own accord, and the hitchhiker climbed in with a cheerful *'Thanks, pal!"* and a slam of the passenger's side door.

The dashboard flickered for the very first time, before stabilizing again, as the Riviera lumbered hesitantly back onto the road.

"Where you headed?" he asked the stranger, who pulled off his cap long enough to run knobby fingers through thinning auburn hair.

"Up the road. Far as you'll take me." There was no hint of the Irish accent that the man's cap and features suggested.

They chatted in a friendly manner for the next few minutes, though strangely, he could not remember what they talked about. The connection of sequential moments was breaking down. Only the radio kept its comforting continuity, with verse after sequential verse belying the dream.

The driver turned once more to ask the man if he realized they were trapped in a dream, within his dream, but now the words refused to come out. Annoyed by the silence, or something darker, the friendly hitchhiker slipped a hand into his worn leather jacket, pulled out a large pistol, and shoved it hard against the driver's head.

"I'm going to kill you now," whispered the stranger, in a tone as flat and cold as death.

The terror was enough to strangle the dream driver into consciousness; a ragged scream he prayed would propel him awake thick and burning in his throat.

****

The next morning found the driver staring down the same road, in the same car, grasping the same black leather steering wheel. Only this time he wasn't alone. His best friend Doug sat in the passenger's seat, extolling the numerous benefits of Miss Manoch's class.

"You and me, and twenty-three nursing students! Twenty-three! Man, how did we get so lucky?"

"That's why we took the class, remember? Odds are in our favor."

Doug merely grinned in response, and scratched his cheek the way he always did when he got caught exaggerating a point. They spent the next fourteen minutes from Waltham to Newton engaging in the same joyously forgettable chatter that guys in college usually spew forth.

Before he knew it, the Buick lumbered toward the corner where he had dreamed the hitchhiker stood the night before, only to find it empty, much to his relief. His great relief.

"Man, I had the weirdest dream last night," he said with a slight tremor in his voice. "I was here. Right here in my car, but it was so real. Or maybe not real. Just freaky, you know?"

Ever the master of expressions, Doug raised an eyebrow, granting permission to continue.

And continue he did, pouring forth every bizarre aspect of the dream, which even now, seemed to replay just behind his eyelids. This very corner. Bruce Springsteen. The crystal clarity of the dashboard. The plodding continuity. And most of all, the stranger who planned to kill him.

Doug listened to detail after exquisitely sharp detail, cocking his head, rubbing his cheek, and raising an eyebrow when any emotional punctuation was required.

After all was said, Doug remained silent for a moment, then uttered his pronouncement.

"Weird," he said, brushing an unseen speck of dust off his leg, before wading back into more comfortable college speak.

And so it went for the next four mornings, until the free air of youthful weekends swept away all memory of the stranger and his threat aside.

But some dreams refuse to lie dormant.

It was the following Monday, and Doug had driven in alone for an early accounting class. The driver once again piloted the big Buick Riviera with sleepy-eyed routine back to the campus, when the feeling suddenly hit him like a silent gasp from someone else's lungs. The dashboard seemed to glow before his eyes, though not in brightness, merely in clarity. Every line, every number razor-sharp and appearing to hovering a fraction of an inch above its firmly fixed position in the dashboard. A zippered tingling ran across the back of his neck, and down his spine, as Jersey power chords burst from the radio in all their terrifying glory.

Bruce Springsteen's harsh-edged vocals pulled him further into that dream-like abyss, though this time, he knew beyond a doubt that he was awake, wide awake, trapped in some strange realm beyond consciousness. Beyond any definition of reality he had ever known.

Time itself slowed to a heavy sludge, along with his heartbeat, along with his breath, along with his ability to link together any cohesive thoughts. He was awake, he had to be, but this wasn't like any consciousness he ever experienced, for he had lost all control of his hands, his body, his will. He could not slow down his car if he wanted to. He could not lighten his foot on the gas pedal. He could not stop the Buick from hurtling toward the corner, that corner, where he knew the stranger would be waiting for him.

He was caught in the unfolding of it all. Paralyzed by a dream that demanded his attention.

A dream that would not let him go.

Even though he begged them not to, his hands, heavy on black leather, turned the steering wheel to the right…and there he stood.

The hitchhiker.

Exactly as he had appeared in the dream.

The same wide, freckled face. The same tweed cap over reddish brown strands of hair. The same worn leather jacket over the orange shirt with the wide brown stripe.

The same friendly grin. The same wagging thumb.

The same man who would soon press a gun to his head and utter the last words he would ever hear.

Except, he didn't.

As the Buick eased towards the hitchhiker, their eyes met; driver and dark passenger; killer and victim. And in that instant of approaching death, the driver suddenly regained control of his limbs and his senses. His hands jerked the wheel away from the curb, just as the hitchhiker started his lopping dash to the door. The Buick growled and leapt back into the center lane, and sped a dozen yards past the hitchhiker.

Then another dozen. And soon he was nearly a block away.

Their eyes met again in the rearview mirror, and in that instantaneous connection, all pretense of friendliness was gone. The coldness in the stranger's stare seemed to resonate with the unspoken message:

Next time…

It wasn't until he rounded another two corners, far beyond where the stranger could see him, that the driver allowed himself to slow the Buick to the curb. He turned the engine off, just as Bruce howled the last lines of his rock and roll lament.

It took four long minutes for his heart to stop pounding in his ears and for his breath to return to normal.

It took another six and a half to stop shaking.

Slowly, the hyper-real details of the dream dissolved back to normal resolution. The dashboard no longer painfully sharp. The radio a comfortable blare, with another inane commercial for a local tire center. The driver took one last look in the mirror to be sure he wasn't followed, then slowly cranked the engine and continued his daily drive back to campus.

He caught up with Doug in the cafeteria after fourth period, and the words exploded from him.

"You remember that dream I told you about last week?!"

"I guess."

"Tell me everything I told you! Every detail. It's important!"

As they sat at the cafeteria's long wooden tables, Doug recounted every point he could remember. Being a detail-oriented accounting major, that turned out to be quite a lot. The unwavering dashboard. The corner on Commonwealth Ave. The Springsteen song. *Born to Run, right?* And the hitchhiker, described to a T.

"I saw him. I just saw him."

"Bullshit."

"Seriously! I couldn't stop shaking."

Doug rubbed his jaw for a long moment. "You didn't pick him up, did you?"

"Hell, no! You think I'm stupid?"

They spent the rest of the period discussing the metaphysical implication of predictive dreams, circular time, or guardian angels with the typical college veneer of deep thought.

For the next three days, they checked every newspaper to see if any bodies were dumped along Commonwealth Ave, before they forgot all about the hitchhiking and the dream, in order to concentrate on more pressing matters of grades, gripes and girls.

****

Years drain away with relentless ambivalence, first slowly, then with increasing ferocity as time left to us dwindles in comparison with decades squandered or surrendered. Soon, the most vivid memories become intangible, amid the pressure of the present and the future's looming finality. With the increasingly circuitous path each life takes, even the closest of friends may find a continent's width of choices between them, as relationships dissolve into memories, and memories slowly, inexorably fade with time.

Doug settled into a comfortable life of fatherhood and finance. The dream driver moved around the country, seeking something he couldn't quite define. Fame? Purpose? Or merely some vague sense of belonging?

For five wonderful years, followed by twenty-two increasingly difficult ones, he remained steadfastly married to a bi-polar woman he thought he could rescue from her inner demons, until he gradually found himself ground down by her endless negativity and sudden bursts of venom. He finally escaped once the children were grown and married themselves, never believing he would be lucky enough to find love again, and doubting he was even worthy of a second chance.

To his surprise, another love emerged to prove him wrong, adding joy to the last chapters of his life.

On this very night, he clung to her in bed, melting into her warmth, synchronizing his breath with hers, and savoring the good fortune that we do not always get what we fear we deserve.

In the darkness, he kissed her sweet-smelling hair and rolled over. He turned his head away from her and opened his eyes, only to find himself inches away from a wide, freckled face.

An impossible face, with cold cruel eyes, staring back at him from the edge of the mattress.

And suddenly, he was back in the 1971 Buick Riviera, with Springsteen still on the radio and the cold steel of a gun pressed hard against his right temple. With suffocating fear, he could no longer tell if he had returned to this terrifying nightmare, or if all the long years since had actually been the dream. A fraction of an instant before the hitchhiker squeezed the trigger, he gasped out a strangled scream to the new wife he so desperately hoped was real:

"Wake me up! Wake me up!"

Mark of a Champion

Some places hold a well of memories as deep or pivotal as any we may experience in our lives. The dimly lit building on West 82nd Street was such a place, though that fact was lost on the ten hard men gathered to watch the massacre currently in progress.

Wham.

A savage right hook struck its target like a fast ball shot from a cannon.

Whack. Bam.

Two more lightning blows powered by angry iron biceps.

Thudda thudda thudda whoomp.

An eye-blurring combination that sent internal organs scrambling wildly throughout the abdominal cavity.

Pow. Pause. Kee-rash.

The final uppercut to the damaged jaw stunned the stocky fighter, and sent him crashing to the blood-splattered canvas.

The kid was good, no question about it. Tonight's sparring partner, Boom Boom somebody or other, had a full six-inch reach on Dyno-Mike Dobson, but after only three gut-punishing rounds, had ended up assuming the same canvas-kissing position as all of Dobson's recent opponents. Even under the most generous damage-per-dollar exchange rate, this latest sparring partner had clearly earned his pay.

As for Dobson, the kid was hot, and he knew it. You could tell by the regal way he climbed in and out of the ring. A dozen sycophantic slap-on-the-backs, followed by a dozen more grinning handshakes and fist bumps marked the breathless entourage of the up-and-coming boxer.

Dobson also know that same faithful mob would dissipate like cheap aerosol spray after his first bruising defeat, only to congeal around the next potential legend.

As well as being talented at taking his opponents apart, the twenty-four-year-old brawler was wise beyond his years. His sinewy, sweat-covered torso glistened like crystallized ebony. A meticulous pattern of self-sculpting perfection remained the sole focus of his concentration.

Amid all the noise and paint-peeling distraction of the old 82nd Street Gym & Boxing Club, Dyno-Mike Dobson could see nothing but the championship title that lay in his future. And nothing was going to stop him from grabbing that belt.

The year was 2003, and the title was still years away. For although Dobson possessed the ambition, the talent, and the charisma, his climb up the boxing hierarchy had been all too brief. Only seven bouts; each abbreviated by a knock-out within the first five rounds. No defeats. No TKO's. No split decisions. Just Dobson's trademark roar of triumph, as another boxer's consciousness and dreams of glory spilled burgundy on an ambivalent canvas.

Dyno-Mike Dobson was a rising star, to be sure, but he needed to develop a bigger following, greater name recognition, and better box office before he could sidestep a veritable army of scarred and seasoned veterans aching to vie for the heavyweight championship title. Like all current sports, boxing was a promotional event. Raw talent alone could not justify multimillion dollar media contracts and worldwide streaming rights. Any Twenty-First Century boxer needed a publicist as powerful as his left jab, a killer manager, and a promotional team to build his online presence. Without that mechanism in place, the modern-day gladiator might never know the glorious, all-consuming hunger that feeds, shapes and eventually devours a world-class contender.

By six-thirty that evening, the 82nd Street Gym & Boxing Club was dark and desolate, save for one incandescent bulb casting an eerie yellow aura around the solitary fighter. Long after his trainer and assistants had gone home, Dyno-Mike Dobson still slammed his accumulated aggressions into the venerable Everlast punching bag.

Some claimed his unchained hostility sprang from the traditional plight of a young African-American boy growing up in the urban battlefields of the Bronx. Yet the simmering rage of Dyno-Mike Dobson was fed by far deeper fires. A white-hot desire to conquer something, anything. To be recognized as the world's best at a single, chosen endeavor. Anything less would have meant personal humiliation to an embittered, anachronistic soul, for whom strength and glory meant more than wealth, more than family, more than self. Each smashing blow that erupted from his lightning fists and coiled steel biceps was an attempt to defeat, not the punching bag, but the limitations - physical, psychological and spiritual - which prevented him from becoming the ultimate warrior, the supreme athlete, whose stunning achievements live on in the awe-silenced memories of generations to follow.

Dyno-Mike Dobson threw every ferocious punch with a single purpose in mind: he wanted to live forever.

"Not bad, kid."

The unexpected voice startled Dobson, and caused his scorching right hook to skim awkwardly off the side of the bag. His own lapse of concentration made the young boxer pivot to face the speaker with a blast of scalding fury.

The large, solidly-built man in the doorway didn't seem to notice.

"It's been a good twenny years or more, since I seen somebody smack a bag like that," he commented casually.

"Old man," sneered Dobson, as he cast a malevolent eye towards the uninvited spectator. "I've torn lungs outa fools stupid enough ta interrupt my workout."

"Yeah. I bet you got a whole locker full of 'em," the old man smiled, as he strolled deeper into the darkened gym. His weary, hooded eyes scanned the walls and worn equipment, as if searching for something familiar, something more tangible than reality. He brushed his fingers along the lowest rope of the ring, closed his eyes, and seemed to pull a memory from its bristly cords. He was silent a moment, before he sighed, and added another "Yeah."

Although Dobson had never seen him before, he could immediately tell the aging stranger felt right at home in the venerable old gym.

But that didn't make him welcome on his practice night.

"I don't know who let you in here, but this is my gym three nights a week. So, take your broke ass outside. I got work to do." Dobson smashed the heavy bag with a fierce combination to emphasize his point. However, the point was lost on the stranger, who broke into another smile as he sauntered even closer.

"You better work on that combo. Your uppercut's looking a bit weak."

"Say what?!"

"You heard me. You're stepping off your left too soon. Cuts your power in half."

"What the hell you know, old man?! I put down Morris Jefferson with that uppercut. Bloodied him up good."

"Jefferson's a chump," the older man snorted. "All ego and biceps. But too stupid to protect his chin." That disarming grin again.

"You got that straight, old dude." But there was a smile creeping in behind Dobson's dark expression. "And yeah, Jefferson was a chump. So, whatta you want, Pops? An autograph or somethin'?"

"Hell, I thought you were just hanging around waitin' for mine."

"Yours? Who the hell are you?"

"Name's Vitale. Nico Vitale. That probably don't mean one ounce of nothin' to you, comin' from a broken-down old slugger like me."

"You baked? Or just some wise ass butt-truffle?."

Vitale shook his head, which did nothing to dislodge his easy grin. "Y'know the biggest problem with passing fifty? You somehow slip past the point where you can tell a compliment from an insult."

Dobson lowered his gloves for the first time since the man walked in. "I'm lettin' you live this long. That's a compliment, comin' from me." Dobson kicked a metal folding chair in Vitale's direction. "Park it, Pops. 'Bout time I take a breather, anyways"

"It's not Pops." Vitale sat down, so that his thick legs straddled the back of the chair, his constantly calculating eyes never moving from the young boxer. "It's Nico. Or Mister Vitale if I scare you that bad."

"It'd take another nine-feet-four of you to scare me, ass-wipe. Don't you know who I am?"

"Little Mickey Dobson."

"Dyno-Mike Dobson! That's my legal name now. Had it changed in court and everything." He pulled up a chair to face the stranger by sitting in the same manner. "And I'm only taking ten to shoot the shit, 'cause this is my cool down time." Dobson looked suspiciously at the older man. "You ain't no regular groupie, old dude. So, what puts your ass in that chair this time of night?"

Vitale ran a meaty paw across his tired face. As he did, Dobson caught a glimpse of the patchwork of scars, the slightly misshapen nose, the drooping right eye. This man had taken some hits in his day. But when he looked up into the younger man's eyes, there was a strange light in his expression.

"I'm here to tell you a story, kid," he said softly.

Dobson stood up with the sudden reflexes of an angry tiger.

"You best not be selling me no religion or no insurance, old man. 'Cuz I'll kick your ass from here to Vegas."

Vitale smiled. He liked this kid. He liked the way he boxed. Liked the way he stood his ground.

"I ain't gonna sell you squat, you candy-assed little punk. I'm gonna tell you a story about Desmond 'Mincemeat' Weaver, a boxer you remind me of. If you're not too much of a chump, you'll listen. When it's over, I'm gonna walk right out that door and you ain't never gonna see me again."

He chewed a chunk of his fingernail, examined it for a while, then looked up at the young fighter with a mischievous glint in his eye. "But I guarantee you ain't never gonna forget me neither," he grinned.

Dobson never liked being played, and his famous temper was nearing the meltdown phase. His voice was cold and menacing as he stalked his way back to the heavy punching bag.

"Save your breath, Pops," he growled. "I don't give a rat's ass about no Desmond Mincemeat Whatsisname. And I don't give a rat's ass about you." He smashed the Everlast with a brutal forearm, and the eighty-pound sandbag swung wildly at the head of the seated stranger. Instead of ducking, Vitale did something which surprised the younger man. He leapt out of his chair, and threw a savage corkscrew punch that tore a gaping hole in the side of the heavy leather bag.

Dobson's jaw dropped as he watched Vitale pull his fist from the bowels of the mortally wounded Everlast, its stream of sand hemorrhaging to the floor.

"Damn, Pops," he whistled with a new sense of respect. "How'd you do that?"

Vitale slowly shook the sand from his scarred knuckles, and slowly sat down again.

"Listen to my story," he said softly. "And maybe I'll show you."

Dyno-Mike Dobson watched the leaking sand form a growing pyramid on the gym floor. He took a chair and nodded for Nico Vitale to unwind his story.

****

"It was 1960 when I first met Desmond 'Mincemeat' Weaver. Some preliminary bout for the district championship, and Mincemeat was already fifteen years past his prime. He was a huge black man, back then we called them Negroes," he waived away Dobson's objection before it cleared his throat. "Hey, it was back in the day. What the hell did we know? Anyways, Mincemeat stood six-foot-six easy, and tipped the scales at three-oh-five. He learned to fight when he was only fifteen. Started the hard way, bare knuckle brawling during the Great Depression."

"Bare knuckles. That's some serious shit."

"You're tellin' me. That kind of fightin' could kill a man real quick. No gloves to absorb the shock or spread out the blow. Just an inch and a half of knuckle bones doin' as much damage as they can before the other guy's knuckles came after your face. Sometimes a real scrapper would let his thumb ride high, so's if he hit you just right, you could lose an eye and never see it comin'. I remember Mincemeat bore his share of scars from back in his knuckle brawling days.

"Mincemeat was a proud man. Refused to take charity of any kind, even when there was no work around for whites or Negroes. His wife was a good, front-pew Southern Baptist from Macon, Georgia. She never much liked the idea of her husband bloodying other men's faces for a living. But Mincemeat had seven kids to feed, and that was about the only job he could do steady. He always said he brought every one of them little Weavers into the world, and had no right to ask anybody else to provide for them.

"In the beginning, he fought because he had to. Then he fought because he loved to. And finally, because he wanted to be the best that ever lived."

"I hear that," Dobson nodded.

"For a while back in the Forties, he just might've been. But Mincemeat Weaver gave away his best boxing years when he volunteered for World War II to fight Germans. He won the Golden Gloves in the Army, but they went and took this natural-born fighting machine and made him a cook." Vitale shook his head and spit on the floor. "That's the army for ya. Seems some of them Southern white boys didn't feel too comfortable serving shoulder-to-shoulder with a Negro carrying a rifle."

Vitale saw Dobson's eyes narrow. "Like I said, it was back in the day, and none of us knew shit about political correctness. We were just second, third or fourth generation idiots ourselves.

"One day, outside Arnhem, Mincemeat's whole squad get themselves pinned down by SS Panzer troops. While his buddies hugged the mud, Old Mincemeat stands up, slings a heavy machine gun over his shoulder, outflanks the German position on his own, and mows down about forty Krauts before the rest of his squad even raised their helmets to see who was saving their scrawny asses.

"After that, nobody felt quite right telling Mincemeat Weaver he had to slop soup for the rest of the war.

"The day the war ended, Mincemeat began planning out his boxing comeback. He had a fire, almost a hatred, that would scare the pants off anyone who faced him in the ring. It was a look he had. An attitude. It made you feel that if the referee weren't standing right there, he'd tear open your throat 'til your head popped off. Once he stepped in the ring, Mincemeat was pure, old-fashioned rage, and if you stepped in there with him, it was you he was pissed at. He got the name Mincemeat because of what he did to people's faces with that right cross of his. But he wasn't just a hitter, or a chump like Morris Jefferson. No sir. He could take your best punch, shrug it off, and still keep comin' at you. At that point, your best bet was to lie down on the mat and play dead.

"The one thing Mincemeat wanted more than anything was a shot at the title. Joe Louis was on top at the time, but he was nothin' compared to old Mincemeat. I saw them both in a boxing demonstration in Queens, when I was just a kid. The Brown Bomber was good, don't get me wrong. But it was Mincemeat who made boxing a battlefield. Like his private little war, roped off from the rest of the world. To a kid like me, too young for World War II, Mincemeat was every American hero rolled into one. The pride and savagery that made Hitler hide in his bunker as GI's like Desmond Mincemeat Weaver drove their Sherman tanks right up to his front door.

"By 1952, Mincemeat's record was forty-six wins, and only three losses. That included twelve knockouts in a row. The big money was on him to take on the undefeated Rocky Marciano, and maybe even be the next World Champion. And that made the big money want a piece of him first.

"They say the mob first came onto him in Trenton. Typical story… We wanna buy out your contract. You give us seventy percent and maybe take a dive when we tell you to…and we let you live."

The old story teller rubbed his chin with the back of his fist. "The fight game was a lot dirtier in those days. Though I hear it ain't a helluva lot better now."

"True 'dat."

"Huh?"

"Just finish up your tale. I got more conditioning to do."

"Relax, kid. That bag ain't going nowhere," he pointed again to the still growing sand stream, nearly turning the heavy bag inside out.

"Anyways, the word around town was Mincemeat took two of their goons apart in his locker room. Real messy like. Snapped one of their necks is what I heard, but you know how these stories get blown up bigger with time. My buddy, Vince, who was workin' the bell that night, says he saw these two gangster types in little piles all over the floor, and Mincemeat looking like he was gonna rip open any white man who said 'boo' to him. The police carted the thugs off to the hospital, and I guess Mincemeat thought it was all over and done with. I was only eighteen at the time, but I coulda told him better."

"He was still black. That don't never end it."

"True enough. The mob guys caught up with him 'bout a week later. He was lucky, I guess. They coulda buried him right then and there, but sometimes, they like to keep guys alive to make a point. So ten of 'em kick down his door in the middle of the night. They ain't stupid twice. This time, they wanna make sure he keeps his temper, so they put a gun to the head of each of his kids. Mincemeat, he's a family man, and he couldn't do nothing if there's a chance his kids are gonna get hurt. So after they smack him around with a baseball bat for a while, they ask him again if he wanted them to buy out his contract.

A pause.

"And..?"

"That stupid sonuvabitch still says no. Can you imagine? Anyway, that's when they did it."

****

There was another long pause as Nico Vitale looked off into the translucent shadows that filled the 82nd Street Gym & Boxing Club.

"Did what?" asked Dyno-Mike Dobson, perched on the end of his seat.

"Huh?" Vitale looked disoriented by the sudden interruption. As if a part of him still dwelt back in the days of mobsters and Mincemeat Weaver.

"What?" pursued Dobson. "What'd they do to Mincemeat?"

"Oh, yeah. Mincemeat. Well, you know these guys don't take rejection too good. So, they took his hands."

"His hands?"

"Yeah. His hands. The one thing a fighter can't afford to lose." Vitale shuddered, unconsciously clenching and unclenching his own fists.

****

"They put two guys on each arm, and one on each leg. Then spread his huge hands up against the wall, palms out. With Mincemeat's kids all scared and crying, the head mobster just sticks his pistol right into old Mincemeat's palm and fires.

Pow. Pow.

"He blows a hole right through each hand. When I met him eight years later, he still had the scars. Big ugly things where the bullets had gone clean through. He told me that after they shot up his hands, they just let him drop to the floor. Mincemeat's wife, Bertie, I think her name was, she just fainted dead away. The kids were all screaming, and there's poor Mincemeat sitting on the floor, blood gushing outa each hand.

"I don't have to tell you, that was pretty much the end of Mincemeat's championship run. Or that's what we all thought. But only two years later, he surprised everyone by coming back to the ring. His fists were never as tight as before, and they hurt him every time he threw a punch, but at least he was able to use them a little.

"The trouble was, after his hands healed, all his power was gone. So was his hunger. It was like he went back to the early days, when he fought just to feed his family. By 1954, Desmond Mincemeat Weaver was a thirty-nine-year-old crippled boxer with no spirit left in him.

"For the next four years, Mincemeat fought whenever he could. He could still take a punch better than any man I ever met, but that was all he seemed to do anymore. He'd stand up for twelve, fifteen rounds like a walking punching bag. Kids who couldn't even climb in a ring with him when he was in his prime were now winning decisions and TKO's on him. Physically, he was still as strong as ever, but his killer instinct was gone. Lou Geary broke three of Mincemeat's ribs in St. Louis. Jake Waschowski cut his right eye so bad, they had to call the fight. When I finally met Mincemeat in 1960, he was a patsy fighter. A sucker bet. A real palooka used by every up-and-comer who wanted to add an easy victory to his stats.

"I met the guy who used to be my idol right here in this gym. Right there in that ring. They called him in as my sparring partner, something he did to raise a little extra money now that his purses were so low. Remember, the guy's nearly twice my age now. At first I just wailed away on him to show my manager and all the little followers, who saw me as the next Rocky Marciano. But even as I was hitting him, I saw something in his eyes. A sadness, I guess. The kind of look I imagine a cow gets as they put her in the slaughterhouse. Right before they hack her to pieces, y'know? For some reason, I just couldn't hit him anymore. This was my idol as a kid. The guy who made me see boxing as a noble sport. And here I was smacking him around any way I felt like.

"I don't know what came over me, but I let my guard down. Not a lot. Just enough to give him an opening. He saw it, and I swear to God, he nodded at me, real subtle-like. Then he slammed me with the same right cross that once knocked out twelve men in a row. Only now it felt like a rookie punch. But you know what I did? I went down. Played it up for the lookieloos. I figured, what the hell...Let the old geezer remember what it feels like to knock a man down again. Hell, it was only a sparring session. It wasn't like anybody outside the gym would ever find out.

"So, there I am, flat on the canvas, looking up at him. The sonuvabitch has a big, fat tear in his eye. The right one. The one that Jake Waschowski cut. Then he throws off his gloves and walks right outa the ring. How about that? I do the guy a favor, and he goes and gets pissed off!

"Later, my manager reads me the riot act. Says I didn't fool him for a second. There's no place in the fight game for sentiment, he says, and if I ever want to make it to the title, I better plan on killing any poor bastard that climbs into the ring with me. I just nod, feeling like a real dip. The crowd that used to hang around me is gone for good by now, looking for the next up-and-comer to suck up to.

"In the locker room, Mincemeat comes up to thank me for what I done. He says he don't believe in charity, but he knew my heart was in the right place. Then he tells me, if I ever take a dive on him again, he'd kill me. And he meant it too.

"What else could I do? I invited him up to my Uncle Paulie's restaurant in Queens for a few beers. That's where he tells me all about what happened to him with the mobsters and all. Mincemeat didn't talk too much, but after six or seven beers, I guess we got to be pretty chatty.

"Anyways, I didn't see him again for about four more years. By that time, he was back on top and two fights away from taking on the heavyweight champ in a title bout..."

****

"Say what?!" Dyno-Mike Dobson shouted. "You tellin' me this beat-up old dude with holes in his hands goes from straight-up patsy to a shot at the title? I mean, this guy's gotta be pushin' forty-five by then!"

"Forty-eight," said Nico Vitale calmly. "Cassius Clay was the champ then, back before he became Muhammad Ali. And Mincemeat Weaver had just won his last six matches in a row. The crowd loves him again, because he gave them something different."

"Like what? Adult diapers?"

"No, kid," Vitale's face darkened, his eyes narrowing to unreadable slits. He took a slow, staccato breath before he continued. "He gave them blood like they ain't never seen before. The last six men Mincemeat fought all died in the ring."

"Bullshit," whispered the young boxer.

"I wish it was," sighed the old man.

****

"It started in '63. Memphis. Some redneck named Bobby Ray Crawley. Just a little warm-up match for the Tennessee State Championship. I didn't see the fight, but I heard all about it. Hell, everyone did. In the third round, Mincemeat gets tired of the names Bobby Ray's calling him — darkie, grandpa, nigger - so he slashes out a right with this new corkscrew punch that goes by so fast, only a few people ever see Bobby Ray get hit. But they sure do see him go down. The papers said there was so much blood pourin' outa that old redneck's head, the front two rows got splashed. There's an official inquiry to see if Mincemeat was hidin' some kind of weight or weapon in his gloves, but they find don't nothin' at all. He split this kid's skull open with a single punch.

"The next match was in Columbus, Ohio. Mincemeat's starting to pull in some crowds, all waiting to see if he can do it again. He takes a few shots and then, *Bam!* Same punch. Same result. I don't even remember the fighter's name, but newspapers all over the country start calling Mincemeat, 'The Man With The Killer Punch.'

"Fight three was right here in the city. Luther 'The Hook' Hagler. Now Luther's runnin' a bit scared, so he dances away from Mincemeat's right. Only there ain't too far you can dance in a ring. Mincemeat clocks him with that corkscrew punch and Luther's head explodes. The Hook lives another twenty-two minutes in the locker room before the ringside doc pronounces him dead as a doornail.

"Now the boxing association don't know what to do, so they suspend Mincemeat, although they can't really come up with a legal what for.

"After the fight, Mincemeat calls me up to see if we can meet at Uncle Paulie's again. I'm the only friend he has left, he says. The only one he can tell his big secret to. My career's pretty hot at this point. I'm walking around with eleven wins and no defeats. Yet I'm scared to be sitting with this guy. My idol who just killed three name fighters with one punch to the head.

"So here we are, puttin' down a big plate of Paulie's spaghetti, when he hits me with it. He says that after a sparring match the year before, he helped rescue some little old Korean grandfather named Kim Yup Park over on West 44th. A gang of about ten or twelve street punks were gathered around the little guy, when Mincemeat walks in the middle of it all. Although his punch is gone, he's still got enough boxing know-how to knock a few toughs on their asses. After a few go down, the rest scatter.

"Park says he's grateful, and offers to pay Mincemeat back by teaching him some crazy secret punch technique. Mincemeat says to himself, what the hell? I ain't got nothin' to lose. So, he spends the next three weeks practicing some sort of mystical physical training, and comes out with this killer punch. A Tsunami Punch, Park calls it, or something like that. The little Korean guy claims he picked it up from some Buddhist priests during the war. Mincemeat tells me it's more magic than martial arts. Like his arm suddenly becomes this living thing he has no control over. Anger sets it off, and once he decides to use it, he can't pull it back. And it always kills. He says this Park guy warns him about that...it always kills. And that scares him to death. So, Mincemeat goes on to tell me how he loses four more fights before Bobby Ray calls him a 'shufflin' nigger,' and that pisses him off enough to try his new Tsunami Punch in the ring.

"Now, picture this. All this time he's talking, I'm chewing on my spaghetti, nodding up and down, and thinking to myself; *Looks like old Mincemeat took one too many shots to the head himself.'*

"But I can't help wondering. I mean, what if it's true? What else could have changed this wrinkled old relic from has-been into a contender at forty-eight? How could a man with ruined hands become so deadly?

"As I sit there, thinking all this shit, Mincemeat keeps rambling on about how he wishes he never learned this punch. He's not out to kill anybody, he says. All he ever wanted was a shot at the title. Now they won't even let him box anymore.

"I tell him don't worry about it, and after another beer or two, he walks himself home at about two in the morning. Me? I lay awake in bed wondering what I'd do if I were in old Mincemeat's shoes?

"By now, even the boxing association can't keep Mincemeat down for long. Joe and Mary America are beating down the doors to buy tickets to whatever fight he's gonna be in. Everyone wants to see if he can kill four men in a row with just one punch. The boxing bigwigs know something good when they see it, so they agree to let him fight again. Only now, nobody wants to climb in the ring with him. All those tough guys who bounced him around for years ain't gonna take a chance against old Mincemeat. Lou Geary wouldn't do it. Neither would Jake Waschowski. He didn't want Mincemeat to remember what he did to that eye.

"Meanwhile, this anti-violence group in Boston starts tryin' to get some law passed that would shut down the whole damn sport. Newspapers claim there's dead boxers from Arkansas to Alaska that Mincemeat is responsible for. Some redneck sheriff down in Louisiana says he'll have Mincemeat arrested for murder if he ever dares to fight in his town. Not that his ant-piss town even has a damn arena. The whole thing becomes one big circus, and that usually means there's big money to be made somewhere.

"With nobody left to face him, the boxing association decides to up the ante. They'll spike the purse, offering a cool quarter mil' to anyone who'll go toe-to-toe with this guy. Back in the Sixties, that was some serious money. Mincemeat says he doesn't want no blood money. Even a quarter million. He says all he wants is a shot at the title. But the head honchos want to milk him for a few more fights. Boost the take, y'know? So, they say they have to make sure it's not just a lucky punch.

"Yeah, right. There's three guys lyin' six feet under, and not one of them feels all that lucky about it, let me tell you.

"Just when it looks like there's gonna be no takers, Pistol Pete Purvis out of Chicago agrees to fight. Pistol Pete was a lot like Mincemeat. Both in their forties, and looking for one last score before they hang up their gloves. Pistol Pete's been getting kicked around the ring by guys twenty years younger for a decade now. He figures, even if he loses, he gets a piece of the quarter million to retire on.

"So, the night of the big fight comes. Atlantic City. Killer Weaver against Pistol Pete. Tickets sell out in three hours flat. Even people who never been to a fight are packing the place, hoping to see Pistol Pete get creamed. Fifteen thousand people guzzling beer, chewing hot dogs and screaming for blood.

"Pistol Pete steps in looking real nervous. The newspaper ran a story about how he drew up his will the night before the fight, but that could've just been a story to goose the crowd. Anyways, everybody cheers when Mincemeat steps into the ring. But the big guy looks as sad as he did the day I took that dive for him four years earlier. Right from the bell, the crowd starts yelling themselves hoarse.

"Boy, are they disappointed. The first five rounds are nothing but two old guys hittin' each other with not enough power left in their bodies to do any real damage. They're boxing right, y'know, but they're just too damn old. Pete's dancing around. Mincemeat is only using his left. By the sixth round, the crowd starts booing. And that starts the promoters panicking.

"By the end of the seventh round, all the promoters and boxing big shots crowd around Mincemeat's corner. They start screaming at him, saying he better start using his right, or they'll never give him a shot at the title. They say Mincemeat is just playing them, and they don't like to be played with. And that's what *really* got him fired up.

"The bell rings for the eighth, and Mincemeat storms right out of his corner. Pistol Pete gets in one shot to the jaw, before…

Bam!

"Tsunami punch!

"Pistol Pete never saw it coming, and then never saw nothin' after that. Mincemeat stomps back to his corner, grabs one of the promoters by the collar - the one who accused Mincemeat of playing them – and the big old boxer and lifts him straight off the ground.

"The promoter turns white as the canvas, and people start to notice a big old wet spot on his trouser leg, as Mincemeat just stares into his eyes with more pure hate than you ever want to see in your life. Finally, Mincemeat just drops him, and storms off to his locker room. He leaves the ring even before the referee announces the winner.

"More than a hundred fighters showed up for Pistol Pete's funeral, plus all the top promoters. It was all a big set up for the press. Pistol Pete never had more than three, maybe four friends in his entire life, but the association thinks all this hoopla will help promote Mincemeat's next fight, which they're already planning.

"Mincemeat was the only one who didn't go to the funeral. He never was much of a hypocrite. But I heard a rumor that he mailed half his winnings to Pistol Pete's widow. That's kinda funny because Pete's old lady was already shackin' up with some young fighter, and starting a promising career as an alcoholic. Still, it's the kinda thing Mincemeat would do.

"In order to get Mincemeat to fight again, they raise the purse to a cool million. It'll be another challenge match. But this time, whoever wins, will go on to face Ali for the heavyweight championship of the world. It was too much for even Mincemeat to resist. One more fight, than a shot at the title. A chance to be remembered as the best boxer in the world. Mincemeat signed on, but refused to grant any interviews, or even show his face in public until the night of the fight.

"Trouble was, they could only find one guy stupid enough to fight him."

"Who was that?" asked Dyno-Mike Dobson.

The police sirens outside the 82nd Street Gym & Boxing Club cried their usual midnight song of violence and passion, but neither man seemed to notice.

"Who'd they get to fight Mincemeat?" he repeated eagerly. "Who'd be that stupid?"

Nico Vitale leaned his chin on the back of the chair he was straddling.

"Me," he sighed heavily.

And Dyno-Mike Dobson's jaw dropped for the second time that night.

****

"Hey, it was too much for me to resist too. Twenty-five years old and a chance at the title. I'd only been boxing a few years, but if I could make it through this one fight, I'd have a chance to go after Muhammad Ali. A chance to be the best in the world.

"I wasn't married. Had no family to worry about. Just this dream to be the best. To be the heavyweight champion of the world. At first I figured, if I could just stay away from his right for a couple of rounds, I might be able to put him down before he caught me with that killer punch. But as the night of the fight got closer, I began to worry that maybe I needed something extra, you know what I mean?

"When Mincemeat found out who he was supposed to fight, he tried to call me on the phone. I just hung up on him. I mean, I already liked the guy too much, and you can't fight somebody you like. Not the way I had to fight this match. It was him or me. One of us would have to be kissing canvas. Hopefully not dead, but you never know. As my manager told me years before, there's no room for sentiment in the fight game. I wanted that title shot more than anything I ever wanted in my whole life. Desmond Mincemeat Weaver was the only thing standing in my way.

"Our fight was scheduled for August 12, 1964. Madison Square Garden. Eighty thousand people bought tickets for a chance to see me murdered up close and personal. Sheiks, earls, baronesses, and who knows what else, flew in from all over the world. They paid ten thousand each for front row seats, secretly hoping to get some of my brains splattered on their thousand dollar suits and gowns. TV cameras also hoping to record something that would shock people at six and eleven, with maybe a special report during sweeps week.

"Me, I was in my locker room throwing up. It's scary to be standing an arm's length away from your dreams and your death at the same time. My trainer didn't say a word. My manager tells me to stay away from his right, like that was some kind of news to me. Those guys were getting their cut whether I walked out of that ring, or was carried out in a body bag.

"I asked for a priest to be in the locker room with me, so he could hear my confession. Father Tony volunteered, a kid I grew up with. I think deep down, he wanted to give me the last rites, but he was afraid it would jinx me. I told him if anything happened to me, he could use my share of the purse to build a gym for the neighborhood kids. I asked him to name it after me. I always kinda wanted to live forever.

"He promised me he would, if things went bad in the ring.

"Then the promoter came in and said it was time to go. I swear, they were drooling, trying to hide their smiles."

Vitale leaned back in his chair. His eyes focused on decades past. When his voice did come, it was a whisper. Dyno-Mike Dobson had to lean in closer to catch every word.

"Let me tell you…the walk to the ring that night was the longest few minutes of my life. Flashbulbs were exploding all around me. Girls I never knew leaning over to give me one last kiss, so they could have a romantic story to tell their friends back home. A few of those anti-violence protesters from Boston try to block my way, but security took care of them pretty quick. I remember how tough it was for me to climb under the ropes and into my corner. I can still see the canvas, still and white as death. I'm pretty sure my face was too.

"Mincemeat climbed into his corner, and the crowd went wild, as usual. He was their hero, just like he used to be mine. Only now, he looked sad. He tried his best not to look over at me, but I could see it in his expression. Old and sad. The kind of look you get when you have to put your family dog down after all those years. That's how Desmond Mincemeat Weaver looked at me that night.

"In my corner, the trainer was all business now. He told me to take Mincemeat out early, before he even had a chance to unload that killer punch on me. And if I saw him winding up with that corkscrew move, to get the hell outa there fast!

"I figured that was some pretty fair advice.

"I did a little sign of the cross in my corner, just as the bell rang to start the first round.

"As he came towards me, I forgot everything and just sort of stood there. He hit me with a left to the jaw, and a right to the stomach that didn't hurt that much. I grabbed him in a clench, because I was too afraid to move. While I'm clenched in with him like that, he whispers something in my ear. Something nobody else heard…

"This is your chance, kid," he says to me. "Take your best shot."

"And that's when I came to life.

"He was right. This was the moment I 'd been training for my entire life. The big fight. The big crowd. The big money. Eighty thousand people, and a few million more watching on their TV sets at home, all waiting to see if

I had what it takes. It was now or never. I'd never get a chance like this again.

"So, I hit him. I smashed him with a left to the jaw that knocked him back a foot. Then a right to the ribs and a left uppercut. I saw blood leak out from his lip. And you know what he did then? The big bastard smiled at me. Then he hit me back hard.

"This was what it's all about. The kind of boxing I loved. Two sluggers, both hungry for glory, going toe-to-toe in front of a screaming crowd. He hit me a dozen times and I hit him two dozen times back. He threw everything he had at me, except that killer Tsunami Punch. I hit him back with every ounce of strength in my body. The crowd was screaming, half for him, half for me. Every stinging punch just made me feel more and more alive. Him, too.

"I think I busted his nose in the second round, and the sonuvabitch smiled at me again.

"By the third round, the TV reporters were saying it was the greatest fight in the history of boxing. But by the fourth, Mincemeat's age was beginning to show.

"I knew that every full power punch he threw was causing as much pain to his crippled hands as it was to my face. We were both bleeding, but the extra twenty-something years he had on me were dragging his arms down like cement. Like he suddenly had this extra tug of gravity pulling down only on him. I was all over him in that fourth round, my combinations chewed up his face like hamburger. When he hit the corner, I knew he wouldn't last another round. And I saw how angry that made him.

"I watched him from my corner, as my trainer tried to close a cut above my left eye. Mincemeat was being screamed at by the promoters again. I was too far away to hear, but I knew what they were saying. The people wanted to see his killer punch, and he better throw it now, or they'd never give him his shot at the title. He'd never get a chance to be the heavyweight champion of the world.

"When they talked about the title, I could see the fire return to Mincemeat's eyes. He'd been in too many fights, took too many punches, suffered too many humiliations to let it slip away. Not now. Not when it was this close. The dream of his life was just one punch away. He looked up at me with hatred, and I saw the muscles twitch in his right arm.

"I knew what he was planning to do.

"The bell clanged for the fifth round, and Mincemeat came charging out of his corner like a freight train. I was watching his right and must have dropped my guard a bit. He hit me with a hard left that stunned me. As my vision cleared, I was staring straight into his eyes, and I saw the battle raging inside him. He was trying not to see me, not recognize me as a friend. If he could see me as some faceless obstacle between him and his dreams, I knew he'd get to the point where he could take me out with that one bloody punch to the head.

"We clenched again, and that's when I saw his eyes grow cold on me. I knew he would throw his Tsunami punch now. The crowd knew it too, and their shouts were deafening. So, I held him in the clench, even while the referee was trying to pull us apart. I was afraid to let go.

"What happened next, I'd remember for the rest of my life. He pushed me from the clench so we were standing face-to-face in the center of that howling crowd. Mincemeat hesitated for a second before throwing his killer punch. Just a fraction of a second. I don't know why. But his hesitation gave me the one chance I needed. I threw my corkscrew punch so hard, it collapsed the left side of his skull.

"And Desmond Mincemeat Weaver was dead before he hit the canvas."

****

"What the hell?!!" shouted Dyno-Mike Dobson, as he leaped out of his chair. "You tellin' me, you killed him with a Tsunami punch?"

"Yeah. I killed him." The memory that took hold of Vitale's wide face seemed to hurt more than any punch he ever took. He ran a thick paw across his scarred jaw. When he finally looked up at Dobson, his aged eyes were red and moist.

"How?" was all the younger fighter could manage.

"Two weeks before the fight, I looked up Kim Yup Park in the phone book. He had a small house on 44th Street, right where Mincemeat said he'd be. I told him about the fight, about how I was afraid Mincemeat would kill me, and how I just wanted to even the odds a little. He looked at me for a long time, didn't say a word, like he was studying the inside of my head or something. Finally, he agreed to teach me the magic punch. I don't think he wanted to, but he probably felt he'd be responsible for my death if he didn't.

"I trained with him, day and night, for one week. My trainer and manager didn't know where I disappeared to. They probably figured I got scared and skipped town. They had a lot of money riding on the fight, so they were real happy when I turned back up again.

"Mr. Park taught me both the physical and mystical side of the Tsunami punch. The philosophy and the technique. The power comes from inside, he kept insisting. But it's more than just a punch...it's something else...something different. Something scary, y'know?

"Mincemeat hesitated and I hit him with it. I guess I'll never know whether I did it in self-defense, or because I was willing to sacrifice anything, even a friend, even my idol, for a shot at the title. Suddenly, I was the guy who killed Desmond Mincemeat Weaver...one of the finest boxers that ever lived. But when he died, my dream died, too."

"What do you mean?" interrupted Dobson. "Didn't you get to fight for the title?"

Vitale let out a laugh, a long one, but there was no humor in it. Then he leaned his thick forearms on the back of the chair.

"I couldn't do it. Every time I'd step inside a ring, even to spar, I'd see Mincemeat lying there on the mat. Head all caved in and bloody. It spooked me. The press and crowds kept following me around. The Man Who Killed The Killer, they called me. The Ringside Slayer, and other stupid names like that. Finally, I just disappeared. Left the fight game behind and took a job in construction. Did pretty well for myself, too."

His sad eyes darted around the shadowy recesses of the 82nd Street Gym & Boxing Club. They moved across the row of Everlast bags, lingered on the weight sets and jump ropes, sought out the speed bags, the ring itself, and eventually found the framed photos of early boxers lining the walls.

Nico Vitale's eyes moistened even more.

"Y'know, this is the first time I been inside a gym in a long time." he whispered. "Still feels right, you know?"

There was a long pause before either fighter spoke. They just stared at one another. Each man a product of a different time, shaped by different fears and experiences. Yet joined by a common hunger. The insatiable desire to be the best.

It was the young fighter who broke the uneasy silence.

"So, what'd you tell me that story for, old man? Am I supposed to learn something from it? If so, I'm not real sure what you're trying to say."

Nico smiled, the warmth returning to his tired face.

"I don't really know myself, Mr. Dyno-Mike Dobson. I guess you just reminded me of a couple of old fighters I used to know. A couple of hard-headed fools who thought wearing the championship belt was the most important thing in their lives, and they'd do anything for it. Guess I didn't want to see you make the same mistakes we did."

Dobson rose from his chair, and walked over to another heavy bag. He smashed it with three piston-like punches, then steadied it again. He studied its rough canvas texture, blood stains from a hundred desperate knuckles. Then, he turned to face the older man.

"I'm gonna win me that title someday," he said.

"I know you are."

"You gonna teach me that killer punch?"

Nico hesitated. "If you really want me to. It'll probably get you a title shot in half the time."

Dobson looked at the sorrowful stranger now standing by the ropes of the sparring ring. Slowly, his gaze fell down to his own gloved hands.

"No, thanks, Pops," he said at last to Nico Vitale. "I'm gonna do this on my own."

"I'm glad to hear you say that, kid," the older man grinned. "I think Old Mincemeat would've been, too."

He turned toward the doorway.

"Keep your guard up, kid!" was the last thing the aging storyteller said before he disappeared into the shadows.

Dyno-Mike Dobson worked the bag for a long while after Vitale had gone, but he realized his mind was no longer on his training. He toweled the sweat from his forehead, then noticed the photos on the wall, as if for the first time. While the clock chimed 1:30 am, he scanned each framed face, all the pugilistic stances, every forgotten name.

Way off in the far right corner of the room, he found the one he was looking for.

'Desmond 'Mincemeat' Weaver', read the hand-printed caption. 'The Man With The Killer Punch.' 55 wins, 27 losses. Died August 12, 1964, Madison Square Garden.'

Beside it rested another framed photo, a younger boxer with a hungry look and familiar grin. Dobson shuddered as he read the caption aloud.

"Nico Vitale. 'The Ringside Slayer.' 19 wins, 2 losses."

As the young fighter reached for the photograph, a small scrap of paper slipped out from behind the frame, and fluttered to the floor. The yellow newspaper clipping was from a 1986 edition of the Pensacola Sentinel. The brief obituary detailed the story of a local construction foreman, who plummeted to his death from the top of a high-rise office tower still under construction. The terse obituary also mentioned that the man had once been considered a championship contender, but gave up boxing after the death of an unnamed opponent in 1964. It went on to list the name of a widow and his surviving children and grandchildren.

Dyno-Mike Dobson, the man who would one day be heavyweight champion of the world, studied the faces that stared back at him from their glass-covered resting place. He pulled the workout towel from his shoulders, and gently wiped the dust off the framed faces of the forgotten legends.

Then, the young fighter returned each photograph to its place of honor on the wall of the 82 Street Gym & Boxing Club, and headed back to the speed bag for another few hours of work.

Monster

The first time I saw it, it slunk up out of the kitchen drain when it thought everybody in the house was gone off to church. I was home sick that morning, with another one of those damn killer migraines that start right behind my eyeballs and send knife stabs of pain through every square inch of my skull.

It didn't know I was home, because I was sitting at the kitchen table not moving a muscle, just sitting there like I do sometimes, almost dead. That's how I get when these damn killer migraines hit me. I can sit like that for hours. Not moving. Not blinking. Just staring straight ahead all day, like someone made a damn wax statue out of me. Only I'm not wax, least I don't think so. I just sit there, like that. The pain in my head gets so bad, what else can I do?

Anyway, this, I don't know, this thing...it slithers right up out of the sink with a hiss that sounds like something between television static and screeching babies, and I'm watching it watching me, but not seeing me. I can see it slowly move its one slimy eye around to scan the kitchen for any sign of life. It doesn't notice me at first, because I ain't movin' a muscle, like I said. Maybe I'm not even breathing, hell, I don't know. I get like that sometimes. Then its one slimy eye moves right over me like some cold, icy shadow. I can feel its hateful eye reach way straight down into the back of my skull, but I still don't move, 'cause I'm smarter than whatever that thing is, and I know there ain't many people on this planet that ever saw something like this, and the hell with the headaches, the longer I can see it without it knowing I'm alive, the smarter I'll be, y'know what I'm saying?

So, here's this, like I said...this thing, thinking it's safe and all, oozing its way out of the sink, and right up onto my kitchen counter, where we keep all the bread and half-empty bags of potato chip. I can tell it's up to no good by the way it sucks in everything with its one slimy eye, like it's trying to figure out some way to kill us all in our sleep.

Then I start to get angry. I mean, what right does this thing have to come into my kitchen and think about killing my family, y'know what I'm sayin'? And as I get really mad, my hand clenches into a real tight fist, until my knuckles are turning white as a corpse. You know how things turn almost transparent when all the blood gets squeezed out of them? That's what my knuckles are like. And I start to breathe heavy, because I'm so damn mad at this thing in my kitchen that's slithering all over my counter. I know any second it's going to turn and catch me shaking with rage, so I jump up before it can see me, grabbing a fork off the table as I go.

I'm up to the kitchen counter in two steps, but that thing has already swung its one yellow eye around to me, and raised up like a snake. But it ain't got no chance, because I'm fast and I'm pissed, and I stab at it with my fork right where its face shoulda been, if it had a face and wasn't so damn ugly and wormlike. The fork sinks in deep and it just hangs there in mid-air, like it's surprised I can hurt it as bad as I know I got it hurtin'.

Then it has the nerve to look at me. It looks at me with like pure hate. Pure inhuman hate pouring outa that one slimy yellow eyeball, and that really makes me mad. I mean what the hell right does it have to hate me? Other then I'm sticking a fork in it, and I'm only doing that because this ugly S.O.B. snuck its way into my damn kitchen.

So I twist the fork to see whether it can feel pain like I'm feeling in my head all the time, and when I do, it lets out this really loud shriek. Man, you ain't never heard anything like this shriek. If you take all the pain and fear and anguish of all the people who ever lived on this planet, distill it down from the very last second of their lives when they finally realize they're just about to die and all, and then you wrap up all that pain and fear and anguish into one single scream...that would be what that shriek sounded like.

Only worse.

This thing's shriek is so terrible, I have to hold my ears to keep my head from busting apart. What else can I do?

But as soon as I let go of the fork to hold my ears, that thing moves. Moves faster than anything I ever seen. So fast, it's almost back down the drain in the kitchen sink before I can take my hands off my ears. But it forgets the fork I jammed into its neck. It can't get back down the drain, 'cause this fork's sticking out of it, so it can only get its eye halfway down the hole. And I'm standing there thinking, *"You stupid piece of slimy shit! Where the hell you think you're going with that fork stuck in your damn throat?"* But it keeps on wriggling and shrieking and trying to get back down the drain, so I take a handful of plates and start smashing at its disgusting snakelike body.

I guess I hurt it again, because it starts to leak this clear, slimy goo outa one part of its body that's not wriggling anymore. I keep smashing at it and smashing at it, and it keeps wriggling and wriggling and shrieking, until it does something I never woulda expected...

It just up and disappears! Turns invisible right before my eyes!

Who woulda thought they could do something like that?

It takes me a second to realize that even though it may be invisible, I can still see the fork wriggling around in the sink. So I say, *"What the hell?"* and reach out and grab this invisible creature thing and yank it right outa the sink. Maybe it was only three or four feet long, with no arms and legs and all, but it sure was heavy. It took everything I had just to pull it out and smash it against the wall. It was heavy and slimy and cold, too. Like you was shaking hands with Death himself. But I knew I had to destroy this evil thing before it kills my family in the middle of the night, while they're all sleeping.

And I can't let it do that.

So I start swinging its invisible body around the room like a crazy man. I swing it by its invisible tail and I hear its invisible head smashing into the refrigerator, and then the walls and the microwave. Each time it hits something, it makes this sickening, squishy sound, and I can just picture all its invisible guts flying all over the kitchen, and I'm thinking, *"Hey, I hope we have some Lysol disinfectant cleaner for when I get through killing this thing."*

And finally after, I don't know, maybe twenty minutes of smashing this thing against every sharp corner in the kitchen, its shrieking gets softer, and then stops. Just stops. I feel it go limp in my hands, and even though it was ice cold, it starts to get even colder, if that's possible. I know it's dying, and I know it knows I know it's dying, so it gives up and drops the invisibility game.

This thing thought it was so much smarter than me, but now one of us is dying, and it sure as hell ain't me!

I let the disgusting, evil thing drop to the floor with a squishy, sickening thud. My arms are real tired by now, as you can imagine. I think even Dwayne Johnson woulda had trouble wrestling this thing for twenty minutes. My head is still aching like a grenade keeps exploding inside my skull, and my heart is beating so loud, I'm afraid the neighbors are going to call the cops to complain about the noise, like they usually do.

Well, I sit right down on the floor next to this dying thing. I mean, I'm pretty exhausted, what else can I do?

I look down at it, squirming pitifully, and in some strange way, I start to feel sorry for it. I mean I know it's ugly and all, and probably not from this planet, or something that's been buried down deep in the Earth for centuries and stuff. And I know it would have killed me if I hadn't killed it first, but what the hell? Maybe it couldn't help itself. Maybe killing was the only way it knows how to survive, you know? Like vines that wrap around your favorite roses, and choke them to death, because that's what they have to do to survive.

As I'm staring at this ugly, half-invisible worm-thing, it slowly raises its slimy eye to look me right in the face. And I look back at it, and say *"You sure are one ugly S.O.B."*

Then it does something else that surprises me. It jumps right into my mouth before I can finish my sentence. The whole slimy thing leaps straight in and slides up the back of my throat, straight to my skull, where I can feel it start to wrap around my brain, and squeeze my frontal lobes so hard, all I can see is white flashes and pain. This thing I half-killed, and felt sorry for, is now crushing my brain to finish me off!

I know I'm gonna die, if I don't do something fast. So I start slamming my head against the refrigerator as hard as I could. Slamming it again and again, until I dent the Frigidaire's heavy steel door, and there's blood from my own skull all over that shiny white enamel front. I just smash and smash my skull, until I feel it crack and crumple like an eggshell. I mean, it's the only way to kill that thing inside me. What else can I do?

And that's how my family found me when they came home from church.

The kitchen cabinets tore up real bad.

Every dish and glass we own in little sparkly pieces on the floor.

And me still smashing my bloody, broken skull against the Frigidaire.

Of course, the thing had turned back invisible in my skull before it died, so even the emergency room X-rays never showed any sign of it.

But I know it's in there.

I know it will always be there.

And I know the evil that thing can do...

All its squishy, slimy insides must have turned invisible, too, because there was absolutely no sign of it in the kitchen when my wife got home. That's why nobody believes me.

My own family didn't believe me.
My own family didn't heed my warnings.
They're blind to the monster inside my head.
And that's why my family is in real danger.
We all are.

When they finally let me outa this place, the first thing I'm gonna do is buy me a shotgun. A big 12-gauge, double-barreled job. Then I'm gonna sit up and keep close watch over my family all night long. Just in case one of those things decides to come back.

I don't need the sleep.
I don't care if I never sleep again.

I have a job to do.

And if I see one of those invisible things trying to sneak inside my family's mouths while they sleep, I'm just gonna point my 12-gauge, and do what has to be done to protect my family.

What else can I do?"

That Healing Touch

Larry Myers took the shattering news as well as could be expected. He turned to his wife of forty-three years, clutched her hand tightly, pressed his lips to her silver hair and tried to hold back the tears she could not.

"We'll get through this, honey," he whispered. "We'll beat this thing. We always do."

The touching scene was all too familiar to Dr. Christine Reynolds. She hated being the official lens of mortality, the messenger of death. This was the worst part of her job, something they had never adequately trained her for in medical school. Her instructors had told her to be dispassionate: sympathetic, but detached. Yet for all her reputed skill as a surgeon, she felt wretchedly inadequate telling people the lives they usually took for granted would suddenly be measured not in decades, but in weeks or days.

She saw the tears tracing sorrow down the cheek of Larry Myers, felt in her own heart the sobs which racked his wife Alice's slender shoulders, and wondered again whether she was strong enough to practice medicine.

She knew physicians here at the hospital who could rattle off phrases like "quadruple bypass" and "twenty-percent success rate" with all the emotion of an overly stuffed diner ordering a second desert. She envied their detachment nearly as much as she despised their apparent lack of humanity.

These were people's lives, damn it. Not charts and cases...but living, breathing patients. Each clinging tightly to their uniquely personal collection of dreams, anxieties, memories and emotions. Yet as attending physician, it was Christine's responsibility to let patients know the terrible truth that the day-to-day infinity of their lives was little more than a cruel illusion. That just to wake each morning was a desperate luxury to be celebrated, not squandered. And that only if they were willing to entrust all their hopes and fears to her frustratingly fallible hands, could they eke out even a slim possibility of survival.

Christine Reynolds allowed Alice Myers to release the floodgates of forty-three years of emotion, while she watched the distraught woman's tearful husband rub her heaving back with gentle circles. Despite her calm, professional front, the young doctor's heart went out to the Myers, and the uncertain future they faced.

Larry was a particularly painful case. At sixty-seven years old, he had worked his way up from bitter poverty, built a business that he could never quite retire from, raised three successful children, and spent the remainder of his time volunteering for the local church community and a half-dozen charities. He had battled his way through nine major operations, so that, one day, he could enjoy the golden years with his beloved wife.

But that was not to be. The damage to his aorta was too great. Only a risky surgery could prolong his life.

Here he sat, trying to absorb the heartbreaking news that those golden years he dreamed of were still beyond his grasp. That the battle was far from over, and his struggles would continue. Yet his only thoughts were of his wife, and how he had somehow let her down once again.

Christine offered the couple a handful of tissues from a box she always kept positioned on the corner of her desk.

"We can schedule surgery a week from Tuesday," she said, a soft tremble in her voice. "I really don't think we should put it off much longer than that."

Larry Myers looked up at the young doctor, his broad face and generous smile hidden beneath a mask of stoic anguish. He nodded silently, then turned to Alice and whispered once more.

"We got this, sweetheart. We got this..."

****

The operating room at Marymount Community Hospital buzzed with all the technological wizardry mankind had created, in a desperate attempt to stave off the inevitable thirst of Nature to reclaim its own. Laser cameras, high intensity surgical lamps, cauterizing tools, electronic monitors, video displays, and a diverse array of other beeping, clicking and flashing equipment all paid tribute to the fierce creativity of the human mind in its ongoing battle with the finite limitations of the body.

Dr. Christine Reynolds was flanked by the six men and women in the drab green scrubs that made up the rest of her surgical staff. Each of them ticked off a last-minute inventory of the tools and equipment they would wield in a tightly choreographed dance of surgical precision. All that was missing was the patient, who would be wheeled in momentarily.

Her face already covered by a surgical mask, Christine scanned the operating room for Lorinda, the head surgical nurse, who was rearranging an assortment of scalpels, clamps and forceps on a tray. She looked up to see Christine staring at her, and nodded. The two women shared a weary dedication to their careers.

Another day, another life to try and piece back together.

With a thump and whoosh, the double steel doors abruptly parted, and the patient was wheeled in. The surgical gurney skidded to a stop beneath the huge, overhead panel, which would soon illuminate the inner cavities of his beating heart. Larry Myers looked pale, too pale, a strange, ashen pallor had invaded his skin. As the gurney was secured, Christine tried to reassure him with her eyes.

"How do you feel, Larry?"

A hesitation, then…

"The truth?"

"Sure."

"I'm tired, Dr. Reynolds," he sighed. "So damn tired of all this. I mean, I've tried to live a good life. And then all this…It's just not fair."

She could see the exhaustion in his eyes. Nine major operations, now once more into the breech, with no promise it would ever get easier. Christine laid a gentle hand on his well-scrubbed shoulder, and tried to absorb all his fear through her surgical glove.

"It's just not fair," he muttered again.

She smiled at him, though it was hidden behind her mask. Leaned closer and spoke something in his ear that no one else in the operating room could hear.

"Courage…" she whispered.

Then gestured for the anesthesiologist to begin.

****

Dr. Christine Reynolds threw open the operating room doors, tearing off her blood-stained gloves as she went. She tore the mask from her face, the paper cap from her long hair, and tossed them into a steel trash barrel without missing a step. She needed something. A steaming cup of coffee maybe, before she could face Alice Myers. She needed to hide within its bitter warmth, in order to dispel the deathlike chill clawing at her insides, the way it always did after something like this happened.

With trembling hands, she poured the black liquid into the white Styrofoam cup, remembering the preciousness of simple acts. She loved and hated these moments, as she drank in the comforting aroma her patient would never again experience.

Larry Myers had been right. It wasn't fair. None of it. Why did the good ones always have to suffer? Why did the rest of us get a free ride? She took a hard gulp of coffee in frustration, burnt her tongue, dropped the scalding liquid on her surgical scrubs, collapsed in the corner, and let hot tears shatter the fragile barrier of professionalism that held all those long-suppressed feelings of wretchedness and inadequacy.

For the next half hour, Dr. Christine Reynolds, Marymount Community Hospital's premier heart surgeon, curled up in the back corner of a surgical supply closet and sobbed like a frightened child. Despite her tightly closed eyes, she could not escape the look of shock, then agony on Alice Myers' face. It was all there in her expression; the sorrow, the accusation, the feeling of being cheated, the bone-crushing despair, and the knowledge that a major part of her life had been clinically removed and discarded like so many surgical sponges. Alice Myers had screamed so loudly that Dr. Reynolds had to call Lorinda to administer a sedative.

"You killed him! You killed my Larry!" the suddenly widowed woman cried, even as the sedative took effect. And perhaps she was right. The young doctor replayed every detail and procedure of the four-hour operation in her mind. Maybe there was something she had done wrong? No, each pre-op process, every incision, every stitch had been carried out with surgical perfection. Larry Myers had simply given up. Lost the will to fight, and who could blame him? That thought led to another, more disturbing question. In her rush for technical precision, had she ignored the real function of the human heart? Just because physicians have developed the technology to squeeze out added months in what are clearly terminal cases, is it right to prolong a patient's life beyond their own desires, or their particular threshold for suffering? Was she attempting to serve the patient, or improve the surgical staff's track record? Or worse, was her own ego the only thing she was trying to heal?

In the darkened corner of a hospital supply closet, Christine Reynolds continued to weep bitterly. She wondered if she could ever escape the agonized expression of Alice Myers, and all the other husbands and wives over the years, who had become widowed by her pitiable inability to save every single heart she touched. Those who found their lives devastatingly suddenly empty because of her guilt-ridden hands.

Maybe she just wasn't qualified to be entrusted with other people's lives. Or their hearts.

"Why are you crying?"

A voice, that seemed to come out of nowhere, startled her. A strange voice, so faint and brimming with innocence.

She looked up to see a young, scrawny boy staring at her with wide, inquisitive eyes. He appeared to be around eight years old. His ebony skin seemed to radiate light in the oppressive shadows of the supply closet, but she realized it was only the fluid prism of her tears that created the effect.

"Why are you crying?" he asked again.

Christine struggled to her feet, embarrassed by her childish position in front of the small boy. She dabbed at her eyes, but couldn't seem to wipe away the emotions they revealed.

"What are you doing here?" she snapped, and immediately regretted the harshness of her tone. "You aren't supposed to be in here."

"I heard you crying. I came to help."

Such innocence. She started to say something doctorly, but softened as the boy studied her face, curiously, in that special way children possess; an ability to see something entirely without judgment or accusation.

"Thanks," she sighed. "But unless you have a stainless steel heart, I don't think you could give me the kind of help I need."

"Why would you want a stainless steel heart?"

"Sorry. I'm being ironic."

Ironic? More like idiotic. She was talking to a child, for Christ's sake. She rubbed harder at her eyes, tried to steady her breath.

"Sometimes I just get sad, I guess," she admitted.

The boy nodded. He accepted her answer, again without judgment. There was something in his small brown face that reflected a kind of serene wisdom. How beautiful to be young, she thought. Before we learn to incrementally collapse in terror over our own mortality.

"Did it have anything to do with that man who died?" the boy asked.

The question was a scalpel, and Christine recoiled as it found its mark.

"What man?" she snapped again. "Who told you about that?" Her arms crossed, subconsciously trying to make herself appear more authoritative.

The boy shrugged, her tone and posture unable to dent his curiosity. "I saw them wheel him out of the operating room. Is that why you're crying?"

"Yes," she whispered, before she realized the answer had escaped her mouth. "It's not easy being a doctor," she sighed.

"But you're the best."

"That's what they tell me. That's not always how it feels." What was it about this strange child that made her admit to such things. She looked into his startlingly clear eyes, knowing he could never fully comprehend her agony.

"What's your name, little man?"

"Malcolm."

"And where are your parents, Malcolm? You didn't leave them in the waiting room, did you?"

"They're dead." No pain. No fear. Just a child's unquestioning answer.

"I'm sorry."

"Don't be. You didn't kill them." She felt herself warmed by his guilelessness. "You didn't kill anyone."

"That's not what it feels like." This was ridiculous. She was propped up in a closet, divulging her deepest fears to a lost child. But she couldn't seem to help herself. It had been so long since she had someone, anyone to confess to.

"Sometimes I feel so empty, Malcolm."

"That's because you need this." he smiled.

The boy reached into the pocket of his unwrinkled jeans and pulled out a small, circular object that glowed oddly bright in the dim supply closet.

"Take it." He held it out to her in tiny, cupped hands. "It's for you."

"What is it?"

She stared at the small glowing orb, or was it merely a circle with no depth? It was hard to discern its shape in the supply closet's half-light. It was two inches in diameter, or maybe three, and must have some sort of LED to make it glow and pulse with so many different colors. It was a plastic child's toy out of a gumball machine, but on closer examination, it seemed incredibly crafted and wildly expensive.

"Take it, Dr. Reynolds. It's for you."

She cupped her hands and held them out to the boy. Gently, he let the glowing orb roll onto her outstretched palms. It wasn't plastic, she realized. Not glass or crystal, or even solid. It seemed to have no weight at all. Yet it tingled as she held it.

Then it disappeared, forcing her to laugh at her own shock.

"That was fantastic, Malcolm!" she clapped with delight. "Some kind of magic trick?"

"Kinda. It made you smile, didn't it?"

"Yes, it did." And she was telling the truth. This simple sleight of hand distracted her from the wretched self-loathing that had threatened to engulf her soul only moments before. She had to admit, it was a pretty impressive trick for a small boy.

"I suppose you won't tell me how you did that?"

"I can't."

"That whole 'magician's never reveal their secrets' thing?"

"Something like that," he smiled, only this time with such a lack of innocence, his eyes seemed almost devious. It made her like him even more. She tried to sneak a peek at his hands, his sleeves and his pockets, to see where he might have palmed the strange device. But all she could find was his mischievous smile.

"Well, you tricked me good, Malcolm," she said, and briefly wondered why her hands were still tingling. She flexed her fingers with sudden concern. Hands, after all, were the most important thing to a surgeon. And this prickly sensation was beginning to border on the uncomfortable.

"Did you spill something on me?" She sniffed her hands to see if she could detect any trace of acetone or astringent. "That's not very safe, you know. Doctors have to remain sanitary."

"I didn't spill anything, Dr. Reynolds." The strange child moved closer, his large soft eyes never moving from hers.

"I just gave you what you want. That's all." His sincerity quickly returned the tears to her eyes. She wanted to hug him, but held back. These days, one never knows what accusations could be made when children are involved. Instead, she reached out for his small, delicate fingers.

"What I want, Malcolm…" His hand felt so comfortable and comforting in hers, like childhood returned. "…what I really want is to never, ever have to look at another person and tell them that their wife or husband is dead. Does that make sense?"

The boy considered this for a moment.

"This is better," he said at last.

She had to smile. How simple life seems at that age. How complex and cruel it becomes, once the comforting curtain of youth slips from our eyes.

"I'm sure it is," she squeezed his tiny hands. "Now don't you think we both better climb out of this silly old closet and find someone to take you home?"

"Okay. Don't feel empty anymore, Dr. Reynolds."

"Thanks, Malcolm. I'll try not to."

"You won't," he said simply.

Dr. Christine Reynolds opened the supply closet door, straightened her scrubs and stepped awkwardly out into the hallway. She was holding the door open for her small companion, when she felt a hand on her shoulder.

"There you are, Christine. I've been looking all over for you."

She turned quickly to see the Head of Surgery for Marymount Community Hospital, the last person she wanted to see after losing a patient. Dr. Wesley Edgehill was tall, abnormally so, which allowed him to loom over subordinates with well-practiced condescension.

"Dr. Edgehill. I didn't see you there."

"I assumed that." Edgehill had a way of making every word sound like a disappointment, which he felt was a valuable trait in an administrator. "Why are you holding that door?" he asked.

"For Malcolm."

"And who is this Malcolm?"

"He's…" Christine poked her head inside the supply closet and saw it was empty. The small boy had slipped past them both, while she was distracted by Dr. Edgehill. She shook her head. "…a magician. Apparently, a very good one."

"Uh-huh."

Dr. Edgehill eyed her curiously, then appeared to grow bored with his appraisal. He dismissed any further conversation with a wave.

"I need your report on the Myers case. Have it on my desk by nine AM, along with a detailed explanation of everything that went wrong."

"Nothing went wrong. It was just…" but the head of surgery had already stomped a good distance down the hall. To Christine, Dr. Edgehill embodied the businesslike sterility of modern medicine. Yet it was that very aloofness she needed to develop, or she would be doomed to a career of endless meltdowns in a variety of hospital supply closets.

Dr. Christine Reynolds wiped her still-tingling hands on her drab green surgical scrubs and quickly put Malcolm out of her mind.

****

The Kroger supermarket was unusually quiet for a Friday night, and Christine Reynolds enjoyed the brightly colored solitude of the deserted aisles. She was in the mood for mindless consumerism, comforted by the knowledge that the only important decision she would have to make tonight was which brand of spaghetti sauce would ultimately end up in her shopping cart. When even this proved too taxing, she grabbed whatever was nearest to her outstretched hand.

Friday night shopping had become a ritual with her, the closest thing to a social life since medical school. She enjoyed watching from a distance; the young lovers with their hungry, hurried kisses; the middle-aged parents endlessly sharing the latest triumphs or frustrations of their children; even the elderly couples, no longer aware they were holding hands because a lifetime of shared memories had meshed their hearts as comfortably as their intertwined fingers. She envied the peace they found in each other's presence. She admired their sublime obliviousness to the headlong rush of fate, which would someday subject their hard-won relationship to the razor edge of a scalpel. Her scalpel.

Each self-absorbed pair insulated themselves with the promise of togetherness, while she saw only its bloody end. As she pushed her shopping cart past the produce counter, Christine's eyes were once more ambushed by untimely emotion.

Christine took her place in the checkout line behind a pair of leather-clad teenagers, and a short, gray haired woman, who tried to put as much distance between herself and the teens as the rows of cash registers would allow. The youths threw down a handful of crumpled bills and snatched up the two packs of unfiltered cigarettes in one swift motion, then left the store with a crescendo of guttural laughter. The elderly woman finally allowed herself to breathe with their absence, before moving to unload her groceries onto the checkout counter. The bored cashier watched the gray-haired woman struggle with the twenty-pound bag of dried dog food in her cart, without offering to help. It was then that Christine noticed the pulsating splotch on the front of the elderly woman's blouse.

"Excuse me, but I believe you have something on you," Christine offered helpfully.

"Do I? Why thank you, dear." The woman brushed at her chest, but could not seem to wipe off the fluorescent spot. After a few abortive attempts, she turned back to Christine with a confused expression. "Where?"

"Right there. That glowing yellow spot."

"Yellow spot?"

"Right by your heart."

The gray-haired woman seemed even more confused. She looked up at the lethargic cashier, who merely shrugged.

It was none of his business.

"I have a tissue in my purse, if you want…" but the woman's sudden anger stopped the young doctor in mid-sentence. She turned her back to Christine and refused to look at her until the groceries were paid for and she was halfway out the automatic glass doors. At that point, the gray-haired woman turned back to Christine and gave her the finger.

The cashier forgot his boredom long enough to squeeze out a single blast of derisive laughter.

****

"Doctor Blue to the Emergency Room. Doctor Blue."

The call for assistance sent five trauma specialists dashing down the hospital hallways. 'Doctor Blue' was a code used by Marymount, so patients would not become unnecessarily alarmed. But every hospital employee knew what it meant.

Doctor Blue.

'Dying Patient, Respond Immediately.'

Christine, who had just arrived for her Saturday morning shift, charged through the Emergency Room doors with only one sleeve in her smock. The trauma team was already swarming about a table with the panicked efficiency that had earned them the highest survival rate in the state.

"Status!" Christine yelled, as senior physician present.

"Massive myocardial infarction!" Nurse Hemming shouted. "Approximately seventy-year-old female. Ambulance just brought her in."

"Breathing?"

"Negative."

"Pulse?"

"Lost it twenty seconds ago."

"Prep for voltage!" Christine directed the well-rehearsed cacophony without thought. This is what she trained for, and if truth be told, what she lived for. These precious few seconds between life and death. Her only chance to make a difference in this world.

Arnold Gersh grabbed the defibrillator paddles and raised them ominously above the table.

"Clear!" he yelled.

The attending staff stepped back in unison, as the powerful electrodes convulsed the patient's chest, flinging her body up off the table for an anxious millisecond. The electrodes retreated and the staff rushed in anew, searching for any telltale sign of life.

"No pulse."

"Hit her again," ordered Christine.

"Clear!" barked Arnold Gersh.

For a second time, the stricken body jerked under the powerful current. But the woman's heart still refused to beat. Christine examined her face, then gasped.

It was the elderly woman from the grocery store.

The one who had given her the finger.

"Pulse?"

Nurse Hemming felt the carotid artery. Nothing.

"Initiating CPR!" Christine said, then suddenly held up her hand to prevent Nurse Hemming from initiating the emergency procedure. "Wait! What's that on her?!"

It was the same luminescent mark, only larger now. It completely covered the woman's heart.

And it was dangerously brighter.

"What the hell is that?!" Christine yelled.

"What?" shouted Nurse Hemming. "What is what?"

"That glow."

Every face turned to look at Christine, not the spot.

"What glow?" asked the anesthesiologist.

"There! Right there!" Christine placed her hand directly on the spot, and was suddenly hit with a torrent of heat and dizziness. Her vision wavered and she staggered back a step. Arnold Gersh was inches from her face, yelling something. She saw his lips move, but all she could hear was the heavy pounding of her own heartbeat. She realized she had stopped breathing, but could not remember how long ago.

Then, just as suddenly, the heat, the dizziness and the pounding ceased.

"Dr. Reynolds, if we don't initiate CPR now, we will lose this patient!"

Christine looked at him, then at the patient, and finally at the flickering light that somehow only she could see. Everything became hyper-defined, as if she were trapped in a dream, or a virtual reality simulation. And just as suddenly, she knew exactly what she had to do.

To the shock and horror of everyone in the surgical theater, she pulled off her gloves and stepped closer to the patient.

"Give me room!" she ordered, before placing her hands over the ghostly illumination on the dying woman's chest.

A fierce wave of nausea washed over her, followed by a sharp, stabbing pain that ran from her fingers to her chest and stomach. The acrid odor of electrical discharge filled her nostrils. The emergency room seemed to blink and fade around her, until only its brightest colors penetrated the translucent veil that fell over her vision. Every noise muffled and slowed, like the sound one hears from the bottom of a swimming pool.

Christine saw the light from the woman's chest pass through her own hands, then slowly recede. It wasn't until the strange glow dissipated, and was no more, that she removed her hands. The room, or her perception of it, immediately returned to normal.

"We have a pulse!" shouted Nurse Hemming.

"Respiration, too!" yelled Arnold Gersh.

"Blood pressure ninety over sixty and climbing. We got her back!"

As the trauma team buzzed with excitement, Dr. Christine Reynolds stumbled to a far corner of the room and tried to contemplate the enormity of what she had just experienced.

****

Thirty minutes later, the door to the physician's lounge flew open. A very agitated Dr. Edgehill filled the doorway, hands on his hips.

"You have exactly sixty seconds to explain yourself, Dr. Reynolds."

Christine shook her head.

"I'm not sure I could explain if you gave me sixty years," she said softly, then took another long comforting swallow from her coffee cup.

Edgehill yanked at an empty chair in front of Christine. He threw himself into it, his face tinted with frustration.

"As I understand it," he began in a steel-edged voice. "You prevented CPR on a patient with no vital signs, so that you could *lay your hands* on her like some kind of side show preacher!"

Christine could only nod.

"And what precisely caused you to violate standard surgical procedure and leave this hospital open to a massive negligence suit? Please tell me what made you suddenly decide to become an irresponsible fanatic when a patient's life was at stake?!"

"I... I saw a light."

"This is hardly the time for joking."

"I'm not joking. I saw a light over her heart and something...compelled me to touch it."

"Compelled you to touch it?"

"That's right."

"Do I look like an idiot to you, Dr. Reynolds? Do you think you can play me for some kind of fool?!"

Christine stood, her eyes flared with indignation.

"Look, Dr. Edgehill. You asked me what happened down there, and I told you. I have absolutely no scientific explanation for any of it, but dammit, it happened!"

"And now you think you're some kind of miracle worker, eh, Dr. Reynolds?"

"Of course not. But I'm not crazy either. The whole trauma team saw it. Ask them yourself."

"I already did," he spat out each word with careful precision. "And not one person present admits to seeing any kind of 'magical' light."

"They might not have seen it, but they saw the results. We ran tests. Dozens of tests! That woman was in complete cardiac arrest, but now she has the heart of a twenty-year-old. No evidence of damage whatsoever!"

Dr. Edgehill pursed his lips and was silent for nearly two full minutes. When he stood, he towered over his younger subordinate. Although she tried to hold her ground, Christine squirmed under his icy gaze.

"As of this moment, you are temporarily suspended, pending a full investigation."

"What?!"

"Dr. Marlowe will take over your patients until a meeting of the hospital's medical board can be convened."

"But that's not fair!"

"Perhaps. But it's cautious. We can't have you soiling the reputation of this institution with some New Age faith healing. So I'm recommending you home, Dr. Reynolds." He walked to the door, then turned to face her.

"And for Christ's sake, try not to perform any more goddam *miracles!*" Dr. Edgehill bellowed, as he slammed the door behind him.

****

For a long while after he left, Christine sat alone in the normally crowded physicians' lounge. From time to time, other doctors would poke their heads in, excuse themselves with poorly hidden derision and exit as quickly as they could.

She didn't blame them. After all, she was a freak. What she had done defied every scientific principal she had ever learned. It was the stuff of charlatans and TV evangelists, who traded in the commerce of illusion, so they could bilk the faithful out of well-intentioned donations.

To Dr. Edgehill and her coworkers, Christine, with her mysterious light and healing touch, had even less credibility.

She was a medical practitioner.

A woman of science.

She, of all people, should know better.

And perhaps they were right. Maybe through some freak electrical discharge or random alignment of circumstances she *had* saved the woman's life. But what did that prove? She had saved hundreds of patients throughout her career. And done it the proper way, with scalpel, clamps and sutures. She could even understand Dr. Edgehill's position, in this era of TV lawyers eager to sue physicians without the slightest provocation. If the woman were to suffer a relapse, what then? What medical chart would the next attending physician be able to read? What surgery or treatment could she claim to have performed?

Dr. Edgehill was right. She was a danger to the hospital and her patients. Best to go home, take a few weeks off. Maybe she could...

The door swung open again with an authoritative whoosh and clatter. A familiar figure stared down at her with stern brown eyes.

"Get off your butt, Doctor," ordered Nurse Lorinda. "We have some big time experimenting to do."

****

The two medical professionals moved the hallways of Marymount Community Hospital, in search of patients with strange glowing lights.

"This is ridiculous, Lorinda," Christine whispered. "Even if I see another one of those...those marks, what am I supposed to do? Heal somebody?"

"That is the profession you chose, Dr. Reynolds."

"No. I chose *medicine*. Not magic."

Lorinda stopped. The large nurse grabbed her superior by the shoulders and stared harshly into her face. "What are you afraid of, Christine? That you just may have some miraculous gift? Some inexplicable ability to save people's lives?"

The young doctor's face paled. Her bottom lip slipped between trembling teeth.

"No," she mumbled. "I'm afraid I won't be able to..."

****

Cardiac Care Ward, Room 17.

Patient: Armando Poncé, 39.

Chain smoker.

Three heart attacks of varying severity.

Scheduled for quadruple bypass.

Prognosis: dim.

Distinguishing Characteristics: large, glowing yellow light, invisible to everyone, except Dr. Christine Reynolds.

Armando Poncé stretched out motionless on the hospital bed, tubes running up his nose, in his arms, and electrodes connected to flashing monitors throughout the room. The patient's mouth hung dryly open, his tobacco-stained teeth chewing at nothing in particular, while his wife Theresa, and teenage daughters sniffed sorrow into embroidered kerchiefs.

Lorinda approached the sobbing women with a gentleness Christine had never seen in the gruff and efficient surgical nurse.

"Mrs. Poncé, you know your husband is very ill. I would like your permission to try something...unusual. It may not work, but I believe it is worth a try. For your husband's sake." She spoke in Spanish, a quiet insistence to her words.

"Qué haria ustéd?" asked distraught wife. "What would you do?"

The large nurse gestured to Christine. She raised her palms in the universal symbol for bafflement, yet never lost her smile. Theresa Poncé, who had grown up with a poor woman's unshakable faith, understood. She turned to her stricken husband, clutched his gray hands with affection. What followed was a long, whispered conversation in Spanish, with everyone in the room throwing furtive glances at the nervous surgeon, who shuffled uncomfortably under their gaze. Their voices grew louder, and the two daughters tried even harder to hide their newly flowing tears behind their embroidered kerchiefs.

After a long pause, the solemn wife nodded her permission. Lorinda clutched Theresa's hands and passed the nod to Christine.

"You're on, Dr. Reynolds." she said.

Dr. Christine Reynolds felt every bit as nervous as the day she performed her first surgical operation. Yet today, she was not wielding a scalpel, something tangible, something she could believe in. Today, she was wielding a dream, a childhood wish that frightened her to the core, because whatever happened in the next few moments, she was sure it would change her life forever.

Christine shuffled over to the bed. She removed a tangle of wires and electrodes from Armando's ribcage. The patient looked up at her with unblinking faith, a man to whom every doctor was a miracle worker. His confidence in her abilities unnerved her even more.

After an extended serrated breath, she spread her palms and wavering fingers over the pulsating glow, which spread ominously across his chest.

Again came the waves of dizziness, the acrid smell, the stultifying nausea. The hospital room melting away into a thick liquid wash of colors and movement. Sounds slowing, amplifying, savaging her ears. A searing pain migrating from her hands, to her arms, then invading her own breast and stomach with stabbing insistence.

She might have been screaming, she wasn't sure. The only thing she could be sure of was the luminescence that joined their souls, and the free-floating eyes of Armando Poncé that glowed with joy and amazement.

As before, the glow flickered, then gradually receded from her hands in a brief ballet of pinpoint sparks. When the light was gone, the room slowly returned to its normal shape and sharpness. Christine Reynolds threw her back against the wall for support, and let her agonizingly heavy hands collapse to her sides.

Lorinda rushed forward to check the patient's vital statistics.

"Pulse 75 and strong. No murmur or erratic beating. Blood pressure one-ten over seventy."

Theresa Poncé and her daughters executed a sign of the cross in unison. They began excitedly whispering something in Spanish that sounded vaguely like 'miracle.'

Lorinda's voice rose. "Near as I can tell, his vital signs, as well as all these monitors here, say Mr. Poncé is as strong as a horse!" She then translated her rampaging enthusiasm into Spanish.

The three Poncé women erupted in laughter and tears. The younger girls hugged their Papa, while Theresa gingerly lifted Christine's fingers and kissed each one.

"Gracias" she whispered, with an appreciation that sliced through the surgeon's own uncontrollable laughter and tears.

****

For the next two hours, they moved through the cardiac wing, extinguishing each of those strange glowing lights only Christine could see.

Room after room. Patient after patient. Nurses, interns, janitors, and a joyous mob of grateful family and visitors accompanied the healing procession through the halls of Marymount Community Hospital. They knew they were part of something rare and wondrous, and the contagious exuberance spread through each spectator like a turbocharged New Year's Eve celebration.

Eleven patients. Eleven times she descended into that between-world of stabbing pain and liquid reality. When the last glow was extinguished, she was nearing collapse, and Lorinda had to strong-arm her past the cheering, worshipping crowd. Still they pursued her, eager to touch her jacket, kiss her hands. But what Dr. Christine Reynolds wanted more than anything else was sleep, the blissful comfort of temporary oblivion.

Lorinda stood guard outside her office and swore to let no one in until her unofficial patient awoke, not even Dr. Edgehill himself.

Christine Reynolds slept with her head on the cold oak desk, dreaming of a strange child named Malcolm, and the precious gift he had given her.

"It's what you always wanted," he had said.

But even now, she was not sure that was true.

****

Dr. Christine Reynolds stood before the fourteen members of Marymount Community Hospital's Board of Directors, in a scene reminiscent of the Spanish Inquisition. The nine men and three women arrayed in front of her scowled at the reports Dr. Edgehill had prepared for them. Then every face turned their scowls to her.

Nurse Lorinda, whose conduct was also being investigated, sat quietly in the back of the room, awaiting her turn.

The board members whispered angrily amongst themselves. Dr. Jeffrey McFarlane, the eighty-two-year-old Chairman of the Board, motioned the rest of his panel to silence. He stared at Christine with piercing black eyes.

"Dr. Reynolds, it seems you have created quite an uproar here at Marymount."

"That was clearly not my intention."

"I'm sure it wasn't. Tell me, Dr. Reynolds..." he leaned forward, sharp elbows punishing the huge walnut conference table. "Do you truly believe you are a miracle worker?"

The question took Christine by surprise. She hadn't really thought of it in those terms. A phrase like that was the antithesis of everything she had been trained to believe as a physician and scientist. Her answer had to be carefully phrased.

"I consider myself a medical anomaly, yet to be adequately explained," she replied slowly. "Nothing more."

"Still, the things you have accomplished seem pretty miraculous, wouldn't you say?"

"With all due respect, Dr. McFarlane," she raised her chin. "I would prefer not to say."

He smiled in reply. A chilling grin, fully devoid of warmth.

"I understand completely, Dr. Reynolds. However, your recent behavior does create some problems for our medical facility."

Dr. Edgehill, on the far end of the long conference table was the first to speak. "Dr. Reynolds' actions, aside from being bad medicine and wholly insubordinate, leaves us open to a frightening degree of liability. These 'healings'...and I use that term loosely...carry an implied promise of full recovery. If any of these eleven patients were to have a relapse, they would find a thousand salivating lawyers eager to press malpractice claims against us. Our insurers will not consider the hospital acted responsibly in allowing Dr. Reynolds' voodoo displays to overrule sound medical practice. And the fact that I had just suspended her at the time..."

"It's not voodoo, Dr. Edgehill!" Christine fumed. "And I do not consider saving lives acting irresponsibly!"

Dr. Julia Thorngate, head of Physicians' Services, chimed in.

"Neither do we, Dr. Reynolds," she said with saccharin formality. "But even if we were to assume your...gift...is genuine, what kind of example are we setting for the younger doctors? This is, after all, a teaching hospital. Shall we ask each of them to ignore the knowledge and skills we are trying vigorously to impart, just so they can simply 'lay their hands' on a few patients and await a miracle?"

"I, for one, hope we are witnessing genuine miracles here," Dr. Irving Rosenblum added with a gentle smile. "But as a professional with more than thirty years in medicine, I am trained to be skeptical. I understand, Dr. Reynolds, that you only treat cardiac cases. Could you tell us why?"

"I'm not really sure, Dr. Rosenblum," Christine said softly. "I don't really understand any of this myself. I just go where the light leads me. And up until now, I have only witnessed it in cardiac patients."

"Do you understand how this might adversely affect our other departments, such as Oncology and Intensive Care?"

"Yes, sir. But I can't seem to do anything about that." She was genuinely affected by her limitations, and it showed in her face. "I guess as far as miracles are concerned, I've become something of a heart specialist..."

Her attempt at humor generated more scowls and silence.

"What I'm most concerned with..." interrupted Dr. Hiram Plotkin, head of the Finance Committee. "...is how we are supposed to bill for these treatments? Even if they do prove to be legitimate cures, how can we charge for what she does? What rate applies to non-medicinal healings?"

Dr. Peter Renfrew, Public Relations. "There's an even bigger problem I see here. Of the eleven people she allegedly healed, seven were white, three were Hispanic, and one was Pakistani. There were no Asians and no African Americans on the list. Can you imagine what the NAACP will do to us on this one?"

"Don't be absurd," Christine shouted. "I can only treat those who have that odd light. If they don't have it, I can't help them. And you want to make this a racial thing?"

"So you are implying that Asians and African Americans don't have your special light?"

"I don't know. I'm sure they do. But there were none present in the ward yesterday."

"How do we know that for sure? What if a minority patient did have that special light, but you simply chose not to treat them? After all, we have only your word that one patient can be healed and another cannot."

"So I'm a racist miracle worker trying to discredit science and bankrupt this hospital with non-billable cures? Is that what you're saying?!"

Dr. McFarlane stepped in. "Dr. Renfrew is saying no such thing. Merely that your preponderance of miracles along specific ethnic lines could be misinterpreted by the media to the detriment of this facility."

"Fine." Christine's face burned with exasperation. "So I'll go down to the West End and heal as many people as I can find. Don't you understand that I'd be happy to do that?! Don't you see that all I want to do...all I ever wanted to do...is save lives?! Black, white, none of that matters! These are patients we are talking about. Real people. Not quotas or statistics!"

Dr. Juanita Georges, Government Compliance. "I think we should also conduct a comparative analysis on the annual incomes of the eleven patients that were treated. Especially in light of the new federal health care proposals, we cannot be seen as favoring the affluent or middle-class..."

"We still haven't addressed the problem with billing," Dr. Plotkin interjected. "We could lose our Medicare funding because of this!"

The assembled directors began arguing amongst themselves. Christine wanted to throw something at them, to smash the heavy wooden conference table that distanced these experts from the real world. The world of gasping last breaths and squealing newborn infants. The world of life as it exists off-paper, in flesh and blood and dreams. She was about to heap upon them all her fiery opinions, when a new voice echoed across the large conference room.

"You sanctimonious, tunnel-visioned plutocrats!" Nurse Lorinda shouted at the stunned board members. "You've crawled so deep inside your bureaucratic specialties that you've lost sight of what made you become doctors in the first place! Like it or not, this woman saved lives. Saved lives that you couldn't. I don't know how and neither does she. It doesn't even matter how she did it. The point is, she made a difference! And you're all so concerned with your petty lawsuits and quotas and federal regulations that you..."

Yet even Lorinda stopped her tirade and fell into silence, when Christine Reynolds rose to her feet and reached out her hands, as if in a trance. She stumbled to the head of the long conference table. There, on the chest of Dr. Jeffrey McFarlane, Chairman of the Board of Directors, directly over his heart, appeared a large luminescent spot. It pulsed so vividly, that every person in the room could now see it. Each one gasped, but none more loudly than Dr. McFarlane himself.

Almost against her will, Dr. Christine Reynolds kicked aside a chair, crawled up onto the conference table and gently placed her hands on the glowing mark. For some inexplicable reason, they all felt it like a sledgehammer to their accepted reality. The acrid smell, the distorted vision. The nauseating dizziness. The aching, muffled sounds.

And the terrifying pain spreading from each of their splayed hands to their own heaving chests.

Nobody moved to stop her.

Nobody moved at all.

They held their breath and prayed to their various gods or science that it would stop.

Please let it stop.

Then they witnessed the terrifying glow evaporate from the quivering chest of Dr. McFarlane, and pass straight through the young surgeon's hands, before disappearing from their sight. In an instant, their familiar reality crashed in on them again.

When it was over, Dr. Georges and Dr. Rosenblum were crying. Everyone else was silent, or gasping for breath. They knew they had been witness to an inexplicable healing that, for all their medical knowledge, for all their surgical skill, they would never again experience in their lifetimes.

When she finally recovered, Dr. Christine Reynolds lightly patted Dr. Hiram McFarlane on the chest.

"On the house," she said with a wry smile. "You'll have my resignation in the morning."

The room was silent for a long time after she left, until the intercom buzzer broke the spell. Dr. McFarlane picked up the conference room phone, and his face drained of blood.

As he disconnected the line, he announced to the assembled Board of Directors:

"It seems we have a television news crew, and a roomful of reporters outside." He slumped back in chair. "Eager to interview the miracle worker of Marymount Community Hospital..."

****

Christine Reynolds placed a comforting arm around twelve-year-old Sha'Lethea, and dried the child's frightened eyes with a tissue.

"Your mother's going to be fine," she smiled. "Just fine."

As if to provide evidence to her words, Belinda Lincoln sat up on the hard metal cot and slowly stretched her arms in the air. Christine examined her eyes, then checked her pulse and blood pressure.

"How do you feel, Belinda?"

"Tired. Bone tired. But twenty years younger!"

"The fatigue will pass. It always does." She helped the large woman to her feet. "Now you stay away from those fried foods, and try to get a little rest now and then."

"Thank you, Dr. Reynolds."

"It's Miss Reynolds now. I'm no longer a licensed physician, remember?"

"That's their loss, Dr. Reynolds. Their loss. Far as I'm concerned, you're a miracle worker."

"Shhhhhh!" Christine whispered to a giggling Sha'Lethea. "That'll be our little secret."

The mother and daughter pushed their way through the tattered white curtain that separated this half of the cramped trailer from the equally small waiting area up front. Grateful for the silence, Christine Reynolds plopped down heavily into the rickety metal chair.

It had been an exhausting day, but a satisfying one.

She had just rested her tired hands on her lap, when Lorinda walked in.

"That's the last of them for today. How do you feel?"

"Drained."

"Are you sure you're up for the nursing home tomorrow?"

Christine smiled. Even without her official Marymount scrubs, Lorinda couldn't help but be the consummate nurse.

"I'm fine. Lorinda. But are you sure this date thing tonight is really necessary? I mean, I don't even know this guy, and there's so much I have to do."

The big woman placed her hands firmly on her hips. "Listen to me, miracle worker," she said sternly. "I've already set the whole thing up. And in matters of the heart, *I'm* the miracle worker around here."

Miss Christine Reynolds, former heart surgeon, surrendered to her friend's fierce loyalty. She leaned her weary head against the wall, and once again thrilled to the life-affirming tingle in her weary hands.

The Promise

Comfortably enveloped in darkness, Patrick LeBlanc once again let his mind drift back to that fateful night nearly twenty years ago.

He thought of his father, of course, the soft-spoken little man who had once been his idol and protector, but who, fault by accumulating fault, gradually became frailer, more human, and finally, ridiculous as Patrick approached his teenage years.

Patrick's father, Martin LeBlanc was quiet, almost pathologically unassuming. His receding hairline had at last retired to the back of his skull, leaving only thin tufts of wiry brown hair above each ear. His gold wire-rimmed glasses made his narrow, bird-like eyes appear even smaller. It was easy to tell he was destined to become no more than a career bureaucrat, a mole-like functionary buried deep in the bowels of a government job that had long since lost any sense of purpose.

His assignment involved overseeing the stockpiling of helium gas for the federal government. Following World War I, the U.S. Army needed to ensure it had enough of the lighter-than-air gas to float their anticipated armada of military zeppelins, blimps and dirigibles. More than sixty years had passed since the army actually flew a blimp for military purposes, and market forces proved far more capable of supplying enough helium for any commercial needs. Yet in true government fashion, a perpetuation of idiocy is always preferable to the sudden shock of fiscal responsibility. Money must be paid out, for no other reason than it had been paid out in the past. Programs had to continue simply because someone had allowed them to continue up until now. And staff size and budgets must grow each year, whether they need to or not. Such is the government way; the enemy of practicality and common sense. And so, the underground stockpiling of helium for outdated war machines continued, and the program's budget automatically expanded by ten percent per year. Martin LeBlanc's tireless efforts allowed him to percolate up the rank to Third Undersecretary in charge of the largest, and most superfluous, subterranean gas hoard in the world. And he was damn proud of it.

Martin was dedicated, to be sure. And meticulous to a fault. Some might even say compulsive. Coworkers whispered that his persnickety nature was probably the main reason his wife had left him, the poor bastard. Miriam LeBlanc had run off to Montana on the arm of an elderly pseudo-cowboy with bad teeth, shortly after the birth of their son.

The pain of his wife's departure forced a sudden transformation in Martin. He became overly protective of his son. Fiercely so. Every night, he tucked the small boy in bed, kissed him good night, and repeated the same promise...

"I'll never let anyone else hurt you, Patrick."

For his part, Patrick LeBlanc remembered his father always being by his side, a source of comfort and pride for a small child, but a growing cause of agony and embarrassment for an emerging teenager. Patrick could still envision the look in his father's eyes the day he insisted it was uncool to kiss your Dad once you reached the eighth grade. His father spoke not a word, but his small eyes could not conceal the depth of his anguish.

Every night after that, Martin LeBlanc would say goodnight to the young man he had raised by himself through all those lonely years. He would maintain a respectful distance and repeat his promise.

"I'll never let anyone else hurt you," he would whisper into the darkened room.

"Yeah, right," young Patrick would snicker to himself, as the door to his bedroom would swing softly shut. "Some protector. Conan the Librarian."

Then, the frustrated youth would fall asleep and dream of real heroes.

****

It was a suffocating late August, and the air that night felt as soggy and sodden as an invisible sponge hanging over the small Baltimore apartment. The searing summer heat refused to surrender even after the sun escaped the horizon. The stars themselves seemed to glisten with sweat, tiredly twinkling in a sky thick and black as used motor oil.

Martin LeBlanc, the diminutive man who made punctuality feel like a four letter word, was nearly three hours late from work. But Patrick wasn't concerned. He had just turned fourteen, and proudly stood eye-to-eye with his stoop-shouldered father. It's about time he had a night to take care of himself for a change.

Patrick wolfed down a frozen dinner of rubberized turkey and a pasty something purported to be mashed potatoes, then belched out loud, simply because he was alone and he could. He watched the beginning of a horror movie on TV, but decided he was too grown up to be scared, so he turned it off. Just to show his father how responsible he was, he decided he would go to bed early. Maybe his Dad would be impressed and leave him alone in the house more often.

That night, there was no little man to turn off the bedroom light. No fatherly goodnight. No ritual promise. Patrick LeBlanc closed his fourteen-year-old eyes and managed to convince himself that growing up was a good thing. Before he drifted off, the newly designated man of the house briefly wondered if he had remembered to close and lock the outside door.

He was sound asleep by the time the knife sliced through the screen door in the back of the house.

The two intruders pulled 9 mm Glocks out of their black hoodies and stepped quietly into the house.

****

A mile and a half away, members of the Washington, DC fire department pulled the dazed truck driver from his shattered vehicle. There was no doubt the man would live, which proved once again, that the universe possessed a well-developed sense of irony. The high level of alcohol which coursed through the man's veins shielded him from the panic of last-second impact, and in so doing, helped him walk away unscathed from an accident that would have pancaked a sober man. Of course, if he had been sober, his eighteen-wheeler might have stayed in the lane he had been traveling, so no accident would have occurred at all.

The drunk driver, freed from his crumpled cab, stumbled to the grassy shoulder and immediately threw up.

Officer Kinslow of the State Police cuffed him, mid-vomit.

The driver of the other vehicle had not been so lucky.

The aging Volkswagen Beetle sideswiped by the swerving truck sat crumpled in the highway like a discarded ball of aluminum foil. The wrinkled hood stuck straight up in the air, like a final salute of defiance mere inches from the shattered windshield. The driver of the Volkswagen looked as bad as his car. The driver's head was awash in blood, his wire-rimmed glasses twisted and broken, with one lens piercing his small right eye. Officer Kinslow called for the jaws of life. They would have to pry what's left of this one from his vehicle, the poor bastard.

A flurry of firemen attached the vise-like claw to the buckled door of the VW bug. The metal groaned and screamed as the door bent back under the massive metallic fingers. Half the mangled body fell sideways out the door, its semi-collapsed head bouncing off the asphalt with a disquieting splat. The legs remained pinned by the dashboard shoved halfway to the headrests.

"Jesus," groaned Officer Kinslow. "This one better get a closed casket, the poor bastard. Scrape him up, will ya?"

"Almost there," wheezed one of the burly fireman, adding more torque to the mechanical jaws.

"Would you speed it up, please?" came the softly spoken voice from halfway under the screeching mechanism.

"Christ!" screamed the fireman, as all three of the rescue workers jumped back as one, causing the huge groaning contraption to fall squarely on the shattered torso, which inexplicably began to lift itself off the bloodied asphalt.

"He's alive! Get that thing off him!" screamed Officer Kinslow, in a far higher pitch than he was used to. "Move it! Move it!"

All three rescue workers overcame their shock, and dove back in to rescue the impossibly mangled man, now observing them patiently from below the car, while half his body was still wedged inside.

"I appreciate your assistance," he said with a soft, unassuming voice.

The smashed passenger door was torn off its hinges, clattering to the pavement below. The diminutive driver used his crushed and contorted right arm to pull his head into something close to upright, and then began to thread the rest of his body through the narrow opening.

"Excuse me," he said.

The rescue workers stepped back, not knowing what else to do.

"Give him space," one whispered.

"Hell, yeah…" another shuddered, as they watched what should have been another bloody traffic casualty attempt to plant his twisted feet on the ground, then slowly begin clomping unsteadily away from the wreckage. The rescue workers stepped back even further, but the small man with the semi-crushed head paid them no notice. It wasn't until he was throwing a contorted leg over the highway guardrail that Officer Kinslow approached him warily.

"Sir… Beg pardon, sir!"

But the man kept on walking, growing ever steadier the further he moved from the crumpled hulk of his vehicle. Kinslow had no choice but to pursue.

"Listen, buddy. You better sit down. The ambulance is coming."

The man stopped. Turned to Kinslow with strangely dulled eyes. "I have to get home," he said in a soft, confused voice.

In nine years as a State Trooper, Kinslow had seen many examples of shock, and this guy bore all the signs.

"You can't go anywhere," he reassured the injured man. "You've just received a terrible trauma. It's amazing you made it out of that wreck alive!"

"I must go home," the man repeated in a daze. "I promise I'll come back. However, I simply have to go home now."

Officer Kinslow encouraged the man into a sitting position with a gentle, but irresistible downward force. He yelled at one of the nervous firefighters to throw a wool blanket over the man, and get something to stop all the blood from spilling out of his gaping head wound.

The rest of his words were swallowed up by the sudden roar of the Volkswagen Beetle exploding in flames.

The crippled car breathed its last with an impressive fireball of gas and burning upholstery. Kinslow helped the firemen unstring their hoses in a half-hearted attempt to contain the blaze. When the fire at last died down, Kinslow returned his attention to the victim.

"Where the hell did he go?" Kinslow asked the nearest fireman.

"I dunno," shrugged the soot-faced man. "But he said he'd be back."

****

The menacing footsteps pounding up the stairs yanked Patrick LeBlanc from his dreams of semi-innocent lust.

Something was wrong, his brain shrieked in silent alarm. Those were not his father's carefully measured footsteps. They were rougher, heavier.

More threatening.

His chest spasmed with sudden terror.

With all the speed of frightened prey, the fourteen-year-old dove into the bedroom closet and quietly pulled the door shut behind him. He tried to silence his panicked breath, as the heavy footsteps clomped down the hall, stopped, then invaded his room. The terrified teen sat in the darkened closet, frantically wishing he was safely cocooned in the far less frightening world he had known as a child.

He bit his lower lip to keep from sobbing out loud.

He knew the stranger with the heavy footsteps wouldn't be fooled so easily. The bed sheets were rumpled and tossed, the mattress still warm. He hoped the stranger with the heavy footsteps would just take all his Dad's money and leave him alone.

Patrick's heart sank as the heavy steps approached the closet door.

Even in the darkness, he could see the knob begin to twist.

The closet door was flung open and the terrified boy stared straight into the lethal black tunnel of a 9mm automatic. He could not look away from the mesmerizing gun barrel, even when the stranger with the heavy footsteps' gruff and bitter voice echoed in his ears.

"Anybody else home, kid?"

Patrick tried to answer, but no words could escape his painfully restricted throat. There was not enough air in his lungs to force the words out. After a moment, his eyes watched the terrible weapon swing lazily upward, then come crashing down on the side of his face. There was a merciful few seconds free of pain, before a searing agony rippled across his swelling cheekbone.

"I said," the gruff voice sneered at him. "Anybody else home?!"

"Nobody. Nobody else...My Dad, he didn't...didn't come home yet."

Another voice, higher in pitch, but just as brutal, called from the hall.

"It's clean. Bed's still made. Kid's tellin' the truth."

And then that horrible, hypnotic gun barrel once more took over Patrick's entire visible world. The bone-numbing click of the hammer being pulled back reverberated in the frightened boy's skull.

"Bad luck for you, kid..." The gruff voice muttered, an instant before it screamed in surprise.

The whole thing happened so quickly, Patrick had trouble later recounting the story to the police. First, he was staring down the barrel of the gun, gasping out his final, desperate prayers. Then the gun fell away, and he watched the stranger with the heavy footsteps crash to the floor, a large carving knife buried deep in his back. Another knife flashed an arc of silver death, as it sunk its sharpened blade into the man's thick neck. A splattering stream of dark blood flew into the closet, spattering onto the face of the terrified boy.

Patrick looked up.

Silhouetted by the moonlight pouring into the hallway, he saw a small mangled figure, whispering words he had heard a thousand times.

"I won't let anyone else hurt you, Patrick," came the soft, lifeless voice. "I promise."

Patrick could do nothing more than sit in the hellish closet and stare at the surprised mask of death on the stranger with the heavy footsteps. Then he heard three sharp gunshots, followed by an agonizing scream. The young boy closed his eyes and prayed. The sound of a body hitting the floor wafted up from the kitchen below.

His heart froze in his chest. He wanted nothing more than to be a little boy again.

After what seemed like hours, but could have been minutes, or even seconds, Patrick's mind flooded with images of his father. The frail, stooped nothing of a man with ridiculously small eyes. The little bureaucrat with the rounded shoulders.

The man who had just saved his life.

Patrick knew what he had to do. He willed his legs to move, and carefully climbed to a standing position. He suffered through another icy moment of paralysis before he could bring himself to step over the huge body creating a black puddle of blood on the floor in front of him. He stretched his throbbing legs over it, half-expecting the stranger with the heavy footsteps to rise up at any second, like the unkillable monster in so many low-budget horror movies.

But this wasn't a movie.

This was life.

This was death, in all its ugliness and terror.

As his grateful feet touched down on the other side of the dead body, Patrick grabbed the baseball bat by his bed, gulped hard, then made his way towards the stairs. He decided he would rather be found with a baseball bat in his dying hands, then crumpled and cowering in his bedroom closet.

He was his father's son. And he had a favor to return.

But Patrick LeBlanc never got the chance.

On the downstairs kitchen floor lay the stranger with the high-pitched voice. A cleaver stuck out from the two separated sections of his throat. A look of almost silly surprise on his dead face.

Patrick stared at the body in disbelief. Reality was never this graphic. Nightmares never so frightening.

A burgundy trail of splatters led straight to the open front door and beyond. Step by terrified step, the young boy followed it outside, his junior league baseball bat still clutched in his trembling hands.

"Dad! Dad!" Patrick's cries poured out with all the hot anguish in his heart. But his father was already limping halfway across their neighbor's lawn. For a moment, he thought he saw the small man turn to face him, but there were way too many tears clouding Patrick's vision.

By the time he wiped his eyes clean, his father was gone.

Patrick LeBlanc sunk to his knees, his thin body wracked by sobs. A moment later, the sobbing figure in the doorway was bathed in alternating red and blue lights, as police cruisers squealed up to the curb in front of his open door.

****

The morning papers broke the story that dominated national headlines for the next few weeks. The stranger with the heavy footsteps and his high-pitched accomplice were wanted in several states for a string of burglaries, home invasions and murders. Yet their gruesome deaths were less easily explained. The story from the frightened child witness made no sense. The bloody fingerprints on the knives which killed the two alleged robbers belonged to the homeowner, Martin LeBlanc, government bureaucrat, yet he was trapped in a car a mile and a half away. Witnesses at the scene of that accident spoke of a little man with small eyes, who crawled back into what little remained of a wrecked and smoldering Volkswagen Beetle, put his shattered head down on the charred steering wheel, and then never moved again.

Neither Officer Kinslow, nor the team of firefighters and rescue workers could explain how a man with the traumatic injuries Martin LeBlanc sustained could possibly have walked three miles to his house and back. The county coroner had to be served a subpoena before he would nervously testify that all indications suggested Martin LeBlanc had died instantly at the scene of the accident. The exasperated coroner would not even venture a guess as to how the victim also came to receive three bullet wounds to the chest, all delivered post-mortum. Ballistics confirmed the bullets in Martin LeBlanc's body were fired from a pistol clutched in the hand of a stranger hacked to death in a home a mile and a half away.

Weeks passed. The funeral was one of the largest a mid-level government bureaucrat had ever received. Patrick was sent off to live with his grandparents, who tried in vain to shelter him from the tabloid press.

Eventually, the bizarre mystery of Martin LeBlanc: 'Dead Man Walking' - faded from the public consciousness, resurrected only in urban legends that began with, "I know a guy, who knew a guy, who had a friend, that swore he saw..."

****

Now, twenty years later, Patrick LeBlanc stood silently in the shadow-filled room, listening to the soft breathing of his three-year-old son. A childish nightmare of flying alligators soothed back to gentle slumber by the warm presence of a loving father. After he was sure the small child was safely asleep, Patrick LeBlanc leaned over the bed and kissed his son's sweet-smelling hair.

"I will never let anyone hurt you, Martin," he whispered to the slumbering child.

"I promise."

Buried Alive

"Do you really have to go tonight?"

Kelly Miller looked up from her Calculus II textbook and directed her question to the open bedroom door. Wrinkles of concern encroached upon her soft green eyes, as they always did when she had 'that feeling' about something. She was only twenty-four, but had learned long ago not to dismiss her dark premonitions too easily. Women's intuition or excessive anxiety, whatever it was, had served her well over the years.

That time in Atlantic City, for example.

The door swung open and Kevin angled his head in, so that only his upper body was visible. She loved to look at his unkempt blond hair, his lanky shoulders, his quirky smile. She drank in his presence, as he tried to wrestle a passable knot into the new tie she had bought him for their sixty-day wedding anniversary.

"What did you say, sweetheart?" That quirky smile again that melted her heart. God, how she loved this man. She bit her lower lip to concentrate on the problem at hand.

"I said, do you really, really, really have to go there tonight?"

"Of course, I do, sweetheart," he replied with transparent enthusiasm. "We need this extra income. At least until you graduate from Princeton and become the world's highest paid mathematician."

The feeling of hovering dread hit her again, a prickly wave that crawled crablike across her neck and shoulders. "You know that place gives me the creeps," she shuddered.

"Well, that's what Calculus does to me." The tie finally conceded the match, allowing itself to be yanked into position around his throat. Mission accomplished, he eased over to her desk and slipped a gentle arm around his new wife's slender shoulders. They had been married just long enough for the touch to instantly suggest memories of shared passion that shot tingles of excitement up his arm. With all the comfort he could muster, he said, "Look. It's only three nights a week. I could sleepwalk through this gig. All I have to do is circle the perimeter once every two hours. Then, I can spend the rest of my time curled up with my Ancient Civ book."

It was not the answer she wanted to hear, and he knew it. But he knew her well enough to gently kiss the worry lines from her forehead and lips, which then led to a flurry of soft kisses on her chin, her cheeks, her eyelids. He loved the smell of her hair, as well as the sweet, endearing way she knocked him on his butt whenever he tried to distract her from studying.

"Rein in the hormones, buster. Romance and mathematics don't mix."

"I don't know about that." he moved closer again. "After all, one goes into one..."

"Not tonight, it doesn't." Her low growl meant she reverted to Serious Kelly again, and he backed off, which immediately made her feel guilty; such is the wonderfully empathetic choreography of the newly married.

"I don't like this job, Kevin." She feared she was being foolish, or worse, a nagging wife like her overbearing mother had been to her dad. The memory made her shudder, then soften, but she couldn't let it go. "I just don't like it."

"What's the big deal?" he shrugged, grabbing a Yankees cap his old college roommate had left behind. He tried it on, scowling in the mirror, then tossed it aside. "I'm a night watchman. No biggie."

"It's a graveyard, Kevin!"

"No, it's not... It's a cemetery. And a very nice one at that."

"You'll be surrounded by a bunch of dead people."

"That's usually the way it works. If you bury live ones, they tend to complain."

She sighed, tapped her frustrations out on the textbook with a mechanical pencil. They had been through this all before. Way too many times. Money was tight, and she knew they really had no choice. One of them had to work, and her course load was much harder than his. Besides, the salary was astoundingly good, and that sleazy Dominic character did tell Kevin he could study between his nightly rounds.

Still, she couldn't shake this icy feeling tingling her hairline.

Damn these premonitions...

"It just doesn't feel right," she frowned again.

He held her tightly from behind, felt the concern knot up in her shoulders. Tried to coo and kiss it away, and eventually succeeded.

"Married only three months," she purred under his touch. "...and already my husband is spending the night with other women."

She reached up behind her to stroke his tousled gold hair, the back of his neck. "And dead ones at that," she murmured between sighs, as she slowly retracted her argument against distraction.

****

The first thing visitors usually noticed was that there were no woods in the ironically named Mount Forest Memorial Park, and no mountain either. Merely a few slightly raised mounds caused by the burial of large family groups over the decades.

It was also clear that the physical decay of this once magnificent garden cemetery could be traced to its questionable change in ownership.

Mount Forest had once been the premier resting place in New Jersey. The cemetery of choice for much of the East Coast's upper crust families. Its manicured lawns, diverse botanical wonders and exquisite statuary evoked images of an idyllic afterlife, where the souls of the dear departed became one with the enduring tranquility of this garden paradise.

Albert H. Whitcombe, who founded the cemetery back in 1898, helped popularize the shift from stark graveyards and potters' fields to the gentle ambiance of the stately memorial park. The serenity of death had been his life's obsession, and it was manifested as much in his own ornate mausoleum, as in the beauty of the cemetery itself. Here, death was merely a pastoral stroll between life and eternity. Those who had passed through that golden portal could commune with nature's splendor, before inevitably completing their journey to the wondrous beyond.

That is, until three decades ago, when the Strazelli family took over. Nobody quite understood why the Strazellis, who had made a fortune in the construction business, would be interested in buying a century-old cemetery. Yet the decline of Mount Forest began the very day Dominic Strazelli, Sr. walked through the elaborate iron gates of the venerable memorial park.

The lush and diverse gardens, which once earned the praise of botanists around the country, soon withered and died due to lack of care. Lawns were mowed haphazardly, and even the amount of space between graves was greatly reduced. The elegant funeral processions of the Nineteen-Thirties and Forties gave way to the "dig a hole and plant 'em" style which characterized the Strazelli family stewardship.

The Eastern Quadrant, which opened in 1997, was particularly wretched. Crooked tombstones, uneven plots, gnarled, overgrown trees and slapdash burials brought back Gothic images of medieval graveyards. Families who once boasted of having relatives at Mount Forest no longer found pride or solace in the final resting place of their loved ones. Some even whispered that "Big Dom" had purchased the cemetery, just so he could one day dig up the Eastern Quadrant and cover it with a strip mall.

But that was only a rumor.

****

Kevin Miller arrived for work promptly at 10:50 PM, clad in the standard gray and green jacket of the Mount Forest night watchman. Yet his punctuality did little to placate the surly mood of his new boss.

Dominic Strazelli, Jr. or 'Little Dom,' was an imposing bear of a man, with a carpet of black chest hair that tried to escape through the neck of his shirt. His wide, flat face was chiseled with a permanent scowl, made more severe by an ambush of thick eyebrows. His exquisitely tailored designer suit was not enough to dispel the frightening impression of a man more suited to sending people to graveyards than overseeing their burial. As he held court in his dark wood-paneled office, he repeatedly drummed a squadron of sausage-like fingers on the top of his black metal desk.

Kevin had trouble taking his eyes off those constantly pounding digits.

"So, kid," Dominic began, as he always did, regardless of the age of the listener. "First night on the job. Think you can handle it?"

"No problem, Mr. Strazelli." Kevin tried to project the boundless enthusiasm of the newly hired. "It's only a night watchman job. I've done a lot worse."

Strazelli's face darkened. "Only a night watchman, huh?" His thick fingers stopped drumming, spread out flat and pressed down hard on the desk. "You get this straight, kid. We take the cemetery business very serious around here. If I find out you don't, I'll kick your sorry ass to the curb! You hear what I'm sayin'?"

Kevin had never seen a person's disposition turn so ugly so fast. Strazelli's malevolent intensity forced him back in his chair. "I'm sorry, Mr.

Strazelli," he sputtered. "I meant no disrespect to you, or to the establishment. Really."

There was an uncomfortable, squirming silence as the large man stared hard at his new employee. Slowly, his scowl seemed to break, which did nothing to make his expression less intimidating.

"Good," he finally said, as he leaned back in his chair. "I don't take no disrespect from nobody. Dead or alive."

Little Dom looked at his Rolex. It was time to leave.

"I'll give you a piece of advice, kid. Stay awake and make your rounds every two hours. And if you hear anything...anything at all...you'd be smart to ignore it. You get me?"

"Hear anything? Like what, sir?"

Little Dom became uncomfortable again. His huge fingers danced an impatient rhythm on the metal desktop. "I dunno," he mumbled. "Voices maybe."

"I thought I was going to be the only one here tonight?"

"You are." The big man stood, and began pacing the room like a caged gorilla. His graveled voice grew more distant. "But y'know, cemeteries at night tend to spook some people. Especially new graves, like we got out there in the Eastern Quadrant." Little Dom tried to dismiss Kevin's confusion with a wave of his massive hand. "Forget about it, kid. Just be smart and ignore anything you hear. Think you can do that?"

"I think so, sir."

"Don't just think. Be sure," Little Dom growled.

He reached his huge paw into the second drawer of his desk, and pulled out a worn leather holster wrapped around a large black revolver. He casually tossed the weapon into Kevin's hands, which had risen instinctively to catch it. "Part of your uniform," he smiled.

"A gun?"

"Don't tell me you ain't never used one before?"

"Well, a Daisy air rifle when I was a kid."

Little Dom chuckled, though his face remained as threatening in laughter as in anger. "Let me tell ya, kid. This baby's got a hell of a lot more kick than some toy pop gun." He smiled at the weapon like an old friend. ".357 Magnum. Real reliable, too."

"Nobody mentioned anything about guns during the job interview."

His discomfort infuriated Little Dom. The big man leaned over the metal desk to within inches of Kevin's face. Kevin could feel harsh breath on his cheek.

"That gun might be the only thing that keeps you walking above ground, instead of planted in it! You hear me? You keep it with you whenever you make your rounds. Especially out there in the Eastern Quadrant."

Kevin's eyes narrowed. He measured his words carefully.

"Where the voices are…" he said softly.

Little Dom smiled. The kid was catching on. That was the hardest part about hiring a new night watchman. Making them understand things better left unsaid.

"You listen to me, kid," he said as he slapped a meaty paw on Kevin's shoulder. "And there ain't nothin' gonna happen to you. Capiche?"

"Yes, Mr. Strazelli."

"Then the place is all yours for the night." Little Dom threw a massive set of keys into Kevin's lap.

He was halfway out the door, when he turned back to Kevin.

"Good luck, kid. Keep your ears closed and your mouth shut, and you'll do just fine," he said, before stomping out into the night air.

****

Kevin Miller rested his elbows on the small metal desk, and once again tried to concentrate on his Ancient Civilizations textbook.

He failed.

He looked up at the sixteen black and white monitors mounted on the wall of the security room. With just a glance, he could see every corner of the Eastern Quadrant of Mount Forest Memorial Park. The monitors revealed a gloomy, but motionless expanse of headstones and statuary. Their very presence made him nervous. Why did a cemetery need such elaborate surveillance equipment? Why were all the cameras only in the Eastern Quadrant? And what possible need could there be for a gun when everybody else is already dead?

Kevin studied the weapon that lay menacingly on the desk beside him. He scratched his furrowed brow and tried not to think of Kelly's premonitions. He picked up the heavy revolver, felt the weight in his hand, and nervously wondered what exactly had he gotten himself into.

His thoughts were scattered by the sudden shriek of the old landline telephone. He picked it up quickly, unable to hide the tremor in his voice.

"Mount Forest." he said into the receiver.

"Hello." A woman's voice. A soft velvet purr. "Is there a cute and sexy night watchman on duty tonight?"

Kevin felt all his built-up tension melt away in an instant.

"That's all we hire, Ma'am," he answered with a smirk that he was sure carried straight through the telephone wire.

"Terrific. After he makes his nightly rounds, I have something else I'd like him to inspect."

Kevin sighed happily. "Why are you still awake, Kelly? It's after midnight. And you have class first thing in the morning."

His gentle scolding was insincere, for he was truly glad she called. The warm sound of his wife's voice placed a blanket of comforting reality over the ill-defined dread of this unholy place.

"I know. I know," she continued. "I'm lying here alone...in this big, old empty bed, and I couldn't help thinking of you. I just wanted to hear your voice before I fall asleep."

"I love you, wife-of-mine."

"I love you, too, Mr. Night Watchman." She was getting sleep-silly, like she always did when she had been studying all night. "My bold protector of the recently interred."

"Hey, no matter what happens, never forget I love you."

"What do you mean by that?" Suddenly, the game was over. She sensed that in his voice. "What's wrong, Kevin? What can happen?"

"I don't know yet, but I..."

And then he saw it.

Monitor Twelve.

Movement.

Almost imperceptible, but there it was.

"I have to go now, Kelly," his voice grew icy.

"Kevin, you're scaring me. What's going on?"

"Nothing. It's okay. Guess night reading about Ancient Druids is getting to me." No need to panic her. "I'll kiss you when I come home."

"Kevin...?"

"Love you, babe. Gotta run."

He hung up the receiver without ever taking his eyes off the monitor. He tried to convince himself that he hadn't seen anything, but deep down, he knew better. It was on the new grave, barren of grass and life. A mound of dirt piled so high, that over time, it would settle into level conformity on the body interred below. But there it was again, on the top of the mound. A small vibration in the soil. Then a small clod of rolling down the side into the adjoining grass.

Packed dirt doesn't move by itself, a voice in his head kept telling him. *It needs something, to move it. Or someone.* The implications of that constricted the muscles in his throat.

Before he bolted out the office door, Mount Forest's newest night watchman grabbed the large black revolver.

And prayed to God that it was loaded.

****

The battery powered golf cart shuddered and bumped its way over the night-streaked contours of Mount Forest Memorial Park.

Kevin rolled past the older, landscaped section of the cemetery into the Eastern Quadrant, an area devoted to the recently interred. There was something about a cemetery at midnight. Something sinister. The few electric lights that fought off the darkness were all mounted in the Eastern Quadrant, another fact he had failed to notice before. Why light a cemetery? And why only this section? His flesh crawled, as he imagined shadows rising behind every tombstone.

The air seemed to blow colder here, although Kevin knew that logically, the temperature had to be the same. Yet the prickling hairs on the back of his neck refused to be persuaded.

It was more than a transition between old and new, sculpted lawns and dirt craters, darkness and eerie artificial light. Where the original garden sections of the cemetery were designed to suggest the tranquility of life gently transitioning into eternity, the desolate Eastern Quadrant exuded an aura of death that refused to bend a knee.

From the dubious safety of his golf cart, he swung his high-intensity flashlight to chase away shadows from every grave and gnarled tree. He glanced at the seat beside him, once again making sure the weapon Little Dom gave him was still there. He inched the slow-moving cart toward the strange grave that had lured him from the safety of his office, and pulled him to the center of this unnatural realm. He strained his eyes for something he hoped not to see. Something he dared not imagine.

Then he heard it, though his mind immediately tried to deny the sound.

But there it was again.

An eerie whisper softer than the wind. More desperate than the cry of a wounded animal. The unmistakable sound of a human voice, muffled by a mound of soil and mystery.

Two terrifying words:

"...help me..."

'Oh God,' thought Kevin as he ran, stumbling to the grave. *There's someone alive in there!*

And he immediately began clawing at the dirt with handfuls of terror.

****

Try as she might, Kelly could not shake the vague sense of dread that suddenly hit her from all directions at once. There was something in Kevin's voice that frightened her. Something that had frightened him.

Although they had only been married two months, she knew Kevin was too maddeningly practical to be unnerved by the simple presence of a graveyard. Yet something was wrong. Horribly wrong. She could feel it like a dead weight in the pit of her stomach.

In the terrifying emptiness of her queen-sized bed, Kelly Miller pressed her eyelids closed and tried to pray her husband safely home beside her.

****

Nineteen miles away, Kevin Miller pressed a soiled hand to his chest to keep from shaking. His frantic attack on the dirt mound had torn precious flesh from his fingers and palms, leaving his hands a bloody mess.

"Are you there?! Can you hear me?!" he screamed to the silent grave before him. "Are you still alive?!"

Nothing.

Long moments of nothing.

Then…something…

A tinny response, barely audible, rose from beneath his feet. The sound of it pierced his bloodstream, and sent distilled horror racing through his veins.

"I'm here!" cried the muffled voice. "In here!" Growing louder. "Thank God you found me!"

****

In the study of his palatial Jersey estate, Dominic Strazelli, Jr. studied the black and white video monitors mounted on his wall. He was keeping an eye on Mount Forest. His cemetery. The Eastern Quadrant. With that new kid trying to claw his way into Lillian's grave.

Then that kid, that stupid kid, grabbed a shovel from the back of the golf cart and attacked the mound with added ferocity.

With a sneer of disgust, Little Dom Strazelli jerked open the cabinet that held his vast gun collection. He grabbed his AR-15 assault rifle, the special one that had never let him down before. Checked the magazine clip for ammo, added a few more hollow point rounds, then slammed the magazine back into place.

Little Dom scowled, as he slung the automatic weapon under his arm.

"Kid shoulda listened," he grumbled, before slamming the door shut behind him.

It was time to go hunting again.

In Mount Forest's Eastern Quadrant.

****

"Please hurry…" the voice from the grave grew weak and desperate. A woman's voice, strangled with fright. "Air…there's not much left in here!"

"Hang on! I'll get you out!" Kevin Miller dug furiously. Getting closer to her with each frantic shovel full of moldy dirt. He sensed the panic in her voice, knew he had to keep her talking. "What's your name? Tell me your name!"

"Lillian....I'm Lillian."

"I'm Kevin."

"Don't leave me, Kevin… Please don't leave me here!"

"I won't. I promise!" His arms had never worked so hard in his life. Six feet of dirt. The foul blanket of the dead. How had they compacted it so quickly? What if he didn't reach her in time?

It was taking too long, and he knew it.

"Lillian," he cried through jagged breaths, "You still with me?"

 pause, then…

"...yes..."

"Hang on! Promise me you'll hang on!"

".... hurry...please, hurry..."

She's alive in there! They buried her alive! His thoughts shrieked as he dug. What kind of animals could do that to another human being? What terror she must be feeling now!

"Hang on..." he said again, as much to his own aching arms as to the terrified woman in the coffin below. His chest felt like it was exploding, but he attacked the rank soil with desperate ferocity. The hole was nearly three feet deep now. He had to fall inside the grave to dig deeper. He tried not to think of what would happen if he did not reach her soon. He had to focus his thoughts. And hers.

"Lillian, who did this to you? Why did they do this to you?"

"...Little Dom..."

"Mr. Strazelli?"

"I... I used to...work for him..."

Talking seemed to calm her, but an edge of insanity was slowly tearing the shards of her voice.

Keep her distracted. Keep her alive. Dear God, help me keep her alive!

"What did you do for him, Lillian?"

"I...I was the night watchman..."

Kevin stopped, stiffened. *I should have trusted my wife's instincts. I should have listened to her!* Tears began to overwhelm his eyes, as he felt the muscles in his back and shoulders begin to give out. Still, he kept digging. He had to keep digging.

"Why did he do this, Lillian? Why would he bury you alive?"

"I don't know…" The voice was fading. Weakening. "…maybe I saw too much," she sobbed softly.

Four and a half feet. Maybe five. Was it true what they say about six feet under? His breath seared his lungs, but he would not rest. He could not let her die. Not this way. Not buried alive. The shear horror of it scorched his consciousness and spurred him on.

"Better not talk anymore." he gasped. "Save your air."

The panic flooded back into her voice. "Please don't leave me, Kevin! You can't leave me in here!"

"I won't…leave you…I'm still digging…"

"You can't imagine what it's like…" Her voice was cold, strangely dead. "What it's like to be buried alive…It's so cold…suffocating. I can feel the dirt pressing down on my chest. Right through the casket…I can feel it… squeezing the life out of me!"

Tears filled his eyes. He slammed and speared his shovel into the dirt again and again and again.

"…almost there, Lillian…"

"The blackness, Kevin…the horrible blackness! Like you're already part of the earth. Like you're being swallowed up. Like you're…" And then the madness set in. Her voice lost all human tone, the tortured cry of an animal. "Get me out of here! Get me out of here now!!!"

"Almost there… I'm almost there!" But Kevin knew he was lying. His arms were on fire and were now too heavy to lift. He had dug down nearly six feet. but in a single hole only two feet wide. By the time he excavated the full length of the coffin, the woman would suffocate. Or maybe Little Dom would find him trying to save her, and he too, would end up buried alive in some adjoining grave.

He pushed forward with his last ounce of strength, and suddenly thought of Kelly. How could he have ruined her life like this? Widowed after only two months.

But he couldn't think like that. He had to keep digging. He had to…

The shovel clanged against something solid.

The coffin lid.

He was there.

"I've reached the casket, Lillian!"

No reply.

Was he too late already? Had he come this far only to kill her by his own weakness? And how was he to open the six-foot casket?

There was only one thing to do. Break a hole in the lid, and hope she had enough strength left to crawl out of the coffin. That is, if smashing a hole in the thick coffin lid with the metal shovel didn't decapitate her.

"...Lillian, are you still with me...? ...I have to..."

"Smash the lid! Just smash it!" A savage voice of gnashed teeth and fury. "Get me out of here! I can't stand it anymore!"

"Okay...Roll over to the hinged side of the coffin."

"Get me out of here!" The woman's voice again. Desperate. Pleading. "Please, Kevin...Please!"

"I will. Just roll onto your left side! Press your body against the hinged side as much as you can…"

"...please, Kevin..."

"Are you on your left side?"

"...I don't know..."

He smashed the casket lid with the shovel, but only dented the surface.

Time had run out. He ran back to the golf cart, grabbed a heavy iron pick from the back, and leapt back into the hole. With all his remaining strength, he smashed the pick into the top corner of the wooden coffin, and prayed to anyone who might be listening that Lillian's head would not be there.

The pick crashed through, stuck in a small hole. He was overcome by the hiss and spray of escaping air.

"Lillian?"

No response.

"Lillian?! Are you okay?!"

But there was no answer. Kevin strained as hard as he could to yank the brutal pick free, but something held it fast and it would not budge. He fought back a momentary nausea at the thought of a smashed woman's skull under his pick. The horrible image and rank air weakened his legs.

Then, slowly, his hands slipped from the wooden handle. He stumbled back against the side of the hole he had dug, like a man trapped in a nightmare he can't escape.

The nausea didn't subside with the fading image of Lillian's mutilated skull. It was triggered by something else, something far more horrifying. For out of the small hole caused by the jammed pick seeped a foul and pungent odor universally recognizable.

The acrid smell of death.

He needed to fill his aching lungs with oxygen, but he did not want to breath in that putrid, tainted air. From his vantage point inside the ghastly pit, he could barely make out the engraving on the tombstone above him.

Lillian Harcourt, it read. He had to squint in order to see the date of death. But there it was, in all its ghastly implications. August 30th of this year. She had been buried for more than six weeks. He could feel the blood drain from his face.

"Open the lid, Kevin..." The voice from the casket was calmer now. No longer frightened. And no longer human.

Kevin's mind exploded with questions too terrifying to answer. How could she survive six weeks in an airtight coffin? And how could he have heard her voice through six feet of solidly packed dirt? How could...

Then something in what was left of his rational mind spoke to him.

It told him to run. Told him to be anywhere else on earth other than standing in this six-foot, freshly dug hole after midnight. Standing on a casket that contained...

"Kevin!" The animal growl again. Only stronger. More threatening. And unquestionably evil.

His own mind screamed again. *Run!*

Kevin Miller tried to scramble up the scar in the earth he had just dug, only to have the loose dirt walls crumble beneath his hands and feet. Behind him, he could hear the sound of the casket lid splintering, but he dared not look. He had to escape before she came.

Lillian...

Whatever she was.

Suddenly, the pick that had been firmly lodged in the thick wooden lid exploded upwards twenty feet in the air, landing, blade first by his scrambling feet. The aroma of death invaded his nostrils and eyes. Dirt from the collapsing wall filled his gasping mouth.

Then a loud crack. The sickening sound of thick wood being torn apart by impossibly powerful hands.

Lillian was breaking free.

Kevin grabbed the pick by his feet, swung it as hard as he could into the dirt cliff above him. This time it held. He grabbed the wooden handle to pull himself up, just as the wall collapsed beneath him.

But he was out of the hole at last.

He ran, stumbling blindly through the darkened cemetery. Assaulted by shadows and unseen abominations, the victim of some obscene and horrible joke. The orange vapor of the few sodium bulbs cast an eerie, Halloween glow on the tooth-like tombstones, as if Hell itself had risen this night to enfold him in its demonic grasp.

Pure terror pushed him on.

He was only fifty or sixty yards from the grave, when behind him arose an unearthly howl, followed by a deafening explosion of wood, that shattered the still night air. Kevin turned in horror to see a ghastly shape rise up from the hole he had just dug.

A woman, once. But no more. The skin was gray and withered on her skull. Half of it collapsed by the pick he had swung. The lips that had been sewn together during embalming were now ripped open at the roots, as they dangled from the torn flesh of her furrowed cheeks. The eyelids were rotted or eaten off, leaving her desiccated, semi-decayed eyes in a macabre and permanent stare. Those dead eyes were looking for someone, now.

"Kevin!" roared Lillian, with a voice as cold as the crypt. "You promised you would never leave me!"

There was no room for words in Kevin's throat. He scrambled to his feet and ran, crashed into a headstone, felt the blood leak from his side, then rose and ran some more.

As he gasped for each panicked, rib-crushing breath, he could feel a tangible animosity well up around him. It rose from every fresh grave he trampled on. From every lifeless, concrete statue that marked a body. He was the invader here. A living being in the realm of the dead.

"Kevin!"

He heard Kelly's voice now, a frighteningly evil mockery. He ran blindly, smashed his knee into a marble tombstone and crashed, face first, onto another newly dug grave. As his viciously pounding head pressed against the moist dirt, he heard another soft voice rising up through the soil.

"...help me..." it pleaded.

Kevin Miller screamed. He shrieked for every nightmare he had ever suffered. Every morbid and threatening vision come to life. Somehow, he found himself back on his feet again, but he could feel the frigid draft of insanity behind him. It wasn't running. There were no footsteps. But it was gaining on him. He knew he was only a heartbeat away from Lillian's foul clutches. His legs reached out for blessed earth, even though he felt his lungs would explode. He ran, because he knew the alternative was death.

Suddenly, something grabbed him. Something of unearthly power and hatred. A withered hand, with long, yellowed fingernails that bit hungrily into his shoulder. The dead hand spun him around like a rag doll, until he came face-to-face with her.

Not with her. With *it*.

The corpse come to life.

He was overpowered by the putrid smell of the grave on its obscene breath. Saw close-up, how the pick had shattered its cheek. And he could feel the unadulterated loathing for all things alive pour from its awful, decayed eyes. This savage monstrosity was Lillian, the thing he had foolishly loosed upon the world. The foul creature that was not buried alive...only buried. She grinned at his fear through torn and decaying lips. The gray and desiccated flesh dangled from her exposed skeleton. One dead hand held him firmly. The other reached out to clutch his throat.

"Kevin," it whispered, like some hellish serpent. "You promised you would never leave me." The cruel, bony hand squeezed, choking the breath out of him. "Now you can feel what it's like to be buried alive!"

The pain in his throat, the horrible stench of the thing, its look of pure hatred, these were the images that filled Kevin Miller's mind as the lack of oxygen smothered his vision with a splash of velvet blackness.

As he slipped inexorably into unconsciousness, he thought he heard the sound of a gunshot...and a familiar voice.

"Get your hands off of my husband, bitch!"

The first bullet that Kelly Miller fired shattered the right shoulder of the monster that was choking her husband. She saw Kevin collapse to the ground, and prayed she wasn't too late. She had arrived just in time to witness that thing...that dead thing...rise out of the hole Kevin had opened for it. When she saw the creature chase her husband, a new instinct prevailed. Viciously protective, she knew she could not watch her husband die in the claws of some unholy corpse. Although in shock, she retained enough presence of mind to grab the large revolver from Kevin's cart.

That corpse turned its ruined face to her now.

Kelly fired again, and another large chunk of dead flesh exploded off the creature's side. It howled in pain, then turned, and flew straight for her. She squeezed the trigger again and again, emptied all her bullets into its ghastly frame. It oozed a putrid slime from the wounds, lost flesh and bits of bone, but it could not be stopped. It flew relentlessly towards her, decaying face mad with vengeance.

The evil entity swooped down upon her. Saw her doom reflected in the eyes of the inhuman monster. Its yellowed claws were within inches of her face, when the creature's head suddenly exploded in a savage shower of bone chips and decayed membrane.

The evil thing collapsed to the ground, lifeless bones shattering with the impact.

From behind a large granite tombstone, Dominic Strazelli, Jr. clutched his semi-automatic rifle and spit derisively on the ground. He stomped over to Kelly's side, and looked with contempt at the once-again lifeless creature at his feet.

"You gotta pop 'em in the head," he sneered. "My old man taught me that."

****

Back in his dark, wood-paneled office, Little Dom Strazelli shook his head at Kelly and her badly scarred, but only recently conscious husband.

"Drink this." he muttered, as he handed her a bottle of transparent liqueur. "Anisette. It'll put life back into your bones."

Kelly hesitated, then took a deep swallow from the bottle. She felt it burn a soothing path into her chest and stomach. She handed the bottle to Kevin, who waved it away.

"What...was that thing?" he asked with a shudder.

"That? That was Lillian. She usedta work here. Long-time employee. Died a coupla month back."

"But how could she…?"

Little Dom could barely contain the anger in his voice. "I told you not to pay any mind to the voices! But you smart-ass college types always have to go poking your noses into other people's business!"

Kelly's eyes were still dilated by the nightmare images she had confronted. "Excuse me, Mr. Strazelli…" she said carefully. "I don't mean to be pushy, but you're saying that thing…that thing that nearly killed us…was dead?"

"Uh-huh."

"It was dead…and it tried to kill us."

Little Dom settled his massive bulk into the black leather upholstery of his executive chair. "They do that sometimes. Scared the shit outa my father the first time he saw one of 'em. Here he thought he was buying a nice, pretty cemetery to plant the relatives, and instead, he finds a buncha talking stiffs complaining about being buried alive. After that, he lost all enthusiasm for the place."

The big man took his own swig of Anisette, wiped a thick forearm across his lips. "Can't say I have much left in me either."

"You mean this happens all the time?"

Little Dom shrugged. "About one out of fifty. For some reason, those two percent can't seem to accept the fact that they're dead. So they try to con some poor sap, like your pretty boy husband here, into digging them up. Usually, they settle down and shut up after a day or two, but Lillian? She's been chattering for nearly two months now." He locked his massive hands behind his head. "Of course, if you had known Lillian before she died, you wouldn'ta been too surprised."

Kevin sat up and sputtered. "But this whole thing… It's impossible!"

"That so? You felt its hands on your throat. If I hadn't figured you'd probably screw up, there's a two percent chance you or your wife here mighta been the next ones chattering out there in the Eastern Quadrant."

Kevin slunk back into his seat, overwhelmed by the thought. Kelly leaned forward, intrigued. "Have any of these things ever escaped?"

"Naw. We timed one once. They can't last more than ten or twelve minutes above ground before their brain realizes it's supposed to be dead and shuts down. Me, I say we should just pop 'em all before we bury 'em. Save us all a hellofa lot of trouble. But families get real annoyed if they open up the casket sometime down the line, and find Uncle Louie's head all blown off."

"Does anybody else know about this?"

"Sure. Graveyard owners throughout history have kept their dirty little secret. Bad for business, if people found out their loved ones are trying to get out. Besides, can you imagine what the Internet would do with this? Some candy-brained bloggers would probably call them 'living impaired,' and demand some new government program to help these things come to grips with their 'death anxiety.'"

Little Dom shook his head with disgust, then washed it away with anther healthy chug of the fiery liqueur.

Kevin looked at his torn and bleeding hands. "This is all just so hard to believe," he groaned.

Little Dom leaned forward, "There are more things in heaven and earth, Horatio, than are dreamt of in your philosophy."

"That's Shakespeare!" Kevin said in surprise.

"So?" Little Dom sneered. "Just 'cause I own a cemetery, don't mean I'm brain dead."

ABOUT THE AUTHOR

Vin Morreale, Jr. is an award-winning author, screenwriter, acting teacher and internationally produced playwright.

He was awarded the prestigious *Al Smith Writing Fellowship*, and his scripts, stage plays, documentaries, museum exhibits and radio comedy have received hundreds of productions around the world, and have been translated into multiple languages, including Chinese, Italian, Russian and Spanish.

Vin has sold material to network and cable television networks, had feature screenplays optioned and produced, and his work has been seen on screen or stage in more than 15 countries. He was named a top screenwriter by both The International Screenwriters Association and The Blacklist.org.

Vin was a founding member of the San Francisco Playwrights Center and the Senseless Bickering Comedy Theatre. His book on theater, *BURNING UP THE STAGE: Monologues, Short Scenes & Audition Pieces for Actors From Six To Seventy* is distributed worldwide through Dramatic Publishing, which also carries a number of his published plays.

You can find more of his books at academyartspress.com.